New York Times bestselling author **Maya Banks** lives in southeast Texas with her husband and three children. When she's not writing, she loves to hunt and fish, bum on the beach, play poker and travel. Escaping into the pages of a book is something she's loved to do since she was a child. Now she crafts her own worlds and characters and enjoys spending as much time with them as possible. She loves to hear from her readers and can be found on Facebook, or you can follow her on Twitter (twitter.com/maya_banks). Her website, mayabanks.com, is where you can find up-to-date information on all of Maya's current and upcoming releases.

Books by Maya Banks

Harlequin Desire

Pregancy & Passion

Enticed by His Forgotten Lover
Wanted by Her Lost Love
Tempted by Her Innocent Kiss
Undone by Her Tender Touch

The Anetakis Tycoons

The Tycoon's Pregnant Mistress
The Tycoon's Rebel Bride
The Tycoon's Secret Affair
Billionaire's Contract Engagement

Visit the Author Profile page
at Harlequin.com for more titles.

#1 *New York Times* Bestselling Author

Maya Banks

Undeniable

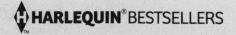

Recycling programs
for this product may
not exist in your area.

ISBN-13: 978-0-373-40111-6

Undeniable
Copyright © 2015 by Harlequin Books S.A.

The publisher acknowledges the copyright holder
of the individual works as follows:

Tempted by Her Innocent Kiss
Copyright © 2012 by Maya Banks

Undone by Her Tender Touch
Copyright © 2012 by Maya Banks

HARLEQUIN®
www.Harlequin.com

Printed in U.S.A.

CONTENTS

TEMPTED BY HER INNOCENT KISS

For Dee and Lillie

Chapter 1

There came a time in a man's life when he knew he was well and truly caught. Devon Carter stared down at the brilliant diamond solitaire ring nestled in velvet and acknowledged that this was one such time. He snapped the lid closed and shoved the box into the breast pocket of his suit.

He had two choices. He could marry Ashley Copeland and fulfill his goal of merging his company with Copeland Hotels, thus creating the largest, most exclusive line of resorts in the world, or he could refuse and lose it all.

Put in that light, there wasn't much he could do except pop the question.

The doorman to his Manhattan high-rise hurried to open the door as Devon strode toward the street, where his driver waited. He took a deep breath before ducking into the car, and the driver pulled into traffic.

Tonight was the night. All of his careful wooing—the countless dinners, kisses that started brief and casual and became more breathless—was a lead-up to tonight. Tonight his seduction of Ashley Copeland would be complete, and then he'd ask her to marry him.

He shook his head as the absurdity of the situation hit him for the hundredth time. Personally he thought William Copeland was crazy for forcing his daughter down Devon's throat. He'd tried everything to sway the older man from his aim to see his daughter married off…to Devon.

Ashley was a sweet enough girl, but Devon had no desire to marry anyone. Not yet. Maybe in five years. Then he'd select a wife, have two-point-five children and have it all.

William had other plans. From the moment Devon had approached him, William held a calculated gleam in his eye. He'd told Devon that Ashley had no head for business. She was too softhearted, too naive, too… everything to ever take an active role in the family business. He was convinced that any man who showed interest in her would only be seeking to ingratiate himself into the Copeland fold—and the fortune that went with her. William wanted her taken care of and for whatever reason, he thought Devon was the best choice.

And so he'd made Ashley part and parcel of the deal. The catch? Ashley wasn't to learn of it. The old man might be willing to barter his daughter, but he damn sure didn't want her to know about it. Which meant that Devon was stuck playing stupid games. He winced at the things he'd said, the patience he'd exerted in his courting of Ashley. He was a blunt, straightforward person, and this whole mess made him grit his teeth.

If she was part of the deal, he'd rather all parties know that from the outset so there would be no misunderstandings, no hurt feelings and no misconceptions.

Ashley was going to think this was a grand love match. She was a starry-eyed, softhearted woman who preferred to spend time with her animal rescue foundation over board meetings, charts and financials for Copeland Hotels.

If she ever found out the truth, she wasn't going to take it well. And hell, he couldn't blame her. Devon hated manipulation, and he'd be pissed if someone was doing to him what he was doing to her.

"Stupid old fool," Devon muttered.

His driver pulled up to the apartment building that was home to the entire Copeland clan. William and his wife occupied a penthouse on the top floor, but Ashley had moved to a smaller apartment on a lower floor. Various other family members, from cousins to aunts and uncles, lived in all places in between.

The Copeland family was an anomaly to Devon. He'd been on his own since he was eighteen, and the only thing he remembered of his parents was the occasional reminder not to "screw up."

All this devotion William showered on his children was alien and it made Devon uncomfortable. Especially since William seemed determined to treat Devon like a son now that he was marrying Ashley.

Devon started to get out when he saw Ashley fly through the door, a wide smile on her face, her eyes sparkling as she saw him.

What the hell?

He hurried toward her, a frown on his face.

"Ashley, you should have stayed inside. I would have come for you."

In response, she laughed, the sound vibrant and fresh among the sounds of traffic. Her long blond hair hung free tonight instead of being pulled up by a clip in her usual careless manner. She reached for his hands and squeezed as she smiled up at him.

"Really, Devon, what could happen to me? Alex is right here, and he watches over me worse than my father does."

Alex, the doorman, smiled indulgently in Ashley's direction. It was a smile most people wore around her. Patient, somewhat bemused, but nearly everyone who met her was enchanted by her effervescence.

Devon sighed and pulled Ashley's hands up to his waist. "You should wait inside where it's safe and let me come in for you. Alex can't protect you. He has other duties to attend to."

Her eyes sparkled merrily, and she flung her arms around his neck, startling him with the unexpected show of affection.

"That's what you're for, silly. I can't imagine anyone ever hurting me when you're around."

Before he could respond, she fused her lips hungrily to his. For God's sake the woman had no sense of self-control. She was making a spectacle here in the doorway to her apartment building.

Still, his body reacted to the hunger in her kiss. She tasted sweet and so damn innocent. He felt like an ogre for the deception he was carrying out.

But then he remembered that Copeland Hotels would finally be his—or at least under his control. He would be a force to be reckoned with worldwide. Not bad for a man who had been told that his sole ambition should be not to "screw up."

Carefully, he pulled her away and gently offered a reprimand.

"This isn't the place, Ashley. We should be going. Carl is waiting for us."

Her lips turned down into a momentary frown before she looked beyond him to Carl, and once again she rushed forward, a bright smile on her face.

He shook his head as she greeted his chauffeur, her hands flying everywhere as she spoke in rapid tones. Carl grinned. The man actually *grinned* as he handed Ashley into the car. By the time Devon made it over, Carl had already reverted back to his somber countenance.

Devon slid into the backseat with Ashley, and she immediately moved over to nestle into his side.

"Where are we eating tonight?" she asked.

"I planned something special."

As expected she all but pounced on him, her eyes shining with excitement.

"What?" she demanded.

He smiled. "You'll see."

He felt more than heard her faint huff of exasperation and his smile broadened. One thing in Ashley's favor was that she was extraordinarily easy to please. He was unused to women who didn't wheedle, pout or complain when their expectations weren't met. And unfortunately, the women he usually spent time with had high expectations. *Expensive* expectations. Ashley seemed happy no matter what he presented her with. He had every confidence that the ring he'd chosen would meet with her approval.

She nestled closer to him and laid her head on his shoulder. Her spontaneous demonstrations of affection still unbalanced him. He wasn't used to people who were so…unreserved.

William Copeland felt that Ashley needed someone who understood and accepted her nature. Why he thought Devon fit the bill Devon would never know.

When they married, he would work on getting her to restrain some of her enthusiasm. She couldn't go through her entire life with her emotions on her sleeve. It would only get her hurt.

A few minutes later, Carl pulled up to Devon's building and got out to open the door. Devon stepped out and then extended his hand to help Ashley from the car.

Her brow was creased in a thoughtful expression as she stared up at the building.

"This is your place."

He chuckled at her statement of the obvious. "So it is. Come, our dinner awaits."

He ushered her through the open door and into a waiting elevator. It soared to the top and opened into the foyer of his apartment. To his satisfaction, everything was just as he'd arranged.

The lighting was low and romantic. Soft jazz played in the background and the table by the window overlooking the city had been set for two.

"Oh, Devon, this is perfect!"

Once again she threw herself into his arms and gave him a squeeze worthy of someone much larger than herself. It did funny things to his chest every time she hugged him.

Extricating himself from her hold, he guided her toward the table. He pulled her chair out for her and then reached for a bottle of wine to pour them both a glass.

"The food is still hot!" she exclaimed as she touched the plate in front of her. "How did you manage it?"

He chuckled. "My superpowers?"

"Mmm, I like the idea of a man with super cooking powers."

"I had someone in while I was gone to collect you."

She wrinkled her nose. "You're horribly old-fashioned, Dev. There was no reason to collect me if we were spending the evening at your apartment. I could have gotten a cab or had my father's driver run me over."

He blinked in surprise. Old-fashioned? He'd been accused of a lot of things, but never of being old-fashioned. Then he scowled.

"A man should see to his woman's needs. All of them. It was my pleasure to pick you up."

Her cheeks pinkened in the candlelight, and her eyes shone like he'd just handed her the keys to a brand-new car.

"Am I?" she asked huskily.

He cocked his head to the side as he set his wineglass down. "Are you what?"

"Your woman."

Something unfurled inside him. He wouldn't have considered himself a possessive man, but now that he'd decided that she would be his wife, he discovered he felt very possessive where she was concerned.

"Yes," he said softly. "And before the night is over, you'll have no doubts that you belong to me."

A full body shiver took over Ashley. How was she supposed to concentrate on dinner after a statement like that? Devon stared at her across the table like he was going to pounce at any moment.

He had the most arresting eyes. Not really brown, but a warm shade of amber. In the sunlight they looked golden and in the candlelight they looked like a mountain lion's. She felt like prey, but it was a delicious feeling, not at all threatening. She'd been waiting for the moment when Devon would take their relationship a step further.

She'd longed for it and dreaded it with equal intensity. How could she possibly keep pace with a man who could seduce a woman with nothing more than a touch and a glance?

He'd been a consummate gentleman during the time they'd been dating. At first he'd only given her gentle, nonthreatening kisses, but over time they'd become more passionate and she'd gotten a glimpse of the powerfully sensual man under the protective armor.

She had a feeling that once those layers were peeled back, the man behind them was ferocious, possessive and…savage.

Another shiver overtook her at the direction of her thoughts. They were fanciful, yes, but she truly believed her assessment. Would she find out tonight? Did he plan to make her his?

"Aren't you going to eat?" Devon prompted.

She stared down at her plate again. What was it anyway? She wasn't sure she could eat a bite. Her mouth felt as if it was full of sawdust, and her entire body trembled with anticipation.

She moved the shrimp with her fork so that it gathered some of the sauce and slowly raised it to her lips.

"You aren't a vegetarian, are you?"

She laughed at the look on his face, as if the idea had just occurred to him.

"Tell me I haven't been serving you food you won't eat all this time," Devon said with a grimace. "You would have said something, wouldn't you have?"

She put the shrimp into her mouth and chewed as she put the fork down. When she'd swallowed she reached over to touch his hand.

"You worry too much. I would have told you if I was a vegetarian. A lot of people assume since I'm so active in my animal rescue organization that I refuse to eat meat of any kind."

The relief on his face made her laugh again.

"I'll eat chicken and most seafood. I'm not crazy about pork or the more uppity stuff like veal, foie gras and stuff like that."

A shudder worked over her shoulders.

"There's something about eating duck liver that just turns my stomach."

Devon chuckled. "It's actually quite good. Have you tried it?"

She wrinkled her nose in distaste. "Sorry. I have a thing about eating any sort of innard."

"Ah, so no cow's tongue for you then."

She held up her hands and shook her head back and forth. "Don't say it. Just don't say it. That's beyond disgusting."

"I'll make a note of your food preferences so that I never serve you animal guts," he said solemnly.

She grinned over at him. "You know, Devon, you're not as stiff as everyone thinks you are. You actually have quite a sense of humor."

One finely arched eyebrow shot upward. "Stiff? Who thinks I'm stiff?"

Realizing she'd put her foot solidly in her mouth, she stuffed another shrimp in to keep the foot company.

"Nobody," she mumbled around her food. "Forget I said anything."

"Has someone been warning you off of me?"

The sudden tension in his voice sent a prickle of unease over her.

"My family worries for me," she said simply. "They're very protective. Too protective," she finished with a mutter.

"Your *family* is warning you about me?"

He acted as though it was the very last thing he expected. Was he so sure that her entire family was pushing for a match between them?

"Well no, not exactly. Definitely not Daddy. He thinks you hung the moon. Mama approves but I'm sure it's because Daddy does. She thinks he can do nothing wrong so if you have his stamp of approval you have hers."

He seemed to relax in his chair. "Who then?"

She shrugged. "My brother wants me to be careful, but you have to understand he's been saying the same thing about all the guys I've ever dated."

Again that eyebrow went up as he raised the glass of wine to his lips. "Oh?"

"Yeah, you know, you're a philanderer, a player. Different woman on your arm every week. You aren't serious. You just want to get me into bed."

A blast of heat surged into her cheeks and she ducked her head. Stupid thing to blurt out. Stupid!

"Sounds like a typical older brother," Devon said blandly. "But he's right about one thing. I do want you in my bed. The difference is, once you're there, you're going to stay."

Her lips popped into an *O*.

He smiled, a lazy, self-assured smile that oozed male confidence.

"Finish eating, Ashley. I want you to enjoy your meal. We'll enjoy…each other…later."

She ate mechanically. She didn't register the taste. For all she knew she *was* eating cow's tongue.

What did women do in situations like these? Here was a man obviously determined to take her to bed. Did she play it cool? Did she go on the offensive? Did she offer to undress for him?

A bubble of laughter bounced into her throat. Oh, Lord, but she was in way over her head.

Firm hands rested on her shoulders and squeezed reassuringly. She yanked her head up to see Devon behind her. How had he gotten there?

"Relax, Ash," he said gently. "You're wound tighter than a spring. Come here."

On shaking legs, she rose to stand in front of him. He touched her cheek with one finger then raised it to her temple to push at a tendril of her hair. He traced a line over her face and down to her lips before finally moving in, his body crowding hers.

He wrapped one arm around her waist, and cupped her nape with his other hand. This time when he kissed her there was none of the restraint she'd seen in the past. It was like kissing an inferno.

Hot, breathless, so overwhelming that her senses shattered. How could one kiss do this to her?

His tongue brushed over her lips, softly at first and

then more firmly as he forced her mouth to open under his gentle pressure.

She relaxed and melted into his embrace. Her body hummed. Her pulse thudded against her temples, at her neck and deep in her body at her very core. She wanted this man. Sometimes she felt like she'd been waiting for him forever. He was so…right.

"Devon," she whispered.

He pushed far enough away that he could see her, but he still held her firm in his embrace.

"Yes, sweetheart?"

Her heart fluttered at the endearment.

"There's something I need to tell you. Something you should know."

His brow furrowed, and he searched her eyes as if gauging her mood.

"Go ahead. You can tell me anything."

She swallowed but felt the knot grow bigger in her throat. She hadn't imagined it being this difficult to say, but she felt suddenly silly. Maybe she shouldn't say anything at all. Maybe she should just let things happen. But no, this was a special night. It needed to be special. He deserved to know.

"I—I've never done this." She gripped his upper arm with nervous fingers. "What I mean is that I've never made love with a man before. You…you'd be the first."

Something dark and primitive sparked in his eyes. His grip tightened around her waist. At first he didn't say anything. He kissed her hungrily, his lips devouring hers.

Then he pulled away, savage satisfaction written on every facet of his face.

"I'm glad. After tonight you'll be mine, Ashley. I'm glad I'm the first."

"Me, too," she whispered.

Some of the fierceness in his expression eased. He leaned forward and kissed her on the brow and held his lips there for a long moment.

His hands ran soothingly up and down her arms, stopping to squeeze her shoulders. "I don't want you to be afraid. I'll be very gentle with you, sweetheart. I'll make sure you enjoy every moment of it."

She reached up on tiptoe to wrap both arms around his neck. "Then make love to me, Devon. I've waited so long for you."

Chapter 2

Ashley stared up at Devon, unsure of what to do now. He didn't suffer any such problem. Dropping another kiss on her brow, he bent and lifted her into his arms and carried her to the large master bedroom in the corner of the apartment.

She sighed as she laid her head on his chest. "I've always dreamed of being carried to bed when the big moment came. I probably sound silly."

Soft laughter rumbled from his chest. "Glad I could fulfill one of your fantasies before I even get you naked."

She blushed but felt a giddy thrill at the idea of him undressing her. That was number two on her fantasy list for when she lost her virginity.

After listening to so many girls in high school and college talk about how utterly unremarkable their first times were, Ashley had vowed that her experience would be different. Perhaps she'd been too picky as a result, but she'd been determined to choose the right man and the right moment. So she was feeling pretty damn smug because it didn't get any more perfect than Devon Carter right here, right now.

He set her down just inside the doorway and she glanced nervously around his enormous bedroom. A person could get swallowed up in here. And the bed was equally huge. It looked custom-made. Who needed a bed that big anyway? Unless he regularly hosted orgies and slept with ten women.

"I'm going to undress you, sweetheart," he said in a husky voice. "I'll go slow and you stop me if you feel uncomfortable at any time. We have all night. There's no rush."

Her heart melted at the tenderness in his voice. He seemed so patient, and she warred with appreciating this unerringly patient side of him and being frustrated because she wanted to be ravished.

It's your first time only once.

She could hear herself issue the reprimand. And she was right. She had plenty of time for down-and-dirty, hot monkey sex. But she would only have this night once and she wanted it to be a night she'd always remember.

"Turn around so I can unzip your dress."

Slowly she turned and closed her eyes when he gently moved her hair over one shoulder so he could reach the zip. A moment later, the light rasp of the zipper filled the room and the dress loosened precariously around her bust.

She slapped her hands over the strapless neckline just before it took the plunge down her body.

Devon's hands closed around her bare shoulders and he kissed the curve of her neck. "Relax."

Easy for him to say. He'd probably done this a hundred times. That thought depressed her and she made herself swear not to dwell on how many bed partners he may have had.

He turned her back around, his smile tender enough to melt her insides. Carefully he pried her fingers away from their death grip on her dress until it fell down her body, leaving her in only her panties.

She flushed scarlet. Why, oh, why hadn't she just worn the strapless bra? She felt like a hussy for not wearing anything but it wasn't as if she had a huge amount of cleavage and the dress fit tightly over her chest so she hadn't been in danger of flopping out of it.

And it wasn't as if she knew she was going to be seduced tonight.

She'd hoped. But then she'd hoped every time Devon took her out. She'd given up on trying to predict when or if the day might come.

"Very sexy," Devon breathed out as his gaze raked up and down her body.

Thank goodness she'd worn the lacy, sexy panties and not the plain white cotton ones she sometimes wore when she was feeling particularly uninspired or just didn't give a damn whether she felt girly and pretty or not.

"You're beautiful, Ash. So damn beautiful."

Some of her trembling stopped as she absorbed the look in his eyes. The eyes didn't lie and she could read arousal and appreciation in those golden depths.

He took her shoulders, gently pulled her to him and kissed her again. Hot. Forceful. In turns fierce and then gentler as though he had to remind himself not to overwhelm her.

She wanted to be overwhelmed.

She might be a virgin but she was no stranger to lust, desire and extreme arousal. She wanted Devon with a force that bordered on obsession. He'd fired many a fantasy that had kept her up at night.

And it wasn't as if she hadn't been tempted in the past. She'd been courted by other men. Some she felt absolutely no desire for but with others she'd experienced a kernel of interest and had wondered if she should pursue a sexual relationship. In the end, she hadn't been sure and if she wasn't absolutely sure, she'd promised herself she wouldn't take the plunge.

Not so with Devon. She'd known from the moment he introduced himself to her in that husky, sexy-as-hell voice that she was a goner. She'd spent the last weeks breathless in anticipation of this night. Now that it was here, her entire body ached for him to take her.

He pulled away for a moment and she stared at him with glazed eyes. He touched her cheek, tracing a path down her face with his fingertip. Then he kissed her again. And again.

Hot. Breathless. His tongue slid between her lips and feathered over her own. Warm and decadent, his taste seeped over her tongue and she drank him in hungrily, wanting more.

His harsh groan exploded into her mouth and the rush of his exhalation blew over her face. "You make me crazy."

She smiled, some of her nervousness abating. That

she had this effect on this gorgeous, perfect man infused her with a sudden rush of feminine confidence.

He fastened his mouth to her jaw and kissed a line down to her neck. He pressed his lips just over her pulse point and then lightly grazed his teeth over the sensitive flesh.

Shivers of delight danced over her shoulders. His hands glided up her arms and then gripped her just above the elbows. He held her in place as his mouth continued its downward trek. Over the curve of her shoulder and then down the front.

He went to his knees in front of her so that his mouth was barely an inch from her nipple. She sucked in her breath, afraid to move, wanting so badly for him to touch her there. His mouth, lips, tongue… She didn't care. She just knew she'd die if he didn't touch her.

He lowered his head and kissed her belly instead. Just above her navel. She sucked in her breath, causing her stomach to cave in. He moved up an inch and kissed her again, tracing a path between her breasts until finally he pressed a kiss directly over where her heart beat.

A slow smile turned his lips upward, the movement light against her skin.

"Your heart's racing," he murmured.

She remained silent. It didn't require acknowledgement from her—her heart *was* beyond racing. It was damn near about to explode out of her chest.

But her hands wouldn't remain still. Drawn to the light brown wash of his hair, she threaded her fingers through the short strands. In a certain light, she could see the shades of his eyes. Amber. Golden. That warm, liquid brown.

Her fingers moved easily through his hair. No styling

products stiffened the strands. A little mussed. Never quite the same from day to day. He paid as little attention to his hair as he did to the other things he deemed inconsequential.

He glanced up, her fingers still thrust into his hair. "Are you afraid?"

"Terrified," she admitted.

His gaze softened and he wrapped his arms around her body, pulling her into his embrace. The shock of her naked body against his still fully clothed one sent shivers up her spine.

"I'd feel less afraid if you were naked, though."

He blinked in surprise and then he threw back his head and laughed. "You little tease." He pushed upward to his feet until he towered over her. "I'm happy to accommodate you. *More* than happy to accommodate you."

She licked over suddenly dry lips as he pulled away and began unbuttoning his shirt. He tugged the ends from his slacks and unfastened his cuffs before shrugging out of the sleeves.

She swayed precariously because oh, Lord, was the man mouthwateringly gorgeous. He was lean in an "I work out" way but he wasn't so muscled that he looked like he got carried away with the fitness regimen. He was hard in all the right places without being a neckless, snarling, swollen, knuckles-dragging-the-ground caveman type.

A smattering of light brown hair collected in a whorl in the center of his chest and then tapered to a fine line that drifted down his abdomen and disappeared into the waist of his pants.

She wanted to touch him. Had to touch him. She

curled her fingers until they dug into her palms and then she frowned. There weren't rules to seduction, right? She could touch. No reason for her to stand here like a statue or an automaton while he did all the work. While taking things slow did have its good points, there was simply too much she wanted to experience to stand idly by while seduction *happened*. She wanted to take an active part.

He'd only begun to undo his pants, when she slid her hands over his chest and up to his shoulders. He went still and for a moment closed his eyes.

His response fascinated her. Did her touch bring him as much pleasure as his touch brought her? A sudden rush of power bolted through her veins, awakening the feminine roar inside her.

She moved in closer, wanting to feel his naked flesh against hers. Hot. She gasped when her breasts pressed against his chest. It was an electric sensation that was wildly intoxicating. She wanted more. So much more.

"What are you doing?" he asked hoarsely.

"Enjoying myself."

He smiled at that and remained still, his hands still gripping the fly of his pants. She ran her palms openly over his chest, exploring each muscled ridge, enjoying the rugged contrast between his hardness and the softness of her own body.

"Take them off," she whispered when her hands drifted perilously close to where his hands were positioned.

"Has the blushing virgin turned temptress?"

On cue, she flushed but he smiled and then let go of his pants to frame her face in his palms. He kissed her, nearly scorching her lips off with the sudden heat. "You take them off me," he murmured into her mouth.

Sudden nerves made her fingers clumsy as she fumbled with his pants, but he stood there patiently, his hands caressing her face, gaze locked with hers as she pushed his pants down his legs.

Swallowing, she chanced a look down to see his erection straining hard against the cotton of his briefs. Plain, boxer briefs. Somehow she'd imagined something a little more… She wasn't sure. She just knew she hadn't imagined plain boxer briefs but then he was a no-fuss kind of guy. Yes, he wore expensive clothing, but it was comfortable expensive clothing. The kind you only knew was expensive because you recognized the label. Not because it looked terribly pricey.

Simply put, Devon Carter looked like a man who'd made money but wasn't overly concerned with appearing as though he was wealthy. It wasn't as if he couldn't look the part. She'd seen him in full business attire with the sleek designer labels and the polished, arrogant look to match. But she'd spent much more time with him privately. When he was relaxed. Less guarded. That was the word. In public situations, he was intensely guarded at all times. Almost as if he was determined to let no one in. It thrilled her that he trusted her enough to see his more casual side.

"Put your hand around me," he coaxed in that low husky tone that had her melting.

Tentatively she slid her fingers beyond the waistband of his underwear and delved lower until she encountered the velvety hardness of his erection. Emboldened by the immediate darkening of his eyes, she curled her fingers around the base and slowly slid upward, lightly skimming along his length.

His hands left her face and he impatiently pushed his underwear down until he was completely nude, cupped in her hands as she gently caressed him.

Having nothing but stolen glimpses of illicit photos to compare him to, he seemed to measure up adequately in the size department. At least he didn't look so huge that she feared compatibility issues.

He gently took her wrists and pulled her hands away from his erection. Then he pulled her hands up until they were trapped between them against his chest. His thumb lightly caressed the inside of her palm as he stared into her eyes.

"You, my love, are driving me slowly insane. It was me who was supposed to do the seducing and yet you utterly enslave me with every touch."

She flushed with pleasure, her skin growing warm under the intense desire blazing in his eyes.

He kissed her again, and he pressed in close until he walked her backward toward the bed. He stopped when the backs of her legs brushed against the sumptuous comforter.

He wrapped his arm around her waist and lowered her back until she was lying on the mattress, him hovering above her.

His expression grew serious and he brushed her hair from her forehead in a tender gesture. "If at any time I do something that frightens you, tell me and I'll stop. If at any time you simply want to slow down, just let me know."

"Oh," she breathed out. Because it was impossible to say anything else around the tightness in her throat.

She reached for him, pulled him down to meet her kiss. She felt clumsy and inept but it didn't seem to matter to him. She wished she was more artful. More practiced. But she couldn't wish for experience because more than anything she was glad she'd waited for this moment. For him.

"I love you," she whispered, unable to hold back the words that swelled and finally broke free.

He went still and for a moment she was terrified that she'd effectively thrown a wet blanket over a fire. She drew away, eyes wide as she searched his face for something. Some reaction. Some indication that she'd breached some forbidden barrier.

Trust her to ruin what would have been the most exciting, wonderful, splendiferous moment of her life by opening her big mouth. She'd never been able to re-strain herself. She tried. Most of the time.

"Devon?"

His name came out in a near croak. Her lips shook and she started to withdraw, already feeling the heat of embarrassment lick over her with painful precision.

Instead of answering her, he moved over her in a powerful rush. He took her mouth roughly, devouring her lips as his tongue plunged inside, tangling with hers.

Her body surged to life, arching up into his. She wrapped her arms around his neck as he gathered her tightly against him. Their bodies were as fused as their mouths. Between her legs, she could feel him so hard. Hot.

His hips jerked, almost as if he could barely contain the urge to push inside her. She gasped for air, partly out of excitement, partly out of sudden, delicious fear and anticipation.

His hands and mouth were everywhere. A sensual assault on her senses. Magic. Gentle caresses mixed with firmer, rougher touches. He slid down her body until his mouth hovered over one taut nipple. And then he flicked his tongue out and licked the tip.

She cried out, nearly undone by the shock of such a simple touch. Pleasure rocked over her and she shuddered violently, her fingers suddenly digging into his flesh, marking him.

Not satisfied with the intensity of her reaction, he closed his mouth over the rigid peak and sucked strongly.

Her vision blurred. She gasped but couldn't seem to draw air into her lungs. Oh, but it was heaven. So edgy. She couldn't even find the words to describe such a decadent sensation as his mouth sucking at her breast.

But then his hand slid between them, over the softness of her belly and lower.

She held her breath as his fingers tentatively brushed through her sensitive folds and then he found her heat, teasing, touching. He knew better than she knew herself exactly how to pleasure her. Where to touch her. *How* to touch her. Each stroke brought her to greater heights.

It was as though she was being wound tighter and tighter. Tension coiled in her belly. Low. Humming through her pelvis. She wasn't ignorant of orgasms, but this was nothing like she'd ever experienced before. It was powerful. Relentless. Nearly frightening in its intensity.

His fingers left her and he carefully parted her legs. His hand glided soothingly up the inside of her thigh and then he stroked her intimately again as he positioned himself above her.

His mouth left her breasts and she moaned her protest. He covered her lips once more with his own and then whispered softly to her.

"Hold on to me, love. Touch me. I'm going to go inside you now. I'll be gentle. There's nothing to be afraid of."

She trembled from head to toe. Not in fear or trepidation. She was so close to release that she feared the moment he pushed inside her the barest inch that she'd go over the edge, and she wanted it to last. She wanted to enjoy every single moment of what was to come.

"Wait," she choked out.

He went still, the tip of his erection just touching the mouth of her opening. Strain was evident in his face as he stared down at her, but he held himself in check.

"Are you all right? Did I frighten you?" he asked urgently.

She shook her head. "No. No, I'm fine. I just needed a second. I'm so close. Just need to catch up."

He smiled then, his eyes gleaming with a predatory light. "Tell me when."

She reached up once more, feathering her hands over his shoulders and to the bunched muscles of his back. Her gaze met his and she drowned in those beautiful amber eyes. "When."

He swallowed hard and his lips tightened into a harsh line. Then he closed his eyes and flexed his hips, pushing into her inch by delicious inch.

At one point he stopped and she stirred restlessly, a protest forming.

"Shh," he murmured as he kissed the corner of her mouth. "Give me just a moment. I don't want to hurt you. Better to have done with it quickly."

She nodded her agreement just as he surged forward, burying himself to the hilt.

Her eyes widened and a strangled sound escaped her throat as she sought to process the sudden wash of conflicting sensations that bombarded her from every angle.

He was deep. Impossibly deep. She surrounded him. He surrounded her. Their hips were flush against each other. His body covered hers possessively. There was a burning ache deep inside her, and she couldn't discern whether it was pleasure or pain.

She just knew she wanted—needed—more.

She whimpered lightly and struggled, not against him, not in protest. She wanted something she couldn't name. She wanted…him. All of him.

"Easy," he soothed.

He kissed her, stroked his tongue over hers and then deepened the kiss just as he began to move inside her. Gently. He was so gentle and reverent. He lifted his body off of her and arched his hips, pushing deep then retreating.

Then he levered himself down, resting on his forearms, never breaking away from her eyes.

"Okay?"

She smiled. "Very okay."

"You're beautiful, Ash. So very beautiful. So innocent and perfect and mine."

His. The possessive growl in his voice thrilled her and sent another cascade of pleasure through her body.

"Yes, yours," she whispered.

"Tell me how close you are. I want to make sure you're with me. I can't hold off much longer."

"Then don't." Her voice shook. She was nearly beyond the ability to think much less speak. Her body was taut. Her senses were shattered and she was so very close to losing all control. Just one touch. One more touch...

He gathered her close and thrust again. And then again. He forced her thighs farther apart, plunged deeper and she lost all sense of herself.

She cried out his name. Heard him murmur close to her ear. Soothing. Comforting. Telling her beautiful things she could barely make sense of. She was spiraling at a dizzying speed, faster and faster until she closed her eyes.

It was the single most beautiful, spectacular sensation she could imagine. She'd wanted wonderful, but this far surpassed even her most erotic fantasies.

When she regained at least a modicum of sanity, she was firmly wrapped in Devon's embrace and his mouth was moving lightly over her neck. For that matter she was on top of him. Her hair was flung to one side while he nuzzled at the curve of her shoulder, moving up and down to just below her ear and back to her shoulder.

She raised her head to stare down at him, still feeling a little fuzzy around the edges. "How did I get here?"

He smiled and slid his hands over her naked body. They stopped at her behind and he squeezed affectionately. "I put you here. I like you covering me. I could get used to it."

"Oh."

He raised one eyebrow. "Speechless? You?"

She sent him a disgruntled look but was too wasted to follow up with any sort of admonishment. Okay, so obviously she was speechless.

He chuckled and pulled her down against him. She

settled over him with a sigh and he rubbed his palm over her back, stroking and caressing as she lay draped over him like a wet noodle.

"Did I hurt you?"

She smiled at the concern in his voice. "No. It was perfect, Dev. So perfect I can't even find the words to describe it. Thank you."

He lifted a strand of hair and lazily twined his fingers around it. "Thank you? I don't think I've ever been thanked by a woman after sex."

"You made my first time special," she said quietly. "It was perfect. You were perfect."

He kissed the top of her head. "I'm glad."

She yawned against his chest and cuddled deeper into his hold.

"Go to sleep," he murmured. "I want you to sleep here tonight."

Her eyes were incredibly heavy, and she was already drifting off when his directive registered in her consciousness.

"Want to sleep here, too," she mumbled.

His fingers stilled in her hair and then his hands wandered down her body, bold and possessive. "That's good, Ash, because from now on, you'll sleep every night in my bed."

Chapter 3

Devon woke to the odd sensation of a female body wrapped around him. Not just wrapped but completely and utterly surrounding him.

Ashley was draped across him, her legs tangled with his, her breasts flattened against his chest, her arm thrown across his body and her face burrowed into his neck.

He…liked it.

He lay there a long while watching the soft rise and fall of her body as she slept soundly across him. She was really quite beautiful in an unsophisticated, effervescent way. She lit up a room when she walked in. You could always pick her out of a crowd. She was extremely… natural. Perhaps a bit too exuberant and unrestrained but in time with the proper guidance, she'd be an excellent wife and mother.

He ran the tips of his finger lightly up her arm. She was pale. Not so pale she looked unhealthy, but it was obvious she wasn't a sun bunny, nor did she indulge in salon tanning. Perhaps what he liked most about her was that she looked the same no matter when he saw her. Though she wore makeup, she didn't wear so much that she was transformed into someone completely different when they went out.

Glossy lips and a touch of coal to already long, lush lashes seemed to be all she did, but then he was hardly an expert on women's gunk.

But she didn't seem fake. At least not that he could tell. Yet. Who knew what the future would bring. He liked to think she wasn't an accomplice in this ridiculous plan of her father's even when he knew it was best for all parties involved to know the entire story from the start.

The selfish bastard in him liked the idea that she felt affection for him, free of machinations. If her words from the night before weren't merely a result of being overwhelmed in the moment, *affection* was perhaps the wrong term. She'd said she loved him.

It both complicated the matter and gave him a certain amount of satisfaction.

While he might approach the marriage as a matter of necessity, convenience and a chance at a successful business venture, the idea that she would be coming into the marriage for the same reasons bothered him immensely.

It made him a flaming hypocrite but he was happy for her to want him because she desired him and yes, even loved him.

First, however, he had to get the preliminaries out of the way. One of which was making their upcoming nuptials official. She didn't know it yet, but she would become Mrs. Devon Carter.

He carefully extricated himself from the tangle of arms and legs, but he needn't have worried because she slept soundly, only wrinkling her nose and mumbling something in her sleep when he slipped away completely.

He pulled on his robe and glanced back at the bed. For a moment he was transfixed by the image she presented. The sun streamed through the window across the room and bathed her in its warm glow.

Her blond hair was tousled and spread out over his pillow. One arm shielded most of her breasts from view, but there, just below her elbow, one nipple peeked out. The sheet slid to just over her buttocks but bared the dimple just below the small of her back.

She was indeed beautiful. And now she was his.

He dug into the pocket of the jacket he'd discarded the night before to retrieve the box with the ring in it and then quietly left the room. When she awoke, he'd put into place the next part of his carefully orchestrated plan.

Ashley stirred and stretched lazily, blinking when the sun momentarily blinded her. She kept her eyes shut for a moment, simply enjoying the warmth and comfort of the sumptuous bed. Devon's bed.

She sighed in contentment. As virginal deflowering went, that had to top the list of all-time most awesome. How could it possibly have been any better? A wonderful night. Romantic dinner for two. Devon staring at her with those gorgeous eyes and murmuring that she would now be his. Oh, yeah, perfect.

Then she realized that he was no longer in bed with

her and she opened her eyes with a frown. Only to see him standing just across the room. Staring at her.

He was clad in a robe, though it dangled loosely, open just enough that she could see his bare chest. He was leaning against the doorway to the bathroom and he was simply watching her. For some reason that sent a giddy thrill up her spine.

Then a flash of color caught her eye and she glanced downward to see a lush red rose lying on the sheet next to her. But it was the tiny card propped next to a dazzling, truly spectacular diamond ring that took her breath away.

Blood rushed to her head and she stared openmouthed at the items before her. She pushed to her elbow and reached for the ring, hands shaking so badly that she was clumsy, nearly dropping the small velvet box where the ring rested.

Then she glanced at the note again, sure she'd misunderstood. But no, there it was. In his neat, distinctive scrawl.

Will you marry me?

"Oh, God," she croaked out.

She looked at the ring, looked at the note and then back up to him, almost afraid that he'd be gone and that she'd imagined this whole thing.

But he was still there, an indulgent smile carving those handsome features.

"Really?" she whispered.

He nodded and smiled more broadly. "Really."

She dropped the rose, the ring, the note—everything—and flew out of bed, across the room, and launched herself into his arms.

He stepped back and laughed as she kissed his face,

his brow, his cheek and then his lips. "Yes, oh, yes! Oh, my God, Devon, yes!"

He made a grab for her behind before she could slide down him and land on the floor. Then he hoisted her up so they were eye level. "You know it's customary to actually put the ring on."

She glanced down at her hand and then over her shoulder to the bed. "Oh, my God! Where is it?"

Shaking his head, he carried her over to the bed then set her on the edge while he reached behind her.

A moment later, he took her hand and slid the diamond onto her ring finger. She sucked in her breath as the sun caught the stone and it sparkled brilliantly in the light.

"Oh, Dev, it's beautiful," she breathed.

She threw her arms around his neck and hugged him tightly. "I love you so much. I can't believe you planned all this."

He gently pulled her arms down and then collected her hands in her lap as he stared into her eyes. "I don't want a long engagement."

Was this supposed to worry her? She beamed back at him. "Neither do I."

"In fact, I'd prefer to get married right away," he added, watching her all the while.

She frowned and chewed at her bottom lip. "I wouldn't mind. I mean if it was just me, but I don't know how my family would take that. Mama will want to plan a big wedding. I'm her only daughter. It's not that I care about a big fuss—I don't. But it would hurt her if she wasn't able to give us a big wedding."

He touched her cheek. "Leave your family to me. I assure you, they'll be on board with my plans. You and

I will have the best wedding—one that your mother will be more than satisfied with. I think you'll find they won't object to our plans at all."

Excitement hurtled through her veins until it was nearly impossible to sit still. "I can't wait to tell everyone! Won't this just be amazing? Everyone will be so thrilled for me. I know Daddy despaired of me ever finding a suitable man and settling down. He always says I'm too unsettled, but really, I'm still young."

He gave her an amused smile. "Are you saying you don't want to get married?"

She stared at him in shock. "No! That's not at all what I was saying. I was merely going to say that I was waiting for the right man. In this case, you."

"That's what I like to hear," he murmured.

He leaned forward to kiss her brow. "How about you take a long bubble bath to recover from last night's activities and then we'll have breakfast together."

She flushed red. She had to be flaming. But she nodded, eager to discuss their future.

Mrs. Devon Carter. It had such a nice ring to it. And speaking of rings… She glanced down, transfixed by the radiance of the diamond that adorned her finger.

"Like it?" he asked in a teasing voice.

She looked back up at him, suddenly serious. "I love it, Dev. It's absolutely gorgeous. But you didn't need to get me something so expensive. I would have loved anything you gave me."

He smiled. "I know you would. But I wanted something special."

Her heart did a little dance in her chest. "Thank you. It's just perfect. Everything is perfect."

He kissed her again, long and leisurely. When he

pulled away, his eyes were half-lidded and they were glowing with desire.

"Go draw your bath before I forget all about breakfast and make love to you again."

"Breakfast?" she whispered. "Were we planning to eat?"

He made a sound in his throat that was part growl, part resignation.

"I don't want to hurt you, Ash. As much as you tempt me, I'd rather wait until you're fully healed from last night."

She pushed out her bottom lip.

"As adorable as you are when you pout, it won't move me this time. Now get your pretty behind out of bed and hit the bathroom. Breakfast will be served in forty-five minutes. Plenty of time for you to soak."

She sighed. "Okay, okay. I'm going."

She got up and walked toward the bathroom but just as she got to the doorway, something he'd said the night before came back to her. She paused and turned around, her head cocked to the side.

"Dev, what did you mean last night when you said I'd be sleeping here with you every night from now on?"

He rose and pulled his robe tighter around his waist. He stared back at her, his gaze intense and serious.

"Exactly what I said. I'll want you to move in as soon as possible. I'll arrange to have what you need transferred from your apartment. You're mine, Ash. From now on, you'll spend every night in my bed."

Chapter 4

"Well, you finally took the leap," Cameron Hollingsworth said as he stared across the room to where Ashley stood with a group of women.

Devon took a sip of the wine, though the taste went unappreciated. He was too distracted. Still, he forced some of it down, hoping it would at least take the edge off.

The official announcement would be made in a few moments. By Devon himself. Ashley's father had wanted to do the honors, but Devon had preferred to do it himself. William Copeland had already orchestrated entirely too much of Devon's relationship with Ashley. From now on, things would be done his way.

Though everyone in attendance was well aware it was an engagement party they had been invited to, Ashley had insisted on waiting until all the guests had arrived before their engagement was announced.

"Cold feet already?" Cam asked dryly. "You haven't said two words since I got here."

Devon grimaced. "No. It's done. No backing out now. Copeland has all but signed off on the deal. After the ceremony he'll fax the final documents and we'll move forward with the merger. I'll want to meet with you, Ryan and Rafe as soon as I return from the honeymoon."

Cam arched an eyebrow. "Honeymoon? You're actually going on one?"

"Just because this marriage is part and parcel of a business deal doesn't mean Ashley has to have any less of a marriage or honeymoon," Devon murmured.

Cam shrugged. "Good idea. Keep her happy. If she's happy, Daddy's happy. You know what they say about Daddy's girls."

Devon frowned. "Don't be an ass. She's…"

"She's what?" Cam prompted.

"Look, she has no idea what her father's done. She thinks this is a wildly romantic courtship that culminated in an equally romantic marriage proposal. If I don't take her on a honeymoon, it's going to look strange."

Cam groaned. "This can't end well. Mark my words. You're screwed, my friend."

"Anyone ever tell you what a ball of joy you are?"

Cam held his hands up in surrender. "Look, I'm just trying to warn you here. You should tell her the truth. No woman likes being made a fool of."

"And have her tell me to go to hell and take my proposal with me?" Devon demanded.

He sighed and shook his head. Yeah, he knew Cam had been through the wringer in the past. He couldn't blame his friend for his cynicism. But he wasn't in the mood to hear it right now.

"This deal is important to all of us. Not just me," he continued when Cam remained silent. "Marriage isn't my first choice, but Ash is a sweet girl. She'll make a good wife and a good mother. Everyone gets what they want. You, me, Ryan and Rafe. Ashley, her father. Everyone's happy."

"Whatever floats your boat, man. You know I'm behind you all the way. But remember this. You don't have to marry her to make this work. We'll find another company. We've suffered setbacks before. Not one of us expects you to martyr yourself for the cause. Rafe and Ryan are deliriously happy. There's no reason you shouldn't hold out for the same."

Devon snorted. "Turning into quite the rah-rah man. I'm fine, Cam. There is no love of my life. No other woman in the picture. No one I'd rather marry. I'll be content with Ashley. Stop worrying."

Cam checked his watch. "Your intended bride is looking this way. I think you're on."

Devon glanced over to where Ashley stood surrounded by friends and relatives. He could never sort out who was who because there were so many. She smiled and waved and then motioned him over.

He handed Cam his wineglass and made his way through the throng of people until he reached Ashley.

She sparkled tonight. She wore a radiant smile that seemed to captivate the room. But then she always drew people. She'd talk to anyone at all about anything at all.

As soon as he approached, she all but pounced on him, took his hand and dragged him into her circle. He smiled at each of the women in turn, but their names and faces kind of blended. After a moment he bent to murmur in Ashley's ear. "It's time, don't you think?"

She all but quivered in excitement. Her eyes lit up and she smiled as she squeezed his hand.

"Excuse us, ladies," he said smoothly as he drew Ashley away and back in Cam's direction. There wasn't anyone standing around Cam. Cam had that effect on people. It was the perfect place to call for attention and announce their engagement.

"Hi, Cam," Ashley sang out as they walked up to his friend.

She let go of Devon's hand and threw her arms around Cam's neck. Cam grinned and shook his head as he attempted to extricate himself from her embrace.

"Hello, Ash," he said before dropping an affectionate kiss on her cheek. "Come stand by me while Devon makes a fool of himself."

Devon sent a glare Cam's way before taking Ashley's hand and pulling her to his side. Laughing, Cam handed him a fresh wineglass and a spoon.

"What, are you kidding me?" Devon asked. "You want me to bang on a wineglass to get attention?"

Cam shrugged then tossed the spoon aside. Then he put his fingers to his lips and emitted a shrill whistle. "Everyone, I'd like your attention please. Devon here has an announcement for us."

"Thanks, Cam," Devon said dryly. Then he turned to face the room filled with Ashley's friends and relatives. And they were all staring at him expectantly. All wanting him to make this moment perfect for Ashley. Hell. No pressure or anything.

He cleared his throat and hoped like hell that he'd manage to get through it without sticking his foot in his mouth.

"Ashley and I invited you all here tonight to join

us in celebrating a very special occasion." He glanced fondly down at Ashley and squeezed her hand. "Ashley has made me the happiest of men by consenting to marry me."

The room erupted in cheers and applause. To the right, Ashley's mom and dad stood beaming at their youngest child. William nodded approvingly at Devon while Ashley's mother wiped at her eyes as she smiled at her daughter.

"It's our wish that you'll all attend our wedding to take place four weeks from today and help us celebrate as we embark on our journey together as man and wife."

He held up his wineglass and turned again to Ashley whose entire face was lit up with a breathtaking smile. "To Ashley, who's made me the luckiest man alive."

Everyone raised their glasses and noisy cheers rang out again as everyone toasted Devon and Ashley.

"Quite an eloquent speech there," Cam murmured in Devon's ear. "One would almost think you meant every word."

Devon ignored Cam and slid an arm around Ashley as they braced for the onslaught of well-wishers pushing forward.

His head was spinning as he processed face after face. Bright smiles. Slaps on the back. Admonishments to take care of "their girl" as everyone in the family seemed to have a claim on Ashley.

She was everyone's younger sister, daughter, best friend or person in need of protection. It bewildered him and annoyed him in equal parts that everyone in Ashley's family seemed to think she was incapable of taking care of herself. Nothing in his relationship with

Ashley had led him to believe this was an accurate assessment.

Yes, she was flighty. She was too trusting, definitely. She was a bit naive. He grimaced. He supposed he could understand that in a family of business sharks she was an anomaly, and perhaps they were right to worry that she'd be swallowed up.

But it didn't mean she was totally incapable of taking care of herself. It just meant she needed someone who'd look out for her best interests and occasionally protect her from herself. Someone like him.

Her hand feathered over his arm and she leaned up on tiptoe. He immediately lowered his head, realizing she wanted to tell him something.

"We can leave anytime," she whispered. "I know my family is a lot to take."

He almost laughed. Here he'd been thinking of how she needed his protection and she was busy protecting him from her overwhelming family.

"I'm fine. I want you to enjoy yourself. This is your night."

Her brow furrowed and her eyebrows pushed together as she stared up at him. "And not yours?"

"Of course it is. I only meant that you're surrounded by your family and friends and I want you to enjoy yourself."

She smiled, kissed him on the cheek and then settled back at his side as they were besieged by more congratulations.

"Ashley! Ashley!"

Devon turned to see a young woman barreling through the crowd practically dragging a man in her wake. He looked a bit harried but wore an indulgent smile. Devon stared a moment and then realized that whomever the woman was, she bore a striking resemblance to Ashley and she had every appearance of sharing many of the same personality traits. Probably one of her many cousins.

"Brooke!" Ashley cried. She put out her hands just as Brooke careened to a halt and Brooke grabbed hold, beaming from ear to ear.

"Guess what, guess what?" Brooke said breathlessly.

"Oh, don't make me guess. You know I'm horrible at it!" Ashley exclaimed.

"I'm pregnant! Paul and I are going to have a baby!"

Ashley's shriek of excitement could be heard over the entire room. Devon winced then quickly glanced around as everyone stared their way.

"Oh, my God, Brooke! I'm so excited for you! When? How far along are you?"

"Just ten weeks. I had to tell you as soon as I found out, but then you've been so busy with Devon and then I heard you guys were getting married and I didn't want to intrude—"

"You should have texted me at least," Ashley said. "Oh, Brooke, I'm so thrilled for you. I can only imagine how excited I'll be when I become pregnant. I hope our babies are close together and can be playmates!"

Ashley had grown louder and louder, her exuberance drawing the attention of the others, who cast indulgent smiles in Ashley's direction.

She was animated and talking a mile a minute, throwing her hands this way and that, and nearly crashed into a passing waiter. Only Devon's and Cam's quick lunge for the tray of drinks prevented complete disaster. Ashley continued, oblivious to the chaos around her.

Then she impulsively hugged Brooke again. For the third time. Then she hugged Paul. Then she hugged Brooke again, the entire time wringing her hands in excitement.

Cam chuckled and shook his head. "You've got quite the chore on your hands, Dev. Keeping up with her is going to wear your stick-in-the-mud ass out."

"Don't you have somewhere else to be and someone else to torture?" Devon muttered.

Cam glanced Ashley's way once more and Devon swore he saw genuine affection in his friend's eyes.

"She's cute," Cam said as he put his wineglass aside.

"Cute?"

Cam shifted uncomfortably. "She's sweet, okay? She seems…genuine and you can't ask for more than that."

Devon stared agape at his friend. "You like her."

Cam scowled darkly.

Devon laughed. "You like her. You, who doesn't like anyone, actually like her."

"She's nice," Cam muttered.

"But you don't think I should marry her," Devon prompted.

"Shh, she's going to hear you," Cam hissed.

But Ashley had already drifted away from Devon and was solidly ensconced in a squeal-fest with Brooke as others had heard the news and had descended. She wasn't going to hear an earthquake if a fault suddenly opened up under the building and sucked everyone in.

"If you think she's so cute and nice, why the big speech about not being a martyr and getting married, et cetera?" Devon persisted.

Cam sighed. "Look, I just hate to see her get hurt and that's what's going to happen if you aren't straight with her. Women have a way of knowing when men aren't that into them."

"Who the hell says I'm not into her?"

Cam arched an eyebrow. "Are you saying you are? Because you don't act like a man who's into his future bride."

Devon frowned and looked around, making sure they weren't overheard. By anyone. Least of all Ashley's overprotective family. "What do you mean by that? You, Rafe and Ryan know the real circumstances of my relationship with Ashley but no one else does. I've given no one reason to suspect that I'm marrying her for any other reason than I want to."

Once again Cam shrugged. "Maybe you're right. Maybe because I know the real story it's easier for me to see that you aren't as excited as your lovely bride to be is over your impending nuptials."

"Damn it," Devon swore. "Now you're going to have me paranoid that I'm broadcasting disinterest."

"Look, forget I said anything. I'm sure it'll be fine. It's none of my business anyway. She just seems like a sweet girl and I hate to see her get hurt."

"I'm not going to hurt her," Devon gritted out. "I'm going to marry her and I'm damn sure going to take care of her."

"And you're being summoned again," Cam said, nodding in Ashley's direction. "I'm going to take off. I'll walk with you over to Ashley so I can offer my congratulations again and say good night."

Devon started in Ashley's direction then listened attentively while she introduced him to one of her cousins—one of the many in attendance—and then waited while Cam said his goodbyes and kissed her on both cheeks.

But the entire time, his mind was racing as he processed his conversation with Cam. Was he coming across as someone who was less than enthused about his upcoming marriage? The very last thing he needed to do was drop the ball when everything was so close to being in his grasp. Finally.

He'd worked too damn hard and long to allow any slips now. If he had to wed Satan himself to seal this deal, he'd don the fire retardant suit and pucker up.

Chapter 5

No matter how many nights she'd already spent in Devon's apartment, she still got butterflies when she entered his bedroom to get ready for bed. Granted she'd only been here a week and it was still a little uncomfortable and awkward because she still didn't feel any sense of ownership when it came to his home.

She was pulling on her satin nightgown when Devon's chuckle broke the silence in the room. She turned quickly, her brow furrowed as he regarded her in amusement.

"What's so funny?"

"You. Every night you spend so much time putting on that lovely nightgown only for me to promptly take it off you when you come to bed. By now one would think you wouldn't bother."

She flushed. "It seems...presumptuous...to think you want...I mean to assume you'd want..."

"Sex?" he finished for her.

She nodded, her cheeks flaming.

He grinned and pulled her toward the bed. "I think it's a safe presumption that I'll always want sex with you. Feel free to assume all you want. I assure you…" He bent and kissed her lingeringly. "That I'll never ever…" He slid his mouth down her jaw to her neck and nibbled at her ear. "*Not* want…" He licked the pulse point at her neck, and her knees buckled. "To have sex with you. Unless I'm in a body cast and even then I'll be thinking about it."

Her nose crinkled and she shook with silent laughter. "It's true then. That sex is all a man ever thinks about?"

"We occasionally think about food."

She laughed aloud this time. "My mother is scandalized that I've practically moved in with you."

"Not practically," he said as he slid one strap over her shoulder. "You *have* moved in with me."

She shrugged. "Well she was aghast. My father told her to stop being such a worrywart, that you and I were getting married and it was only natural that we'd want time together before the big day to see if we were compatible. Eric, on the other hand, seemed pretty ticked. He thinks Daddy's nuts to *allow* me to move in with a man who's boned half the city—his words, not mine."

Devon straightened his stance and stared at her with an open mouth. "Do you *always* do that?"

She sent him a perplexed frown. "Do what?"

He shook his head. "Blurt out whatever comes to mind."

Her frown grew deeper. "Well, I guess. I mean I haven't really thought about it. It *is* what he said. I mean I didn't really pay any attention to him. He's just really protective of me and he always gets snarly when a guy starts paying attention to me."

"I hardly think me asking you to marry me can be compared to some random guy paying attention to you," he drawled.

"Well, but I'm living with you now so he obviously knows we're having sex and he doesn't like to imagine his little sister having sex. With anyone."

Devon shuddered. "Who would?"

She grinned. "My point is, he's just being Eric and he had to get his two cents in."

"For the record, I have not *boned* half the city."

She wrapped her arms around his neck and pulled him down to kiss her. "As long as I'm the only one you'll…well, you know, in the future? I don't really care about the past."

"The future? Oh, yeah. And the present. Like right now."

She shivered as he lowered her to the bed. For having been a virgin a mere week ago, her education was no longer sorely lacking. Every night he'd taken her to places she'd only halfway imagined, and others she hadn't even known existed.

If this was a precursor to how life with him was going to be, she was going to be one very happy woman.

"Joining our meeting via video conference call this morning are Ryan Beardsley and Rafael de Luca," Devon said as his two friends' faces flashed up on the monitor on the wall. "Ryan is on location at our site build on St. Angelo Island, where our flagship resort is in its first stage of development. When completed, this resort will be the standard for every new Copeland property. Good morning, Ryan. Perhaps you could give us a progress report on the construction."

Devon tuned out Ryan and glanced over at Cam, who was slouched in a chair. Devon knew well the progress on construction. He got daily and sometimes hourly reports. Though Ryan was on site, his focus was on his very pregnant wife, who could deliver at any moment. To that end, Devon kept in contact with the foreman so that any issues that arose could be swiftly dealt with.

Cam hadn't dressed for the occasion. He'd never quite bought in to the idea that image is everything in the business world. But then he didn't really care what others thought or didn't think. It was easier for Cam, though. He'd been born to this world, while Devon had to claw and dig his way in, one torn fingernail at a time.

Cam looked like a man who could be heading to the beach for the day or at the very least planning to spend the day kicked back with a beer in one hand and a cigar in the other. But then Cam didn't drink or smoke. The man had no vices. He was disgustingly perfect in his imperfection.

Members of Tricorp's staff listened attentively to Ryan's report. Jotted down appropriate notes. The secretary took detailed minutes. There was an air of expectancy in the room. Everyone knew it was a matter of time before the big merger was announced.

Devon thought it kinder to wait. Maybe he was getting old and soft. Maybe he didn't even deserve to be on the verge of the biggest coup of his career. Because at the very moment when he stood to gain everything he'd ever wanted, he'd actually gone to William Copeland and suggested that they postpone the announcement for six months. He thought it would be kinder to

Ashley if she were to think that business had nothing to do with their marriage and that the merger came after. William wouldn't have it, however. He insisted that things proceed as planned.

He thought Devon worried too much about Ashley's potential reaction. She loved him, wasn't that enough? It had made Devon cringe that apparently the whole world knew she was madly in love with her husband to be.

Besides, William pointed out that as disinterested in the family business as Ashley was, the chances of her actually putting it all together were slim. William's advice to Devon? Keep her busy and happy.

Suddenly in the midst of Ryan's report, a sound jangled over the room. There was a series of starts as his employees looked down and then around. Devon frowned. What the hell was it? It sounded like a ring tone, but it wasn't one he'd ever heard before.

Then slowly everyone's gaze turned to him and it was then he realized it was his phone going off in his pocket.

"What the hell?" he muttered.

Cam snickered.

Devon yanked his phone out of his pocket to see Ashley's name on the LCD. He nearly groaned aloud.

"Excuse me a moment," he said as he rose. "I'll take this outside."

He hurried out the door, irritated by Cam's look of amusement. He knew damn well who was calling Devon.

As soon as he was outside the conference room he punched the answer button and brought the phone to his ear. "Carter," he said tersely.

Ashley wasn't even remotely put off by his greeting. Or lack of one.

"Oh, hi, Dev! How's your day going?"

"Uh, it's good. Look, was there something you needed? I'm kind of in the middle of something here."

"Oh, nothing important," she said cheerfully. "I just wanted to call and tell you I love you."

An uncomfortable knot formed in his stomach. What was he supposed to say to that? He cleared his throat. "Ash, did you change the ring tone on my phone?"

"Oh, yeah. I did. I downloaded one so you'd know when I'm calling. Neat, huh?"

Devon closed his eyes. The cheerful cascade of noise that sounded like a cross between Tinker Bell sneezing fairy dust and a waltz at some damn princess ball would make him the laughingstock of the office in short order. Not to mention that Cam would never, ever let him live this down.

"Neat," he lamely agreed. "Look, I'll see you tonight, okay? We still on for dinner at nine?"

"Yes, that's perfect. I'm at the shelter until eight so if it's okay I'll just meet you at the restaurant."

He frowned. "Do you have a ride?"

"I'll get a cab."

He shook his head. "I'll send a car for you. Stay put at the shelter until it arrives. I'll arrange it for eight."

She sighed but didn't argue further. "Have a good day, Dev. Can't wait until tonight!"

"Thanks. You, too," Devon said but she'd already hung up.

He stared at his phone for a long moment and then punched a series of buttons. How did you even change the ring tone? He'd never designated a special ring tone for a person. His phone rang, the contact showed up, and if he wanted to answer he did. If he didn't, he let it go to voice mail. No way he wanted sparkly Tinker Bell music to play every time Ashley called him. What if she made a regular habit of it?

To his never-ending grief, she called him every single day. It baffled him that her timing was utterly impeccable. She always managed to catch him right in the middle of a meeting or when he was with a group of people.

After the second instance, he began silencing his phone and putting it on vibrate, but on two occasions, he simply forgot and his entire meeting was treated to Tinker Bell on crack.

After two weeks, he began to get amused, indulgent looks from some. Sympathy from others. Delighted grins from the women personnel. And Cam laughed his fool head off.

Ashley simply called whenever the mood struck, and unfortunately for him, he could never be sure when she would be moved to call him. Sometimes she wanted advice on wedding details. Like flowers. How the hell did he know what the difference between a tulip and a gardenia was? And invitations. Elopement to Vegas had never looked so enticing as it did right now.

Rafael and Ryan hadn't gone through all of this for their weddings. They'd both had exceedingly simple affairs. Devon was in hell. A wedding that was being planned by the entire Copeland clan.

He was ready to throw his cell in the Hudson.

Chapter 6

"Dev?"

Devon stuck his head out of the bathroom then proceeded toward the bed, rubbing his hair with a towel. She was laying stomach down on the bed, feet dangling in the air as her jaw rested in her palm.

There was a slight frown marring her delicate features, which told him she was thinking about something. He almost didn't want to ask because he'd quickly learned that Ashley's thoughts ran the gamut.

He sat on the edge of the bed and rubbed his hand over her back. "What's up?"

She turned slightly so she could stare up at him. "Where are we going to live? I mean after we get married. We haven't really talked about it."

"I assumed we'd live here."

Her lips turned down just a bit and her brow wrinkled. "Oh."

"That doesn't sound like a good 'oh.' Do you not like the apartment? It's bigger than yours so I naturally thought it would accommodate us better."

She scrambled up and sat cross-legged beside him. "I do like it. This is a great apartment. It's a little manly-looking. More like a bachelor pad. It's not really appropriate for children or pets."

"Pets?" he croaked out. "Uh, Ash, I don't know about pets."

Her frown deepened, which he found distressing. Ashley rarely pouted about anything, which was good, because it was damn hard to resist her when she looked unhappy. Maybe it was because she was rarely ever anything but happy.

"I've always wanted a house in the country. A place for kids and pets to run and play. The city isn't a good place to raise a family."

"Lots of people raise families here," Devon pointed out. "You were raised here."

She shook her head. "Not always, no. We didn't move to the city until I was ten. Before that we lived on this really great farm. Or at least it was a farm before my father bought it. It was such a beautiful place to live."

The wistful note in her voice was a shot to the gut.

"It's something we can discuss when the time comes," Devon said by way of appeasement. "Right now, my focus is on making you my wife, having a week of uninterrupted time with you on our honeymoon and getting you permanently moved into my apartment."

She smiled and leaned up to brush her lips across his jaw. "I love it when you talk like that."

He raised a brow as she drew back. "Like what?"

"Like you can't wait for us to be together."

She snuggled against him and wrapped her arms around his waist. And again he was assailed by an unfamiliar nagging sensation in his chest. It wasn't comfortable. He wasn't sure he liked it even as he didn't want it to go away.

"It won't be long now," he said. And then some strange urge to continue on and at least make a token effort to lift her spirits pushed stubbornly at him. He stroked a hand over her silky hair and pressed a kiss to the top of her head. "We can always revisit the issue of where to live later. Right now, though, I want our concentration to be on each other."

She squeezed him tighter and then pulled away as she'd done before to stare up at him, her blue eyes shining. "Can we talk about one other thing?"

"Of course."

"When you say you want our concentration to be on each other, does that mean you'd prefer to wait to start a family? We've talked casually about children. I've made it no secret that I'd love to become pregnant right away but you haven't said what you want in that regard."

A sudden picture of her swollen with his child and her radiant, beautiful smile flashed through his mind. It shocked him just how gratifying the image was. He was assailed by a surge of longing and possessiveness that baffled him.

He'd always viewed marriage, a wife and eventual children with clinical detachment. Almost as if they were components of a to-do list. And maybe they had been. Right underneath his goals of business success.

Now that he was suddenly faced with all of the above, he had a hard time thinking rationally about what he wanted. It was a very damn good question.

At some point he'd stopped looking at marriage to Ashley as the chore it had begun as. He'd resigned himself to the inevitability and honestly, he could do so much worse. She was intelligent, good to her core, sweet, affectionate and tenderhearted. She'd make a perfect mother. Much better than his own had ever been. But would he make a good father?

"Dev?"

He glanced down to see her staring at him with worry in her eyes. It was instinctual to want to immediately soothe the concern away. He kissed her brow. "I was just thinking."

"If it's too soon to be having this conversation, I'm sorry. Daddy always says I get too far ahead of myself. I just can't help it. I get excited about something and I just want to reach out and grab it."

He couldn't help but smile. It was such an apt description of her. She embraced life wholeheartedly. And she didn't seem to much care if she stumbled along the way. He wondered if anything ever got her down at all. People like her were a puzzle to him. He didn't understand them. Couldn't relate to them.

He pulled her onto his lap until she was astride him. "What I think is that you'll be a perfect mother. I was just imagining you pregnant with my child and decided I quite liked the image. I also had the thought that I've never used protection, which is hugely irresponsible of me even given the fact that we both have clean histories and are safe, which makes me wonder if subconsciously I was hoping to get you pregnant all along."

She sighed and went soft, melting into his chest as she leaned toward him. "I was hoping you'd say that. I mean about wanting children. It's not that I *have* to have them right away. A small part of me realizes it would probably be better to wait but I've always wanted a large family and I don't want to be old when they're graduating high school."

"You realize we've done nothing to prevent pregnancy so far," he said in a low voice.

"Do you mind?" she asked anxiously. "I mean would you be upset if I was actually pregnant before we got married?"

He chuckled. "It would be the height of hypocrisy for me to be upset over something I could have very well prevented."

"I just want to be sure. I don't want us to have a bad start. I want everything to be…perfect."

He touched her nose and then traced a path underneath her eye and down the side of her face. "Do you suspect that you're already pregnant, Ash? Is that why you're bringing this up tonight? I don't want you to be afraid to tell me anything. I'd never be angry with you for something that is equally my responsibility, if not more so. You were an innocent when I made love to you. Birth control absolutely should have been my responsibility."

She shook her head. "No. I mean I don't know. I don't think so anyway."

He rested his forehead on hers and thought for a moment that they already acted like a married couple who were at ease in their relationship. Strangely, he trusted Ashley and felt comfortable with her. There was a sense of rightness that he couldn't deny. Maybe William Copeland had known what he was doing after all.

"Well, if you are, then fantastic. Really. I want you to tell me if you even suspect you could be. And if you aren't? We'll work on remedying that. Deal?"

She grinned and a delicate blush stained her soft cheeks. "Deal."

"Now what do you say we go to bed so you can have your evil way with me?"

Her cheeks grew even redder and he smiled at the shy way she ducked her head.

He leaned in to nibble at her ear and then he whispered so the words blew gently over her skin. "I'll do my very best to make you pregnant."

To his surprise, she shoved him forward. He landed on his back on the mattress with her looming over him, a mischievous grin dimpling her cheeks. Then her expression grew more serious and her eyes darkened. "I love you so much, Devon. I'm the luckiest woman on earth. I can't wait until we're married and I'm officially yours."

As she lowered her mouth to his, he was gripped by the feeling that she was completely and utterly wrong. It wasn't she who was the lucky one.

Chapter 7

"Ashley, if you don't sit still we're never going to get your hair and makeup right," Pippa said in exasperation.

"I still think she should have just called in a stylist," Sylvia said as she eyed the progress Tabitha was making on Ashley's hair.

"Tabitha *is* a stylist, silly," Ashley said. "She's the best and who doesn't want the best on their wedding day? And who knows more about makeup than Carly?"

Pippa snorted. "That's so true. I'm convinced cosmetic companies should just pay her to endorse their products."

"Close your eyes, Ash," Carly said. "Time for mascara. Just a bit, though. Don't want you looking clumpy on the big day."

Ashley frowned. "Definitely not clumpy."

"Darling, are you almost done?" Ashley's mother sang out from the doorway. "You're on in ten minutes."

"Ten minutes?" Tabitha shrieked. "No way. Can you stall them, Mrs. C.?"

"I'm not going to be late to my own wedding," Ashley said firmly. "Just hurry faster, Tab. My hair will be fine. Just put the veil over the knot."

"Just put the veil over the knot," Tabitha grumbled. "As if it's that easy."

Sylvia rolled her eyes, pushed between Tabitha and Ashley and quickly affixed the veil to the elegant chignon. "There, Ashley. You look beautiful."

"Lip gloss and we're done," Carly announced. "Make a kissy face."

Ashley smacked her lips and a moment later, Carly pulled away to allow Ashley to see herself in the mirror.

"Oh, you guys," she whispered.

Her best friends beamed back at her in the mirror.

"You look beautiful," Pippa said, her eyes bright with tears. "The most beautiful bride I've ever seen."

"Absolutely you do," Tabitha said.

The four women crowded in to hug her.

"Girls, time for you to go. Your escorts are waiting. We don't want to make the bride late," Ashley's mother called.

Her friends scrambled toward the door, bouquets in hand.

"Your father is coming to get you now," her mother said as she walked over. She paused when she got to Ashley and then smiled, tears glittering in her eyes. "My baby, all grown up. You look so beautiful. I'm so proud of you."

"Don't make me cry, Mom. You know I have no willpower."

Her mom laughed and reached for her hands. She squeezed them and then helped her to her feet.

"Let me fix your gown. Your father will be pacing outside the door. You know how he hates to be late for anything."

She fussed with Ashley's dress and then there was a knock on the dressing room door.

"That will be him now. Are you ready, darling?"

Sudden nerves gripped Ashley and her palms went sweaty. But she nodded. Oh, God, this was really it. She was about to walk down the aisle and become Mrs. Devon Carter.

She threw her arms around her mom and hugged her tight. "Love you, Mom."

Her mother squeezed her back. "Love you, too, baby. Now let's go before your father wears a hole in the floor."

She went ahead of Ashley to open the door and sure enough, her father was outside checking his watch. He looked up when he heard them and his expression softened. A glimmer of emotion welled in his eyes and he held out his hand to take hers.

"I can't believe you're getting married," he said in a tight voice. "It seems like only yesterday you were learning to walk and talk. You look beautiful, Ash. Devon is a lucky man."

She leaned up to kiss his wrinkled cheek. "Thank you, Daddy. You look pretty spiffy yourself."

The wedding coordinator hurried up to them and motioned with rapid flying hands. She shooed them toward the entrance to the aisle and then spent a few seconds arranging the train of her dress.

Ashley's mom was escorted down the aisle and

seated, which only left Ashley to be walked down the aisle with her father.

The music began, the doors swung open and every eye in the church turned to watch as Ashley took her first step.

Her bouquet shook in her hands and she prayed her knees would hold up. The dress suddenly seemed to weigh a ton and despite the cold outside, the church felt like a sauna.

But then she caught sight of Tabitha, Carly, Sylvia and Pippa all standing at the front of the church, their smiles wide and encouraging. Pippa winked and held a thumbs-up then pointed toward Devon and made a motion like she was fanning herself.

And finally her gaze locked on to Devon and she forgot about everyone else. Forgot about her nervousness, her sudden doubt. Nothing but the fact that he awaited her at the front of the church and that from now on, she'd belong to him.

It gave her a warm, mushy feeling from head to toe.

And then her dad was handing her over to Devon. Devon smiled reassuringly down at her as they took the step toward the priest and the ceremony began.

It pained her to later admit that she didn't remember most of the ceremony. What she did remember was Devon's eyes and the warmth that enveloped her standing next to him as she pledged her love, loyalty and devotion. And the kiss he gave her after they were pronounced husband and wife scorched her to her toes.

Suddenly they were walking back down the aisle, this time together, as a married couple. They ducked into an alcove to await the others and Devon pulled her close into his side.

"You look absolutely stunning."

He kissed her again. This time slower. More intense. Long and lingering. He took his time exploring her mouth, and when he pulled away, she swayed and caught his arm to steady herself.

Around her, the noise of well-wishers grew and she realized that guests were coming out of the church.

"Darling, they need you back inside the church for pictures," her mother called as she hurried towards Ashley and Devon. "All your attendants are already gathered. The others are going ahead to the reception. The car is waiting to take you and Devon after you're finished with all the photos."

Devon looked less than happy at the idea of posing for so many photographs but he gave a resigned sigh and took Ashley's hand to lead her back into the sanctuary.

"It'll be over soon," she whispered. "Then we can be off on our honeymoon."

He smiled down at her and squeezed her hand. "It's the only thing making the next few hours bearable for me. The idea of you and me locked in a hotel suite for days."

She flushed but shivered in delight at the images his words invoked. She too couldn't wait for them to be alone.

But at the same time, this was her day and she was going to enjoy every single moment of it. She smiled as she was swarmed by her friends. She was surrounded by countless cousins, her uncles and aunts, her parents, her brother, distant relatives, friends.

It was truly the happiest day of her life.

Devon collected a glass of wine while Ashley's brother took his turn on the dance floor with her. Devon should probably be dancing with one of her family members but she had so many female relatives that he couldn't keep track.

Cam immediately found him and Devon whistled appreciatively to mock the formal tuxedo his friend wore.

"Only for you would I wear this getup," Cam said darkly. "I didn't wear this for Rafe's wedding and Ryan married Kelly so fast we were lucky to get a phone call saying the deed was done."

"You weren't *required* to wear one for Rafe's wedding," Devon pointed out.

Cam shrugged. "True, but then I wasn't required to wear one for yours, either. I didn't want to disappoint Ash. She thinks I look hot."

Devon shook his head. "I can't believe you've stuck around this long. Not like you to be out of your cave for such an extended period of time."

Cam made a rude noise. "I'm supposed to convey my congratulations or commiserations, whichever you need or prefer, from Rafe and Ryan. They were both sorry they couldn't make it but with wives about to drop the package at any moment, they understandably remained at home by their sides."

"You have to cut it out," Devon said. "My getting married isn't the end of the world. You didn't give Rafe and Ryan this much grief."

"Oh I did," Cam said with a grin. "I totally did. But they deserved it. They were both total douche bags."

"Like you're a shining example of chivalry, Mr. I-hate-everyone-and-women-in-particular."

Cam sobered. "Don't hate women at all. I like them too much if anything. Kind of sucks if you ask me. Besides, it's fun to give you hell. I think Ashley is perfect for a stuffy stick-in-the-mud like yourself."

"I didn't mean that, man," Devon said wearily. "I'm just on edge. I'll be glad when this is all over with. Too much stress. I've worried on a daily basis that she'd find out the truth and tell me to go to hell. The sooner we can get the hell out of here and on the plane to St. Angelo, the better I'll feel."

"For what it's worth, I wish you well," Cam said. "I think you made a huge mistake marrying someone over a business deal, but she's a sweet girl and you could certainly do worse. It's not you I worry about anyway. It's her."

"Gee, thanks," Devon said dryly. "Glad you've got my back on this one."

Cam's gaze found Ashley on the dance floor as her brother spun her around. She laughed and her smile lit up the entire room. It was clear she was having the time of her life.

"At least you won't suffer a broken heart," Cam said in a low voice. "Can you say the same for Ashley?"

"I'm not going to break her heart, damn it. Can we drop this? The last thing I need is for someone to over-hear us."

"Yeah, sure. Think I'll go cut in on Ashley's brother, pay my respects to the bride before I head back to the cave you accuse me of crawling out of."

Devon watched as Cam sauntered onto the dance floor. A moment later, Eric relinquished Ashley into Cam's arms.

"You've made my little girl very happy," William Copeland said.

Devon turned around to see his father-in-law come

up behind him. William smiled broadly and clapped Devon affectionately on the back. "Welcome to the family, son."

"Thank you, sir. It's an honor."

"You take Ashley and you two have a good time. Don't worry a thing about the business. We'll have plenty of time to focus on what needs to be done when you get back."

Devon nodded. "Of course."

"Ashley's mother wanted me to tell you that the car taking you and Ashley to the airport is waiting outside. Now tradition is that you stick around, do silly stuff like cut the cake and stuff it into each other's faces, but if it were me and I'd just married one of the sweetest girls in New York City, I'd duck and make a run for it. You could be to the airport before anyone notices you're gone."

Devon smiled. "That sounds like the best plan I've heard all night. You'll cover my exit?"

William smiled back conspiratorially. "That I will, son. Go on now. Go collect your bride. Everyone here will be more than happy to eat the cake for you. No groom I ever knew gave a damn about cake anyway."

Devon laughed and then waded into the crowd to go retrieve Ashley from Cam.

Chapter 8

The sun was sinking over the horizon when Devon carried Ashley through the doorway of their suite. As soon as he put her down, she ran to the terrace doors, flung them wide and gasped in pleasure at the burst of color splashed across the sky.

"Oh Devon, it's beautiful!"

He came up behind her, slipped his arms around her body and pulled her into his chest. He nibbled at her ear and she sighed in pleasure.

"I can't believe this is our view for the next week. Do you know how long it's been since I've been to the beach? I was a little girl."

"What?" he asked in mock horror. "You don't go to the beach?"

"I know. Terrible, isn't it? I don't know why. It's just not where our family ever went on vacation and my friends aren't really beachgoers. I just haven't made it a point to go and yet here we are and it's so fabulously gorgeous that I don't even have the words to describe it," she said breathlessly.

He chuckled. "Sounds to me like you have plenty of words. But I'm glad you like it."

She turned in his arms, allowing his hands to drop to her waist as he held her there. "How on earth did you find this place? I'd never heard of St. Angelo."

"We're constructing a resort here. We broke ground several weeks ago. Ryan and Kelly live here, remember?"

Her nose wrinkled. "Oh yes, you told me about them. I remember now. I've never met them. I've only met Cam."

"A situation I'll remedy soon. Bryony and Kelly are both very near to their due dates and so they aren't able to travel. We'll have dinner with Ryan and Kelly while we're here and I'm sure we'll have the occasion to meet Rafe and Bryony before long."

"I can't wait."

"I couldn't care less about them at the moment," Devon murmured. "I'm more interested in our wedding night."

Heat exploded in her cheeks at the same time a delicious shiver wracked her spine. "I have to get ready," she said in a low voice. "I have something special. It's a surprise."

"Mmm, what kind of surprise?"

"Umm, well, it was a gift from my girlfriends. They assured me no man alive would be able to resist me in it."

"Oh hell, remind me to thank them."

She raised an eyebrow. "You haven't seen me in it yet."

"I'll like it. I'm sure I'll like it. I'd like you in sack-cloth. Whatever it is they bought you, I'm sure I'll appreciate it. Right before I peel it off your delectable body."

She all but wiggled in excitement. She was barely able to contain herself. "Okay, you wait here. Give me fifteen minutes at least. I want to look perfect. And no peeking!"

He held up his hands. "Would I do such a thing?"

Her eyes narrowed. "Promise me."

He sighed. "Okay, okay. But get moving. I'm going to go down and arrange for a very good bottle of wine and also give them our breakfast order for the morning. You have until I get back to do your thing."

She went up on tiptoe, kissed him and brushed past him into the suite. She waited just until he walked by and out of the bedroom before she hurriedly retrieved the bright pink, totally girly gift box from her suitcase.

At her lingerie shower, her girlfriends had delighted in making her eyes grow wide at all the things they'd bought her. The gifts had ranged from totally classy and elegant to absolutely outrageous and daring.

For her wedding night, she'd chosen a gown that was the perfect blend of elegant and sensual. It was sexy without being over-the-top siren material, although Ashley had no objection over the siren part. Being a seductive temptress for an evening had its merits and she was determined that she'd eventually work up the nerve to pull that one off.

She hurriedly changed and then went to survey herself in the mirror in the corner. The gown was beautiful. She felt like a princess and she liked that feeling very much. A pampered, cherished princess.

She reached for the clip holding her hair up and let the strands tumble down onto her shoulders. She fluffed it a bit, ran her fingers through the ends to straighten it and then took another step back to survey her reflection.

The bodice plunged deep between her breasts and offered just a hint of a view of the swells. If she turned just right, her nipple was almost bared. Almost, but not quite.

The skirt of the gown was sheer and it shimmered over her legs like a dream. Maybe she'd underestimated the siren quality of the lingerie. It seemed innocent enough in the box, but on her…? It took on a more seductive air and made her look less innocent and more brazen.

Not a bad look to achieve on one's wedding night.

She flashed herself an impish grin and turned away from the mirror. Impulsively, she swirled around, outstretching her arms as she pretended to dance with an imaginary partner.

Humming lightly she twirled again, sighing dreamily as she performed the steps to the waltz she and Devon had danced at her reception. He was a good dancer. He didn't seem entirely comfortable with dancing as a rule, but he'd been more than adept at it. He moved like a dream. Commanding. Graceful with a hint of arrogance that made her all giddy inside.

She closed her eyes and whirled again. Her outstretched hand smacked against something hard and pain flashed over her knuckles at the same time a crash jolted her out of her fantasy.

Devon's laptop that had been resting on the mantel of the fireplace along with his wallet, keys and the contents of his pockets, was now lying on the floor in pieces.

She dropped to the floor, groaning her dismay. It looked as if the battery had just popped out but how could she be sure? What if she'd broken it? Who knew what all-important, irreplaceable things he had on his laptop. If he was anything like her father and brother and countless other family members, his entire life was in the damn thing.

Okay, she knew her way around computers. She may not spend her life on one, but she was capable of working one. Or determining whether or not she'd just broken her husband's.

She put the battery back in, checked for further damage and then pressed the power button, praying that it would come on. After a moment, the black screen of death remained and she let out another groan.

In frustration, she punched several buttons on the keyboard, willing something—anything—to come to life. The problem was, as soon as she began pressing the keys, the monitor blinked and she was treated to a dozen programs opening and flashing in rapid succession.

At least the damn thing worked.

She bit her lip in consternation and began closing the programs down. There were lots of Excel spreadsheets, countless charts and graphs that made her head swim. Halfway through she was struck by the fear that none of these were saved or that she was losing valuable information.

As much as she didn't want to ruin the moment, she'd be better off telling Devon what happened and let him sort out his laptop. That way tomorrow when he opened it up, there would be no nasty surprises.

She downsized the pdf that looked to be more a mammoth-sized report when her name caught her eye. She slowed down to read, her fingers pausing on the keyboard. It was an email from her father and she smiled as she saw the reference to her as his baby. But what she read next halted her in her tracks.

I've had time to consider your reservations in regard to Ashley and perhaps you were right to be concerned. I don't want you to think I discounted your intuition, but rather I want you to understand that I want her protected at all costs. Her knowing the truth of our arrangement isn't necessary even as I understand why perhaps you're uncomfortable with it. She's my only daughter and I love her dearly. The truth is, I'd rather she never know that the marriage is a condition of the merger. You are a welcome addition to this family and I trust that you'll always act in her best interests, which is why I implore you to remain silent as to our agreement.

Stunned, Ashley stared at the screen, sure that she couldn't have understood this correctly. She was jumping to conclusions, something her mother had always accused her of.

She admonished herself to remain calm even though her pulse was racing so hard that she could literally feel it jumping in her neck and in her temples.

She returned to the email, forcing the blurry words to focus.

"Ashley?"

She yanked her head up, startled as Devon suddenly loomed over her.

"It fell," she croaked out. "Off the mantel. I was afraid it was broken. The battery fell out of it. When I put it back together and started it back up, all these programs opened and I was trying to shut them all down."

He reached down to take the laptop, but she held on to it, with bloodless fingers.

He swore when he caught sight of what she was reading and he wrested the computer from her grip.

"Give it back, Devon. I want to know what it says."

He closed it with a sharp snap and tucked it underneath his arm. "There's nothing you need to see."

"Don't lie to me," she grit out. "I read most of it. Or at least the important parts. I want to know what the hell it means."

Devon stared back at her, his lips drawn in a thin line. He looked as though he'd rather be anywhere but here, doing anything but having this conversation with her. Too bad. She wasn't about to back down.

"Nothing good can come of it, Ash. Just forget it, okay?"

She gaped at him. "Forget it? You want me to just forget I saw an email from my father basically admitting he bought me a husband? Or at least manipulated you somehow into marrying me? This is my wedding night, Devon. Am I supposed to pretend I didn't see that email?"

Devon cursed and ran his hand through his hair. "Damn it, Ashley, why the hell did you open the laptop?"

"I didn't mean to! Believe me I'd give anything not to have knocked the damn thing down. But the fact is I did and now I want to know what's going on. What kind of a deal did you strike with my father? Tell me the truth or I swear I'm walking out of here right now."

"This is precisely why you're your own worst enemy

at times, Ash. You're too impulsive. You don't think before you act. You just go around wading into situations and you end up getting hurt. If it enters your mind, you simply do it. That quickly. At some point you have to learn some control."

She gaped at him, openmouthed, as his frustrated, angry words bit into her. How was she the bad guy here? What the hell had she done? This wasn't her fault. She hadn't entered this marriage under false pretenses. Devon knew precisely where she stood. God knew she'd told him enough times.

His eyes flashed and he turned his back. He walked across the room to the dresser and slapped the laptop down on it. For a long moment, he stood there, not facing her, silent. Tension rose sharp and so thick it was uncomfortable. Fear struck a deep chord within her because she realized that she was about to learn something truly terrible about her life. Her fate. Her marriage.

"Devon?" she whispered.

She thought back on their relationship. The whirlwind courtship. Suddenly the blinders were off and she began to analyze every date. Everything he'd said to her. How much of it had been a lie? Was any of it true?

She didn't want to ask. She wasn't sure she could bear to know the answer to her most burning question, but she also realized she had no choice.

He turned around and his eyes were shuttered. His expression was impassive almost as if he hoped to quell any further discussion.

Suddenly the circumstances of her marriage didn't matter to her. There was only one thing she absolutely had to know. The most important thing. The one thing that would determine her future. And whether she had one with him.

"Just answer me one question," she said faintly. "Do you love me?"

Chapter 9

Dread had a two-fisted grip around Devon's throat. He stared at Ashley's pale, stricken face and he knew his time had come. Maybe he'd always known that this moment would come. He'd never really believed that it was possible to prevent Ashley from finding out the truth and furthermore it was stupid to try to keep it from her.

Damn fool of an old man. William Copeland didn't want his precious daughter hurt and yet he'd set her up for the biggest fall of her life. Nice. And now Devon was going to look like the biggest bastard of all time.

"I care for you a great deal," he said evenly.

Anger and fear warred with one another in her eyes. His answer sounded lame even to his own ears but he couldn't bring himself to destroy her even further. Hadn't she endured enough already?

"Let's have the truth," she demanded. "Don't patronize me or pat me on the head while whispering pretty words to pacify me. It's a very simple question, Devon. Do you love me?"

His nostrils flared. "The truth isn't always a pretty thing, Ash. The truth isn't always pleasant to hear. Be careful when you ask for the truth because it can hurt far more than not knowing."

If possible she went even paler. Her eyes were stricken and all the light vanished from their depths as if someone had extinguished a flame. For a moment he thought she'd let it go, but then she squared her shoulders and said in a low, dead voice, "The truth, Dev. I want the truth. I need to hear it."

He bit out another curse and thrust his hand into his hair. "All right, Ashley, no, I don't love you. I care about you a great deal. I like and respect you. But if you want to know if I love you, then no."

She made a broken sound of pain that was like a knife right through his chest. Why couldn't he have just lied to her? Because she would have known the truth whether he admitted it or not and she'd already been deceived enough.

And maybe now they could finally go forward with complete and utter honesty and he could stop feeling like the worst sort of bastard at every turn.

She started to step backward, but she swayed precariously and flailed out one arm to catch herself on the mantel. He bolted forward, caught her shoulders and then guided her to the bed, forcing her down into a sitting position.

He took one step back and then heaved out a breath. Before he could launch into what he wanted to say, she found his gaze and he flinched at the raw vulnerability reflected in those eyes.

"What a fool I've made of myself," she whispered. "How stupid and naive. How you must have laughed."

"Damn it, Ash, I've never laughed at you. Never!"

"I loved you," she said painfully. "Thought you loved me. Thought we were getting married because you wanted me, not my father's business or whatever it was he offered you. How much did I cost you, Dev? Or should I ask how much my father offered you to marry me?"

Furious at the senseless direction this was heading, he yanked the chair out from the desk, turned it around and sat so he faced her.

"Listen to me. There's no reason we can't have an enjoyable marriage. We're compatible. We get along well together. We're good in bed. Those are three things many married couples don't have going for them."

She closed her eyes.

"Look at me, Ash. This may be painful to hear but maybe it's for the best if we get it all out in the open. You're far too emotional. You wear your feelings and your heart on your sleeve and it's only going to get you hurt. Maybe it's time for you to grow up and face the fact that life isn't a fairy tale. You're too impulsive. You dash about with no caution and no sense of self-preservation. That's only going to cause you further pain down the road."

She shook her head in utter confusion. Her eyes were cloudy and it was clear she was battling tears. "How could I possibly ever hurt as much as I do now? How can you be so…so…*cold* and calm and so matter-of-fact as if this is nothing more than a business meeting where you're discussing figures and projections and sales and a whole host of other things I don't understand?"

His gut twisted into a knot. He'd never felt so damn helpless in his life. He wished to hell it was as simple as telling her to be harder and for her not to let this destroy her, but he knew it was pointless because Ashley was one of the most tenderhearted people he knew and he was an ass to sit here and tell her to get over it.

She covered her face in her hands and he could see her throat working convulsively as she tried to keep her sobs silent. But they spilled out, harsh and brittle in the quiet.

He lifted his hand to touch her hair but left it in the air before finally pulling it back. She wouldn't welcome comfort from him, of all people. If it were any other woman, she'd have already come after his nuts and he'd deserve everything she dished out and more.

"Ash, please don't cry."

She lifted her ravaged face and pushed angrily at her hair. "Don't cry? What the hell else do you suggest I do? How could you do this? How could my father? Tell me, Devon, what was the price put on my future? What do you get out of the bargain?"

He stared at her in silence.

"Tell me, damn it! I think I deserve to know what my happiness was traded for."

"Your father wanted me to marry you as part of the merger between Tricorp Investments and Copeland Hotels," he bit out. "Happy now? Can you tell me what possible good it does for you to know that?"

"It doesn't make me happy but I damn well want to know what I've gotten myself into, or rather what my father got me into. Did I ever even have a chance? Did you study up on all the ways to worm your way into my heart?"

"Christ, no. Look, it was all real. It's not like I faked an attraction to you. It wasn't exactly a hardship to pursue you. If I hadn't wanted to marry you, no merger or deal would have persuaded me differently. I thought and still think that we'd make a solid marriage. I don't see why love has to be the be-all and end-all in this equation. Mutual respect and friendship are far more important aspects of a relationship."

"Maybe you can tell me how the hell I'm supposed to respect a man who doesn't love me and who manipulated me into a marriage based on deception. Does everyone think I'm a brainless twit who should be pathetically grateful that a man sweeps into my life and offers to take care of me? I've got news for you and my family. I hadn't married yet because it was my choice. I hadn't had sex with a man yet because I had enough respect for myself that I wasn't going to be pressured into something I wasn't ready for. It's not like I haven't had men interested in me. I'm not pathetically needy nor was I going to waste away if I wasn't married by the ripe old age of twenty-three. I was happy. I had a good life."

"Ashley, listen to me."

He leaned forward, caught her hands and stared until she quieted and returned his gaze.

"Right now you're upset and you're hurting. But don't discount the possibility that we could enjoy a comfortable, lasting marriage. Don't make a snap decision you may regret later. Take some time to think about it when you've calmed down. When you're not so volatile, you'll be able to look at the situation more objectively."

"Oh screw off," she snapped. "Could you be any more patronizing? 'Don't be so high-strung, Ashley. Don't be so stupid and naive. Don't expect ridiculous things like love and affection in a marriage. How perfectly absurd would that be?'"

"I don't think we should have this conversation any longer," he said tightly. "Not until you've had time to calm down and think about what you're saying." He stood abruptly and she looked hastily away but not before he saw the silver trail of her tears streaking down her cheeks.

He wanted more than anything to pull her into his arms and let her cry on his shoulder. He wanted to comfort her, hold her, soothe her fears and tell her it would be all right. But how could he when he was the sole reason she was devastated?

"I'm sorry, Ash," he said hoarsely. "I know you don't believe that, but I'm more sorry than you'll ever know. I would have done anything at all to spare you this pain."

"Please, just go away and leave me alone," she choked out. "I can't even look at you right now."

He hesitated a moment and then sighed in resignation. "I'll take the couch in the living area. We'll talk more in the morning."

It took every ounce of his willpower to turn around and walk out of the bedroom. His instincts screamed at him not to leave her alone. To take her in his arms and force the issue. Make her listen to him. To not relent until she agreed that their marriage could and would work if only they could set aside the emotional volatility that always seemed to accompany declarations of love.

He had only to point at his friends to know this was an inevitable truth. Their lives were emotional messes brought on by the letter *L*.

All that angst and suffering in the name of love. Rafe

and Ryan had spent more time in abject misery and all because they'd been ripped to shreds by...love.

Devon grimaced and sank onto the couch in the dark living room. What a wedding night this had turned out to be. Maybe he'd always known that it was inevitable that she learn the truth. How could she not? But he'd hoped they'd have a lot more mileage behind them. Then she could see that their marriage wasn't defined by love or emotion, volatility or vulnerability.

Friendship, companionship, trust, respect.

Those were all things he was on board with.

Love? Not so much. It was a messy, raw emotion he had no desire to embroil himself with.

Chapter 10

Ashley sat on the private veranda and stared over the ocean as the sun began its hesitant rise. She felt empty. Wrung out. She felt stupid and so horribly naive that she cringed. It still baffled her that a life she'd thought was so perfect just hours before was a complete facade.

All night she'd sat huddled in an uncomfortable chair trying to come to grips with the fact that she'd been lied to at every turn. She'd been used and manipulated, not just by Devon, but by her own father. And all over a business deal.

She couldn't wrap her head around it.

Why? Why had it been so important for Devon to marry her? Was her father so unconvinced of Ashley's ability to manage her own life that he'd all but hired a man to be her husband? She winced at the thought, but it was appropriate. At the very least, she'd been used as a bargaining chip.

She rubbed at eyes that felt full of sand. She'd cried all that she was going to allow herself to cry. She be damned if she shed another single tear over her husband.

A dry laugh escaped her. Her husband. What was she going to do about her marriage? Her complete and utter farce of a marriage.

She closed her eyes against the humiliation of it all. What a fool she'd made of herself over the last month. She wanted to die from it.

Had he laughed at her the entire time? Had he joked with his friends about what a gullible idiot she was? She didn't like to imagine he could be so cruel, but the man she'd faced down the night before and demanded the truth from had been brutally honest. At her insistence, but crushingly forthright all the same.

"It's time you had the cold hard truth, Ashley," she whispered. She'd been living a fantasy.

She rubbed at her temples, willing the vicious ache to go away. But the pain in her head was nothing compared to the unbearable ache in her heart.

Should she leave him? Should she ask for a divorce? They could have the shortest marriage on record. She could go back home. Chalk it up to a lesson learned the hard way. It was doubtful at this point that her father would pull the plug on the deal because Devon had lived up to his end of the bargain. It wasn't Devon who was unhappy with the result. It was her. Everyone had evidently thought she was the very last person who should be consulted about her life.

But the idea of divorcing Devon held as little appeal as living in the cold, sterile state her marriage now existed in. She deeply loved him and love wasn't something you could switch off at will. She was hurt beyond belief. She was angry and she felt horribly betrayed. But she still loved him and she still wished that they could go back to the way things had been before she'd found out the damnable truth.

It was true what they said about ignorance being bliss. She'd give anything at all to go back to being that innocent little girl who still believed in happily ever after with Prince Charming. For just a little while Devon had been that prince. He'd been perfect. She'd built him into something he wasn't, and that wasn't entirely his fault. He couldn't be blamed for her utter stupidity.

No, she didn't want a divorce. But neither did she want to live a life with a man who didn't love her.

She thought back to all the things he'd said to her the night before. His criticisms had stung. They'd stunned her. She'd never imagined that he'd thought of her in such a negative way. But maybe he was right.

Maybe she was too impulsive, too flighty, too exuberant. Perhaps she should be more controlled, more guarded, show more of a knack for self-preservation.

It was evident that he didn't want the person she was. It was evident he didn't love flighty, impulsive, tenderhearted, animal-loving Ashley Copeland, who called him at work just to say she loved him.

If he didn't want or love that person, then the only two options left to her were to walk away and get a divorce or to *become* someone he could love.

Could she make him fall in love with her? Her family always worried that she was too trusting. Too naive. Too everything. Apparently they were right.

The only person who didn't seem to think anything was wrong with who Ashley Copeland was, was Ashley herself. And it was becoming increasingly clearer that her judgment stank.

It was time for one hell of a makeover.

But the idea didn't excite her. It didn't infuse enthusiasm into her flagging spirits. It was a bleak thought and she dimly wondered if Devon was worth such an effort.

Would his love be enough, provided she could even make him fall in love with her?

A voice in the back of her mind whispered that it was time for her to grow up. It was a voice that sounded precariously close to Devon's. He thought she should grow up. Her father evidently thought the same. Maybe they were both right.

She stiffened when she heard a sound on the terrace. She knew it was Devon but she wasn't ready to face him yet.

"Have you been out here all night?" he asked quietly.

She nodded wordlessly and continued to stare over the water.

He walked to the thick stone railing that enclosed the private viewing area, shoved his hands in his pockets and for a moment stared over the water as she was doing. Then he turned to face her and leaned back against the stone.

He looked as bad as she felt, though she had no sympathy. His hair was rumpled. He was still in the same clothes as the night before.

"Ash, don't torture yourself over this. There's no reason we can't have a perfectly good marriage, no matter the circumstances of *how* we came to be married."

He was starting to repeat his arguments from the previous night and the truth was, she couldn't stomach hearing again how she was naive and impulsive and whatever else it was he'd said when he outlined all her faults.

She bit her lip to keep the angry flood from rushing out because at this point it did her no good and she didn't have the emotional energy to spare.

She held up a hand to stop him and cursed at how it trembled. She put it back down and tucked it into her gown, blinking as she realized she was still in her sexy, lacy lingerie that she'd so painstakingly picked out for her wedding night.

Unbidden tears welled again in her eyes as she realized just what a disaster her wedding night had been. What should have been the most special night of her entire life would forever be a black hole in her past no matter what happened in the future.

"I agree," she said before he could launch into another list of her shortcomings.

He promptly shut his mouth and then stared at her, his brows drawn together in confusion. "You do?"

She nodded again because the words seemed to stick in her throat. Almost as if they were rebelling. It took her a few moments to force out what she wanted to say.

"You're absolutely right. I was being silly. I had unrealistic expectations and I shouldn't allow them to get in the way of marriage."

He winced but remained quiet.

"I am agreeable to at least a period of time in which we see how things progress."

He frowned at that but she looked up with dead eyes. "Be glad I'm not on a plane home with an appointment to see a divorce lawyer."

He pushed out a breath and then slowly nodded. "All right. How long do you think this test period will last?"

She shrugged. "How would I know? I can't exactly put a time frame on when I can give up all hope of having a happy marriage."

"Ash."

The low growl in which he said her name only served to make her angrier. She curled her fingers into tight balls, determined not to give in to the urge to scream at him. She was determined to get through this, no matter how excruciating it was.

"I'm not trying to punish you, Devon. I'm trying to get through this without losing what little pride I have left."

He went pale and pain flickered in his eyes. And shame. Though that hadn't been her intention, either. She wasn't trying to make digs at him because that wouldn't make this go away. It wouldn't give her back her happiness. It would only make her more miserable than she already was.

"You seem to think we can have an enjoyable marriage. I personally find no joy in being married to a man who doesn't love me, but I'm willing to try. You're probably right in that I shouldn't allow something so silly as love to enter the equation."

"Damn it, I care a lot for you—"

"Please," she bit out, halting his words in midsentence. "Just don't. Don't try to make it better by offering me platitudes. It was hard to hear your assessment of my faults. Does anyone ever like to hear that about themselves? But I'm willing to work on not being so impulsive and exuberant or whatever else it was that you mentioned. I'll try to be the best wife I can be and not disappoint you."

He bit out a sharp curse but she ignored him and plunged ahead before she lost all her courage and fled.

"I just have one thing to ask in return," she whispered.

She was trying valiantly not to break down again. She'd already made such an idiot of herself in front of him. She was forever making a total cake of herself with him.

His lips were thin. His eyes were dark with raw emotion. At least he wasn't totally unaffected by her distress.

"I find the situation I'm in immensely humiliating. I'll make every effort to be a wife you'll be proud of. All I ask is that you please not embarrass me in front of my family by making our issues known to anyone. What I'm asking you to do is pretend. At least with them."

"God, Ash. You act as though I despise you. I'd never embarrass you."

"I just don't want them to know you don't love me," she choked out. "If you could just act like—like a real husband in front of them. You don't have to go overboard. Just don't treat me with indifference now that you don't have to pretend in order to get me to marry you anymore."

And then another thought occurred to her that very nearly had her leaning over to empty the contents of her stomach.

"Are you all right?" Devon asked sharply. Then he swore. "Of course you aren't all right. You look as if you're going to be ill."

"Is there someone else?" she croaked out. "I mean did you ever plan to be faithful? I won't stay married to you if you're going to sleep around or if you have a mistress on tap somewhere."

This time the curses were more colorful and they didn't stop for several long seconds. He closed the distance between them, knelt down in front of the lounger she was curled up in and grasped her shoulders.

"Stop it, Ashley. You're torturing yourself needlessly. There is no other woman. There won't be another woman. I take my marriage vows very seriously. I don't have a mistress. There's been no other woman since well before you entered the picture. I have no desire to sleep around. I want *you.*"

Her shoulders sagged in relief and she leaned away from him so that his hands slipped from her arms.

"Damn it, I wanted to tell you the truth from the very beginning but your father wouldn't hear of it. My mistake. I should have told you anyway. But it doesn't change anything. I still want to be married to you. If I found the idea so abhorrent, I'd simply wait until the deal was done and begin divorce proceedings. There wouldn't be a damn thing your father could do at that point."

She closed her eyes wearily and rubbed at her head. The sun's steady creep over the horizon was casting more light onto the terrace and each ray speared her eyeballs like a flaming pitchfork.

"Do you have one of your headaches?" he asked, his voice full of concern. "Did you bring your medicine?"

She opened her eyes again, wincing as she tried to refocus. "I want to go home."

Devon's expression darkened. "Don't be unreasonable. What you need is to take your medicine and get some sleep. You'll feel better once you rest and eat something."

"I won't stay here and pretend. It's pointless. You even brought me to the island where you're building a resort, I'm sure so you could keep up with the progress. So don't tell me I'm being unreasonable for wanting to dispense with the fairy-tale honeymoon. You and I both know at this point it's a joke and we'll just spend all week staring awkwardly at each other or you'll just spend most of the time at the job site."

His jaw ticked and he stood again, turning briefly away. Then he turned back, irritation evident in his gaze. "You wanted me to pretend in front of your family. Why can't you pretend now?"

"Because I'm miserable and it's going to take me a little time to get over this," she snapped. "Look, we can say I wasn't feeling well. Or you can make up some business emergency. It's not as if anyone in my capitalistic family would even lift an eyebrow at the idea of business coming first. Right now my head hurts so damn bad, we wouldn't even be lying."

Some of the anger left Devon's gaze. "Let me get you some medication for your headache. Then I want you to get some rest. If…" He sighed. "If you still want to leave when you wake up, I'll arrange our flight back to New York."

Chapter 11

She slept because the pill Devon gave her would allow her to do no less. She rarely resorted to taking the medication prescribed for her migraines for the reason that it made her insensible.

When she awoke, she was in bed by herself and it was nearly dusk. Her headache still hung on with tenacious claws and when she moved too suddenly to try to sit up, nausea welled in her stomach. Her head pounded and she put a hand to her forehead, sucking air through her nostrils to control the sudden wash of weakness.

The room was blanketed in darkness, the drapes drawn and no lights had been left on. Devon had made sure she had been left in comfort, only a sheet covering her and the air-conditioning turned down so it was nearly frigid in the room.

Before, his consideration would have been endearing. Now, she could only assume he was operating out of guilt.

She pushed herself from the bed and sat on the edge for a moment, holding her head while she got her bearings. After a moment, she got to her feet and wobbled unsteadily toward the luggage stand, where her still-packed suitcase lay open.

She ripped off the silky gown she'd so excitedly donned the night before and tossed it in the nearby garbage can. If she never saw it again, it would be too soon.

She dug through the suitcase, bypassing the chic outfits, the swimwear and the other sexy nightwear she'd purchased, and pulled out a faded pair of jeans and a T-shirt. She briefly contemplated shoes, but the idea had formed in her head to take a long walk on the beach. Maybe it would clear her head or at least stop the vile aching. For that, she wouldn't need shoes.

Having no idea where Devon was, or if he was even still in the suite, she opted to leave through the sliding glass doors to the veranda. The breeze lifted her hair as soon as she walked outside the room and she inhaled deeply as she took the steps leading down to the beach.

The night was warm and the wind coming off the water was comfortable, but she was cold to her bones and she shivered as her feet dug into the sand.

It was a perfect, glorious night. The sky was lit up like a million fireflies had taken wing and danced over the inky black canvas. In the distance the moon was just rising over the water and it shimmered like a splash of silver.

Drawn to the mesmerizing sight, she ventured closer to the water, hugging her arms around her waist as the incoming waves lapped precariously close to her toes.

At one point, she stopped and allowed the water

to caress her feet and surround her ankles. There she stood, staring over the expanse of the ocean, stargazing like a dreamer. It would take a million wishes to fix the mess she was currently in. And maybe that was what had gotten her into this situation in the first place.

Stupid dreams. Stupid idealism. She'd been a fool to wait for the perfect guy to give her virginity to. She'd always been somewhat smug and a little holier-than-thou with her friends who'd given it up long ago. But they at least had gone into the situation with their eyes wide open. They hadn't confused sex for love. They weren't the ones on their honeymoon with the migraine from hell and a husband who didn't love them.

They were looking pretty damn smart for shopping around and Ashley was looking like a moron.

She pulled out her cell phone and stared down at her contacts list. She could use the comfort of a good friend right now but she wavered on whether to send a text. She was already humiliated enough. Could she bear to tell her friends or even one friend the truth about her marriage? Or would she go back home, live a lie and hope that Devon would pretend as agreed.

Could she ever make him love her?

She lowered the hand holding the phone and then she shoved it back into her pocket. What could she say anyway in the limited number of characters allowed by a text message? Or maybe she should just tweet everyone.

Marriage fail. Honeymoon fail.

That would get the message across with plenty of characters left over.

She shoved her hands into her pockets, closed her eyes and wished for just one minute that she could go back. That she would have asked more questions. That she would have picked up on the fact he'd never said he loved her even when Ashley made it a practice to tell him every day.

She'd just assumed he was a typical guy. Devon was reserved. He was somewhat forbidding. But she'd been wildly attracted to those qualities. Thought they were sexy. She'd been convinced that he quietly adored her and that his actions spoke louder than words.

She'd never considered even once that his actions were practiced, fake and manipulative.

Another shiver overtook her and she clamped her teeth together until pain shot through her head.

"Enough," she said.

She had beat herself up for the last twenty-four hours, but it was Devon who was the jackass here. Not her. She'd done nothing wrong. Naiveté wasn't a crime. Loving someone wasn't a crime. She wouldn't apologize for offering her love, trust and commitment to a man who didn't deserve any of it.

He was wrong. She wasn't.

The only thing she could control from here on out was what she did with the truth. It was no longer about what Devon wanted. If he could be a selfish jerk-wad, she could at least focus on what she wanted from this fiasco.

Then she laughed because what she wanted was the jerk-wad to love her. That might make her pathetic.

No, she couldn't text Sylvia or Carly or Tabitha. Definitely not Pippa. Pippa would have her in front of a lawyer in a matter of hours and then she'd likely take out a hit on Devon.

Plus her friends would tell her she was being stupid for wanting to stay in the marriage. And she may well be an idiot, but she didn't want people telling her that. She'd already made one mistake. It wouldn't be the first or last and well, if it didn't work out, at least then she could cite incompatibility and she wouldn't have to tell everyone that the marriage had fallen apart before it had ever gotten off the ground.

She had just enough of an ego to want to save face. Who could blame her?

Feeling only marginally better about taking control over a perfectly out-of-control situation, she turned to retrace her steps. She was hungry but the thought of food made her faintly nauseous and her head was hurting so badly she wasn't sure she could keep anything down anyway.

She was still a good distance from the steps leading to her and Devon's suite when she saw him striding toward her on the sand.

Even now after so much time to think and decide how she wanted to proceed, she wasn't prepared to face him. How could she just go on after finding out he was nothing like the man she'd thought she'd married? It was as if they were strangers. Intimate strangers who would now live together and pretend a loving existence to outsiders.

There weren't manuals for this. Certainly no one had ever given her advice on such a matter. She wasn't good at artifice. She hated lying. But it was what she'd asked him to do. It was what she herself had just decided to do with her friends and family. To the world.

"Where the hell have you been?" Devon demanded as he approached. "I was worried sick. I went in to check on you and you were gone."

Before she could answer, he put his hand around her

elbow and pulled her toward the glow cast from the torches that lined the beach.

She flinched away from the burst of light and he muttered something under his breath.

"Your headache isn't any better, is it?"

She slowly shook her head.

"Damn it, Ash, why didn't you come to me? Or take another pill. You should be in bed. For that matter you've eaten nothing in twenty-four hours. You're as pale as death and your eyes are glazed with pain."

She braced herself as he reached for her again, but his touch was in direct contrast to the tone of his voice. He was infinitely gentle as he pulled her against his side and began leading her back to the suite.

Unable to resist the urge, she laid her head on his shoulder and closed her eyes, trusting him to at least get her safely up the steps. His hold tightened around her and then to her shock, he simply swung her into his arms and began carrying her back.

"Put your head on my shoulder," he said gruffly.

Relaxing against him, she did as he directed and for a few moments, basked in the tenderness of his hold.

Pretending was nice.

He carried her back into the suite, into the still-darkened bedroom, and carefully laid her on the bed.

"Would you be more comfortable out of your jeans?" he asked. But even as he asked, he was unfastening her fly and pulling the zipper down.

He efficiently pulled her pants down her legs, leaving her in her panties and T-shirt. She lay there, cheek resting on the firm, cool pillow, and willed the pain to go away. All of it.

He sat on the edge of the bed and then turned, sliding his leg over the mattress and bending it so he was perched next to her.

"I'll get you another pill, but I don't think you should take it on an empty stomach. It might make you ill. But neither do you look as though you could keep down much so I'll call down for some soup. Would you like something to drink? Could you handle some juice?"

As he spoke, he smoothed his hand over her hair, stroking gently, and she had to bite her lip to keep the hot tears from slipping down her cheeks again. This wasn't going to work if she broke down every time he was nice to her or took care of her.

And it wasn't as if he was doing anything different than he'd done all along. It was one of the things that had made her think he loved her to begin with, even absent of the actual words. He'd been so…good…to her. So caring. Protective. Possessive. A guy couldn't fake all of that, could he?

"Soup sounds good," she said faintly.

He continued to stroke her hair and then his hand went still and he frowned. "Is that bothering you? I wasn't thinking. I'm sure you must be supersensitive to any touch or sound."

"It was…nice."

"I'll be right back. Let me order your soup. You need to get something in your stomach. It might help with the headache, too."

She closed her eyes as he stood and walked across the room. He stepped outside but she could just make out the low murmur of his voice as he ordered room service. A moment later, he returned and gently laid his hand over her forehead.

"It'll be here in a few minutes. I told them to put a rush on it."

"Thank you."

He was silent for a few seconds and then he said in a voice full of resignation, "I'll make arrangements for us to fly home in the morning. Perhaps it's best if you're back in familiar surroundings. I don't want you to suffer with a headache the entire week we were supposed to be here. At least at home, you'll have your family and your friends to surround you and…make you feel better."

She nodded, her chest heavy and aching with regret. It should have been different. They should have spent the week making love. Laughing. Spending every waking moment immersed in each other.

Instead they'd go back home to a very uncertain future in a world that was suddenly unfamiliar to Ashley. Where she'd have to guard every word, every action.

It frightened her. What if she failed? What if even after she removed the annoyances he still felt nothing more for her than he did now?

Then he doesn't deserve you, the voice inside her aching head whispered in her ear.

He didn't deserve her now. The intelligent side of her knew and accepted this. But she wanted him. Wanted his love, his approval. She wanted him to be proud of her.

If that made her an even bigger moron than she'd already been, she could live with that. What she couldn't live with was just walking away without seeing if their marriage could be salvaged.

"It will be better when we get home," she whispered.

His hand stilled on her hair but he remained silent as he seemed to contemplate her words. His expression was grim and tension radiated from his body in waves.

Then there was a distant knock and he rose once more. "That'll be the food. Just stay here. I'll wheel the cart in and we'll get you a comfortable spot made up so you can eat in bed."

He strode out of the room and Ashley lay there a moment mentally recovering from what felt like a barrage of emotional turmoil. Finally she pushed herself upward and sat cross-legged on the bed, with pillows pushed behind her back to keep her propped up.

Devon returned with the rolling table and parked it at the end of the bed. As soon as he uncovered the bowl of soup, the aroma wafted through the air and her mouth watered. On cue, her stomach protested sharply and sweat broke out on her forehead.

"You okay?" Devon asked as he positioned the tray in front of her.

His gaze was focused sharply on her face, his forehead creased with concern. She nodded and reached for the napkin and utensils with shaking hands.

When she would have slid the bowl closer, Devon gently took her hand away.

"Perhaps it would be better if I ladled the soup into a mug so you could sip at it. Less chance of spilling it that way."

She nodded her agreement and watched as he filled one of the cups on the table with the delicious-smelling broth.

"Here. Careful now, it's hot."

She brought the steaming mug to her lips and inhaled, closing her eyes as she tentatively took the first sip.

It was heaven in a coffee cup. The warmth from the soup traveled all the way down to her stomach and settled there comfortably.

"Good?" he asked as he edged his way onto the bed beside her.

"Wonderful."

He watched as she downed a significant amount of the soup and then he took her medicine bottle from the nightstand and shook out another pill.

"Here. Take this. Once you're finished you can lie down and hopefully sleep until morning. I'll wake you up in time to catch the flight. Don't worry about your things. I'll lay out something for you to wear on the plane and I'll pack everything else and have it all ready to go. All you'll have to do is get dressed and head out to the car when it's time."

Even though she was still devastated and angry, she couldn't be so much of a bitch not to recognize or acknowledge that he was taking absolute care of her.

She leaned back against the pillows, cup in hand, and glanced his way.

"Thank you," she said quietly.

A flash of pain entered his eyes. "I know you don't believe this right now, but maybe in time you will, Ash. I never meant to hurt you. I never wanted this to happen. I wouldn't have hurt you for the world."

She swallowed and brought the rim of the cup back to her lips. There wasn't much she could say to that. She did believe that he wasn't malicious. If she hadn't discovered the truth on her own, maybe he would have never told her. She was quite certain he wouldn't have. Maybe he thought he was doing her a favor by keeping it from her.

He pulled the mug away and then cupped her chin and gently turned her until she looked back at him.

"You'll see, Ash. We'll make this work."

She nodded as she lowered the mug the rest of the way down to the tray in front of her.

"I'll try, Devon. I'll try."

He leaned toward her and pressed a kiss to her forehead. "Get some rest. I'll wake you in the morning."

Chapter 12

The next morning was a total blur for Ashley. Devon gently woke her and after ascertaining that her headache wasn't better, he arranged a light breakfast, hovered over her while she ate and then all but dressed her and whisked her into a waiting car.

They drove to the airport and once on the plane, he settled her into her seat and gave her another pill. He propped a pillow behind her head, put a blanket over her and then made sure every single window was shut around her.

She drifted into blissful unawareness as the airplane left the island and traveled back to the cold of New York City.

When they landed, once again Devon ushered her into a waiting car, taking the blanket and pillow with them so she was comfortable in the backseat. She dozed with her head on his shoulder until they reached his apartment and then he gently shook her awake.

"We're home, Ash. Wait inside the car while I get out. I'll help you inside."

Home. She blinked as the looming building floated into her vision through the fogged window of the car. A cold rush of air blew over her as Devon stepped out. He spoke a moment with the doorman and then he reached back in to help her out.

"Careful," he cautioned as she stepped onto the curb.

He wrapped an arm around her and guided her to the door the doorman held open for them. Once inside, he didn't loosen his hold. He kept her close all the way up in the elevator until they reached his apartment. Their apartment. It was hard to keep that distinction in her mind.

Their home was already cluttered with her things. She'd moved completely in before the wedding. Devon had suggested having a cleaning lady come in which said to her that he didn't appreciate the somewhat careless way she kept her stuff. She sighed. One more thing she'd have to work on.

When they entered the bedroom, Devon pulled out one of his workout T-shirts and tossed it onto the bed. "Why don't you get out of your travel clothes and into something more comfortable. I'll wake you for dinner so you eat something."

"I'd rather just lie down on the couch," she said, reaching for the T-shirt.

His expression darkened and for a moment she couldn't imagine what she'd done to draw his disapproval. Then it struck her that he assumed she wouldn't be sleeping in his—their—bed.

It wasn't something she'd given any consideration.

The thought hadn't even occurred to her. In her mind, if she was staying and making an effort to make their marriage work, she just naturally assumed they'd still sleep together.

Perhaps it wasn't something she should assume at all. She sank onto the edge of the bed, still foggy and loopy from the medication. She rubbed wearily at her eyes before focusing back on him.

"I only meant that when I have a headache, sometimes I'm more comfortable propped on the couch so I'm not lying flat. However, it does bring up a point that I hadn't considered. I assumed that we'd continue to…" She swallowed, suddenly feeling vulnerable and extremely unsure of herself. "That is, I just thought we'd continue to sleep together. I have no idea if that's something you want."

Devon stalked over, bent down and placed his hands on either sides of her legs so that he was on eye level with her.

"You'll be in my bed every night. Whether we're having sex or not, you'll be next to me, in my arms."

"Well, okay then," she murmured.

He rose and took a step back. "Now, if you're more comfortable on the couch, change into my shirt and I'll get you pillows and a blanket for the couch."

She nodded and sat there watching him as he walked away. She glanced around the room—to all her stuff placed haphazardly here and there—and sighed. When she got rid of this headache, she'd whip the apartment into shape. She'd been away from the shelter more days than she'd ever been away before but the animals were in good hands and they'd be fine while she got the rest of her life in order.

Devon would no doubt be back to work in the morning, which meant she'd have plenty of time alone to figure out things. She wrinkled her nose. Being alone sucked. She was always surrounded by people. In her family she didn't have to look far if she wanted company. There was always someone to hang out with. And aside from her family, her circle of friends was always available even if for a gab session.

But what was she supposed to talk to them about now? How wonderful her marriage was? Her husband? The aborted honeymoon?

Her head was too fuzzy to even contemplate the intricacies of her relationships right this second. She reached for the T-shirt, shed her own clothes and crawled into Devon's shirt.

She started to leave her clothes just where they'd dropped on the floor, but she stopped to pick them up and then deposited them into the laundry basket in the bathroom. It was technically Devon's basket and he might not want her mixing her clothes with his, but she didn't have a designated place of her own yet. One more thing for the to-do list.

She trudged out to the living room to see that Devon had arranged several pillows and put out a blanket for her. As she started across the floor, Devon appeared from the kitchen. She crawled onto the couch and burrowed into all of the pillows while Devon pulled the blanket up to her shoulders. Then he perched on the edge close to her head.

"Are you feeling any better yet?"

She nodded. "Head doesn't hurt as bad. A few more hours and it should be fine. Just fuzzy from all the medication. I've never had to take three in a row like that."

He frowned as if he realized the significance of her having the worst headache of her life after their confrontation.

"Rest for a few hours then. I'll check on you in a bit and see if you're up for some dinner. I thought we'd eat in, of course. I can order anything you like or if you prefer, I can make something here."

She nodded.

"I have some calls to make. I'll let your family know we're back and why. You just concentrate on feeling better."

Her eyes widened in alarm. "What are you going to tell them?"

He frowned again. "I'm only going to tell them that you came down with a severe headache and that we thought you'd feel better if you were back in your own home."

She sagged in relief and the knot in her stomach loosened. "They'll want to come right over, or at least Mom will. Tell her not to bother, please. Let her know I'll call her soon."

"Of course. Now get some rest. I'll sort out dinner later."

He kissed her forehead, pulled the covers up to her chin and then quietly walked away, flipping off all the lights. She heard the door to his office close and she lay there alone in the darkness.

It wasn't anything she hadn't experienced before. In the evenings when Dev got home from work, he often sequestered himself in his office for a time while she watched TV or ordered in their dinner. But she hadn't felt so alone then. Because she'd known he was just in the next room and that in theory she could walk in there at any time. Only now it was as if a gulf had opened between them and he may as well be on the other side of the moon. She didn't feel as though she had the right to interrupt him.

She lay there as the haze slowly began to wear off. She braced herself for the inevitable onslaught of pain, but there was only a dull ache that signaled the aftereffects of a much worse headache than she'd experienced in at least two years.

For that matter, she hadn't been forced to take the pain medication prescribed for her headaches in months. Emotional stress, the doctor had said, was a trigger for her. The last time she'd battled frequent headaches had been when her mom and dad had briefly separated and she'd feared an eventual divorce.

It was the very last thing she or any of their family had ever imagined because it was so obvious her parents loved each other. The separation hadn't lasted long. Whatever their issues had been, they'd worked through them quickly and her dad had moved back into the apartment with her mom and they'd gone back to being the loving couple that Ashley had always witnessed.

But for the entire period of their separation, Ashley had been deeply unhappy and stressed and she'd battled headaches on a weekly basis. The doctor had counseled her on coming up with more effective ways to manage stress but Ashley had laughed. Now she realized she was as guilty as Devon had accused her of being when it came to wearing her feelings on her shoulder. She absorbed too much of the world around her and it affected her. That wasn't something she could change, could she?

She sighed. If she had any hope of not spending the next year in bed knocked out on medication, she was going to have to harden herself. She couldn't go around being a veritable sponge and reacting so emotionally to everything.

Her husband didn't love her? So what. She'd have to find a way to be happy. As Grammy always said, you make your nest now lie in it. Well, Ashley had certainly made the biggest, messiest nest of a marriage and now it was hers to wallow in.

As the medication wore off, she found it impossible to sleep. Her mind was buzzing with a mental list of everything she needed to do. Or not do. The list of things not to do was every bit as long as the list of things that needed to be done.

Learn to cook. That one popped uninvited into her head. She frowned because how did one simply learn to cook? Even Devon possessed rudimentary know-how in the kitchen. He could prepare simple dishes. She wasn't even sure she could boil water if necessary.

Okay that one should be simple enough. Pippa was a first-rate cook and it wouldn't be strange that Ashley would want to learn to cook a fabulous meal for her new husband. She could say she wanted to surprise him with a romantic meal for two.

And cooking shows. There was an entire television network devoted to cooking. Surely there was something she could watch there that would help.

Cleaning. Okay, she knew how to clean. She just didn't possess the organization skills to do it well. But she could muddle her way through it. It simply required discipline and less of a scatterbrain mentality.

She had to curb her tongue and her reactions. That should be simple enough. Smile and nod instead of shriek and wave her hands. Her mother was an expert at all the social graces but then she'd had to be with all the business functions she'd arranged and managed for her husband.

Ashley could certainly draw on the resources around her. She'd never particularly had a desire to be more like her family. She hadn't really considered that she was so different. She hadn't thought much about how she compared. Why would she? But they could help her. She just had to make sure she employed their help in a way that didn't give away the true reason for her transformation.

The door to Devon's office opened and he stepped out, looked her way and then started toward her.

"Can't sleep?" he asked. "Do you need anything?"

She shook her head and pulled the blanket closer to her chin. "I'm fine. Just getting comfortable."

He took a seat in the armchair across from the couch. Their gazes connected but she didn't look away, as tempted as she was. She couldn't keep avoiding him, no matter how desirable the prospect was.

It was hard for her because humiliation crept up her spine every time she had to face him, but eventually that would go away or she'd harden enough that it would no longer affect her. Or at least she hoped so.

"I spoke to your parents. Your mother is naturally concerned for you. She'd like you to call her when you're feeling up to it. Your father wants to see me in the morning, so if you're okay by then, I'll be out for a few hours."

"I'll be fine," she said softly. "Headache's gone. No reason for you to stay home and babysit me."

"If you need anything at all or if you begin to feel bad again, call me. I'll come home."

Hell would freeze over before she'd ever call him

at work again, not that she'd tell him that. She nodded instead and sighed unhappily. So this is what her marriage boiled down to. A stilted, awkward conversation between two people who were clearly uncomfortable in each other's presence.

"Do you think you could eat something now?" Devon asked, breaking the strained silence. "What would you like?"

Deciding to take the olive branch, or perhaps create an olive branch out of a dinner offer, she shifted and pushed herself up so that her back was against the arm of the couch.

"You could cook, if you don't mind. I could sit at the bar and watch."

He looked surprised by her suggestion, but his surprise was quickly replaced by relief. He looked almost hopeful.

"That would be nice. Are you sure you're up for the noise and the light?"

Again she nodded. She hadn't talked this little since she'd been a nonverbal toddler. Her parents always swore that because she was late to talk she'd spent the rest of her life making up for lost time.

He stood and held down his hand to her. "Come on then. Bring the blanket with you if you're cold. You can sit on one of the bar stools and wrap it around you."

Hesitating only a brief moment, she slid her hand over his, enjoying the warmth of his touch. He curled his fingers around her wrist and helped her from the couch.

She stood up beside him but he waited a moment for her to get her footing.

"Okay?" he asked. "Fuzziness gone yet? I don't want you falling."

"I'm fine."

He didn't relinquish her hand as he started toward the kitchen. He guided her toward one of the stools and settled her down. He wrapped the blanket around her shoulders and tucked the ends underneath her arms.

"What's your pleasure tonight?"

He walked around to open the refrigerator, surveyed the contents and then glanced back at her.

It was probably another sign of her shortcomings that she had no idea what was or wasn't in the fridge. Heat singed her cheeks and she dropped her gaze. Tomorrow she'd take inventory. After she cleaned the house.

"Ash?"

She yanked her gaze back up. "Uh, I don't care. Honestly. I'll eat whatever."

"Oh, good. I've been dying to cook this cow's tongue before it goes bad."

She blinked for a moment before she realized he was teasing her. The memory of the night he'd first made love to her came back in a flash. The dinner they'd had when he'd asked her if she was a vegetarian.

Unbidden, a smile curved her lips. He smiled back at her, relief lightening his eyes.

"No?" he asked.

She shook her head. "No cow's tongue. But I'd eat his flank. Or his tuchus even."

"So you'll eat cow's ass but not his tongue," Devon said in mock exasperation.

Her smile grew a bit bigger and she leaned forward on the counter, resting her chin in her palm. This pretending felt nice. Who said denial was a bad thing?

If she could effectively put out of her mind the whole debacle that had been her honeymoon and take some time to work on her shortcomings, maybe at some point the pretense could become real. He could love her. He was committed to their marriage. It was a step. He was attentive, caring and he obviously hated to see her hurting. Those weren't the characteristics of a man who loathed her. So if he didn't hate her, and he seemed to like her well enough even if she annoyed him, then eventually, possibly, he could love her.

It was a hope she clung to because the alternative didn't bear thinking about. He didn't want a divorce, but she couldn't remain married to a man who could never love her. If she lost hope that he'd never reciprocate her feelings, it would signal the end of their marriage whether he wished it or not.

Devon tossed a package onto the counter and then returned to the fridge, where he pulled out an onion, what looked like bell peppers in assorted colors and a box of mushrooms.

"How about I do stir-fry? It's quick and easy and pretty damn good if I do say so myself."

"Sounds yummy."

She watched him in silence and soon the sizzle of searing meat filled the room. While the meat cooked, he sliced the vegetables. He stopped to give the meat a brisk stirring and then returned to the cutting board.

She decided he looked good in the kitchen. Sleeves rolled up, top button undone, his brow creased in concentration. He was efficient, but then he seemed efficient at everything he did. She wondered if there was anything he wasn't accomplished at. Was he one of those people who could pick up anything and do it well?

"Name one thing you suck at," she blurted out.

Then she promptly groaned inwardly because this

was precisely what she wasn't supposed to be doing. She had to demonstrate more…control. More decorum. Or at least stop blurting out her first reaction to everything.

He glanced up, his brows drawn together as if he wasn't sure if he'd heard her correctly. "Say that again?"

She shook her head. No way. "It was stupid. Just forget it."

He put down the knife, glanced over at the skillet and then returned his gaze to her. "Why would you want to know something I suck at?"

She closed her eyes and wished the floor would just open up and swallow her. So much for her campaign to become less…everything on his complaint list about her.

"Ash? Come on. Don't leave me hanging here."

She sighed. "Look, it was a stupid question. It's just that you seem like one of these people who is good at everything. You know, a person who can pick up something and just do it and do it well. I just wanted to know one thing you suck at. Gives hope to us mere mortals."

He shrugged. "I suck at lots of things. I'm definitely not one of those people who is good at everything. I've had to work hard for everything I've earned."

This was going from bad to worse. "It didn't come out right, Dev, okay? Can we just forget it? I wasn't insinuating that you haven't worked hard. I think it's evident that you've worked for everything you have. That wasn't what I meant at all. Sorry."

She pushed her hand into her hair and focused her stare down at the countertop. Running out of the room seemed overly dramatic even if it was what she wanted more than anything.

"Then what did you mean?"

There wasn't any anger or irritation in his voice. Just simple, casual curiosity. She chanced a peek back up at him to gauge his expression.

"Well, like cooking. You seem good at that. I just wanted to know something you aren't good at. You seemed to me to be one of those people who have a natural ability to pick up on things. You know, like sports. You ever see kids who just pick up a ball and know how to play? I bet you were one of those."

He groaned. "Oh, man. Clearly you've never watched me try to play basketball. And I say try, but that's probably not even an accurate word to use. Rafael, Ryan and Cam like to torture me at least once a year when they drag me down to play a 'friendly' game of basketball. What it really is is an opportunity for them to pay me back for every imagined slight. And then they don't let me forget it for the next six months."

"So you aren't good at basketball? Is that what you're saying?"

"Yeah. That's exactly what I'm saying."

She smiled. "Oh. Well, that's okay because I'm terrible at it, too."

He smiled back at her and then tossed the vegetables into the pan he'd taken the meat out of. "We can be terrible together then."

"Yeah," she said quietly.

He busied himself finishing up the meal and five minutes later, he set a plate in front of her while he stood on the other side of the bar, leaning back against the sink while he held his plate.

She looked up and frowned. "Not going to sit down?"

"I like watching you," he said as his gaze slid over her face. "I'd prefer to be across from you."

Her cheeks warmed and she quickly looked back down at her plate. She had no response for that. It puzzled her that he'd say such a thing.

But maybe he was trying. Like she was trying. Just as she would be trying as she embarked on her to-do list the next day.

It wouldn't happen overnight, but maybe…one day.

Chapter 13

Ashley woke with a muggy hangover feeling but then who wouldn't after two days in a medication-induced coma?

Today was the first day in her bid to take over the world. Well, sort of. Or rather it was her attempt to *not* take on the world quite so much. *Reserve* and *caution* were her two new friends.

There would be no more lying around and feeling sorry for herself.

Devon had exited the apartment early. The previous night had been a study in awkwardness.

He'd crawled into bed next to her and they'd lain quietly in the dark until finally she'd drifted off to a troubled sleep. Sometime during the night, he'd drifted toward her, or maybe she'd attacked him in her sleep. Either way, she'd ended up in his arms and had awakened when he'd gotten up early to shower.

He'd kissed her on the head and murmured for her to go back to sleep before leaving her alone.

"Welcome to your new reality," she murmured as she pushed herself out of bed.

She spent her entire time in the shower lecturing herself on how her situation was what she made of it. It could be horrible or she could salvage it. It was just according to how much effort she wanted to invest in her own happiness. Put that way, she could hardly say to hell with it and stomp off.

She winced when she caught sight of herself in the mirror. She looked bad. Not in one of those ways where she really didn't look so bad but said so anyway. She honestly looked like death warmed over. There were dark circles under her eyes. There was a line around her mouth from having her jaw set so firmly. Her unhappiness was etched on her face for the world to see. She'd never been good at hiding any kind of emotion. She was as transparent as plastic wrap.

Thank goodness for Carly and her never-ending list of tips for any type of makeup emergency. This definitely called for the full treatment.

When she was finished with her hair and makeup she was satisfied to see that at least she didn't look quite so haggard. Tired, yes, but that could easily be explained away by the headache. Surely an ecstatic new bride would smile her way through even the worst of migraines.

First stop was her mother's, since if Gloria Copeland didn't soon hear from her chick, she'd move Manhattan to get there to make sure all was well. After that was tackled, she had work to do. A lot of work.

She took a cab over to her former apartment building and smiled when Alex hurried to greet her.

"How are you, Miss Ashley? How is married life treating you?"

It was a standard question that would likely be asked of her a hundred more times before the week was out. Right after the one where most people would ask her why the hell she was back home after only two nights on her honeymoon.

"I'm good, Alex. Here to see my mother. Will you ring up and let her know I'm on my way?"

A moment later, Ashley stepped off the elevator and into the spacious apartment that very nearly occupied an entire floor. It was where she had spent a large portion of her childhood and it still felt like home to her no matter that she'd moved out on her own some time ago.

"Ashley, darling!" her mother cried as she hurried to greet her daughter. "Oh, you poor, poor darling. Come here and let me see you. Is your headache better? I knew there was simply too much excitement going on with the wedding and your moving and all the other plans. I worried it would prove to be too much for you. We should have spaced out the arrangements better."

Her mom enveloped her in a hug and for a long moment, Ashley clung to the comfort that only a mother could offer when her world was otherwise crap.

"Ashley?" her mother asked in a concerned, hushed tone when they finally pulled apart. "Is everything all right? Come, sit down. You don't even look like yourself today."

Ashley allowed herself to be pulled over to the comfortable leather couch. It smelled like home. She settled back and immediately burrowed into the corner, allowing the familiarity to surround her like a blanket.

"I'm fine, Mama. Really. I think you were right.

There's been so much excitement and stress that when we finally got to St. Angelo I just crashed. Poor Devon was stuck taking care of me while I was insensible from the medication."

"As he should have. I'm glad he took good care of my baby for me. Are you feeling better now? You're pale and there are dark smudges under your eyes."

So much for Carly's awesome makeup tips.

"I'm better. I just wanted to come over so you wouldn't worry. I have to go back soon. There's a lot I need to do in our apartment to get everything squared away."

Her mom patted her on the arm. "Of course. But first, let me fix you a nice cup of hot tea."

"Spiced tea?" Ashley asked hopefully.

Her mother smiled. "With a peppermint."

Ashley sighed and relaxed into the couch, more than willing to allow her mom to fuss over her and baby her before she crawled back into the real world. If only manufacturers could package a mom's TLC into a box of bandages, they'd make millions.

Think of the marketing opportunities. Life sucks? Slap a mom bandage on and everything's instantly better.

A few minutes later, Ashley's mother returned carrying a tray that she set on the coffee table in front of Ashley. She handed her a cup of steaming tea and then unwrapped a peppermint that Ashley dropped into the bottom.

Ashley studied her mom as she settled back onto the couch, her own cup of tea in hand. "Mom? What happened between you and dad?"

Her mom reacted in surprise and cast Ashley a startled glance as she set her teacup back on its saucer. "Whatever do you mean, darling?"

"When you separated that time. I never asked because honestly I wanted to forget it ever happened. But now that I'm married… I just wanted to know. You two have always seemed so in love."

Her mother's eyes softened and she leaned forward to put her cup down on the coffee table. Then she turned and gathered Ashley's free hand in hers.

"It's natural for you to worry about those things now that you're married yourself. But darling, don't dwell on them."

"I know, but it just seems like that if it could happen to you and Daddy that it could happen to anyone. Was he having an affair? Did you forgive him?"

"Oh, good Lord, no!" She sighed and shook her head. "I know it was difficult for you and Eric, but especially for you. I never imagined that you'd think something like that, though. I should have guessed. I was so determined not to drag you children into our mess and thought I was doing the best thing by protecting you from any of the details. I can see I was wrong."

"What happened then?" Ashley asked softly.

"Oh it sounds so silly now. But back then I was convinced that my marriage was over. Your father was doing what he's always done. The difference was, suddenly it wasn't good enough for me. I began to worry. Maybe it's normal to go through a stage where you question what you want out of a relationship or worry that perhaps your partner doesn't love or value you anymore. Your father was working a lot of long hours. He was traveling constantly. You and Eric were adults and were going your own way and suddenly I found myself feeling quite alone and no longer valuable."

"Oh, Mama. I wish I had known," Ashley said unhappily. "That sounds so very awful for you."

Her mom smiled. "It was at the time but it wasn't entirely your father's fault. He was caught completely off guard when he returned home only to discover that I'd moved his things out and he had to find another place to live. He begged me to tell him what was wrong, what he'd done wrong, how he could fix it. But the truth was, I didn't even know myself. I just knew I was unhappy and that I no longer knew what I wanted from my marriage or my husband. If I didn't know, how could he?"

"What did you do?"

"I refused to speak to him for a week. It wasn't that I was angry. I just didn't know what to say to him. I took that time to think about and articulate what it was I wanted to say to him. And during that time, I realized that it wasn't him that I needed to change. It was me. I needed to find what was going to make me happy and he couldn't do it for me.

"When I finally agreed to see him, the poor man looked like death warmed over. I felt so guilty for the way I'd made him suffer but I knew we'd never last if I couldn't get myself together. I asked him for a period of separation. He was adamantly opposed. It wasn't until I gently reminded him that I didn't need his permission and that we were already separated that he backed off."

Ashley frowned. "I always assumed...I mean I just thought that it was Daddy's decision to move out. I always wondered if there was another woman."

Her mom twisted her lips in a regretful frown. "Yes, it's what Eric thought too, unfortunately. He was furious with your father. It wasn't until I explained things to him that he calmed down. Then I think he was angry with me for making your father move out. Eric is very black-and-white."

"Yes, I know," Ashley said with a grimace. She took another sip of her tea and then looked back at her mom. "So what happened? What made you decide to let him move back in?"

Her mom sighed and a faraway look entered her eyes. "We were separated for six months and in a way, those six months were some of the best times of my life."

Ashley's eyes widened. "But Mama!"

"I know, I know, but listen to me. I didn't say they were easy. They weren't. But those six months out- lined to me in clear detail what I wanted my life to be. And who I wanted to spend it with. I had opportuni- ties. There were plenty of men who flirted with me and would have jumped at the opportunity to date or have an affair."

Ashley's mouth dropped open and her mother smiled at her reaction. "Darling, you don't think the need for sex goes away when you hit thirty, do you?"

"Oh, my God," Ashley muttered. "I'm so not hearing my mother talk about all the hot guys she had a chance with while she was separated from my father."

"I had opportunity, yes, but I couldn't do it," her mom said.

"Because you loved Daddy?"

"Because it would have been dishonorable. Your fa- ther didn't deserve it. Because I honestly didn't want to be with anyone other than him. And I realized that I'd been blaming him for my own unhappiness. It was easy to say he'd been neglecting me or that he spent too much time at work. But the truth was, after you children grew up and left the nest, I simply didn't know what it was I wanted to do next. And I took out my frustrations on the closest available target because I didn't want to take responsibility for my own failures and feelings of inadequacy."

"Wow, I never realized…"

Her mom smiled and reached up to touch her cheek. "What, that I'm human like everyone else? That your mom isn't perfect?"

"Well, yeah, I guess," Ashley said lamely. "It's a totally shocking discovery. You may not survive the fall from the mom pedestal."

Her mom laughed and tweaked Ashley's nose. "Such a smart alec like your father. I always thought you were so much like him."

"What? I'm nothing like Daddy. He'd probably be horrified to hear you say that. He despairs of me because I have no head for or interest in business."

Her mom smiled indulgently. "But you have a huge heart like your father does and when you love, you love with everything you have. Just like William. He was devastated when I asked him to leave. And even though I knew I absolutely had to do what I did, it was the most difficult decision I've ever made. Our marriage is better for it. When we got back together, I was a stronger, more confident woman. I didn't need him to make me complete. I wanted him. But I didn't need him and therein was the difference."

Ashley set aside her cup and then impulsively threw her arms around her mom in a hug. "I love you, Mama. Thank you for talking to me. It was just what I needed today."

Her mother stroked her hand over Ashley's hair and hugged her back. "You're welcome, darling, and I love you, too. You know I'm always right here if you need me."

* * *

Devon sat across from William Copeland as William completed his order with the waitress. The two had met at William's favorite place to eat lunch, but Devon wasn't in the least bit hungry.

"You not eating, son?" William asked as the waitress looked expectantly in Devon's direction.

"I'll just have a glass of water," Devon said.

After the waitress left, William leaned back and for a moment looked visibly discomfited.

"I wanted to talk to you about some changes in the organization."

Alarm bells clanged in Devon's already aching head. Two nights without decent sleep and the image of Ashley's tearstained face were wearing on him. The very last thing he needed was the old man to renege on their agreement. Wouldn't that be the height of irony?

He must have seen the wariness on Devon's face because he quickly went on.

"It's not what you think. I want you to take over my position at Copeland. I know the merger with Tricorp wasn't supposed to be splashy, that we agreed to keep the Copeland name and that Tricorp would be more of a silent party, but I'm ready to resign and I want you to take my position."

Devon shook his head in confusion. "I don't understand."

William sighed wearily. "I'm sick, son. I've been having health issues. I've been trying to see to matters because I want my family provided for. I want Eric to have a position but he isn't ready to take over. And the thing is, I'm not sure he wants his future locked into the family business. Lately he's hinted that his interests lie in other areas. And Ashley… It's why I pushed so hard for the marriage to take place. I wanted her settled with a man I trusted and whom I knew would take good care of her. If it got out that my health was failing, the vultures would have descended and she would have been easy pickings."

"Sick?" Devon managed to get out. "How sick?"

"I don't know yet. I won't lie. I've been in denial. I haven't even discussed this with Gloria and she's going to hit the ceiling when she finds out. I'm not ready to die yet, though. I want a lot of years with my children and eventual grandchildren. I spent decades working my ass off to get where I am and now I want to retire and enjoy time with my wife and watch my grandchildren play. But in order to do all that, I have to make sure my company is in good hands. I don't want Copeland to die, which is why I wanted this merger so badly. It wasn't Tricorp I was after. To be honest I could have picked a dozen other companies who would bring as much to the table. But I went with Tricorp because of you. You're who I want for my daughter and my company."

"Jesus, I don't even know what to say," Devon muttered. "This is quite the bomb to drop the day after I return from an aborted honeymoon."

"I know you thought I was a crazy old man for making Ashley part of this deal. And that I'm a manipulative bastard. You'd be right on that count. I knew you wanted this partnership. I knew you wanted the Copeland name for the line of resorts you've envisioned. I also knew what I wanted. It just so happened that our wants aligned perfectly. And my children are provided for."

"Everyone but Ashley," Devon said quietly.

William looked up sharply. "What do you mean?"

"She wanted a husband who adores her, who loves her, who is the embodiment of all she's dreamed of."

"So? Any reason you can't be that man?"

It was a good question and one he wasn't sure how to answer. He rubbed his hand through his hair. "How soon are you wanting all of this done?"

"I want to tender my resignation as soon as everything is done. It won't be a secret that I'll want you to take over. Voting won't be an issue. You'll be the most logical person to take over when I retire. I hold a lot of sway over the board. They'll listen to me. I'm going to make a doctor's appointment and then tell my wife so she can rearrange my teeth for me and then drag me to the doctor. After that, she'll take over and I won't be able to scratch my ass without her permission."

The words were said with wry wit, but it was obvious from the warmth in William's eyes that he adored his wife beyond reason and absolutely didn't mind giving up control to her in his retirement.

The older man seemed totally at peace with his actions and decisions and Devon wondered how much he could really fault his father-in-law for taking steps to ensure that his family was provided for. Even if he didn't agree with the methods. Would he have done the same for his son or daughter?

He liked to think that he'd offer them something better than the occasional reminder not to "screw up."

The image of Ashley, round and lush with his child, conjured a powerful surge of emotion. He realized in an instant that he'd do whatever it took to protect a son or daughter.

"Take care of yourself," Devon said gruffly, suddenly unsteady at the idea of something happening to a man who'd seemed so determined to be a second father to him. "I'll expect you to spoil our children."

William's expression eased into a broad smile. "Planning to provide me with them soon?"

Devon shrugged. "Maybe. That'll be up to Ash. I just want her to be happy."

William nodded. "So do I, son. So do I."

They were interrupted by the waitress bringing William's entrée to the table. For a moment, William fussed over his food and then he looked up at Devon again. "I'd like you to plan a cocktail party. It'll give Ashley a chance to play hostess. I'm thinking a couple weeks out at most. I want to go ahead and announce that I'm planning to retire and that you're my choice to succeed me. I want this all to seem like a natural progression of the merger. A changing of the guard with my blessing."

"We can do that," Devon said. Or at least he hoped. Maybe by that time Ashley wouldn't be quite so upset. Right now, asking her to appear happy for an entire night in front of dozens of guests seemed unreasonable at best.

"Good. We'll talk more later and I'll give you a guest list and of course you'll have your own colleagues to invite. I just want to say again how happy I am to have you as my son-in-law. I knew from the moment I met you that you'd not only be the best thing for my company, but for my daughter as well."

Chapter 14

When Devon walked into his apartment, he immediately noticed the change. There wasn't any clutter. No magazines strewn about. No shoes littering the floor. No purse hanging from a doorknob. And he could smell cleaning solution.

As he walked farther inside, his stomach knotted because not only was everything picked up, but he also realized that the apartment was completely and utterly devoid of Ashley's presence. All of the things she'd moved in and haphazardly decorated with had been put away. No silly knickknacks on the coffee or end tables.

The apartment looked precisely as it had before she moved in.

Has she packed up and left? Had she decided not to give their marriage a chance?

He experienced a faint sensation of illness. His stomach

tightened with dread and the beginnings of panic gripped his throat.

Then he heard a distant sound that seemed to come from the kitchen. He strode in that direction and realized that a television had been left on. But when he reached the doorway, he had to grip the frame to steady himself.

Relief blew through him with staggering ferocity.

She was still here.

She hadn't left.

She was sitting at the bar, her brow furrowed in concentration as she watched a cooking show. She had a notepad and pencil in front of her and she was furiously taking notes.

As his gaze took in the rest of the kitchen, he realized that she'd evidently spent the day cleaning. The surfaces sparkled. The floor shone. The scent of lemon was heavy in the air.

She was dressed in faded jeans and an old T-shirt. Her hair was pulled back into a ponytail and she wasn't wearing any makeup.

She looked absolutely beautiful.

But she also looked tired. The dark circles under her eyes were more pronounced and she had a delicate fragileness to her that made him instinctively protective of her. But he couldn't protect her from himself and it was he who had hurt her.

Drawn to the vulnerable image she presented, he slid his hands up her arms and then lowered his mouth to kiss her on the neck.

She froze immediately then turned swiftly around. "Hi," she offered hesitantly. "I didn't expect you back quite so soon."

"Technically I'm off this week," he said as he pulled away. "I had lunch with your father. We discussed business and now I'm done."

She made a face but didn't comment, which he was grateful for. Anytime her father and business were mentioned, it was going to be difficult, but the more he did it in passing, maybe it would lessen the sting.

"What happened to all your stuff?" he asked casually as he went around to open the fridge. He pulled out a bottle of water and pushed the door closed.

"Oh, I just organized everything," she said. "I didn't really have time before the wedding. Was too busy with other stuff."

"Mmm-hmm," he murmured. "And the cleaning? Should you have been doing all this today? You just came off a pretty bad headache. I wouldn't think all the cleaning stuff would be good for you to be inhaling."

"It was okay. Headache is gone. Just a little residual achiness."

He frowned. "Why don't you go lie on the couch. I'll figure out dinner and we'll watch some TV or just relax in the living room if you don't want the noise."

She rose from the stool. "No, no, I've got dinner planned. Are you hungry already? What time did you want to eat?"

Perplexed by her sudden agitation, he hastily backed off. It appeared she was at least trying for a semblance of normalcy and that relieved him. Maybe after the initial storm passed and she had time to think she'd see that nothing had changed between them.

In light of today's conversation with William Copeland, Devon was on the verge of accomplishing all his goals. And at a much faster rate than he'd ever planned. Five years down the road was here now. Copeland Hotels would be his. His dream of launching a new luxury chain of exclusive resorts under one of the oldest and most respected names in the business would be realized. He'd have a wife. Children. A family. He'd have it all.

The surge of triumph was so forceful he felt drunk with it.

"I'm in no hurry," he soothed. "Why don't we sit down and have a drink. What are you cooking?"

A dull flush worked over her face. "I'm not. At least not tonight I mean. I will another time. I thought I'd call for take-out. It's almost like a home-cooked meal but they bring it and set it up."

"Sounds wonderful. Thank you. I think a nice quiet dinner at home would be fantastic after the week we've had. We didn't really get to see each other much in the days leading up to the wedding. We can start making up for that now."

Pain flashed in her eyes but she remained quiet, almost as if she was dealing with the sudden reminder of their circumstances. He hated it. Wished he could wipe it from her memory. In time, it would fade. If he showed her that they could have a comfortable relationship, some of the rawness of her emotions would settle and they could go back to the easy camaraderie they'd shared before everything went to hell.

She squared her shoulders as if reaching a decision and then tilted her chin upward. "You go on out and have a seat. Would you like wine? Or do you want me to mix up something for you?"

He opened his mouth to tell her that he'd take care of it, but something in her eyes stopped him. There was a quiet desperation, almost as if she was barely clinging to her composure.

"Wine would be great," he said softly. "You choose something for both of us. I like everything I've stocked here so I'm good with whatever you pick out."

He left the kitchen, his chest tight. The next weeks were going to suck as they found their way in the new reality of their relationship. He had confidence that it would work out, though. He just had to be patient.

A few minutes later, Ashley came into the living room carrying two wineglasses and a bottle of unopened wine. She looked disgruntled as she set the glasses down on the coffee table.

"Can you open the wine?" she asked hesitantly. "I couldn't get the bottle opener to work properly. I'm sure I'm not doing it right."

He reached for the bottle and let his fingers glide over hers. "Relax, Ash. Take a seat. I'll pour."

Reluctantly she backtracked and sank down onto the couch. In truth she still didn't look well and it wouldn't surprise him if her head was still hurting her. Her brow was wrinkled and she looked tired. Maybe a glass of wine would ease some of her tension.

He opened the bottle and then poured a glass for her first. After pouring his own, he set the glass on the table and took a seat in the armchair diagonal to where she sat on the couch.

"Your father wants us to host a cocktail party in a week or two," he said.

"Us?" she squeaked. "As in you and me? Why wouldn't he want Mama to host it? She's awesome at hosting parties. Everyone always talks about how much fun they have when she throws a get-together."

"He's going to be announcing some changes at Copeland soon and this is his way of easing into that. Your father is looking at taking a less active role in the managing of things. He's ready to retire and focus on his family."

She looked despondent.

"Ash, this isn't a big deal. Most of the people who'll attend are people we already know. We'll pick a nice venue, have it catered, hire a band. It'll be great."

She held up her hand. "I'll handle it. No problem. I don't want you to worry about it. I just need to know exactly when. I'm sure you and Daddy will be busy with… whatever it is you're busy with. Mama always handled parties for Daddy. No reason I can't do it for you."

The dismay in her voice troubled him. He thought it rather sounded like she would be planning a funeral, but he wasn't about to shut her down when she was making such an effort. That she was so willing to try when it was obvious he'd crushed her endeared her to him all the more.

"I'm sure whatever you come up with, I and the others will love," he said.

She took a long drink of her wine, nearly draining the glass.

"Want to watch a movie?" he suggested.

She nodded as she put her wineglass back on the coffee table. "Sure. Whatever you want to put on is fine."

He picked up the remote but he didn't return to his own chair. He eased onto the couch next to her and put his arm along the top of the sofa behind her head.

For a long moment she sat there stiffly, almost as if she wasn't sure what she was supposed to do. He cursed the awkwardness between them. Before she wouldn't have hesitated to burrow underneath him and snuggle in tight. She'd drape herself over him when they watched movies. She would have kissed him, hugged him and generally mauled him with affection through the entire show.

Now she sat beside him like a statue, tension and fatigue radiating from her like a beacon.

"Come here," he murmured, pulling her underneath his arm. "That's better," he said when she finally relaxed against him and laid her cheek on his chest.

They were silent as the movie played and he was fine with that. There wasn't a lot he could say. There were only so many times he could apologize or tell her he hadn't meant to hurt her.

It wasn't the movie that captured his attention, though. He sat there enjoying her scent. Her hair always smelled like honeysuckle. Even in winter in the city. She had an airy, floral scent that clung to her. It suited her.

And he loved the feel of her next to him. He hadn't realized how much until he'd spent the last several days with a wall between them.

He touched her hair, idly sifting through the strands with his fingers, savoring the sensation of silk over his skin. By the time the credits rolled, he couldn't have even said what the movie was about. He hadn't cared.

"Ash, are you sure you don't want me to go out for some dinner?" He waited a moment. "Ash?"

He glanced down to see that she'd fallen sound asleep against his chest. Her lashes rested delicately on her cheeks and her lips were tight, almost as if she were deep in thought even at rest.

Gently he kissed her forehead and rested his chin there for a long moment. Somehow, someway, he would make it up to her. He was reaching the high point in his life and career where everything he'd worked so hard and so long for was his. And damn it, he wanted her to be on top of the world with him.

Chapter 15

"This is hopeless," Ashley said as her shoulders sagged.

Pippa wrapped her arm around Ashley and squeezed tight. "You're not hopeless. You'll get it down. You're being way too hard on yourself."

"After three weeks, you'd think I'd be able to perform the simplest tasks in the kitchen," Ashley said forlornly. "Let's face it. I'm a culinary disaster."

"Are you all right, hon? You seem really down lately and not just about this cooking stuff. Is everything okay with you?"

Ashley smiled brightly and straightened her stance. "Oh, yeah, fine. Marriage is exhausting work. Who knew? Just trying to get my routine down. I've been spending my mornings at the shelter so I can be at home when Devon gets in from work. I keep hoping one of my meals will actually turn out but I keep having to call in backup."

Pippa laughed. "You're so silly. I don't even know why you're bothering learning to cook. Devon doesn't care if you can cook. The man's obviously crazy about you and you couldn't cook before you got married. I'm sure he's not expecting some miracle to occur."

Ashley bit her lip to keep from crying. The truth was, she was exhausted. Planning that damn cocktail party had turned out to be a giant pain in her ass. She was tempted to call her mother and beg for help but pride kept her from making that call.

The old Ashley would have laughed, thrown her hands up and admitted she was hopeless. The new Ashley was going to suck it up, be calm and get the job done.

"Are you coming to my party?" Ashley asked, suddenly worried she'd be surrounded by a sea of unfamiliar faces.

"Of course I am. I promised you I'd come. I know you're nervous, but really, this is your thing, Ash. You shine at social events. Everyone loves you and you're so sweet."

"Why don't you meet me at Tabitha's place the afternoon before. We'll get our hair done together. I'm aiming for a more sophisticated look for the party. You know, mature and married as opposed to young and flighty."

Pippa snorted. "Flighty?"

Ashley laughed it off but she knew well that Devon considered her a complete ditz.

"I need Carly's makeup skills, too."

"Honey, you aren't holding tea for the queen. You're hosting a cocktail party for friends and business associates. We already love you. And those who don't will. Stop tormenting yourself over this."

"I just don't want to look stupid," Ashley said.

Pippa shook her head. "I swear I don't know what's got into you lately. You're perfect and anyone who doesn't think so can kiss my ass."

"I love you," Ashley said, emotion knotting her throat.

Pippa hugged her fiercely and then pulled away. "Are you pregnant or something? I swear you're not usually so emotional."

"Oh, God, I don't think so. I mean it's possible but I haven't even kept up with my periods. I just remember being thrilled it wasn't going to happen on my honeymoon. You know, the one I ended up cutting short."

"Well, take one of those home pregnancy tests. You're a mess, Ash. Hormones have to be the reason why."

She closed her eyes. No, she couldn't be pregnant yet. Well, she certainly could, but she suddenly didn't want to be. But it was a little too late for that line of thinking. When was the last time she and Devon had made love anyway? Definitely before the wedding. But it was still too soon to tell.

"I'll give it a little more time," she said firmly. "I'm just a wreck over this stupid party. I feel like it's my first big test as Mrs. Devon Carter. I don't want to humiliate myself or him in front of a hundred people."

"Stop it," Pippa chided. "You're going to be awesome. Now, do you want to try this sauce again?"

Ashley sighed. "I'm thinking I should start out with something even easier. Sauces aren't my thing apparently. I keep ruining them."

"Okay, then let's try something different. Name something else you love to eat."

Ashley thought a minute. "Lasagna. That sounds really good right now."

"Perfect! And it couldn't be easier. I'll give you the easy recipe. You can always graduate to fancier once you've mastered the kid-friendly version."

"That's me," Ashley said in resignation. "The kid-friendly version."

Pippa swatted her with a towel. "Grab the hamburger meat from the fridge. I think we're down to the last pack so you better nail this one, girlfriend."

Half an hour later, Ashley put her fist in the air as she and Pippa stood back and closed the oven door on a perfect, if somewhat beleaguered, lasagna.

"I can totally do that on my own," Ashley said as Pippa wiped her hands. "I'm so excited! Maybe I'm not a complete lost cause."

Pippa shook her head. "All it takes is a little time and patience. You're going to be a culinary genius in no time."

Ashley threw her arms around her friend and hugged her tight. "Thanks, Pip. I love you, you know. You're the best."

Pippa grinned. "I love you, too, you nut. Now go home and make your lasagna before your husband gets there. Call me tomorrow and let me know how it went. And take that damn pregnancy test. I'll want to know if I'm going to be an aunt!"

Ashley rolled her eyes. She started to walk toward the door when her cell phone beeped, signaling a received text message. She pulled it out and then frowned as she read it.

"What is it, Ash?" Pippa asked.

"There's a problem at the shelter. Molly is upset but she doesn't give any info. I'll hop over on my way home. It's not too out of the way. See you Friday afternoon at Tabitha's."

"Okay, be careful and call me when you get home so I'll know you made it. You know I hate you going down to the shelter by yourself all the time."

"Yes, mother," Ashley replied. "Later, chickie."

With a wave, she disappeared from Pippa's apartment and headed down to catch a cab to the shelter.

It was later than he'd have liked when Devon entered the apartment. His day had been long and full of endless meetings and his ears were still throbbing from the number of people who'd talked to him.

The only person he wanted to see was Ashley, and he was looking forward to seeing what disaster she'd come up with for dinner.

He grinned as he loosened his tie and headed for the kitchen. The past weeks had been hilarious. Oddly, he hadn't minded the sheer number of ruined meals he'd been served. It had become a contest for him to correctly guess what the meal was *supposed* to have been.

He sniffed as he reached the doorway into the kitchen and the delicious aroma of…something…floated into his nostrils. It didn't smell burned. Or even slightly scorched. It smelled like gooey, bubbly cheese and a hint of tomato.

His stomach growled and he scanned the kitchen area for Ashley. He frowned when he realized she was nowhere to be seen. Deciding he'd better check on whatever was for dinner, he hurried to the oven and pulled open the door.

Inside was what looked to be a perfectly put together and perfectly cooked lasagna. He snagged a pot holder and then reached inside to take out the casserole dish.

After setting it on the stove, he turned off the oven and then went in search of Ashley. As he neared the bedroom, he heard the low murmur of her voice.

She was standing by the window overlooking the city and she was on her cell phone. He started to detour into his closet to change when he heard a betraying sniff.

He spun around, frowning as he zeroed in on Ashley. Her back was mostly to him though she was angled just enough that he could see her wipe at one cheek.

What the hell?

It took all his restraint not to walk over, take the phone and demand to know who the hell had upset her.

"I'll see what I can do, Molly. We can't let this happen," she said.

She wiped her cheek with the back of her free hand and then hit the button to end the call. Then she turned and saw Devon. Her eyes widened in alarm and then she closed them in dismay.

"Oh, my God, the lasagna!"

She bolted for the door, gone before he could even tell her he'd already taken care of it. He was more concerned with what had made her cry.

"Ash!" he called as he hurried after her.

He caught up to her in the kitchen to find her palming her forehead as she stared at the lasagna.

"I'm sorry," she said. "I just forgot it. If you hadn't come in, it would have burned."

"Hey, it's okay," he said. He walked over and slipped

a hand over her shoulder. "It needs to rest a minute anyway. Let me grab some plates and we'll set the table. Then you can tell me what's got you so upset. Who was that on the phone?"

He steered her toward the table, parked her in a chair and then went back to retrieve plates and utensils. After setting the places, he went back for the lasagna and carried the still piping hot dish to the table.

He sat down, picking up a knife to cut into the lasagna while he waited for her to respond. To his horror, her eyes filled with tears and she buried her face in her hands.

He dropped the knife and bit out a curse. Then he scrambled out of his chair and pulled it around so he could scoot up next to Ashley.

"What's wrong?" he demanded. "Did someone upset you?" Obviously someone or something did but he wanted answers. He wasn't a patient man. His inclination was to wade in and fix things. He couldn't do that if he didn't have the story.

"I've had the most awful day," she croaked out. "And I wanted everything to be perfect. I finally learned how to cook that damn lasagna. But then Molly called. I stopped by the shelter and she had terrible news and I don't know what to do. We've been talking about it all evening."

He gently pulled her hands away, wincing at the flood of tears soaking her cheeks.

"Who's Molly?"

She frowned and lifted her gaze to meet his. "Molly from the shelter."

He looked searchingly at her. Clearly this was a person he was supposed to know, but he was drawing a complete blank.

"She's my boss at the shelter."

"Wait a minute. I thought you ran the shelter."

She shook her head impatiently. "I do, mostly, but she's in charge. I mean she runs it but I do most of the legwork and fundraising. She says I have more connections and am the natural choice to go out and pound the pavement for donations."

Devon scowled. It sounded to him as though this Molly person was taking advantage of Ashley. He wasn't certain of the salary that Ashley drew from her position at the shelter. He assumed that her parents still helped her financially since she didn't have a typical nine-to-five job and she'd been living in her own apartment for a while now. He hadn't concerned himself with her finances because he wanted her to be happy and he knew he'd fully support her once they were married. But he sure as hell didn't want her busting her ass in a job where she was being used.

"So what did Molly have to say?" he gently prompted.

"The grant the shelter had is being pulled and without it, we can't continue to stay open. It pays the basics like the utilities, food for the animals and the salary for the vet we have on retainer. We don't raise enough money to stay afloat without the grant."

Her eyes filled with tears again. "If we don't stay open, all the animals will have to be transferred to a city-run shelter and if they aren't adopted out, they'll be euthanized."

Devon sighed and carefully pulled Ashley into his arms. "Surely there's some way to keep the shelter open. Have you talked to your father about sponsoring it?"

She pulled away and shook her head. "You don't understand. Daddy's all business when it comes to stuff like that. He doesn't make emotional decisions. He's more interested in profit and return or it being a cause he sees the value in. He's not much of an animal person."

Ashley's view of her father was clearly wrong. William Copeland had made an emotional decision. A huge emotional decision when he'd opted to go with Tricorp because for whatever reason he'd decided Devon would be the perfect son-in-law and candidate to take over Copeland.

"How long can you continue running as you are now?"

She sniffed. "Two, maybe three weeks. I'm not sure. We're already at maximum capacity but it's hard to say no when a new animal comes in. We just got in a dog and it was so heartbreaking. The poor thing is the sweetest dog ever but he was horribly neglected. I don't understand how people can be so cruel. Would they dump their child out on the street somewhere? A pet isn't any different. They're just as much a family member as a child!"

Unfortunately, there were people who'd think nothing of tossing out their kid, not that Ashley needed to be reminded of that. It would only upset her further.

He smoothed his hand over her cheek and then leaned forward to kiss her forehead. "Why don't you eat something. The lasagna smells wonderful. There's nothing you can do tonight. Maybe a solution will present itself in the morning."

She nodded morosely and he scooted his seat back. He picked the knife back up and cut into the lasagna, spooning out neat squares onto the plates.

"This looks wonderful," he said in a cheerful tone. He wanted her to smile again. She'd been entirely too serious ever since they returned from their honeymoon and he was becoming impatient for her to return to her usual, sunny self.

He handed her a plate and then took his own. When he bit into the gooey cheese and the perfectly al dente noodles, and the savory sauce slid over his tongue, he moaned in pleasure.

"This is awesome, Ash."

She smiled but it didn't quite reach her eyes. There was still deep sadness in those big, blue eyes and it was twisting his gut into a knot.

As good as dinner was, he was anxious to get through it. He had a sudden urge to comfort Ashley and wipe away her pain.

She picked at her food and it was obvious she had no interest in eating, so he hurriedly gulped his down and then collected their plates to dump into the sink. "Come here," he said, holding his hand out to her.

She slid her fingers into his and he pulled her to her feet. He took her into the bedroom, sat her on the edge of the bed and began taking her shoes off.

Crouching between her legs, he slid his hands along the sides of her thighs until his fingers palmed her hips. He held her there, staring intently at her, unable to believe he was about to make her a promise.

The business side of him balked and demanded to know if he'd lost his damn mind. But the side of him that cringed upon witnessing Ashley's distress was urging him on.

"Listen to me," he said, before he could talk himself out of it. "Let me see what I can do, okay? Don't give up hope just yet. We have a few weeks. I may be able to help."

To his surprise she threw her arms around him and

hugged him fiercely. It was the first spontaneous show of affection he'd been treated to since before their marriage.

"Oh, Devon, thank you," she whispered fiercely. "You have no idea how much this would mean to me."

"I have an idea," he said wryly. "You love those animals more than you love people."

She nodded solemnly, not in the least bit abashed to admit it. Then she kissed him full on the mouth.

It was like baiting a hungry lion. He didn't wait for her to pull back in regret. Didn't offer her the chance to change her mind. He'd suffered three long weeks wanting her with every breath and knowing she was emotionally out of reach.

If this was his chance to have her back in his bed without a wealth of space between them, he was going to grab the opportunity with both hands.

He kissed her back, his hands going to her face, holding her there as he fed hungrily on her lips. Tentatively her arms circled his neck and she leaned into him with a soft, sweet sigh that tightened every one of his muscles and made him instantly hard.

He had to force himself to exercise some restraint because what he really wanted to do was tear her clothes off, haul her up the bed and make love to her until neither of them could walk.

"You have far too many clothes on," he said, near desperation as he fumbled with the buttons on her blouse. It was expensive. Probably silk. But ah, hell, he'd buy her another one.

The sound of the material rending and the buttons popping and scattering on the floor only spurred his excitement. He fumbled clumsily with the button on her pants and then began pulling to get them off her. She lifted her bottom just enough that he could slide the material down her legs and then there she was, sitting so dainty and beautiful, clad only in her pale, pink lingerie.

She was the most beautiful sight he'd ever seen. Hair tousled just enough to make her look sexy. Her lips swollen from his kiss. Eyes glazed with passion instead of deep sadness. And her skin. So soft, glowing in the lamplight. Curvy in all the right places. Generous breasts, straining at the lace cups, and hips and behind just the right size for his hands to grip.

He stood only long enough to strip out of his clothes. It wasn't practiced or smooth. He felt like a fifteen-year-old getting his first glimpse of a naked woman. If he wasn't careful, he'd be acting just like one, too.

She stared shyly up at him and he nearly groaned. "Baby, you have to stop looking at me like that. I'm holding on to my control by my fingertips and you're not helping."

She smiled then, an adorable, sweet smile that took his breath away. He forgot all about trying to maintain an air of civility. His inner caveman came barreling out, grunting and pounding his chest and muttering unintelligible words.

He swept her into his arms, hauling her back on the bed. They landed with a soft bounce and he claimed her mouth, wanting to taste her again and again.

"Love the lingerie," he said hoarsely. "I'll love it more when it's off, though."

She wiggled beneath him and he realized she was trying to work out of her straps.

"Oh, no, let me," he breathed.

He pushed himself off her and then maneuvered himself upward so he straddled her body, his knees digging into the mattress on either side of her hips.

Her gaze slid downward to his groin and her eyes darkened. Tentatively she moved her hands slowly toward his straining erection. Color dusted her cheeks and she glanced hastily upward, almost as if she was seeking his permission to touch him.

Hell, he'd give her anything in the world if she'd touch him. He'd buy her twenty damn shelters if that would make her happy. Right now, it would make him delirious if she just wrapped those soft little fingers…

He closed his eyes and groaned as she did exactly what he'd fantasized about. Her touch was gentle. Light and tentative. Like the tips of butterfly wings dancing over his length.

She grew bolder, stroking more firmly, running the length of him with her palm until he was little more than a babbling, incoherent fool. He was supposed to be in control here. She was the innocent. He was the one with more experience. But she literally and figuratively held him in the palm of her hand.

If he didn't put an end to her inquisitive exploration, he'd find release on her belly and he wanted to be inside her more than he wanted to breathe.

Leaning down, her kissed the shallow indention between her breasts and then nuzzled the swell as he reached up to slide the straps over her shoulders.

He loved the way she smelled. It was one thing he missed about the apartment now. Before she had little bowls of potpourri and little scented candles haphazardly arranged throughout. The entire apartment had smelled like…her. Fresh. Vibrant. Like spring sunshine.

Now that she'd gone through in a mad cleaning rush, it was as if her very presence had been expunged.

The cup of her bra slipped over her nipple, exposing the puckered point to his seeking lips. He sucked lightly, enjoying the sensation of her on his tongue. Underneath him, she quivered and her breathing sped up in reaction.

He slipped one hand beneath her back, reaching for the clasp of her bra. Seconds later, it came free and he pulled carefully until it came completely away. Tossing it aside, he eyed the feast before him.

She had beautiful breasts. Just the perfect size. Small and dainty, much like her, but there was just enough plumpness to make a man's mouth water. Her nipples were a succulent pink that just beckoned him to taste. He knew enough about her now to know her breasts were highly sensitive. And her neck. Up high, just below her ear. It was guaranteed to drive her crazy if he nibbled either spot.

Tonight he wanted to taste all of her, though. He wanted her imprinted on his tongue, his senses. He wanted to be able to fall asleep smelling her, the feel of her skin on his.

Palming both breasts, he caressed, rubbed his thumbs across the tips before lowering his head to suck at one and then the other. He nipped lightly, causing the peak to harden even further. Then he slid his mouth down her middle to the softness of her belly, where he licked a damp circle around her navel.

Chill bumps rose and danced their way across her rib cage. She stirred restlessly, murmuring what sounded like a plea for more.

He thumbed the thin lace band of her panties and carefully eased the delicate material over her hips then down her legs and over her feet. Finally, she was completely naked to his avid gaze.

He moved back over her, his head hovering over the soft nest of blond curls between her legs. Then he stroked his hands over her hips and downward. He spread her thighs with firm hands, opening her to his advances.

All that pink, glistening flesh beckoned. He lowered his mouth, pressed his lips to the soft folds and nuzzled softly until she strained upward to meet him.

"Devon," she whispered.

It had been a while since he'd heard her husky sweet voice murmur his name in what was a blend of pleasure and a plea for more. It made him all the more determined that before he was finished, she'd call out his name a dozen more times. She'd find her release with his name on her lips. There would be no doubt in her mind who possessed her.

He licked gently at the tiny nub surrounded by silken folds, enjoying every jitter and shudder that rolled through her body. She was more than ready to take him, but he held back, enjoying his sensual exploration of her most intimate flesh.

Slowly he worked downward until he tasted the very heart of her, stroking with lazy, seductive swipes of his tongue. She began to shake uncontrollably and her thighs tightened around his head. He pressed one last kiss to the mouth of her opening and then moved up her body, positioning himself between her legs.

He found her heat and sank inside her with one powerful thrust. Her chin went up, her eyes closed and her lips tightened in an expression that was almost agonizing.

He kissed the dimple in her chin and then slid his

mouth down her neck and to the delicate hollow of her throat. Her pulse beat wildly, jumping against her pale skin, a staccato against his mouth.

Her slender arms went around him, gripping with surprising strength. Her nails dug into his shoulders like kitten claws.

"Put your legs around me," he said. "Just like that, baby. Perfect."

She crossed her heels at the small of his back and arched into each thrust. Her fingers danced their way across his back, sometimes light and then scoring his flesh when he thrust again. She thrust one hand into his hair, pulling forcefully until he realized she was demanding his kiss.

With a light chuckle, he gave in to her silent demand and found her mouth.

Breathless. Sweet. Their tongues worked hotly over each other, dueling, fighting for dominance. She had suddenly become the aggressor and he was lost, unable to deny her anything.

She was wrapped around him, her body urging him on, arching to meet him and finding a perfect rhythm so they moved as one.

Sex had never been this…perfect.

"Are you close?" he choked out.

"Don't stop," she begged.

"Oh hell, I'm not."

He closed his eyes and thrust hard and deep. And then he began working his hips against hers in rapid, urgent movements. She let out a strangled cry and he remembered his vow.

"My name," he said in a breathless pant. "Say my name."

"Devon!"

She came apart in his arms. Around him. Underneath him. He was bathed in liquid heat and he'd never felt anything so damn good in his life.

"Ashley," he whispered. "My Ashley. Mine."

He unraveled at light speed, his release sharp, bewildering and beautiful. His hips were still convulsively moving against her body as he settled down over her, too exhausted and spent to remember his own name. The one he'd demanded she say just moments ago.

He became aware of gentle caresses. Her hands gently stroking over his back. He was probably crushing her but he couldn't bring himself to move. He was inside her. Over her. Completely covering her. She was his.

He knew this moment was significant. Something had changed. But his mind was too numb to sort out the meaning. Never before had he been so undone after making love to a woman.

It was supremely satisfying and scary as hell.

Chapter 16

Ashley surveyed the guests as they filtered into the upscale restaurant she'd rented out for the night and felt the ache inside her head bloom more rapidly. She was so nervous she wanted to puke. She wanted everything to be perfect and for things to go off without a hitch.

She'd spent the afternoon at Tabitha's getting hair and makeup done. Her friends had been skeptical of the look she wanted but in the end they hadn't argued and then told her how fabulous she looked.

Ashley wanted…sophisticated. Something that didn't scream flighty, exuberant or impulsive. This was her night to prove to Devon that she was the consummate hostess and perfect complement to him.

Her dress was, as she'd been assured, the perfect little black dress. Ridiculous as it sounded, it was the first such dress that Ashley had owned. For Ashley, wearing black was the equivalent of going to a funeral. It made her feel subdued and swallowed up. Somber. She much preferred brighter, more cheerful colors.

As for her hair, she never paid much attention to it and wore it down more often than not, or she just flipped it up in a clip and went on her way.

But Tabitha had spent an hour fashioning an elegant knot, without a hair out of place. Pippa had grumbled that it made her look forty and not the young twenty-something she was.

Carly had applied light makeup using muted shades and Ashley wore pale lip gloss instead of her usual shiny pink. The perfect accompaniment to the dress and hair were the pearls her grandmother had given her before she passed away two years ago.

She wore a simple strand around her neck and a tiny cluster at her ears.

Ashley thought she looked perfect. She just hoped everyone else did as well and that she could pull off the evening with a smile.

Across the room, the jazz ensemble played. Waiters circled the room, offering hors d'oeuvres and a choice of white and red wines. Two bartenders manned the open bar and in addition to the appetizers offered by the waiters, there was an elegant buffet arranged by the far wall.

Lights were strung in the fake potted trees, making the room look festive and bright. Flickering candles illuminated centerpieces of fresh flowers on each table.

Ashley had fretted endlessly over all the arrangements until she was sure she was spouting menu choices in her sleep. She'd tasted each and every one of the appetizers, wrinkling her nose at some, loving others. She'd made Pippa accompany her, though, because Pippa's tastes were more refined. Ashley was pickier and more apt to turn her nose up at fine cuisine.

Now the moment had arrived and though she kept telling herself that these people didn't matter to her and that they were her father's and Devon's associates, she couldn't shake the paralyzing fear that she'd make some huge mistake and embarrass herself and her husband in front of everyone.

"Ashley, there you are," Pippa said as she made her way through the growing crowd.

"Oh, my God, I'm so glad you're here," Ashley said. "Thank you for coming. I'm a nervous wreck."

Pippa frowned. "Ash, there's no reason for you to be so worked up over this. It's a party. Loosen up. Have some fun. Let your hair down from that godawful bun."

Ashley let out a shaky laugh. "Easy for you to say. You aren't facing a hundred of your husband's closest business associates."

Pippa rolled her eyes. "Come on, let's go get a drink."

Ashley let Pippa lead her over to the bar but when they got there, Ashley ordered water. Pippa raised an eyebrow and Ashley sighed.

"I have a doctor's appointment tomorrow," Ashley whispered. "Don't you dare say a word to anyone, okay? I haven't told anyone I even suspect I might be pregnant. I took one of those damn home pregnancy tests and it was inconclusive but I haven't had my period yet and I'm sure I'm late. So until I know, I don't want to drink anything."

"What time is your appointment?" Pippa demanded.

"Ten in the morning."

"Okay, then here's what's going to happen. Carly, Tabitha and I are going to wait for you at Oscar's and you're going to come straight over for lunch after your appointment so you can tell us the news one way or another."

Ashley nodded. "Okay. I'll need the support regardless of the outcome. I'm kind of undecided about this whole thing."

Pippa blinked in surprise. "You mean you aren't sure you want to be pregnant?"

"Yes. No. Maybe. I don't know," she said miserably.

"Ash, what the hell is going on with you lately? All you've ever wanted is to have children."

Ashley bit her lip in consternation as she saw Devon making his way toward her. "Look, I can't talk about it now. I'll see you at lunch tomorrow after my appointment. And don't breathe a word! I haven't told anyone. Not even Dev."

Pippa looked at her oddly but went silent as Devon approached.

"There you are," Devon said when he got to the two women. He kissed Pippa's cheek in greeting and then tucked Ashley's hand in his. "If you don't mind, Pippa, I'm going to steal my wife for a bit. There are some people I want her to meet."

Pippa leaned over to kiss Ashley's cheek. "See you tomorrow," she whispered softly. "Take care of yourself."

Ashley smiled her thanks and allowed Devon to lead her away. For the next hour, she smiled and quietly listened as Devon introduced her around and discussed things she had no clue about. But she pretended interest and glued herself to his every word, nodding when she thought it was appropriate.

Her headache had worked itself down her neck until it hurt to even move it. Her cheeks ached from the permanent smile and her feet were killing her.

The old Ashley would have kicked off her shoes, pulled her hair down and found someone to talk with about things she understood. Finding or starting conversation was never difficult for her.

The new Ashley was going to survive this night even if it killed her.

Devon seemed appreciative of her effort. He'd told her she looked beautiful and he'd smiled at her often as he took her from group to group. Maybe she had imagined it or maybe it was wishful thinking on her part but she'd sworn she saw pride reflected in those golden eyes of his.

"Stay right here," Devon said as he parked her on the perimeter of the makeshift dance floor. "I have to find your father. He's announcing his retirement tonight."

She nodded and dutifully stood where he'd left her even though her feet were about to throb right off her legs and her head hurt so bad her vision was fuzzing.

She was careful to wear a smile and not let her discomfort show. Instead she turned her thoughts to the possibility of her being pregnant.

It was true she'd lived the past week in denial. She hadn't entertained the thought. Hadn't wanted to think about it because if she acknowledged the possibility, then she had to consider the reality of her marriage and whether she was ready to bring a child into such uncertainty.

The previous night with Devon had been... Her smile faltered and she quickly recovered. It had been wonderful. But what was it exactly? Sex? Lust? It couldn't be considered making love. Not when he didn't love her.

He'd been exceedingly tender. She was still embarrassed that she'd lost control of her emotions and cried in front of him. It felt manipulative and she still worried that the only reason he'd had sex with her was because she'd been upset and he wanted to comfort her.

He'd left for work this morning before she'd awakened. She'd overslept—another reason she suspected she was pregnant. She was so tired that some days it was all she could do to remain upright. Twice she'd succumbed to the urge to take a nap simply because she would have lapsed into unconsciousness otherwise.

So she hadn't been able to gauge his mood after they had sex. She had no idea if it changed anything or nothing at all. And she hated the uncertainty. Hated not knowing her place in the world or in this relationship.

Devon had been good to her. He'd been kind. But she didn't want good or kind. She didn't want him to feel sorry for her because he'd broken her heart. She wanted his love.

She could feel the anxiety and rush of anger and confusion crawling over her skin, tightening and heating until the sensation reached her cheeks. She curled and uncurled her fingers at her sides, the only outward reaction she'd allow herself as she sought to calm the turmoil wreaking havoc with her mind.

Maybe it was best she didn't dwell on her possible pregnancy. She was already uptight enough without causing herself full-scale panic.

Her father stepped up onto the elevated platform along with Devon. Ashley's mom stood—just as she always had—by her husband's side. But Devon hadn't wanted Ashley there. He'd wanted her here. All the way across the floor from him. She didn't know if there was any significance to that. Her ego was bruised enough to conjure all sorts of pathetic scenarios that spiked the self-pity meter.

For half an hour her father talked, fondly recounting memories, thanking his staff and his family. She smiled faintly when he singled her out and gave her an indulgent, fatherly smile. Then he went on to say that he was stepping down and that Devon would be succeeding him.

There were surprised murmurs from some. Nods from others who obviously suspected such a thing. A few raised eyebrows but most notably, she noticed that people's gazes found her. There were knowing smiles. A few whispers. Nods in her direction.

Her facade was starting to crack. Her smile was beginning to falter. It was as if the world had put two and two together and said, "Aha! Now we get it."

She just wished she did. She stared around, looking for a possible escape path, but she was surrounded by people. All looking at her. Or between her and Devon. Those damn knowing smiles. The smirks of a few women.

It was the worst night of her entire life. Worse than even her wedding night.

Devon found himself surrounded by a throng of people offering their congratulations. He had only taken one step away from William before everyone had descended. Family members. Staff members. Some offering sincere congratulations. Some clearly wary and uncertain. But that was to be expected. Any time change was announced, fear took hold. It was too early to be offering anyone reassurances. Who knew what would happen over the course of the next few months when a changing of the guard would take place and Devon would be at the helm of what would now be the world's most exclusive line of resorts and luxury hotels.

Tonight, though, Devon was celebrating his own victory of sorts. He'd cornered William before the party had begun and told him that Copeland was going to sponsor Ashley's animal shelter.

William had been opposed until Devon threatened to refuse to take William's place in the company. Devon wanted full sponsorship with a yearly budget allocated to the shelter. He was determined that Ashley wouldn't shed another damn tear over her beloved animals.

His father-in-law grumbled and told Devon he was a besotted fool, but he'd given in, telling Devon he'd just do as he damn well wanted when he took over anyway. Which was absolutely true, but they didn't have that much time and he needed William's cooperation to fund the shelter now so it wouldn't have to close.

Now he just needed the right opportunity to tell Ashley the good news. Tonight in bed after the party seemed perfect. Then he'd make love to her until they were both insensible.

He was yanked from his thoughts when he saw Cam pushing his way through the crowd. He grinned when Cam got to him and he slapped his friend on the back. "Well, we did it. Everything. Copeland. The new resort. Oh, ye of little faith."

Cam ignored Devon's ribbing. His expression was grim and his gaze was focused over Devon's shoulder across the room. "What the hell have you done to her, Dev?"

Devon reared his head back. "Excuse me?" He turned, looking for the source of Cam's attention, but all he saw was Ashley, standing where he'd left her so she wouldn't be swallowed up by the crowd.

Cam shook his head then turned his gaze on Devon. "You don't even see it, do you?"

Devon's eyes narrowed. "What the hell are you talking about?"

Cam made a sound of disgust. "Look at her, Dev."

Again, Devon followed Cam's gaze to Ashley. He studied her a long moment.

"Really look at her, Dev. Take a long, hard look."

Devon battled a surge of irritation. He was about to tell Cam to go to hell when Ashley rubbed her hand over her forehead. The gesture seemed to make abundantly clear what perhaps he'd missed before. Maybe he'd been missing for a while. Or maybe it just took Cam drawing his attention to it.

She was pale, her face drawn. She looked tired and exceedingly fragile. She looked...different. Not at all like the vivacious, sparkling woman he'd married.

He frowned. "She probably has a headache."

"You're a dumbass," Cam said in disgust.

Before Devon could respond, Cam turned on his heel and walked away, leaving Devon baffled by the anger in his friend's voice.

But he didn't have time to figure out Cam's mood or what bug was up his ass. Ashley looked exhausted. Her forehead was creased in pain and she rubbed the back of her neck. He was more convinced than ever that she had one of her headaches.

He pushed his way through the few people standing between him and where William now stood with his son, Eric.

"I'm going to take Ashley home," he said to William. "Please give our apologies to our guests."

William looked up in concern while Eric frowned and immediately sought Ashley out in the crowd.

"Is something wrong?" William asked.

"Everything's fine," Devon said in an effort to calm the older man. "I think she has a headache."

Eric scowled, his blue eyes flashing as he stared holes through Devon. "She seems to be having headaches quite frequently these days."

Devon wasn't going to stick around to argue the point. He nodded at William and then went to collect Ashley.

He found her conversing with two of the people who worked in the Tricorp offices. Or rather *they* were doing all the conversing. Ashley stood smiling and nodding.

"Excuse us please, gentlemen," Devon said smoothly. "I'd like to steal my wife if you don't mind."

The relief on her face made him wince. She was obviously suffering and she'd had to stand here through her father's speech.

His plans for the evening melted away. His primary concern now was getting her home so he could take care of her. The news about the shelter could wait until tomorrow. They'd have dinner together—another of her experimental concoctions, no doubt—and then he'd tell her that her animals were safe.

He drew her in close, noting again the fatigue etched in her features. But more than that, it was as if the light had been doused from her usually expressive eyes.

He experienced a tightening sensation in his chest but he shook it off and focused his attention on her.

"We're leaving."

She looked up in surprise. "But why? The party will be going on for hours yet."

"You're hurting," he said quietly. "Headache?"

A dull flush worked over her features. "It's okay. I'm fine, really. There's no need for you to leave. I can have Pippa take me home or I can just catch a cab."

"The hell I'll have you leave here in a cab," he bit out. "I've done what I needed to do here. The rest is William's night. I won't have you suffering when you could be at home in bed after taking your medication."

Her shoulders sagged a bit and she nodded her acceptance. He put his hand to her back, noting again just how fragile she felt. It wasn't something he could even describe. How did someone feel fragile? But there was an aura of vulnerability that surrounded her like a fog. He wasn't imagining it.

He guided her toward the door, not stopping to acknowledge the people who spoke as they passed.

She was silent the entire way home. She sat in the darkened interior of the car, eyes closed and so still that he was afraid to move for fear of disturbing her.

Once back at their apartment, he helped her undress and pulled back the covers so she could crawl into bed. He leaned down to kiss her brow as he pulled the sheet up to her chin.

"I'll go get your medication and something to drink."

To his surprise, she shook her head. "No," she said in a low voice. "I don't want it. I hate the way it makes me feel. I just need to sleep. I'll be fine in the morning."

He frowned but didn't want to argue with her. She needed to take the damn medicine. She was obviously in a lot of pain. But her eyes were already closed and her soft breathing signaled that she was relaxing or at least trying to.

"All right," he conceded. "But if you aren't better in the morning, you're taking the medicine."

She nodded without opening her eyes. "Promise."

Chapter 17

Devon woke Ashley the next morning long enough to ascertain how she was feeling. Ashley assured him she was fine even though her stomach still churned with humiliation and upset. In truth, she just wanted him gone. The last thing she wanted was a set of eyes on her when she was on the verge of cracking.

After he left for work, she shuffled into the shower and stood for a long time underneath the heated spray. Afterward she didn't linger in the bathroom long. She dried her hair because of the cold, but pulled it back into a ponytail. She was too on edge to worry over makeup and just made do with moisturizer.

She was in turns scared and dismayed over the prospect of pregnancy. At times she firmly hoped she wasn't expecting. Others, she held a secret, ridiculous hope that a pregnancy would... What? She laughed helplessly at just how naive she was. Even as she knew a child would in no way fix a doomed relationship, there was a part of her that wondered if Devon would grow to love the mother of his child.

It angered her that she could even entertain such a notion. Why on earth would she settle for a man loving her because she produced his offspring? If he couldn't love her before that, why would she even care what happened after she popped out a kid?

Unrequited love sucked. There were no two ways about it.

If she had it to do all over again, she'd put a definite "wait and see" on any childbearing. Or at least get through the honeymoon without any life-altering surprises.

She ate a light breakfast to settle her stomach. She couldn't be entirely certain if her queasy morning stomach was due to pregnancy or her rather fragile emotional state of late. Or maybe subconsciously she wanted to be pregnant and so had convinced herself of the possibility. Weren't there women who had false pregnancies?

Her nervousness grew as she got into a cab to go to the doctor's office. The only person who knew what she was doing today was Pippa. And well, now Tabitha and Carly would know as well, but she was counting on them to get her through either scenario. Pregnant or not pregnant.

At the clinic, she filled out the paperwork and waited impatiently for the nurse to call her back. After answering a myriad of questions, she was asked to pee in a cup. They drew blood and then she was asked to wait in the reception area.

For twenty of the longest minutes of her life.

She fidgeted. She flipped through a magazine. Finally she got up to pace as she took in the other women in various stages of pregnancy.

Finally the nurse called her back. Ashley hurried toward the door and was escorted to a private sitting area outside one of the exam rooms.

"Well?" she blurted, unable to remain silent a moment longer.

The nurse smiled. "You're pregnant, Mrs. Carter. Judging by when you say your last period was, I'd say maybe six weeks at most. But we'll schedule a sonogram so we can better determine dates."

Ashley's stomach bottomed out. She broke out in a cold sweat and her head began pounding until her vision was blurred.

"Are you all right?" the nurse asked gently.

Ashley swallowed rapidly and nodded. "I'm fine. Just a little shocked. I mean, I suspected but maybe secretly I didn't really believe I was."

The nurse gave her a sympathetic look. "It takes time to adjust. It can be a little overwhelming at first. The important thing is for you to rest, take it easy. Take a little time to let it sink in. We're doing lab work and will check your HCG levels to make sure they're in an appropriate range. If there's any cause for concern, we'll call you. Otherwise, set up an appointment with the receptionist on way out for your first visit to the doctor. We'll do your sonogram then."

Ashley walked out of the clinic a little—okay, a lot—numb. Again, it wasn't a huge shock. She and Devon hadn't done anything to prevent pregnancy at all. In fact they'd openly embraced the idea—at her instigation—but now she wondered if he was even as open to the idea as he'd let on. How could she be sure he hadn't said whatever was necessary to get her to agree to marry him?

Her mouth turned down in an unhappy frown as she laid her head back against the seat of the cab. She should have asked the nurse what she could take for a headache now that she was pregnant.

But she doubted even the strongest pain medication would help the roar in her ears and the nerves that were balanced on a razor's edge.

The cab dropped her off half a block from the restaurant where she was meeting her friends and she bundled her coat around her as she pushed through people hurrying by. She ducked into the bright eatery and scanned the small seating area for the girls.

In the corner, Pippa stood up and waved. Tabitha and Carly both turned immediately and motioned her over with a flurry of hands.

Ashley nearly ran, desperate to be surrounded by the comfort of her best friends in the world.

"So?" Pippa demanded before Ashley had even had a chance to shrug out of her coat. "Tell us!"

"Are you pregnant?" Tabitha asked.

Ashley flopped into her chair, wrung out from the events of the past weeks. To her utter horror, tears welled in her eyes. It was like knocking the final stone from an already weakened dam.

Her friends stared at her in shock as she dissolved into tears.

"Oh, my God, Ashley, what's wrong? Honey, it's okay, you have plenty of time to get pregnant," Carly soothed.

Tabitha and Pippa wrapped their arms around her from both sides and hugged her fiercely.

"I *am* pregnant," she said on a sob.

That earned her looks of bewilderment all around. Pippa took charge, taking a table napkin and dabbing at Ashley's tears. Her friends sat quietly, soothing and hugging her until finally she got her sobs under control and they diminished to quiet sniffles.

"What the hell is going on?" Pippa asked bluntly. "You look like hell, Ash. And you haven't been yourself. What the hell was that last night with the weird hair and the dress you wouldn't normally get caught dead in?"

"Pippa!" Tabitha scolded. "Can't you see how upset she is?"

"She's right," Carly said in a grim voice. "Besides we're her friends and we love her. We can get away with telling her she looks like crap."

Tabitha sighed. "I think what they're delicately trying to say is you just don't look happy, Ash. We're worried about you."

"Everything's such a mess," Ashley said as tears welled up all over again.

"We've got all day," Pippa said firmly. "Now tell us what's going on with you."

The entire story came spilling out. Every humiliating detail, right down to the disaster of a wedding night and her decision to make Devon fall in love with her.

The three women looked stunned. Then anger fired in Pippa's eyes. "That son of a bitch! I hate him!"

"So do I," Tabitha announced.

"I'd like to kick him right between the legs," Carly muttered.

"You aren't going to stand for this are you?" Pippa demanded.

"I don't know what to do," Ashley said wearily.

Carly grabbed Ashley's hands. "Look at me, honey. You are a beautiful, loving, generous woman. You are perfect just like you are. The only one who needs to change in this relationship is that jerk you married. I'm so pissed right now I can't even see straight. I cannot believe his nerve. I wouldn't change a single thing about you and moreover he doesn't deserve you."

"Amen," Pippa growled. "You need to tell him to take a long walk off the short end of a pier."

Tabitha pulled Ashley into her arms and hugged her tightly. Then she pulled away and gently wiped at the tears on Ashley's cheeks.

"No one who truly loves you should ever want you to change. And no one who wants to change that essential part that makes you *you* deserves a single moment of your time."

"I love you guys," Ashley said brokenly. "You can't even imagine how much I needed you right now."

"I just wish you'd confided in us sooner," Pippa said. "Nobody should have to endure all of what you've endured alone. That's what friends are for. We love you. We would have kicked his sorry ass weeks ago if we'd known."

Ashley cracked a watery smile. "What would I do without you all?"

"Let's not even consider the possibility since you're never going to be without us," Carly said.

"So what are you going to do, hon?" Tabitha asked, her voice full of concern.

Ashley took a deep breath because until right now, at this very moment, she hadn't known. Or maybe she had but had pushed it aside, unwilling to accept the decision that her heart had already made.

"I'm going to tell him I can't do this," she said softly.

"Good for you," Pippa said fiercely.

"You're leaving him?" Carly asked.

Ashley sighed again. "I can't stay with him. I deserve better. I deserve a man who loves me and doesn't want to change me. I'm tired of trying to be someone I'm not. I liked myself the way I was. I don't like this person I've become."

"That a girl," Tabitha said. "And don't you worry even for a minute about the baby. You have us. You know your parents will support you. We'll be with you every step of the way. We'll babysit. We'll go to the doctor with you. We'll even coach you in the delivery room."

"Oh God, stop before you make me cry again," Ashley choked out.

"Do you want one of us to go with you?" Carly asked anxiously. "I don't want you to have to do this alone. Pippa would be awesome to take with you. She can be scary when people mess with someone she loves."

Pippa grinned.

"No," Ashley said, squaring her shoulders. "This is something I have to do on my own. It's time I regained control over my own life and future. I haven't had it since Devon walked into my life."

"I'm so proud of you, Ash," Tabitha said.

"We all are," Pippa said firmly. "If you need a place to stay until you get everything sorted out, any one of us will be more than happy to let you stay as long as you need."

Ashley looked at her three friends and some of the terrible ache in her chest dissolved at the love and loyalty she saw burning in their eyes. She really would be okay. Things would suck for a while, but she was going to be okay. She'd get through this. She had family and friends—the very best of friends—and now she had a child to focus on.

The moment the nurse had confirmed that she had a life growing inside her, Ashley's entire world had changed. Her priorities had shifted and she'd instantly known that she had to do what was best for her and her child.

It had been a powerful moment of realization.

Calm settled over her. Oh, she was still terrified—and heartbroken. That wouldn't change overnight. But now she knew what she had to do and she couldn't escape the inevitability of the path that for once *she* had chosen instead of it choosing her.

Chapter 18

Devon was having a hard time concentrating. He'd already blown three phone calls. He'd sent an email to the wrong recipient and replied to another thinking it was someone else. His focus was completely and utterly shot and he couldn't even pinpoint exactly what had him so out of sorts.

He was concerned for Ashley, definitely. He hadn't wanted to leave her that morning, but she'd insisted she was fine and that he should go into work. Still, he had a nagging sensation tugging at his chest that wouldn't go away.

Something just wasn't right.

He picked up his phone to call Ashley's cell but was interrupted by his door opening. He looked up and frowned. His secretary hadn't announced a visitor and he knew damn well he didn't have an appointment now.

To his surprise, Eric Copeland strode into the room, his expression grim. He stopped in front of Devon's desk and planted his palms down on the polished wood.

"What the hell have you done to my sister?"

Devon pushed back and shot up out of his chair. "What the hell are you talking about? I'm getting damn tired of people asking me what I've done to her. If you're asking why we left the party last night, she had a headache and I didn't want her to suffer needlessly. I took her home and put her to bed."

Eric made a sound of disgust. "You may not know this about Ashley but the only time she gets these headaches with any frequency is when she's stressed or unhappy. I find it pretty telling that she returned from her honeymoon after only two days because of a headache and that since then, she's suffered them on a regular basis."

It was a fist to Devon's gut. He sank back into his chair as Eric stood seething over him.

"My sister looks desperately unhappy," Eric continued. "I don't know what the hell is going on, but I don't like what I see. She's changed and something tells me you have everything to do with that."

"Maybe she's finally growing up," Devon said tightly. "Her family hasn't done her any favors by coddling her and shielding her from the world around her."

Eric gave him a look of pure disgust. The cold fury emanating from the younger man slapped Devon squarely in the face. It pricked at Devon and aroused an instinctive need to defend himself. The idea that his marriage was being picked apart by this outsider roused his ire even as a voice in the back of his mind whispered to him to listen.

"Her family loves her just like she is," Eric bit out.

"She is cherished and adored by us all. She is appreciated for the beautiful, warm, loving person she is and we'd damn well never try to change her. Anyone that would doesn't *deserve* her."

He spun around and stalked toward the door but then he stopped and turned back to Devon, his lips curled into a snarl. "I don't know what the hell kind of deal you struck with my father but he was wrong. Dead wrong. You weren't the right man for my sister. The right man would know and appreciate what a gift he'd been given. I'm putting you on notice right now. I'm watching you. If Ashley isn't more herself in very short order, I'm coming after you with everything I've got. I hadn't planned to take over the business for my father, but if the choices are having you as a part of the family and making my sister miserable or me sucking it up and taking over myself, I'll do it."

Devon's lips thinned but he acknowledged Eric's ultimatum with a tight nod.

With another dark look, Eric stalked out of the door.

Devon stared out his window in brooding silence after Eric's abrupt departure. Then he stared down at his phone, suddenly afraid to make the call he'd planned just minutes before.

It also occurred to him that she hadn't called him at work in weeks. Not once. No more silly Tinker Bell chimes that amused his coworkers to no end. Not even a mushy text message like she'd done so often before.

He hadn't given it much thought. Things had been so busy after the wedding, with William wanting to move into retirement and the new resort going up, as well as the endless planning sessions for the future.

He'd honestly just forged ahead, hoping that with

time, Ashley would get over her initial upset and see that things really hadn't changed that much between them. But a sick feeling settled into his stomach as he realized—truly realized—that everything had changed. And most notably, *she* had changed.

A ping sounded, signaling the intercom, and Devon raised his head irritably. Now his secretary wanted to talk to him? Giving him a heads-up on Eric's arrival would have been nice. But he forgot all about his irritation when he heard what she had to say.

"Mr. Carter, your wife is here to see you."

Adrenaline surged in his veins.

"Send her in," Devon demanded, rising from his seat.

Ashley hadn't ever set foot in his office. Not even when they were dating. She'd called him. Texted him. Sent him sweet emails. But she'd never actually come into his building.

He was striding across the room, fully intending to meet her, when the door opened and she hesitantly walked in. He stopped abruptly, taken aback by the starkness of her features. She was pale, her face was drawn and her eyes were heavy and dull.

An uneasy feeling crept up his spine as she stared back at him.

"Are you busy?" she asked in a soft voice. "Have I come at a bad time?"

"Of course not. Come, have a seat. Would you like something to drink?"

He was suddenly nervous and he hated that feeling. Somehow she'd managed to completely upend his confidence. Much like she'd upended his life.

She shook her head but took a seat on the small sofa

in the small sitting area of his office. "I needed to talk to you, Devon."

It was only natural that any man hearing those words from his wife would dread what followed. But coming from Ashley, they seemed so...final.

"All right," he said quietly. He took a seat across from her and studied the tiredness in her eyes. Those rich, vibrant eyes looked...bleak. Without hope. That was what he'd been reaching for. What had eluded him about the way she looked. He caught his breath, suddenly filled with an impending sense of doom. She looked...hopeless, and Ashley was nothing if not eternally optimistic. Had he ever considered such a thing a flaw? He was ashamed to say he had. Now he just wanted it back.

"I'm pregnant," she said baldly. There was no emotion. No accompanying excitement. No flash of joy. Frankly, he was bewildered by her reaction.

"That's wonderful," he said huskily.

But her expression said it was anything but wonderful. She looked as though she was battling tears.

"I can't do this anymore," she said in a choked voice.

Alarm blistered up his spine and rammed into the base of his skull. "What do you mean?"

She rose and it was all he could do not to tie her to the damn sofa because he had a sudden sense that she was slipping away from him in more ways than one.

Her hands shook but she exerted admirable control over her emotions as she courageously faced him down.

"This marriage. You asked how long it would take to determine whether it would work. The truth is, it was never going to work. It's taken me this long to realize it, but I deserve more. We both do. You deserve to find a woman you can love and that you won't be manipulated into marrying. I deserve a man who adores me and wants to be married to me. Someone who won't try to change me. Someone who accepts me, faults and all. Someone who loves flighty, impulsive Ashley and isn't embarrassed by her."

Tears clouded her eyes and her voice grew thick with emotion. "I thought… I thought I could make you love me, Dev. It was a mistake from the beginning to even try. It was a hard lesson for me to learn but I can't be someone I'm not even if it meant you'd eventually love the new me. Because it wouldn't be Ashley you loved. It would be someone I made up and all the while the real Ashley would be standing there, unloved. I can't do that to myself. And I can't do it to my child. I want to be a woman and a mother I can be proud of first. Before anyone else. I have to love and be at peace with myself, and you know what? I am. I liked me just fine. Was I perfect? No, but I was happy in my own skin and my family and friends accept that person. Someday there'll be a man who'll accept me, too. Until then, I'd rather be alone and true to myself than with someone who places conditions on his ability to love and accept me."

So stunned was he by her declaration that he stood while she walked quietly toward the door. When he realized she'd already slipped by him, he whirled around, calling her name, the lump in his throat so huge that it came out as a mere croak.

But the door had already closed quietly behind her, leaving him standing there so numb…and broken.

Dread consumed him. The realization, the true realization of just what he'd done threatened to completely unravel him. Oh, God. What had he done?

His legs buckled and would no longer sustain his

weight. He staggered back onto the couch and slumped forward, burying his face in his hands.

She was right and so very wrong all at the same time. The realization was as clear to him as if someone had hit him over the head with it.

He'd destroyed something infinitely precious and he'd never forgive himself for it. He didn't deserve forgiveness.

Dear God, was this what he'd done to her? She'd come into his office and delivered the news of her pregnancy in a dispassionate fashion, as if she were telling him that she had a dentist appointment or that she was buying new shoes.

Where she'd once jumped up and down and squealed her joy over her cousin's pregnancy and vowed she'd do the same over her own pregnancy, she'd related the news with dead eyes and a broken spirit.

He'd done that to her. No one else. Him and his high-handed, arrogant opinions of how she should act or not act. He'd taken something beautiful and precious and had spit on it.

He'd suffocated a ray of sunshine and sucked every bit of joy and life from her.

Cam was right. Eric was right. Ashley was right. He didn't deserve her. They'd seen clearly what he'd blithely ignored. In his arrogance, he'd assumed he was right and that he knew what was best for Ashley.

He had tried to change her. And she was bloody perfect just as she was. He hadn't even realized how much he'd missed all the things he professed to be annoyed over. The random calls at work just to say she loved him. The sudden attacks of affection when she'd throw her arms around him. Her exuberance around others.

She hadn't cleaned and organized their apartment because she felt like it. She'd eradicated every hint of her presence there because she'd thought that's what he wanted. She'd tried to become this image of the perfect wife to please him. He himself had thought he wanted her to.

The cooking. The endless trying to kill herself to please him. She'd gone from a vibrant breath of fresh air to a subdued, beaten-down shadow of her former self.

She no longer sparkled. All because he was the biggest ass on the face of the planet.

His pulse ratcheted up and the sick feeling inside him grew as he realized just how long it had been since she'd said she loved him. Since she'd demonstrated any outward affection for him. Since she'd simply smiled and seemed happy.

Tears burned his eyelids. He'd taken something so very beautiful and he'd crushed it. He'd rejected her love. The very gift of herself. He'd arrogantly told her in essence that she wasn't good enough for him. That he knew better. That she wasn't worthy of him.

A low moan escaped him. Not good enough for him? He wasn't good enough to lick her boots.

In clear and startling detail, he realized what perhaps he'd fought from the very first moment he laid eyes on Ashley. He loved her. Not the new, subdued Ashley. He loved the impulsive, passionate, sparkly Ashley. And the very thing he loved the most was what he'd tried to kill.

Rafe and Ryan had nothing on him when it came to being complete and utter bastards to the women who loved them. Devon had surpassed any amount of sin a man committed against someone they claimed to care for.

How could he possibly expect Ashley to forgive him when he'd never be able to forgive himself?

She was pregnant with his child and she was leaving him.

He didn't deserve her. He should let her walk away and find someone who adored her beyond reason and would never ever treat her as he had.

But he couldn't do it. He couldn't be that selfless. *He* adored her beyond reason and if it took the rest of his damn life, he would make it up to her for every wrong he'd done to her.

But first he had to make damn sure she didn't walk out of his life forever.

Chapter 19

Ashley tugged the coat tighter around her as she stepped from the cab in front of her parents' apartment building. She had no desire to face them today but she needed to get it over with and she wanted the comfort only her mother could provide.

Devon had already called her cell a dozen times until finally she'd shut it off so it would stop ringing. She'd expected resistance. She was fortunate that she'd caught him off guard enough that she'd been able to get out of his office without much fuss.

But now he would want to talk to her. No doubt he'd give her another lecture about being impulsive and reckless and whatever other adjectives he'd want to assign to her. Then he'd inform her that there was no reason they couldn't have an enjoyable marriage, blah, blah, blah.

She wanted more than some damn enjoyable marriage. She wanted…awesome. She wanted a man who loved her and celebrated her for who she was. Maybe she'd never have it. But she damn sure wasn't going to settle for someone her father had bribed to marry her.

Which was another reason she'd come to her parents' apartment. Because first she was going to tell her father to stop interfering in her life. Then she wanted a hug from her mother.

She walked into the apartment and took off her coat. "Mom?" she called. "Daddy?"

Gloria Copeland hurried out of the kitchen and smiled her welcome. "Hi, darling. What brings you over today? I wish you'd called. I would have made sure I had tea ready."

"Where's Daddy?" Ashley asked quietly. "I need to talk to him. To you both, actually."

Gloria frowned. "I'll go get him. Is something wrong?"

"You could say that."

Alarm flashed across her mother's face. "Go sit down in the living room. We'll be right there."

Her mom hurried away and Ashley made her way into the spacious living room. Instead of sitting, she went to the fireplace, grateful for the warmth. She was cold on the inside and it felt as though she'd never be warm again.

A moment later, she heard the footsteps of her parents and she turned slowly to face them.

"Ashley, baby, what's wrong?" her father asked sharply.

Both her mother and her father stood a short distance away, impatient and worried. She drew a deep breath and took the plunge. "I've left Devon and I'm pregnant."

Gloria gasped and put her hand to her mouth. William's eyes narrowed and he frowned. "What the hell happened?"

"*You* happened," she said bitterly. "How could you, Daddy? How could you manipulate us both that way?"

Her father threw up his arm in anger and swore. "Damn it, I told him not to tell you."

"He didn't. I found out on my wedding night. Can you possibly imagine how awful it was to find out on my wedding night that my father had all but bought and paid for my husband?"

"William, what on earth is she talking about?" Gloria asked in bewilderment.

It relieved Ashley that at least her mother hadn't known. She wouldn't have been able to handle the double deception.

"He made me part of the Tricorp deal," Ashley said with more calm than she felt. "He forced Devon to marry me or the deal was off the table."

"Damn it, it wasn't like that," her father bit out. "You make it sound like…" He dragged a hand through his hair and closed his eyes wearily. "I just wanted what was best for you. I thought Devon would take care of you. He seemed perfect for you."

"I can take care of myself. I don't need a man to do that. I want a man who wants me for who I am, not because my father waves a lucrative deal in front of him. I want someone who *loves* me."

"Oh darling," Gloria said, finally finding her voice. She rushed forward and enfolded Ashley in her arms. "I'm so very sorry. How awful for you. I had no idea."

Ashley closed her eyes, absorbing the love and acceptance she'd been denied with Devon.

Her mom pulled away and gently stroked a hand through Ashley's hair. "What about you being pregnant? When did you find out?"

"I went to the doctor this morning. Then I went to see Devon."

"Ashley, are you sure about this?" William asked. "I don't believe for a moment that Devon doesn't care about you. Think about what you're doing here, honey. Do you really want to throw everything away because of the way you met? I understand your anger and I take full responsibility. Devon never wanted to deceive you. It was me from the start."

She had to take a moment as she battled tears. "He doesn't like the real me. He thinks I'm flighty, irresponsible, impulsive, too trusting. He wants to change everything about me. How can you possibly think this is a man I'd want to be with? Is that really who you'd want your daughter married to? What would that teach my daughter if I stay with a man who doesn't value me? How can I expect her to have any self-respect if her mother doesn't?"

Her mother wrapped an arm around her shoulders and glared her husband down with furious eyes. "I can't believe you did this, William. What in the hell were you thinking? You may as well have told your daughter that she doesn't matter. You've pulled some stupid stunts in your time, but this takes the cake."

William sighed. "Ashley, please don't be angry with me. I only wanted the best for you. You're my only daughter and I just wanted to see your future secured. I thought that you and Devon would make a sound match. I was wrong and I'm sorrier than you can possibly imagine."

"You aren't pulling the plug on this deal," Ashley said in a low voice. "You won't punish Devon because he can't love me. If you think he's the best choice for the business then leave me out of it. I'd appreciate being able to make my own choices in the future, free of manipulation."

"I do love you, baby. Please believe that. I never meant to hurt you. Devon tried to tell me but I wouldn't listen. I thought I knew better. He wanted me to tell you everything. He didn't want to deceive you but I tied his hands and for that I'm sorry."

Tears welled in her eyes. Who knew what may have happened if they'd just been left alone?

William hesitantly pulled her into his arms and hugged her tight. "You know you can count on me and your mother to help you with whatever you need, and we'll be here for the baby when it comes."

"I know," she whispered. "And I love you too, Daddy. Just let me make my own mistakes from now on. Your heart was in the right place but now I've fallen in love with a man who can never love the real me."

He slowly released her and her mom pulled her into another hug. "Do you want me to send someone over for your things? You know you can stay here as long as you like."

Ashley shook her head. "I'm going to stay with Pippa for a bit until I figure out what my next step is. I need to find a better job. I have a child to consider now. Devon is right about one thing. It's time to pull my head out of the clouds and grow up."

How long could she possibly avoid him? Devon paced his office, though he hadn't gotten any work done in the three days since Ashley had walked out on him. He hadn't slept. He'd worn out his phone trying to call her. He'd called her friends, her parents, every family member he had a number for.

The reception had been understandably chilly.

He didn't care. He had no pride where Ashley was concerned. He didn't care if he came across as the most pathetic, lovesick guy who'd ever lived. He just wanted her back. He wanted her stuff strewn all over his apartment. He wanted to be able to smell her as soon as he walked into a room. He wanted her to be happy again. He wanted her to smile.

When he wasn't at the office, he was at the apartment, waiting. She hadn't returned. Not even to get her things. All her clothes were still neatly hung in the closet. Her shoes—and there were a ton of shoes—were stacked in boxes on the shelves in his closet. Ashley never went anywhere without her shoes and the fact that she still hadn't returned to the apartment worried him.

If only she'd answer her damn phone. Or one of the hundreds of texts he'd sent her. He just wanted to know she was all right. Worry was eating a hole in his gut. She was pregnant. What if she had another one of her headaches? Who would take care of her?

Eric had said she had frequent headaches when she was unhappy. Devon had made her miserable. Her medication was also at the apartment but surely she couldn't take it now that she was pregnant. He could at least hold her, rub her head, make sure it was cool and dark in the room.

If she would just talk to him. Just give him a chance to tell her how much he loved her. He hadn't realized how much he missed the sunshine she brought into his life until it was gone. Snuffed out over careless, thoughtless words he'd thrown at her.

His cell rang and he scrambled for it, nearly dropping it in his haste to see if it was Ashley calling. Disappointment nearly flattened him when he saw it was Rafael. With a heavy sigh, he put the phone to his ear and muttered a low hello.

"It's a girl!" Rafael said in a jubilant voice. "A beautiful six-pound, twelve-ounce baby girl. She was born an hour ago."

Devon's eyes closed and he swallowed back the bitter disappointment. He was so envious of his friend in this moment that it took everything he had not to throw the phone at the wall.

"Hey man, that's great. How is Bryony doing?"

"Oh she's wonderful. What a trooper. I'm so damn proud of her. She breezed right through labor. I think she was a hell of a lot stronger than I was. I was ready to fall over by the time the little one made her appearance. But boy, is she gorgeous. Looks just like her mama."

Devon could practically hear Rafael beaming through the phone.

"Give her my love," Devon said. "I'm happy for both of you."

"Is everything okay, Dev? You sound like hell if you don't mind me saying."

Devon hesitated. He didn't want to dump on Rafael on the day his daughter was born, but he was at the end of his rope and he could use any advice he could get.

"No," he said bluntly. "Ashley's pregnant and she left me."

"Whoa. Back up a minute. Holy crap. I thought she was head over heels in love with you? What the hell happened? And damn, you move fast. How far along is she?"

"I have no idea," Devon said in a weary voice. "I don't know anything. She came to my office three days ago, told me she was pregnant and then announced she was leaving me."

"Ouch. That blows, man. I'm sorry to hear it. Is there anything I can do?"

Devon sank into his chair and rotated around so he could watch the falling snow through the window. "Yeah, you can give me some advice. I have to get her back, Rafe."

There was a prolonged silence. Then Rafael blew out his breath. "Okay, well the first question. Do you love her? Or is this more of a 'you're not leaving me because you're pregnant and we should stay married' type thing?"

Devon swore. "I love her. I screwed up but I love her. Not that she'll ever believe me. I messed up so bad with her, Rafe. I make you and Ryan look like choirboys."

"Oh boy. That's bad. That's really, really bad."

"Tell me about it."

"Well, I'll tell you like a certain gentleman once told me when I was standing around with my thumb up my ass wondering how the hell I was going to get Bryony to forgive me. Either go big or go home."

"What the hell is that supposed to mean?"

"It means you need to pull out the big guns. Do something huge. Make a gesture she can't possibly mis-understand. And then get on your knees and grovel. Trust me. The first time on your knees sucks, but if she takes you back, you'll spend the rest of your life on them anyway so better get used to it now."

"If she'll take me back, I'll gladly stay on them," Devon muttered.

"It pains me that I can't even give you hell about falling hard like the rest of us poor schmucks you liked to rag on. You're too pathetic to pick on right now."

"Gee thanks," Devon said dryly. "Don't you have a daughter to go take care of? She probably needs a diaper change or something."

"She's sleeping with her mama, but yeah, I'm going to get back to my family. It's the best feeling in the whole world, Dev. Get your ass out there and get your family back where they belong."

"I will. And thanks, Rafe."

"Hey, no problem, man. Anytime."

Devon slid the phone back into his pocket and pondered his friend's advice. Go big or go home. Pretty solid advice. Now he just had to figure out how big to go. There was absolutely nothing he wouldn't do to convince Ashley to give him another chance.

Chapter 20

Ashley sat on Pippa's couch, curled underneath a blanket as she sipped hot tea and watched it snow. It had snowed for the last two days, leaving a heavy blanket over the city. She longed for the comfort of her own apartment…or rather Devon's apartment. She bleakly considered that it had never really been her home. But she missed it all the same. Nights like tonight she and Devon would have snuggled in front of the fire and watched a movie.

"Hey, chickie," Pippa said as she settled down the couch from Ash with a bounce. "How are you feeling? Nausea still a problem?"

It was probably the pregnancy hormones—that was what she was blaming anyway—but she got positively weepy over how protective and caring Pippa had been ever since Ashley had moved in. Or sort of moved in, since Ashley hadn't yet worked up the nerve to get her things from Devon's apartment. Instead she'd been borrowing clothes from Pippa. But soon—as in tomorrow—she was going to have to brave going.

"Yes and no. I honestly don't know if it's the pregnancy or the fact I'm upset. I've been so queasy and nothing sounds good. Even my favorite foods have suddenly lost their appeal."

"I'm sure neither is helping," Pippa said dryly. She hesitated a moment as if deciding whether or not to say what was obviously on her mind. But Pippa wasn't one to hold back. "Have you talked to Devon yet, Ash?"

Ashley put her cup down and sighed. "No. I'm a horrible coward."

"No, you aren't," Pippa said fiercely. "It took guts to go to his office and lay it out to him like you did. I'm so freaking proud of you. I so want to be you when I grow up."

Ashley's eyes got all watery again. "Oh, my God. I've got to stop this," she said, sniffling back the tears. "Pippa, you're the most put-together person I know. You've got it all. You're smart. You can cook like a dream. You're gorgeous. And you're the best friend I could possibly hope for."

"And strangely I'm still single," Pippa drawled.

Ashley giggled. "Only because you're a picky bitch, as you should be. I could use some lessons from you."

Pippa shifted forward on the couch, her expression suddenly serious. "Ashley, you have no idea how truly special you are. When the rest of us were struggling to find ourselves, sleeping around and experimenting with all the wrong guys, you were so calm and centered. You knew exactly who you were and what you wanted. You've always known who you were. You valued yourself and you refused to settle for less. Just because Devon turned out to be a prick who tried to change you doesn't mean you did anything wrong. You may have lost your way for a very short time, but ultimately you didn't let him change you."

Ashley smiled but inside she wondered if Pippa was right. Devon had changed her. Irrevocably. No matter that she'd resisted and refused to become someone she didn't like, she'd never truly be who she was before Devon entered her life.

But maybe that was what life was all about. People and circumstances changed you. It was what you did with that change that mattered.

The door buzzer sounded and Pippa made a face. "I swear if that's another salesman I'm going to wet down my steps so they'll freeze and anyone coming up will bust their ass. We've had two already this week."

"Are you expecting a delivery? Maybe it's your groceries."

Pippa grew thoughtful. "No, I'm pretty sure I arranged it for tomorrow. But maybe you're right. I'll be right back."

"You sit," Ashley said as she pushed the blanket back. "You've been on your feet all morning. I've done nothing but sit around and feel sorry for myself."

Pippa rolled her eyes but flopped back on the couch as Ashley padded toward the door. Ashley grinned as she imagined Pippa watering down her steps so they'd become icy. It was something she'd totally do.

She opened the door to the street-level apartment and blinked in shock to see Devon standing on the stoop, snow landing on his hair and wetting it. He wore a coat but had no scarf or cap, and he looked like he hadn't slept in a week.

"Hello, Ash," he said in a quiet, determined voice.

She gripped the door until her fingers went numb. "Uh, hi. What are you doing here?"

He laughed. It was a dry, brittle sound that in no way conveyed true amusement. "I haven't seen my wife in a week. She won't return my phone calls or texts. I have no idea if she's okay or where she's staying and she asks me what I'm doing here when I finally track her down."

She swallowed nervously but she held her ground. It was mean-spirited to make him stand out in the cold, but she didn't want him to come in.

"I was going to come by tomorrow to pick up my things," she said in a low voice that barely managed to hide the tremble. "If that's all right with you."

"No, it's not all right with me," he bit out.

Her eyes widened and she took a step back at the vehemence in his voice.

"Can we go somewhere and talk, Ash?"

She shook her head automatically. "I don't think that's a good idea."

His lips formed a grim line. "You don't think it's a good idea. You're pregnant with my child. We're married. We've only been married a short time. And you don't think we have anything to talk about?"

She closed her eyes and put a hand to her forehead in an automatic gesture.

"Ash? Is everything okay?" Pippa called. Then she came up behind Ashley. "Who is it?"

Ashley turned. "It's okay, Pip. It's Devon."

Pippa's expression darkened, but Ashley held up her hand. Pippa reluctantly turned to go back to the living room but she called back in a low voice, "I'll be right here if you need me."

Ashley returned her attention to Devon. "I know we need to talk. I just don't think I'm up to it right now. This has been hard for me, Dev. I don't expect you to believe that, but this isn't easy."

His expression softened and he took a step forward, snow dusting off his hair as he moved. "I know it's not, baby. Please. There's so much I need to say to you. There are things I need to show you. But I can't do that if you won't talk to me. Give me this afternoon. Please. If you still don't want anything to do with me, I'll take you over to the apartment myself and I'll help you pack your things."

She stared back at him, utterly befuddled by the pleading in his voice. He almost looked as though he were holding his breath. And his eyes. They looked... bleak.

"I—I need to get my coat," she said lamely.

The relief that poured over his face was stunning. His eyes lightened and he immediately straightened, hope flashing in those golden depths.

"And shoes," he said. "I brought some from the apartment. I wasn't sure you had any you loved here."

She gaped at him. "You brought my shoes?"

He shifted uncomfortably. "Six pairs. They're in the trunk of the car. I chose those I thought would be warm and would protect your feet from getting wet in the snow."

Something loosened in her heart and began to slowly unwind.

"That would be great," she said softly. "Let me go

get my coat and my cap. If you brought a pair of boots, that would be perfect."

"I'll be right back. Wait here. I don't want you falling on the ice," he said.

He turned and sprinted back toward the street, where his car was parked. She stood there a moment, staring in bemusement as he popped the trunk and bent over to rummage in the boxes.

He rarely drove his own car. She'd only seen the vehicle once. They always used his car service or hailed cabs.

Realizing she was still standing in the wide open doorway, allowing the bitter chill inside, she hastily withdrew into the apartment and shut the door.

She hurried back into the living room, grabbed a brush from the end table and began pulling it through her hair in short, rapid strokes.

"Ash? What's going on?" Pippa asked cautiously.

Ashley stopped and frowned. "I'm not altogether certain. Devon wants to talk. Asked if I'd give him the afternoon and then he'd take me to the apartment and help me pack if that's what I wanted. He's acting…weird."

Pippa snorted. "Of course he is. You dumped him after telling him you were pregnant with his baby. That has a way of altering your priorities."

"I guess I'll go…talk," Ashley said as she put the brush aside.

"Call me later," Pippa said. "I'll want a full report."

Ashley blew Pippa a kiss and went to the closet to retrieve her coat and scarf. She pulled on a cap and tucked her hair carefully underneath before heading back to the door.

When she opened it, Devon was standing there holding a pair of fur-lined boots. When she would have reached for them, he bent over and said, "Here, let me."

She put a hand on his shoulder to balance herself and stood on one foot while he pulled her boot on the other. After he zipped it up, she switched feet and he put the other one on for her.

When he was done, he straightened to his full height and then took her hand to help her down the steps. He walked her to the car and settled her into the passenger seat.

"Where are we going?" she asked as he pulled away into traffic.

"You'll see."

She wrinkled her nose and sighed. He slid his hand over the center console and tangled his fingers with hers.

"Trust me, Ash. I know it's a big thing to ask and I totally don't have the right to ask it of you, but trust me just this once."

The utter sincerity in his voice swayed her as nothing else could. There was raw vulnerability echoed in his every word and expression. He looked as terrible as she felt, almost as if he'd suffered as much as she had.

It didn't make sense to her. She had no doubt that he wasn't exactly celebrating her departure from the marriage, but with the deal still intact, he was getting precisely what he wanted without the unnecessary burden of a wife.

When they pulled up outside the shelter, Ashley sat there, bewildered. "Why are we here, Dev?"

Devon opened his door, walked around to hers and held out his hand. "Come on. There's something I want you to see."

She allowed him to help her out of the car and they hurried toward the entrance of the older building. As soon as they ducked inside, the sounds and smells of the animals filled her senses. Her heart softened when she saw Harry the cat sound asleep on the reception desk. He was their unofficial mascot and the children who often filtered through the shelter in search of a pet loved to pet him as much as he loved being petted.

To her further surprise, Devon ushered her past the reception area and through the hallway lined with cages. He'd never been here before. How could he possibly know where he was going?

He stopped outside the larger room they used for animal orientation when they'd put pet and new owner together for a period of adjustment before the animal was released to his new home.

He gave her a quick, nervous smile and then pushed the door open. Inside, Molly and the other shelter volunteers stood beaming in a line, and when Devon and Ashley walked fully through the entrance, they let out a loud cheer.

"What's going on?" Ashley asked in bewilderment.

"Say hello to your new staff," he said. "You are now the acting director of the Copeland Animal Shelter."

Ashley's eyes went wide as she stared at Molly and then at the other grinning volunteers. Then she glanced back at Devon. "I don't understand. We aren't closing?"

Molly rushed forward and threw her arms around Ashley. "No, we aren't closing! Thanks to your husband. He gave us the funding we needed to stay running. Not only can we stay open, but we also have the money for improvements and for marketing so we can heighten awareness for the animals we need homes for."

She disentangled herself from Molly's embrace and then turned back to Devon. "You did this for me?"

"I did it before you left," he said gruffly. "I talked to your father about it the night of the party. I threatened to refuse to take his position if he didn't agree to fund the shelter."

Her mouth fell open in shock. She wanted to throw her arms around him so badly, but she knew it wouldn't be what he wanted. But he looked so nervous, as if he worried she wouldn't appreciate what he'd done. How could she not?

"I know how much the animals mean to you, Ash."

Tears blurred her vision and her heart ached. She loved him so much. "Thank you," she whispered. "I can never thank you enough for this. It means the world to me."

"You mean the world to me," he said softly.

Her eyes widened and her heart thumped so hard against her chest that she put a hand over her breast to steady herself.

But before she could question him, he turned to the others and said, "As much as we'd love to stay and celebrate with you, I have to take Ashley one more place."

After saying their goodbyes, Devon ushered Ashley out to the car again. She sat in her seat, bemused and a little hopeful, but for what she wasn't sure. Something was different about Devon. Something that went deeper than simple regret or guilt.

"What did you mean, Dev?" she asked softly as they drove away. "Back there when you said I meant the world to you?"

His hands tightened around the steering wheel and his jaw worked up and down.

"Exactly what I said, Ash. There is so much I need

to say to you, but I'm asking you to be patient with me. This isn't a conversation I want to have in a car when I'm driving and I can't look at you or touch you. So I'm asking you to give me a little while. There's a place I want to take you and then I want us to talk and I want you to listen to everything I have to say."

Her mouth went dry at the intensity in his voice. He was tense. Almost as if he feared she'd refuse and demand he take her back. Wanting in some way to alleviate his obvious stress, she reached over to lay her hand on his leg.

"Okay, Dev. I'll listen."

Chapter 21

Devon continuously had to ease up on the accelerator as he headed out of the city. He was impatient and time was running out for him, but the roads were slick and the very last thing he wanted to do was endanger his wife and child.

His wife and child.

The words and the image were powerful. *His* wife and child. The woman he loved and had hurt so terribly. A child resting inside her womb. Their creation. His family. Something that belonged solely to him.

What would he do if he wasn't granted a second chance to make amends?

He couldn't—wouldn't—focus on that possibility. To do so would drive him insane. It was up to him to make her forgive him or at least agree to give him one more chance to make it all right.

She was so beautiful, but there was an aura of sadness that surrounded her. It was as if a light had been extinguished or a black cloud had crawled across the sun and clung stubbornly as the storms rolled in.

He wanted her to smile again. He wanted her to be happy. But more than anything he wanted to be *why* she was happy. He wanted her to be happy with *him*.

The trip to Greenwich, Connecticut, took longer than he'd like. The drive was silent and tense. They both seemed nervous and ill at ease. By the time he turned onto road that would wind around to the front of the sprawling home he wanted Ashley to see, they only had an hour of daylight left.

He pulled to the curb just before the bend in the private lane and shut the engine off. Beside him Ashley's brow furrowed in obvious confusion.

He walked around to her side of the car and opened the door. He pulled her out, carefully arranged her scarf and cap so she'd be warm and then took her hand and tugged her onto the road.

Snow drifted in the ditches and spread out over the landscape, a pristine covering of sheer white. It reminded him of her. Magical, almost like a fairy tale.

He'd once told her that life wasn't a fairy tale, but damn it, she was going to have one. Starting right now.

"It's beautiful here," she said breathlessly.

Enchantment filled her eyes as she stared out over the rolling hills. Her face had softened into a dreamy smile and he felt a stirring in his heart. This was how he wanted her to look every day. Happy. Sparkling. So damn beautiful she made him ache to his bones.

He pulled her up short just as they reached the sharp bend in the road. He kept hold of her hand and pulled her to face him, his heart pounding damn near out of his chest.

Their breaths came out in visible puffs. Snowflakes began to fall again, spiraling lazily down, some sticking in her hair, some melting and absorbed by the splash of sun in the barren white of winter.

"Ash."

It came out as a croak and he cleared his throat, prepared to fight with everything he had to keep the woman he loved.

She cocked her head to the side and sent him an inquisitive glance.

"Yes, Devon?"

Her voice was sweet and clear in the silence that had settled over the area. Only the distant crack of a tree limb disturbed the calm.

He hated that he stood here, tongue-tied, unable to form a single damn word, his heart in knots. There was so much to say he simply didn't know where to start. Finally his frustration got the better of him.

"Damn it, I love you. I'm standing here trying my best to come up with the words to everything I have to say and all I can think, all that weighs on my mind, is that I love you so damn much and I can't live without you. Don't make me live without you, Ash."

Her expressive eyes widened in shock. Her mouth popped open and then snapped shut again. She shook her head wordlessly as if she had no idea what to say to his sudden declaration.

Then hurt entered her eyes, crushing him with the weight of her pain. Her gaze held the memory of all the terrible things he'd said and done. He couldn't breathe for wanting to drop to his knees and beg her forgiveness.

"Then why?" she choked out. "If you love me, really love *me*, then why would you want me to change? You don't love the real me, Dev. You love the image you have in your head of how the perfect wife should be. Well, I've got news for you. I'm not her. I'll never be her."

She was glorious in her anger. Her eyes came to life and sparked darts of fire. Color suffused her cheeks and her lips pinched together as she glared holes through him.

"Trying to change you was the biggest mistake I've ever made or will make in my life. God, Ash, when I think of how stupid I was I just want to punch something."

He put his hands on her shoulders and stared intently into her eyes. "You are the most beautiful, precious thing that has ever barreled into my life. I didn't see it because I didn't want to see it. When your father suggested the marriage, I was pissed and I resented his interference."

"That makes two of us," Ashley muttered.

"But the thing was, I didn't mind the idea of marrying you. Even when I told myself that I was angry, there was a part of me that didn't at all mind the idea of marriage and settling down. Starting a family. With you.

"I was torn and I was an immature jerk acting out because I felt like marriage was being forced on me instead of when I was ready for it. Even though I didn't mind the outcome, I was resentful on principle. Which is stupid. And then on our honeymoon night I was gutted when you found out because the last thing I ever wanted was to hurt you. I felt cornered. Here you were demanding to know how I felt and my feelings weren't even something I could admit to myself. So I answered out of frustration and I said all that crap about how we could have a good marriage anyway because in my mind I wanted things to go on as they had before but without the vulnerability I felt every time the question of love popped up."

He sighed and released her shoulders, stepping back for a moment as he stared off into the distance. "Your entire family baffles me, Ash. I don't always know how to take them. I'm not used to having this big, huge loving family where dysfunction isn't a way of life. Your dad was always calling me 'son,' and he wanted me to marry you, and all I could think was that I don't fit here. I'm not good enough. I wasn't worthy. And that made me angry because after I left home, I was determined never to feel inferior again."

She was still staring at him like she had no idea what to say.

"You scared me, Ash. You barged into my life, turned it upside down with your take-no-prisoners attitude. You were the one thing I couldn't control, couldn't put in its proper place, and I tried. Oh, I tried. I was determined that you weren't going to be a threat to me. I hated how rattled you made me feel and how I went soft every time you entered a room. I thought somehow if I covered you up that you wouldn't shine quite so brightly and that maybe I could better control my reaction to you or at least I wouldn't feel like my guts had been ripped out every time you smiled at me."

"Wow," she whispered. "I have no idea what to say, Devon. I had no idea I affected you so badly."

He shook his head. "Oh, God, no, Ash. Don't you see? You are the very best part of me. It wasn't you. It was never you. It was me."

No longer able to keep his hands from her, he stepped forward again and pulled her close so that their faces were almost touching and he could feel the warmth of her breath on his throat.

"You are the very best part of my world. You are my life. I cannot imagine an existence without you. I don't want to. What I did was unforgivable. It was the result of ignorance and stupidity of the highest magnitude. I can only tell you that if you let me back into your life that you'll never have cause to doubt me again. I'll spend every single day proving to you that you are the absolute center of my universe. You wanted a man who adored you beyond reason. Someone who accepted you for the beautiful, amazing woman that you are. Look no further, Ash. He's standing in front of you with his heart in his hands. No man will ever love you more than I do. It isn't possible."

Her eyes were huge in her face. Brilliantly blue, sparkling like the most exquisite gems. Her cheeks were brushed with rose and her throat worked up and down as she swallowed. Tears glittered like diamonds, clung to her lashes but didn't fall. He wouldn't let them this time. If she never cried again, it would be too soon for him.

When she opened her mouth to speak, he simply put his lips to hers and kissed her long and sweet. He was shaking as he crushed her to him. For the last week he'd despaired of ever getting this close to her again and now she was warm and soft in his arms and so very precious.

"Don't say anything yet," he whispered. "There's still something I want to show you."

He pulled away, gathered her hand in his and pulled her along the road. She walked with him haltingly, as if she were in a solid daze. As they rounded the sharp bend, she stopped in her tracks and gazed in wonder at the sprawling house on top of the hill.

In the distance, dogs barked and she turned her head, her brow furrowing as she searched for the source of the noise. And then over the hill, two dogs bounded, making a beeline for Ashley.

"Mac! Paulina!"

She dropped to her knees just as the dogs launched themselves at her, licking and barking excitedly as Ashley tried to hug them.

"Oh, my God, where did you come from?" she whispered.

Devon glanced up the hill to see Cam standing there and Devon waved his thanks before turning his attention back to Ashley and the sheer joy in her eyes.

One of the dogs knocked her over and she went laughing to the ground, snow sticking to her coat as she lay gasping for air.

Devon carefully picked her back up and fended off the animals as they tried their best to lick her to death.

"They come with the house," he said solemnly. "Since you're the new director of the shelter, it only stood to reason that some of the animals find their home here."

She brushed herself off and then stared back at the house again. "Is it… Is it yours?" she asked hesitantly.

"No, it's yours."

She turned to stare at him, excitement flashing like fireworks in her eyes. "You mean it? Really? How? Why? When?"

He chuckled indulgently and then because he couldn't help himself, he pulled her into his arms so that he was wrapped solidly around her. They stood staring up at the house as her heart beat solidly against his chest.

"You wanted a home where you could envision children playing and you could be surrounded by your animals. I ignored that because I wasn't ready for anything in my life to change. My apartment was comfortable and I saw no reason we couldn't live there. But the simple truth is, I want to live wherever you are and wherever makes you happy. A good friend told me to go big or go home. I'm going big, Ash. Because I'll do any damn thing in the world to have you back in my life."

"Oh my," she whispered. "I don't know what to say, Dev. You're saying everything I've ever dreamed you saying. I want to believe you. I want it more than anything. But I'm afraid."

He tugged her even closer and rested his forehead on hers. "I love you, Ash. That isn't going to change. I was an ass. I just need a chance to prove to you that you're safe with me and a chance to show you that I'll love and cherish you every day for the rest of your life. You and our children."

"You're okay with the baby?"

"If I was any more okay, I'd burst wide open. I can't think of anything better than this house with you and our son or daughter plus the half dozen or so more we'll fill it with."

"Oh I love that," she said, her eyes lighting up like a thousand suns.

He stroked a strand of her hair away from her face and then he kissed her softly, lingering over her lips as he savored being this close to her again.

"I love you," he said. "I love you more than I ever thought it possible to love another person. I won't lie. It scares the hell out of me, but being without you scares me even more. Give us a chance, Ash. I'll show you that you can trust me again. I swear it."

She wrapped her arms around his shoulders and

moved her forehead down to nestle in the side of his neck. "I love you too, Dev. So very much. You have the power to hurt me like no one else. But you also have the power to make me happier than anyone else in the world."

He inhaled the scent of her hair and hugged her more fiercely. "I want you to be happy. I want you to smile again. I'll do anything to make that happen."

She pulled away and smiled mischievously up at him as the dogs danced around at their heels. "Then why don't you show me my new house?"

He relaxed, going suddenly weak as relief tore through him with the force of a storm. Oh, God. He couldn't even find his tongue because he feared if he tried to speak right now, he'd lose what was left of his composure.

It was several long seconds before he could pull himself together enough to speak.

"The sale isn't final yet but the house has been empty for six months and I've gotten the keys. I'll be happy to show you around."

She threaded her arm through his as they started up the rest of the driveway leading to the house.

"Can't you just imagine our children playing here?" she said wistfully. "And the dogs running after them?"

He pulled his arm loose and wrapped it tightly around her as he leaned down to kiss her temple.

"Know what the best part will be?"

She glanced up at him in question.

"Seeing their mother's smile light up their father's world each and every day of his life."

* * * * *

UNDONE BY HER
TENDER TOUCH

For Huggy Bear

Chapter 1

She shouldn't be so nervous about catering for a bunch of muckety-mucks, but Pippa Laingley wanted everything to be perfect for her friend Ashley Carter's housewarming.

And really, why should she be nervous? Just because the net worth of the assembled guests was more than the national debt shouldn't be cause for her to sweat. Okay, and there was the fact that Pippa was on the verge of opening her own storefront café and catering business and she needed this to go off without a hitch so there would be good word of mouth and maybe a few referrals.

She spun around in Ashley's huge kitchen, mentally taking stock of what was ready to go out. Where were the damn waiters?

On cue, the door swung open, and a guy who couldn't be more than twenty hustled through. Pippa took one look and groaned.

"Where's your uniform?"

He gave her a blank look.

She sighed and closed her eyes. "White shirt? Black slacks? Nice polished shoes? Preferably well-groomed hair?"

His mouth worked and then he snapped it shut. "I'm sorry, ma'am. I'm the emergency fill-in. I just assumed whatever I needed would be here."

Pippa blew out her breath. "First day on the job?"

"Yeah," he mumbled. "A friend told me about part-time gigs that paid good money. I'm sort of filling in for him."

Her gaze narrowed. Great. She wasn't even getting an official employee. Some moron had decided to skip and had worked a deal with his buddy to split the proceeds for a night's work. No way he was going to handle a room full of people. Which meant she was going to have to wade in and help.

So much for having a nice glass of wine with the girls and gushing about Ashley's new house.

Grabbing the kid by the arm, she pulled him toward the stairs. "Come on. You have to get into something better than that."

He blinked but allowed her to drag him all the way to Ashley and Devon's bedroom. She barreled into Devon's closet and hurriedly riffled through his clothing until she found something appropriate.

"Strip," she ordered crisply.

A dull flush rose up the kid's neck.

The sound of a clearing throat was Pippa's first warning that she and the kid weren't alone.

"Perhaps I should come back later."

The low drawl shivered over Pippa's nape and she

squeezed her eyes shut in mortification. Now she and the kid both were blushing fools. She turned to see Cam Hollingsworth leaning lazily against the door, his eyes flashing with amusement.

"Why, Pippa, you cradle robber."

She could never understand why the man always caught her at a disadvantage. She was an intelligent, well-put-together, very articulate career woman. She owned her own business, never took any crap off anyone and people rarely intimidated her. And yet, every single time she crossed paths with Devon's friend, she always made an ass of herself.

No way she was going to let this spiral into a mire of humiliation. She glared at Cam and then stalked over, tossing him the shirt and slacks.

"Get him into this. I need him downstairs in two minutes."

To her utter delight, Cam blinked in surprise. She'd caught him off guard. Then he frowned and looked beyond her to where the kid still stood.

"What the hell? Aren't these Dev's clothes?"

"I need a waiter or no one is going to get food or drink," she gritted out. "He's all I've got. I'm not letting Ashley down tonight and neither are you. So get your ass in gear."

She stomped past him and hurried down the stairs, not waiting to see Cam's reaction to her dictate.

When she got back into the kitchen, she quickly lined up the trays, set wine and champagne glasses out and then grumbled under her breath about having to help ferry food and drinks to Ashley's guests.

She'd asked for three servers. She'd gotten some college kid in need of beer money. Just great.

A moment later, college kid presented himself, and to Pippa's surprise, he'd cleaned up well. The pants and shirt were a bit too large for his lanky frame, but he looked neat and presentable. His hair had been combed back until he looked almost polished.

She gestured him over, shoved a tray of lobster tarts into his hands and then pushed him out of the door toward the living room, where Ashley and Devon were entertaining their guests.

Then she returned to the island and began pouring wine into half the glasses. She filled the rest with champagne.

"Would you like some help?"

She whirled around, still holding the bottle, and darn near tossed the contents onto the floor.

"Help?"

Cam nodded slowly. "Assistance? You look as though you could use it. How on earth did you think you'd manage this on your own? Ashley was nuts for allowing you to cater the event."

Pippa was horrified by the offer and then, as she processed the rest of the statement, she was just irritated as hell.

"I'd hate for you to sully those pretty hands," she snapped. "And for your information, I've got this under control. The help didn't show. Not my fault. The food is impeccable if I do say so myself. I just need a way to deliver it into the hands of the precious guests."

"I believe I just offered my assistance and you insulted me," Cam said dryly.

Her eyebrows drew together. Oh, why did the man have to be so damn delicious looking? Why couldn't he be a toad? Or be bald? Although on the right guy, bald was totally hot. Why could she never perform the simplest functions around him?

"You're Ashley's guest," Pippa said firmly. "Not to mention this isn't your thing. You're used to being served, not serving others."

"How do you know what my thing is?" he asked as he reached for one of the trays.

She had absolutely nothing to say to that and watched in bewilderment as he hefted the tray up and walked out of the kitchen.

She sagged against the sink, her pulse racing hard enough to make her dizzy.

Cameron Hollingsworth was gorgeous, unpolished in a totally sexy way, arrogant and so wrong for her in so many ways, but there was something about the man that just did it for her.

She'd seen him often enough ever since Ashley had become involved with Devon Carter. Cameron and Devon were close friends and business partners in a consortium of luxury hotels and resorts. As Ashley's best friend, Pippa had been to many of the same social events as Cameron. He'd been paired with her at Ashley's wedding, and that had been ten sorts of hell, being close enough to smell him, and him so perfectly indifferent to her.

She sighed. That could be what irritated her the most. He was a luscious specimen of a male and he couldn't be any less interested in her.

Maybe she just wasn't his type. The problem was, she didn't know what his type was. She never saw him with other women. He was either intensely private or he didn't have much of a social life.

She was itching to shake his world up just a little.

Realizing she was spending far too much time mooning over Cam, she grabbed another tray, took a deep breath to compose herself and then headed toward the living room.

Pippa smiled brightly, hoping her lipstick at least was still visible. The rest of her makeup had probably melted off by now. She made her way through the room, relieved to see that many of the guests now held wineglasses. Cameron had indeed delivered the goods.

"Pip, what are you doing?" Ashley hissed.

Pippa jerked around to see her friend staring aghast at her.

"Hey, Ash, how is everything going? All your guests arrived?"

"Stop acting like the hired help," Ashley said with a frown. "Why are you and Cam walking around serving drinks and hors d'oeuvres? And who's the kid wearing Devon's clothes!"

"Don't get worked up, Ash. It's not good for the baby," Pippa said cautiously.

Ashley folded her arms over the noticeable baby bump—really, it was so adorable—and pinned Pippa with her most ferocious stare. Not that anything Ashley ever did could exactly be called ferocious. Could puppies or kittens be ferocious? "Pip, I asked you to do this because I wanted to help. Maybe get the word out about you, but I didn't want you working yourself silly at my housewarming party. I need my best friend beside me, not serving me!"

Pippa sighed and handed Ashley one of the yummy snacks off her tray. "Look, the help didn't show. All you got is me, the kid wearing your husband's clothes and Mr. Mouthwateringly Gorgeous over there."

Ashley's eyes widened. "Cam? You're talking about Cam?"

Pippa gave her an exasperated look. "I'm damn sure not talking about the infant wearing Dev's clothes!"

"Whoa," Ashley breathed. "I had no idea. I mean, yeah, Cam is hot in a broody kind of way, but I had no idea that was your thing."

Pippa couldn't even look over at him without getting a betraying flutter in her belly. "I'd like to lick those brooding lips," she muttered.

Ashley giggled and then clapped a hand over her mouth. Her eyes sparkled merrily.

"Stop staring at him!" Pippa hissed. "You may as well be holding a sign up announcing we're talking about him."

Ashley turned her back to Cam, a grin still flirting with her mouth. "So how'd you get him to help out? Did you bat those gorgeous green eyes?"

"I don't even know," Pippa said in bewilderment. "He offered. I was kind of rude to him."

Ashley snickered. "You? Rude?"

Pippa glowered at her. "Shut it."

Ashley put her hand on Pippa's arm and rose up on tiptoe to look over her shoulder. "I think I'm being summoned. Seriously, though, Pip. I'm not worried about the food so much that I want my best friend to be the serving wench for the evening. Go put the tray up and join us for a drink."

Pippa switched the platter from one hand to the other as she surveyed the room. There were too many important potential clients to just shrug off such an opportunity. Ashley had given her the chance and she wasn't going to squander it.

"I'll check with you later, Ash. I have mingling to do. Your guests look hungry."

Before Ashley could respond, Pippa was off, wading into the crowd, a bright smile on her face.

"Are you out of your mind?"

Cameron turned to see Devon staring at him as if he was nuts. Cameron set the empty tray onto the sideboard and grinned at the look of absolute *what-the-hell?* on his friend's face.

"Wouldn't be the first time I've been asked that."

"You're playing waiter tonight?"

Cameron shrugged. "Pippa needed help. She looked like she was close to melting down. I figured that wouldn't make Ash very happy."

Devon frowned as he studied Cameron for a long moment. "I think you're full of crap."

But Cameron ignored Devon as his gaze caught Pippa melting into the crowd. She moved with effortless grace. She was mesmerizing to watch. He tracked her progress across the room as she smiled and greeted many of the guests. She laughed, and irritation sparked that he hadn't been able to hear what it sounded like.

He'd been watching Pippa for months. She'd drawn his notice the very first time he'd seen her. He hadn't actually met her then. They hadn't been officially introduced until the third time they were at the same event. Even then he'd treated her as he treated most people. Cordial politeness. Faint disinterest. But he'd been anything but disinterested.

She hadn't realized it, but he'd marked her from that very first moment. Like a predator marking prey. He watched and waited for that perfect moment. Working up to when he'd take her to bed and lose himself in that satiny skin and silky mane of glossy dark hair.

He could just feel the strands brushing through his fingers and falling down around them both. Her astride him, head thrown back as he pulled her down onto him again and again.

He muttered a foul curse when his body reacted fully to the erotic fantasy. He was at a housewarming, for God's sake. The focus was supposed to be on babies, happy homes, puppies and rainbows. Not how fast he could get Pippa to his house a half mile down the road so they could indulge in a night of hot sex.

He was certain she was as attracted to him as he was to her. Often when she thought he wasn't looking, her eyes glowed warm with lust as she fixed her gaze on him. He enjoyed those stolen glances because that was when he could see the honesty in her eyes.

The rest of the time she hid behind that brassy fa-cade, the take-no-crap-off-anyone exterior. But inside? He was absolutely sure she was warm and gooey and all feminine purr. He couldn't wait to run his fingers over her body and elicit that throaty sound of pleasure.

"Cam, what the hell, man? Hello? Anyone home?"

He blinked and turned to see that Devon was still standing there. He scowled. "Don't you have a wife to tend to?"

Devon shook his head. "Do you have any idea how pathetic you look mooning over her from across the room?"

Cameron's nostrils flared. "I don't know what the hell you're talking about."

"Keep telling yourself that," Devon said with a snort.

"Good God. Just go over there and get it done with. And then get a room, for Pete's sake."

"Oh, I'll get a room," he said softly. "She's going to be locked in mine the entire night."

Devon made a strangled sound of annoyance and then turned as if he couldn't get away fast enough. Cam was too busy watching Pippa to care, though. He could see that her tray was empty. Her gaze was searching the rest of the room, a slight frown on her face. She was looking for the kid, and she didn't look happy.

Her brow creased in annoyance, she left in the direction of the kitchen. Cameron picked up the empty tray he'd discarded moments ago and hurried after her.

He found her in the kitchen muttering swearwords that would make a sailor wince. He grinned when she threatened to kick the asses of every single waiter who'd stood her up tonight.

"Where's the kid?" Cameron asked.

She jumped, nearly sending the platter she was filling flying in the opposite direction. She whirled around, a ferocious scowl on her face. "Would you stop doing that?"

He held up his hands and took a cautious step back.

"He skipped out," she growled. "He didn't even give Devon's clothes back! How am I going to afford to replace them? The shirt cost more than an entire catering job nets."

Cameron laid his hand on her arm and she went completely still. The slender muscles in her arm rippled and he could hear the quick intake of her breath. He was right. She was satiny soft and yet firm. She either worked out or she was particularly blessed with excellent body tone. He'd lay odds that she worked out. She seemed rather disciplined.

"I'm sure Devon won't miss a white shirt and black slacks," he drawled. "He likely has two dozen more outfits just like it. He's a well-ordered bastard. Not into too much variety, if you know what I mean."

"That's not true," she defended staunchly. "He has a very laid-back wardrobe. Casual. Expensive casual, but still very casual."

Cameron shrugged. "Can't say I've ever made it into his closet."

She suddenly giggled and then stopped herself, but her eyes were full of mirth.

"Glad you find me so amusing."

"It's not you as much as the idea of you poking around in Devon's closet. You have to admit, it's pretty funny."

He rubbed the pad of his thumb in a slow up-and-down pattern above her elbow, and she went quiet again.

"Would you like me to take food out this time or would you prefer I make another round with wine and champagne? Hell, it's Dev's tab. I vote we take some bottles out and let everyone pour up what they like. You and I can circulate with food and watch everyone get wasted."

She studied him a moment, cocking her head to the side. "I never realized you actually had a sense of humor."

He lifted an eyebrow, taken aback by her candor.

Then she blushed and briefly closed her eyes. Just when he thought she'd stammer out an apology, she reopened her eyes and stared evenly at him.

He couldn't help it. He laughed. This time it was her eyebrow that went up.

He pushed in close to her, until their bodies were nearly touching. So close that her scent and soft warmth enveloped him and held him captive.

He brushed his hand over her cheek, pushing back that velvet cascade of hair. And it was every bit as silky as he'd imagined. He wrapped one finger in it, tugging experimentally.

"Here's what I propose," he murmured. "Let's make another pass. Load everyone up on food and drink. Set out a few trays within easy reach and then we ditch this place and go to mine."

Her lips parted and her eyes went glossy, the pale green mesmerizing. "Is that a proposition?"

"Bet your sweet little ass it is."

"Surely you can do better than that."

Both his brows went up.

She narrowed her gaze. "You'll do better or I'm taking my sweet little ass home. Alone."

Ah, but he did love it when she got all sassy.

He leaned in, touched his lips to hers. He cupped the side of her neck, sliding his fingers around the slim column to delve into her hair. He pulled her close, molding his body to hers as he took full possession of her mouth.

Heat slicked through his veins like rapidly flowing lava. He wanted her. To the point of desperation.

When he finally pulled away, they both breathed heavily and her eyes took on a sleepy, drugged look.

"How about I take you home with me and we make love all night long?" he murmured.

She licked those delectably swollen lips. "Now that's better."

Her husky voice shot straight to his gut and he realized he was a short fuse away from taking her right here in his friend's kitchen and damn anyone who saw.

"You get the food," he said in a strained voice. "I'll get the wine."

Chapter 2

Cameron pulled Pippa out the back door and the brisk chill of the winter air blew over her ears. She tugged her hand from Cameron's long enough to pull her coat tighter around her, but he quickly reclaimed her wrist, hauling her ever closer to his car.

He stopped abruptly when they got to a midnight-black Escalade. He turned with a frown, still holding tightly to her hand.

"How did you arrive? Did you drive?"

Drive? She didn't even own a car. Nor did she have a license, which was problematic given that she needed a delivery van to cater events.

She shook her head. "Ashley sent a car for me."

He paused, arching one eyebrow. "And how did you get all that stuff here from New York?"

She flushed, feeling as though he were judging her and her abilities.

"I shopped here. Had the wine delivered. Ashley has an excellent kitchen." Pippa should know since she was the one who'd stocked it from floor to ceiling. Ashley was clueless when it came to cooking, but Pippa was working to rectify that.

Cameron opened the passenger door to the Escalade and all but pushed her inside. "Good enough. It works out perfectly. I'll have a car drive you back to the city in the morning."

With that, he shut the door, leaving her a little disgruntled at how eager he seemed to be to get rid of her before they even had sex.

He stalked around the front, yanked open his door and climbed in, keying the ignition before he'd even settled onto the seat.

Then again, her feminine pride was stroked just a bit over how desperate he acted to get her to his house so the sexing could commence.

She knew he didn't live far. Ashley had commented on the fact that they were now neighbors with Devon's purchase of the new house.

Cameron tore down the driveway, his hands tight around the steering wheel as he navigated onto the paved lane. He drove about a quarter mile before turning into a gated drive. The gate swung open and Cameron accelerated up the winding path to the house.

Pippa couldn't make much out about it in the dark. There weren't any lights on. The mansion loomed in the shadows. It looked unwelcoming. She wondered if it was a hulking monstrosity built from stone like a medieval dwelling. She'd heard Devon tease Cameron about his "cave" and now she was curious.

Just before they got to the house, lights began to flicker on. Pippa realized that Cameron was turning them on remotely from the SUV. She leaned forward, trying to get a glimpse but was prevented as Cam pulled into the garage.

Determined that she wasn't going to succumb to nerves or be caught at any disadvantage, she slid out of the passenger's side and walked around to meet him by the door. He ushered her inside, one hand pressed to the small of her back.

They walked into a sprawling kitchen that made her drool with envy. It was nirvana to someone like her, who'd rather be hard at work over a stove than anywhere else. It was like a showroom, so immaculate that she wondered if anyone ever used it.

He didn't pause or allow her to, either. He pressed ahead, running a gauntlet through a huge living room to the wooden staircase that opened into the foyer where the front entrance was. Tugging her behind him, he mounted the steps. She nearly had to run to keep up.

By the time they made it into the spacious master bedroom, she was slightly winded. But before she could think to catch up, he yanked her to him, molding her body against his. His lips found hers in a ravenous kiss that muddled her senses.

"You are so damn beautiful," he muttered as his mouth skimmed down her jaw to her ear. "You drive me crazy. Across the room. If I even know you're near."

She smiled a tiny smile of satisfaction. What woman wouldn't love to hear this?

He set her apart from him, his hands almost rough

on her shoulders. He stood breathing hard, his fingers curled into her flesh.

"We need to discuss a few things before we get carried away."

Though his words came out calm, his eyes blazed with a wildness that made her shiver. He wanted her. There was no question. She'd never been quite so devoured by something so simple as a man's gaze.

"There are things you should know. Things I need to make clear so there is no misunderstanding."

Her curiosity piqued, she lifted an eyebrow and gently shook away his hands. She eased onto the edge of the bed and then crossed one leg primly over her knee.

"Do go on. I'm listening."

He frowned a moment, as if he couldn't quite ascertain whether she was teasing him. Okay, she totally was, but what could be so important that he'd put a screeching halt to some pretty hot foreplay? Not that they'd really gotten that far into anything yet, but the way he kissed made her feel like they were already having sex.

He wiped a hand over his mouth, cupping his chin for a brief moment before he pinned her once more with that glittering gaze.

"I don't do commitment. I need you to understand that if we go to bed together, this is a one-night stand. I won't call you in a few days. I won't call you, period. I'll expect you to leave in the morning. I'll provide a car for your transport back into the city."

She blinked and then she laughed. It was clear it was the very last thing he'd expected her to do. Had he maybe expected her to stomp out of his bedroom in a huff?

Still smiling, she rose and sauntered toward him.

When she was in his space, she let her fingers trail up the buttons of his shirt and then to his neck and jaw.

"You're way too serious, Cam," she drawled. "I was hardly anticipating a marriage proposal. If you expect me to cling to you and beg for more when this night's over, you're destined to disappointment. What I want is hot sex. Can you give me that?"

Relief flared in those gorgeous blue eyes and his nostrils quivered as his breaths came in harsh spurts. He was reaching for her when she put a hand to his chest.

"Not so fast, hotshot. I have a few things I'd like to get out of the way, too."

He looked caught off guard and his brows furrowed in quick reaction.

"I assume you've got condoms. Or rather, I'm not assuming anything. No condoms? No sex. I'm clean, in case you're wondering. It's none of your business when the last time I had sex was or who with, but it's been long enough that I've had blood work done since. And I never have unprotected sex."

"I've got them," he growled. "I'm clean. I don't give a f—" He cleared his throat. "I don't care who you had sex with last or when. Been a while for me, too. I'm clean and I always use condoms."

She reached for him, bunching his shirt into her fist, and then she yanked him forward. "Then we have nothing else to talk about," she said just before she dragged him down to meet her kiss.

Lust gripped Cameron by the throat and squeezed until he was light-headed. She was everything he'd imagined and a whole hell of a lot more. She was sweet, spicy, feisty as hell and she was seducing him in his own bedroom.

He loved how impatient she was, yanking at his shirt, pulling it from his pants. He was used to being the aggressor in bed, but it was a huge turn-on to have Pippa boldly staking her claim.

When her fingers slipped into the waistband of his slacks and began undoing the fly, he nearly lost it. He took in deep breaths, trying to calm the adrenaline boiling through his veins.

But then, as soon as the fly was loosened, she reached down and cupped his erection.

Oh, hell.

She leaned up on tiptoe to kiss him, all the while caressing his length with soft, silky fingers. "You know, I'd love nothing more than to drop to my knees and give you the best experience of your entire life, but not the first time. I'm a little more demanding the first time with a new guy. I expect him to rock my world first."

If that wasn't a challenge, he didn't know what was. He pulled her away from him enough that he could walk her back to the bed. He pulled just as impatiently at her clothing until she was wearing nothing more than the sexiest damn lingerie he'd ever seen up close and personal.

She was an absolute siren in black. Black hair and wicked black lacy panties and bra that barely covered her nipples. Her hair was delectably mussed, giving her that just-out-of-bed look. And her eyes. So sultry with liquid eroticism. She wasn't just beautiful. She was bloody amazing.

He tumbled her onto the mattress, enjoying the way she sprawled, laid out for him, a feast for his senses. And he wanted to indulge them all. Touch, sight, smell... He wanted to hear her whisper his name and her throaty sounds of passion. But most of all he wanted to taste every inch of her skin.

Knowing if he didn't take care of the condoms now, he'd never stop in the heat of the moment, he fumbled in the nightstand, pulled out the entire box and tossed it on the bed.

Then he came down over her, captured her mouth and molded her soft body to his.

It was like being struck by lightning. An electrical charge surged through his body, tightening every one of his muscles. She returned his kiss every bit as passionately as he kissed her. Her hands roamed over his back, exploring every inch of his flesh.

Remembering the vivid fantasy he'd had earlier that night, he rolled, taking her with him until she was positioned astride him.

The reality far surpassed the weak fantasy he'd spun in his head. Nothing compared to having her here, in his arms, her thighs pressed to his sides.

"Undress for me," he said hoarsely. "Right here where I can watch."

A wicked smile glimmered on full, kiss-swollen lips. Slowly she reached behind her and began to unclasp her bra. Instead of letting it fall immediately, she held the tiny lace confection to her chest and then allowed the straps to slide down her arms inch by inch.

He was barely capable of breath. The anticipation was killing him. And then finally she pulled the bra away, baring her full breasts to his avid gaze.

And they were perfect breasts. Perfectly shaped. Perfect size. Just the right amount of bounce. Firm. High. Delectable nipples that just begged for his mouth.

"I'll need your help with the panties," she murmured, her eyes flashing mischievously.

He couldn't even stammer out a reply. He nodded, but then right now he'd agree to damn near anything.

She leaned forward, pushing her gorgeous breasts mere inches from his mouth. Then she slid one leg over him so she was no longer straddling his hips. She turned then and began working her panties slowly down her buttocks.

He wasn't at all sure what he was supposed to help with, but he was game. He turned over on one elbow and reached to steady her waist with his free hand, letting his fingers wander down the small of her back, enjoying the feel of so much silky flesh.

When the underwear was down to her knees, trapped there by the mattress, she turned on her back and stretched her legs over his chest.

More than happy to accommodate, he took over, pulling the panties the rest of the way until they came free of her feet. He tossed them across the room and went after her like a starving predator.

He slid over her body, the sensation of skin on skin nearly undoing him. He kissed her neck, nibbled, tasted and teased and then worked down, wanting nothing more than to have her breasts underneath his tongue and lips.

She was utter perfection. Curvy, sweet, not too slim, not too heavy. Just…perfect.

A sigh escaped her when his lips closed over one straining nipple. It was an intoxicating combination of hardness and velvet. Luscious. So very soft. He sucked gently at it, rolling it between his lips. He flicked his tongue repeatedly over the point, bringing it to an even harder bud.

Then he slid his mouth over the hollow between her breasts to the other nipple. For several seconds he played, idly toying with it. She twisted restlessly beneath him, her breaths coming more rapidly now.

"You are so damn perfect," he murmured. "I can't get enough of you. You taste better than anything you could possibly cook."

He looked up to see her lips form a pout. "You haven't tried my cooking, then," she said. "I'm a wonderful cook."

He laughed. "It was a compliment, or at least it was meant to be."

"I think you're doing just fine without the compliments," she said in breathy delight.

He cupped her breast in his palm, shaping it, watching as the nipple hardened again. "You like this. What else do you like, Pippa? Tell me how to please you."

"Oh, you're doing fine. No complaints here. I love it when a guy takes his time and doesn't just think about his own pleasure."

"Oh, but this is my pleasure," he murmured. "I love touching you. I love tasting you. Love watching you respond. How your eyes go a darker green when you're really turned on. And that little vixen smile that tells me I'm in for one hell of a good time."

"On second thought, keep on with the compliments. I'm liking this very much," she purred.

"Where do you like to be touched?" he whispered.

Her eyes darkened again. She reached for his hand and slid it down her belly to the juncture of her legs. She guided his fingers over her softness to the tiny bundle of nerves at the apex and gently stroked the tip over it.

Then she moaned when he took over himself. Oh, yeah, she liked that. A lot.

He could be just as wicked as she could. Still stroking through the soft, velvet folds of her femininity, he lowered his head and sucked her nipple into his mouth.

She let out a cry and arched upward, her hands tangling in his hair. She was forceful. Nothing dainty about her. She knew what she liked and demanded it. He loved that about her.

He stroked his thumb over her clitoris one last time and then he pulled his hand away long enough to snag a condom. He leaned down to kiss her as he parted her legs. He wanted it to last, too, but he also knew this wouldn't be the only time tonight. There was no way he'd get enough and he planned to use every single minute she was here to his advantage. Neither of them would be able to walk the next day but he was more than okay with that.

He nibbled at the corner of her mouth. "Are you ready for me?"

She responded by wrapping her legs around his waist and arching upward. He smiled at her impatience.

He planted his forearms on either side of her shoulders. "Guide me in, Pippa. Show me how you want it."

Her pupils flared and then she reached down, circling him with her fingers. She positioned him against her opening and arched just enough that he slid in the barest inch.

They both let out an anguished sound and he could hold back no longer. Flexing his hips, he drove deep. At first he thought he'd hurt her, but then she dug her fingers into his shoulders and all but roared at him not to stop.

He grinned, kissed that ferocious mouth and then began to move in a frantic rhythm. There was no style, no grace. Their lovemaking couldn't be described as polished or smooth. Far from it.

It was animalistic, with Pippa taking every bit as much as she gave. She demanded everything he had and more. He'd never made love to a woman more fierce than her, and he loved every minute of it.

She fused her mouth to his. Then she nibbled at his jaw and moved her mouth lower to sink her teeth into his neck. He'd wear her marks for days and it stroked his male pride to think of someone else being able to see the marks of her possession.

But she wouldn't be without marks of her own. Oh, hell, no.

"Are you with me, Pippa?" he panted out. "I need you with me. I'm close."

"Sooo there," she said from behind clenched teeth. "Go hard, Cam. Don't let up. Please just don't let up."

As if he could.

He let out a roar of his own and began driving into her with powerful, quick strokes. He wasn't aware of anything but her. Only her. Writhing beneath him. Surrounding him with her sweetness. He smelled her, heard her, could still taste her on his tongue. And, oh, man, he felt her all the way to his bones.

"Cam!" she cried out.

Her fingers gripped his shoulders and she shuddered violently beneath him. He gathered her in his arms and let out a shout of his own as his body seemed to fracture and break into about a million pieces.

The next thing he knew he was flush against her, all his weight atop her body. It felt so damn good even though he had to be crushing her. But she wasn't complaining. In fact, she was wrapped so tightly around him that he couldn't have moved if he wanted to.

He lay there several long seconds while he caught his breath, and then with a groan, he rolled to the side so he could dispose of the condom.

When he looked back, Pippa was sprawled rather indelicately on her back, her expression dazed.

"I think you killed me," she murmured. "When can we do it again?"

Chapter 3

Pippa dragged her eyes open and stared dumbly at the white cloud enveloping her head. Her body felt as though it had been hit by a freight train, but, oh, man, was it a wonderful feeling.

It took her a moment to realize she was facedown on the pillow. She lifted her head, her hair falling like a curtain over her eyes. Impatiently, she shoved it back and propped herself up on her elbow.

The bed was empty. Well, almost. At the end, her clothing was neatly folded, a nice subtle reminder that she was to depart as soon as she awakened. She wrinkled her nose. Cam certainly hadn't stuck around. She couldn't even tell he'd been in bed with her. No indention in the pillow. No lingering scent. No warmth. Nothing at all to indicate that they'd spent the entire night tearing up those wonderfully luxurious sheets.

With a sigh, she pushed herself up farther, holding the sheet over her breasts. Then she snorted over the realization that she was being unreasonably modest. He'd made himself clear. He wanted no awkward next-morning encounters. She didn't have to worry about him barging in unannounced. And even if he did, it wasn't as if he hadn't seen her boobs already.

Not only had he seen them but he'd licked them, kissed them, nibbled at them and worshipped them over and over.

A shiver stole over her and her skin prickled, her nipples hardening at the memory of just how hard and often they'd made love through the night. She'd be lucky if she could manage to dress herself and get down those damn stairs.

She was tempted to take a really long hot shower. Her last attempt at a shower had been interrupted, and, well, she'd just gotten sweaty all over again. Many times again after that shower with Cam. But he wanted her out and she wasn't going to delay things.

She checked her watch and groaned. It was past nine. She should have been up and out a lot earlier but she hadn't drifted to sleep until well into the morning.

Nothing like wearing out her welcome.

She scrambled out of bed, wincing as all of her muscles protested the movement. Hell, she hurt in places she'd never even used before.

After pulling on her underwear, she slipped the dress over her head and put on her shoes, beating a hasty path to the bathroom to try to do something with her hair. She had makeup in her purse but she wasn't going to bother. She had no one to impress and the car would drop her outside her apartment.

After brushing the tangles from her hair, she twisted it into a loose knot and fixed it in place with a large clip she'd pulled from her purse. She perched her sunglasses on her nose, satisfied that she didn't look like such a fright.

Taking a deep breath, she exited the bedroom and quietly walked toward the stairs. She had no idea if Cam was even here, but the last thing she wanted to do was draw attention to her late exit from his bed.

She tiptoed down the stairs and when she reached the bottom, she was greeted by a tall, somber-looking man who was an indeterminate age somewhere between forty and seventy.

"Miss Laingley, the car is out front waiting to take you into the city."

She winced. "I'm sorry. Has it been waiting long? I'm afraid I overslept."

The older man smiled kindly at her. "Not at all. There's no need to offer an apology. Come, I'll see you out."

He offered his arm, but that was awkward so she pretended not to see and walked ahead of him toward the massive double front doors. She paused when she got there, suddenly realizing she hadn't gotten her coat. With a frown, she turned, only to see the man holding it open for her.

"Thank you," she murmured.

No matter what Cam had said about it being a while, it was obvious she wasn't the first woman he'd given such a spiel to. His butler or whatever the hell this guy was had the whole process way too down pat.

She slid her arms into the sleeves and then pulled the coat closed as the man opened the door. Cold air billowed in and Pippa blinked at the sudden white. Then she smiled. "It snowed!"

"Indeed it did. At least six inches according to the weather."

This time when he offered his arm, Pippa took it to descend the steps. She still had on those toothpick heels she'd worn the night before, and while they were sexy beasts for shoes, they weren't appropriate for icy conditions.

He was solicitous of her the entire way, ushering her into the back of the sleek black sedan that was already warm and toasty. He hung there a moment, staring into the backseat as he held on to the door.

"Have a safe trip, miss."

"Thank you," she murmured.

He closed the door and the driver pulled down the drive that had already been cleared of snow. She turned in her seat, staring back at the house she hadn't gotten a good look at the night before.

It was a hulking piece of construction, but it wasn't as looming or intimidating as she thought it might have appeared. It looked entirely normal. In keeping with the other mansions that dotted this area.

It was, however, extremely private and surrounded by thick woods on all sides. There was no way to tell the total acreage, but she guessed it was a lot. She couldn't see another house or even the road as they wound their way down the drive.

Yes, it did appear that Cam was Mr. Reclusive as Devon had suggested. Now that she'd had a taste of all that dark, broody passion, it made her wonder just how often Cam ventured out to lure a woman back to his cave.

She nearly laughed. She made it sound like he was

the Beast, sulking in his lair while he waited for Beauty. But if anything, Cam was Beauty. The man was sinfully gorgeous and forbiddingly perfect.

And he could make love like a dream. She'd wear and feel the effects of his lovemaking for a week. A sharp tingle snaked down her back, invading her limbs, bringing awareness and arousal all over again.

She gave one last look to the imposing structure as the car turned the final bend of the driveway. Then with a sigh, she leaned her head back and closed her eyes.

Cam stared through the slat in the blinds of his upstairs office as the car bearing Pippa back to the city drove away. For several long seconds, he continued to stare, even when it disappeared from view.

He turned away and stood for a long moment, hands thrust into his pockets. It annoyed and bewildered him that he had no idea what he was going to do next. He experienced a sudden surge of restlessness, an urge to go do something, although what, he had no idea. He only knew that being here, alone, in his too-quiet house was suddenly...unbearable.

He scowled. It was the damn woman. He'd been caught off guard by everything about her. Maybe he'd expected someone more like Ashley. Sweet, shy, innocent, naive, a bit vulnerable, in need of protection. Maybe his ego had been stroked by offering Pippa a night in his bed. Maybe he thought he'd been granting her a favor while indulging in what he'd wanted to do from the moment he'd met her.

Instead, she'd rocked his world. This was a confident, self-assured woman who wasn't afraid to reach out and take what she wanted, and she'd wanted *him*. His ego should be assuaged by that. But he found himself disgruntled because…the damn roles had been reversed.

It was almost as if she had been the one to say, *Hey, I want you but I don't want any strings*. She'd taken control.

He'd acted like an out-of-control, desperate, raging sex fiend. Nothing like the composed, commanding man he liked to present to the rest of the world.

And that…well, that bothered him. A lot.

Shaking his head, he walked down the hall back to his bedroom. He entered hesitantly, which *was* stupid given that he'd seen her drive away, but somehow her presence was still firmly imprinted. He could smell her.

His gaze traveled over the rumpled bed linens, the mussed pillows. One of the sheets was barely clinging to the bed. Most of it was on the floor.

He should have taken her to one of the guest rooms. He didn't bring women to his bedroom. Ever. If he'd actually been thinking the night before, he would have remained downstairs where she wouldn't have breached the areas private to him at all. But the only prevailing thought he'd had was to get her into bed, however fast he could do it.

Lust was a bitch.

A controlling, fickle mistress from which there was no escape. At least not when it came to Pippa Laingley. Maybe now that he'd had her six ways to Sunday, his blood would cool and he wouldn't lose his damn mind every time she came within a hundred feet.

His gut told him this was in no way true, but for his peace of mind, he was going with it.

He walked into the bathroom, wincing at the mess facing his cleaning lady. The shower door was still open. Towels had been discarded on the floor. The countertop was a mess thanks to his impatience. He'd swept the surface bare with a quick hand right before lifting Pippa onto the edge so he could have her again.

There were at least two discarded condoms on the floor.

He gingerly leaned down to toss the one by the sink into the nearby trash can and then went for the one on the floor by the shower. He used a tissue to pick it up and started for the trash can when he noticed something that sent panic knifing through his stomach.

He froze, unable to even process the evidence before him. Then a string of obscenities blistered the air. His stomach balled into a knot. Sweat broke out on his forehead and his mouth went completely dry.

He closed his eyes, willing it not to be so, but when he reopened them, he saw irrefutable proof in his shaking hand.

The condom had torn.

Chapter 4

Pippa was tempted to throw her cell across the street, but only the knowledge that she'd have to replace it kept her from giving in to the urge. What else could possibly go wrong today?

She'd found the perfect place for her bakery and catering business. It was in a nice area. The terms were satisfactory. It had already been outfitted with the necessary facilities. All she'd need was a little remodeling to the front to accommodate eat-in customers and she'd be set.

After so long doing word-of-mouth events, she was ready for a more solid step. One that would give her a steady income versus never knowing when she'd land her next gig. Her meager savings had kept her in her current apartment, but if she didn't start bringing in a regular income, it would be gone in a year.

She was certain she could qualify for a small-business

loan, but in order to get the necessary funds, she needed a signed lease. Which she had, at least until her Realtor had called her to inform her that there was a problem.

Suddenly her dreams of cute cupcakes, yummy little pastries, intricately decorated bonbons and delicious-smelling breads evaporated.

She blew out her breath in a cold fog and mounted the steps to her apartment. She fumbled with the lock just as her cell phone went off, which only renewed her desire to toss it into oncoming traffic.

She managed to push inside to where it was a great deal warmer, and after kicking the door shut with her foot, she glanced down at her phone. It wasn't a number she recognized, but given that she'd handed her number out to potential clients, she couldn't afford not to answer the phone.

With a sigh, she punched the receive button and put it to her ear. "Pippa Laingley."

She was in the midst of trying to shrug out of her coat when she heard Cam's voice over the line.

"Pippa, it's Cam."

She paused and then chuckled, leaving her coat dangling from the arm that was bent to her ear. "Well, hello, Cam. What a surprise. I distinctly remember you saying you wouldn't call. To what do I owe this honor?"

"One of the condoms broke," he said tersely.

She quickly switched the phone to her other hand so she could shake away the coat. She left it there in the doorway and walked toward her living room, sure she hadn't heard him correctly.

"Say that again," she said shakily.

She sank onto the couch, clutching the phone tightly to her ear.

There was an indistinguishable sigh and then he said, "The condom we used in the shower. It broke. I didn't discover it until after you'd left. Since we were in the shower, there would have been no...evidence...at the time. I didn't notice."

Her heart lodged solidly in her throat and she closed her eyes. No, she wouldn't have noticed, either.

He'd been insatiable, but then so had she. The very last thing she'd considered at the time was whether the condom had performed as expected. Obviously if it would have happened at any other point, they would have known. But in a shower?

"Pippa, are you there?"

The strident demand shook her from her thoughts.

"I'm here," she said faintly.

"There are things we have to discuss."

She frowned. "Why are you only just now calling me? When did you discover this?"

There was a pause. "I found it yesterday after you left."

"And you're only just now telling me?" she shrieked. "This would have been good to know yesterday when there was something I could have done."

Even as she was furious at him, she wasn't sure what she would have done. A morning-after pill? It would have been a bit late for that, but what did she know about such things? She could have at least done some research and made an informed decision.

"Calm down, Pippa."

The condescension in his tone just pissed her off even more.

"Don't tell me to calm down," she seethed. "You aren't

the one who has to live with the consequences of that broken condom."

"Don't I?" he snapped. "If you think an unplanned pregnancy doesn't affect me every bit as much as it does you, then you're delusional. Now quit shouting at me so we can discuss our options like adults."

She bit hard into her lip to prevent the outburst straining to break free.

"Now, I assume from your reaction that you aren't on any sort of birth control."

"No one can ever accuse you of being stupid."

"Cut the crap, Pippa. I get that you're scared and caught off guard. This isn't a picnic for me, either. You taking this out on me helps neither of us."

Realizing she was doing exactly as he'd accused, she went silent, her grip still tight around the phone. She should have thrown it when she'd had the urge. If she had, she wouldn't be having this harrowing conversation right now.

"I think you should move in with me, at least until we know if you're pregnant."

Her mouth fell open and her brow creased in disbelief. "What?"

He sighed again. "Perhaps this isn't a conversation we should be having over the phone. I can pick you up in an hour."

She got her wits back in time to utter a hoarse, "No."

"Then what's your preference?" he asked impatiently.

She put her hand to her temple and dug her fingers into it, massaging the increasing ache.

"Look, Cam, I'm not moving in with you. That's about the most absurd suggestion I've heard. We don't need to talk face-to-face. Right now, I have no desire to see you. I'm in shock. I need time to figure out my options. I don't need you breathing down my neck. If it turns out I'm pregnant, I know where to find you, and believe me, you'll be hearing from me then. Until that point, I'd appreciate it if you just backed off."

"Damn it, that's not what I want. Look, Pippa, I need to know that you and the…baby…are safe. If there is a baby, I mean. The best way to do that is for you to be close where I know you're taken care of."

There was quiet desperation in his voice and an odd detached tone that suggested to her he wasn't even focusing on the real issue at hand. His head seemed to be somewhere else and that annoyed her all the more.

He was worrying about her and a theoretical baby's safety, and at this point she was just worried that there *was* a theoretical baby.

"I don't care what *you* want," she said evenly.

She pulled the phone away from her ear and punched the end button. Then realizing that Cam was the persistent sort, she turned it off and thrust it away.

She sat there for several long minutes, staring into nothing as she tried to absorb the implications of that broken condom. She wasn't stupid enough to laugh it off and say something absurd like, *Who gets pregnant from that one time?* There were any number of pregnant women who'd naively asserted the same thing. She wasn't one of them.

She shot to her feet, needing to do something. Information. Probabilities. She knew the timing was probably good, but she hurried to her bedroom to dig out her diary where she kept information on her menstrual cycle.

Any single, sexually active woman was a moron if she didn't keep track of such things.

She slipped to the page where her last entry had been written and then calculated the days in her head. Then she let out a harsh groan. Could the timing have been any better? Not that she could possibly predict when she was ovulating, but if she went with averages, there was a good possibility that this weekend had been her prime baby-making window.

Okay, so it was entirely possible. The next thing she needed to do was figure out her options, if she had any.

She went back to that damnable phone, turned it on and ignored the cacophony of sounds signaling missed calls, voice mails and text messages. They were probably all from Cam. The man was likely on his way here.

She punched in Carly's number and hoped like hell her friends were available.

A moment later, Carly's sunny voice spilled over the line and Pippa sagged in relief.

"Pip! How's it going? Have your lease all straightened out? I have to tell you I'm so excited for you! How did Ashley's housewarming go? I was so sorry to miss it. I hope she wasn't too disappointed."

Pippa flinched from the onslaught and waited to get a word in edgewise. "Carly, are you free? I need the girls. This is an emergency."

There was a brief silence and then Carly said, "Pip, are you all right? What's happened?"

"I'll tell you when we're all together," Pippa croaked. "Can you call the others?"

"You bet. Oscar's?"

Pippa hesitated. "Yeah, but make sure we get a private table."

"Do you want me to call Ashley?" Carly asked. "Is she still in Greenwich?"

As much as Pippa wanted and needed Ashley there, she wasn't sure if it was a good idea. But she was just selfish enough to see if Ashley would make the trip in for her.

"See if she can make it," Pippa said in a low voice. "But make sure… Tell her I want her to be careful."

"If she knows you need her, she'll be there," Carly said in a comforting voice. "We'll all be there, Pip. You know that."

"Yes, I do, and I love you all for it."

"Give me some time to get everything ironed out and then I'll text you with a time everyone can meet. In the meantime you know you can come over. I only have one appointment this afternoon. You can always hang out here at the salon. I'll even do your nails."

Pippa smiled. "Thanks, Carly, but I'll just meet you guys later. I need to figure some stuff out."

Pippa could practically see her friend's frown.

"I'm worried about you, Pip. Be careful, okay? I'll see you as soon as possible."

Pippa hung up the phone, relief so great she was shaky with it. She had the best friends in the world. Smart friends. They'd be able to help her figure this out.

In the meantime, she wasn't sticking around the apartment in case Mr. Broken Condom decided to make an appearance. The very last thing she wanted right now was to face the potential father of her potential child.

Chapter 5

Pippa lengthened her stride as she neared Oscar's. There was a mix of snow flurries and tiny pellets of sleet in the air, stinging her cheeks as she walked.

She'd hoped the cold would bring her around. Make some of the shock wear off. But she was still reeling from Cam's phone call and all that was going to help her right now was an emergency session of the girl-friends' round table.

She opened the door to Oscar's and unwound the scarf she'd hastily thrown around her neck. She scanned the room, relief easing some of the awful tension when she saw her friends already seated in a corner booth way in the back. It was perfect.

As she made her way through the maze of tables, Tabitha looked up and waved fiercely. Sylvia, Carly and Ashley quickly turned. Carly rose as Pippa approached.

She got hugs from everyone and finally she squeezed into the booth beside Ashley, who looked at her with concern.

"What's wrong, Pip? Carly called us all but she wouldn't say what was the matter."

"I haven't told her yet," Pippa said ruefully. "I may be jumping the gun here, girls. But I'm freaking out and need your help sorting through my options."

"Oh, my God, what is it?" Tabitha exclaimed.

Sylvia frowned. She was the older and more serious-minded of the group. Not to mention ultrapractical. She'd have solid advice. Pippa would bet any amount of money on it.

Pippa drew in a deep breath. "I could be… Well, there's at least a slim possibility that I'm pregnant."

"What?"

Pippa winced as all four of her friends exclaimed at the same time.

Ashley's eyes rounded and she stared at Pippa in question. "Oh, Pip, how sure are you?"

"I had a one-night stand the other night." She glanced up at Ashley and grimaced. "With Cam. We left Ashley's party together. He took me to his house and we had sex. *Lots* of sex."

Ashley looked robbed of speech. Sylvia just kept wearing that frown. That damn disapproving frown that reminded Pippa way too much of how a mother would look. Well, Pippa's mother wouldn't look that way. She'd congratulate her daughter on snaring a wealthy baby daddy and then tell her to milk him for all he was worth. Not exactly mother-of-the-year material.

Oh, Miranda wasn't evil. She wasn't even a bad mother. She was just superficial and very mercenary. Pippa supposed she could even admire her mother for being so shrewd when it came to relationships. Miranda Laingley was out for number one and number one only. And she refused to apologize to anyone for it.

"I'm not following," Tabitha said slowly. "Maybe I'm dense here. If you *just* had sex with him, why on earth are you worried about pregnancy?"

"Because one of the condoms broke and the timing is perfect in my cycle," Pippa replied.

"Cam?" Ashley squeaked. "Okay, I knew you were kind of crushing on him, but you and him? Really?"

"You needn't look so flabbergasted," Pippa muttered. "The attraction was mutual, I assure you."

Ashley looked immediately contrite and threw her arms around Pippa, hugging her tightly. "Of course it was, sweetie. Oh, my gosh, poor you!"

"I'm so unbalanced by all of this. The timing couldn't be worse. Oh, my God, you guys don't even know this yet. With the pregnancy scare, I just blanked it out, but the lease on the building space fell through. I don't have a place for my shop. And now this. I'm trying to get my business off the ground. I have no health insurance and I'm in no way prepared to be a mother. I just want to cry, but I know that solves nothing."

"You cry, honey," Carly said fiercely. "We'll figure this out."

"You know we'd do anything for you," Ashley said. "You all helped me so much when I was going through such an awful time with Devon. I can never repay you for that."

Pippa sniffled, trying to hold back the tears that threatened. "You never have to repay me, Ash. I love you. We all do. I love all of you guys."

"When exactly did you have sex?" Sylvia interjected.

"Saturday night. All of Saturday night. Well into Sunday morning."

Sylvia reached for Pippa's hand. "You can go to your doctor and have him advise you of the alternatives."

"I'll pay for you to go to the doctor, Pip," Ashley said. "I'll take you myself."

An uneasy flutter settled into Pippa's chest. She rubbed absently at the discomfort. It was the way she felt when she imagined taking measures to prevent a pregnancy that could already have begun.

"Pippa?" Sylvia asked gently.

"Oh, God, I feel so stupid," Pippa whispered. "I can't make that kind of decision in an instant. How can anyone?"

"Okay, what is your gut telling you?" Carly asked. "What are you afraid of? Is it the pregnancy itself that scares you? Or is it the idea of being an unwed mother and not being able to support yourself and a baby?"

"You aren't making any of it sound appealing," Pippa muttered.

"You don't have to make a decision right this minute," Tabitha broke in. "Taking a morning-after pill or getting a shot aren't your only options. You could totally wait and see if you even are pregnant and then pursue your options then. Women have many choices these days, Pippa."

Ashley squeezed Pippa's hand and stared urgently at her friend. "If you want this baby, if there is a baby, you have to know we'd help. All of us. You wouldn't be alone. I just want you to make the best choice for you. But whatever that is, you have our absolute support."

Pippa could no longer hold back the tears. They

streamed down her face as she stared at her best friends in the world. "I don't know what I'd do without you guys."

"You forget one important part of the equation," Sylvia pointed out.

Everyone looked at Sylvia.

"The father. Obviously you'll have us, but is he going to take responsibility in this matter?"

Pippa nodded. "He would. I have no doubt he would. I told him I'd let him know if I was pregnant and until then to back off. I just had to process all this, you know?"

"Yes, honey, we know," Carly said sympathetically.

"This probably sounds crazy to all of you, but from the moment I realized there was a possibility, everything changed for me. I began to imagine this tiny life inside me and even though I could take a pill and it would all go away…" She took a deep breath. "I'm not sure that's what I want."

She looked up at each friend in turn, but she saw no judgment or condemnation in their eyes. All she saw was unwavering love and support. Determination. Loyalty.

"If… If there's a baby. I think I want it." She swallowed the knot in her throat and then spoke with more conviction. "I know I want it."

"Take some time to get used to the idea," Sylvia advised. "There's no hurry. You don't have to make up your mind today or even tomorrow."

But Pippa knew the more the initial shock wore off, the more firmly she'd be entrenched in the idea of having and keeping her baby.

Her baby.

Already she felt fiercely protective of it.

Out of the wreckage of her shock and confusion came the very firm realization that she'd never do anything to end the pregnancy. Nor would she ever give up a child she gave birth to. Her possessiveness and the strong surge of love she already felt were shocking in their intensity, especially because she didn't even know if she was pregnant.

If she was, whatever happened, she would keep the child. She'd go to Cam and together they'd work out an amicable solution.

Maybe she was being stupidly naive, but until he showed her differently, she was going to believe wholeheartedly in his sense of responsibility.

Her hands shook as she raised a glass of water to her mouth. After taking a long drink, she put it back down and then leveled a stare at her friends.

"Okay, girls, how long do I have to wait before I can take a pregnancy test?"

Chapter 6

Pippa paced the floor of her living room, trying not to stare at the little stick lying on the coffee table just a few feet away.

"It isn't time yet," Ashley said when Pippa stopped and hesitated.

"Why does it have to take so long?" Pippa exploded.

She couldn't take not knowing another minute. The past weeks had been ones of unimaginable stress with Cam breathing down her neck, asking her every few days if she knew anything yet. The last time he'd asked, she'd all but screamed at him to back off. Maybe he'd finally gotten the hint or maybe she'd just sounded that desperate because he hadn't been in contact for the past couple of days.

The hell of it was, he acted concerned. It almost seemed as though he was acting on the assumption that she *was* pregnant and had made it his mission to "check on" her frequently.

He was making her insane.

"It's only been two minutes," Ashley soothed. "It doesn't do any good to sit and stare at it. It won't make things go any faster."

Pippa sank onto the couch. "You're right. It's driving me crazy, though. I just feel it. In my gut. I'm pregnant. And don't tell me it's some psychological crap and that I'm imagining all the symptoms. I'm just telling you that I feel different. My boobs are sore. I'm queasy. My smell is off. Weird stuff gets to me. Like the smell of cupcakes. Who the hell gets sick smelling a cupcake?"

Ashley smiled. "I don't think you're imagining anything, sweetie. Let's wait for the results and then we'll tackle the solution together. Okay?"

Pippa groaned and closed her eyes. The past three weeks had been a form of torture she never wanted to repeat. She changed her mind from day to day. One day she thought having a baby would be great. She and Ashley would have little playmates. On other days she thought she was solidly out of her mind and was terrified by the prospect.

And, well, she felt a little stupid. An unwanted pregnancy at her age? She wasn't some stupid teenager playing around with unprotected sex. She'd always been so damn careful. Always!

She'd never considered herself terribly old-fashioned, but still, she'd preferred to have children within the boundaries of a loving, committed relationship.

"Okay, you can look now."

They both stared at the stick on the coffee table like

it was an ugly bug neither of them wanted to get close enough to squash.

Pippa's stomach curled into a vicious knot. "You look. I don't think I can."

Ashley reached over and took Pippa's hand, squeezing hard. "Just remember, that no matter what the outcome, it'll be okay. I promise."

Pippa nodded, then slammed her eyes shut as Ashley reached for the stick. She didn't even want to see Ashley's reaction. Her heart thundered until she could feel it jumping into her throat.

"Pippa," Ashley said gently. "Open your eyes."

Pippa cracked open her eyes to see Ashley's solemn expression. Ashley laid the stick back onto the table, her gaze still centered on Pippa.

"What?" Pippa demanded, unable to stand it any longer. Ashley's expression told her nothing. Nothing at all! "Am I pregnant?"

"According to the test you are," Ashley said slowly.

Pippa deflated in a whoosh, sagging forward as she reached for the test, wanting to see the confirmation herself. It was a bit blurry and she blinked rapidly to bring it into focus.

And there it was. A big, glaring plus sign that pretty much said, *Yes, you're pregnant.*

"Oh, my God," she whispered.

Ashley looked uneasily at her. "You aren't going to do something crazy like faint on me, are you?"

Pippa managed to close her mouth, but she was numb from head to toe. It was as if Ashley was talking from a mile away and Pippa was having this surreal out-of-body experience. The entire room seemed to slow down and become a big void of white noise.

Pregnant.

With Cam's baby.

Mr. I Don't Do Relationships.

Mr. I Won't Call You.

As screwups went, this one was epic.

She closed her eyes again and groaned. "What am I going to do, Ash? Cam is going to freak. He gave me this long speech about how he didn't do commitment, it was just sex, blah, blah, blah. A baby is definitely a commitment."

"Take a few days. Let yourself come to terms with the shock. Then talk to Cam," Ashley advised.

"I need to talk to him now."

Ashley frowned. "Pip, you're upset. You aren't thinking rationally. The last thing you need is to go up against Cam. He can be... He's intense, okay? He'll bulldoze over you."

"No one's going to bulldoze me. I need to talk to him now. Other than me, this affects him the most. He deserves to know so he can start planning accordingly. It's not like I'm going to wait a week and then suddenly decide not to tell him. The result will be the same no matter when I talk to him, so why wait? Besides, he's been blowing up my phone for weeks now. No sense holding off any longer."

Ashley sighed. "I just don't want you to make any impulsive decisions. He can be persuasive. That's a nice term for it. He can be ruthless."

"I can hold my own with him. I'm not afraid. This is as much his problem as it is mine. I'll be damned if I spend the next week agonizing over my future alone. If I suffer, so can he."

A laugh escaped Ashley and her eyes danced merrily. "Okay, you just convinced me that he won't rip you to shreds and have you for dinner."

"Damn right he won't," Pippa muttered. "If he even tries, he won't ever have to worry about fathering another child."

Ashley laughed again and then impulsively leaned over to hug Pippa. "You know, this is going to be just fine, Pip. We'll be pregnant together for a little while at least. Devon and I will do anything we can to help, and you have Tabitha, Carly and Sylvia. Oh, and my mother. She views you as another daughter, and when she finds out you're pregnant, look out. She'll have you packed in so much bubble wrap you won't be able to breathe."

Pippa grinned. "I love your mama."

"And she loves you."

Pippa sighed and then rose from the couch. "Not to be rude, Ash, but I need to do this before I end up losing my nerve. I just want to get it over with so I don't have to live with unnecessary stress."

"Get your coat, then. We'll ride together over to Cam's office and then I'll have the driver take me home."

"Thanks, Ash. For everything. For holding my hand and being with me so I didn't have to do this alone."

Ashley hugged her again. "I seem to remember a time when you held my hand a lot longer."

"Okay, let's do this," Pippa said as she went for her coat.

Cam sat staring out his office window. There was a mixture of rain, sleet and snow, although soon the temperatures would drop enough that it would turn entirely to snow. His mood was as foul as the weather.

He'd largely ignored work even though he'd been a steady presence in the office. He sat in on meetings with Devon and their other two business partners and friends, Rafael de Luca and Ryan Beardsley. Their newest hotel, the flagship resort for the newly formed merger between Tricorp and Copeland Hotels, was coming along at a rapid pace. Things were on the upswing. He should be on top of the world.

But the past weeks had been the worst sort of hell as he tortured himself with the thought of Pippa being pregnant. The thought that she wasn't taking care of herself, that something would happen.

Worry, guilt and anxiety had taken over his every waking moment and his dreams, as well. And he only had himself to blame. He should have never given in to such temptation. He damn sure should have been more careful with the birth control. He should have just left Pippa the hell alone.

Then he wouldn't be sitting here feeling gutted with worry over losing something precious for the second time in his life.

The fact that he hadn't heard from her should have reassured him. Because if she was pregnant, he would have heard. She'd promised to let him know, and he trusted her to do that. Nothing about her had led him to believe otherwise.

But the longer he went hearing nothing, the crazier he got.

It had become a regular habit since their night together for him to reach into his desk drawer—the only one he locked—and pull out a small folding picture frame.

It contained two photos. One of Elise and one of Colton.

He stood staring at them now, his fingers tracing the lines of Elise's smiling face. Colton was merely a day old in his picture. Tiny. Wrinkled. Still red and he had a misshapen cone head, but Cam had never seen such a beautiful sight in his life.

All these years later, just looking at the two people he'd loved and lost had the power to stop him breathing.

He couldn't do it again. He couldn't bear it. He didn't want to set himself up for that kind of agony. He'd never wished for anything as hard as he wished for Pippa not to be pregnant.

With each day that passed without him hearing from her, some of his tension eased. He could breathe a little easier.

She wasn't pregnant. He had to believe that.

His secretary buzzed him, interrupting his thoughts.

"Mr. Hollingsworth, there is a young woman here to see you. She doesn't have an appointment."

"Did you get her name?" Cam asked impatiently.

His secretary put him on hold to inquire. Why the hell hadn't she asked already? He was about to tell her he wasn't to be disturbed when she came back on.

"Pippa Laingley. She seems sure you'll agree to see her."

There was a disdainful sniff in Mrs. Milton's voice that told Cam she'd probably already tried to get rid of Pippa.

"She would be right. Send her in at once."

Cam shot to his feet, his gut in knots as he fixed his gaze on the door. A moment later, Pippa showed herself in, pausing at the threshold as she searched the room for him.

He watched her closely, examining her every nuance, searching for a sign that she was in some way... different. His hands knotted into tight fists but he kept them behind his desk, not wanting her to see how on edge he was. His instinct was to go to her. He wanted to haul her into his arms and hold on tight. Promise her that things would be all right. But he'd learned long ago that nobody could make those promises.

He had to play this cool if he had a prayer of making it through this encounter.

"Pippa," he greeted. "Sit down. Please. Would you like something to drink?"

As she drew closer, he could see the paleness of her features. The shadows under her eyes. She even looked as though she'd lost weight. With sudden guilt, he realized the past weeks had been far more stressful for her than they had been for him.

"I hope I'm not interrupting something important," she said quietly. "I had to come and see you right away."

The knot grew larger in his stomach and he swallowed hard so his voice wouldn't crack.

"Not at all. I'm all yours. What would you like to discuss?"

He cringed at the obliviousness in his tone. No one was that stupid. Denial didn't make everything go away. Dread mounted with every breath until he wanted to just yell at her to say what it was she wanted to say.

"I'm pregnant," she said baldly.

Something inside him withered and died. Dismay weighed down on him like the heaviest of burdens. Grief welled deep in his chest and he stood there, motionless, because if he so much as twitched, he'd crack and crumble right there in front of her.

Finally managing to find his voice and his composure, he asked, "Are you certain?" But he knew she was. There was no denying the truth in her eyes. If only he could go back.

She nodded grimly, then hesitated. "As certain as I can be without a doctor's confirmation. I took a drugstore test. They're supposed to be ninety-nine percent accurate, or something like that."

He cleared his throat. "I'm sure it's right. We knew it was a distinct possibility."

She stood there, her hands shoved into her coat, her uneasiness obvious.

"Are you all right? Have you been well?"

He hated the distance in his voice even as he embraced it, wanted it. He didn't want the intimacy that two people who'd created a child should have and enjoy. He hated that she'd already adamantly turned down his offer—or rather, his demand—that she move in with him. Not that he could blame her. He was certain he came across as some unbalanced freak. Pushing her away, then yanking her back.

But as badly as he didn't want to allow himself any sort of closeness with her, he had to be certain she was provided for. That she had everything she needed, the best medical care, emotional and physical support. He couldn't have anything happen to her…their…*his* child. Never again.

Maybe it was the coldness of the arrangement that had put her off. Maybe she wanted…more. He cringed even as he thought it, but marriage? Maybe it was the best solution. A practical solution. She'd certainly benefit and he'd get what he most wanted. Peace of mind.

"I'm just tired. And worried," she admitted. "It will

be better now, regardless. It's just a relief to finally know so that decisions can be made."

Alarm skittered up his neck, prickling every one of the hairs. "Decisions? What kind of decisions?"

She lifted one shoulder in a shrug. He really wished she'd take that damn coat off but he wasn't certain he wanted her to stay. He damn sure knew he didn't want her to leave. What a mess this entire situation was.

Deciding to take charge, he took a step back from his desk and turned sideways, keeping her in sight. "We have a lot to work out. I will have a lawyer draw up papers. We should think about living arrangements."

She held up a hand to stop the flow of conversation. Her other hand went to her temple and rubbed even as she shook her head.

"I refuse to have any sort of a conversation about my future or your future or the baby's future in some damn office where who knows what can be overheard. I'm still struggling to come to terms with this. I just thought you should know, so that maybe you'd have time to come to grips with this, as well. I thought we could talk later. After we've both had time to think. I just... I just needed to tell you. I couldn't wait."

"I don't think—"

She raised her gaze to meet his and her eyes sparked with quick anger. "I don't care what you think. I'm going now. If you'd like to discuss this later, you can come to my apartment. Right now I'm going to have lunch. Alone. I'll be home by six."

If she'd just been snappish and churlish he probably would have wanted to wring her neck. But what he saw was a woman valiantly trying to maintain control.

She was rattled—every bit as rattled as he was—and it looked as if she would shatter at any moment.

He couldn't push her. It would be unconscionable. Even as the thought of allowing her to walk out without having anything settled made his stomach knot. It was all he could do to slowly nod his agreement.

"All right," he said quietly. "I'll be at your apartment at six. Don't worry about dinner. I'll bring something."

Chapter 7

It shouldn't have surprised Pippa to find Cam waiting for her on the stoop of her apartment, but when she looked up and saw him there, her eyes widened in shock. Then she checked her watch, wondering if she'd lost more time than she'd thought on the walk home. But nope, he was just really damn early.

He was wearing a long coat, but no hat or scarf, and his hair was damp from the drizzle that still couldn't decide on whether it wanted to be snow or not. His mouth was drawn into a grim line, but his expression softened when he saw her. She could swear she saw relief glimmering in his eyes.

She quickly dug into her pocket for her keys and mounted the steps. He moved to the side, frowning as she fumbled with the lock.

"Did you walk all this way?"

She pushed open the door, welcoming the instant warmth. Cam came in behind her and helped her with her coat before removing his. She started to take them, but he shook his head and asked, "Where do you want them?"

She gestured toward the closet door. "There is fine."

She waited until he'd finished and then led him into the living room.

"You didn't answer my question. Did you walk all the way home in the rain? It's frigid out there."

"Just the last ten blocks. I rode with Ashley to your office and then hopped a cab to the restaurant where I had lunch. There was little sense in getting one home since it's so close."

His frown didn't go away but he eased his large frame into one of her too-small chairs. He looked enormous in her tiny living room. His presence overpowered everything else and she had the instant sensation of not being able to breathe.

He seemed nervous and on edge. Guilt for her earlier unreasonableness ate at her. She'd been a bitch with the way she'd dumped the news on him at his office and then left in a snit.

He dragged a hand through his hair, then glanced her way again. "I know I'm here early, but perhaps you'll understand my impatience to get this matter settled."

"Settled?" she echoed. She eased down onto the edge of the couch. She should be offering him a drink or... something...but somehow it seemed silly because neither of them cared for observing social niceties at the moment. "I don't see that this will ever quite be settled. It's not something to *be* settled."

He sat forward, his body language tense and impatient. He dragged a hand through his hair several more times as he seemed to be trying to figure out what to say next.

"I'd like to know your plans."

She gave a jerky laugh, then closed her eyes because she was teetering on full-on bitch mode again. "You and me both. You have to give me a break, Cam. I only just found out this morning."

"Do you want the baby?"

"Yes!" she said fiercely. "Yes," she said again, calmer this time. "I've battled that question constantly over the past weeks, and no matter how stressed, worried, panicky or dismayed I may currently be, I do want this baby."

Was it relief that flashed in his eyes? It was hard to tell because the rest of him was so intense.

She rose, unable to sit still another moment. She paced away, keeping her back to him for a long second before finally turning to face him once more.

"I don't have a plan, Cam. Does anyone ever plan for something like this? Obviously I'm going to need your help. I don't have health insurance."

"You'll have the best available care," he cut in.

Her shoulders sagged forward. "Thank you. I've been trying to get my business started and health insurance is one of those pesky little details I haven't sorted out yet."

His expression was somber, his eyes serious. "You won't have to worry there. I'll want you and our child to be well taken care of."

Okay, maybe this wouldn't be so bad. He seemed to be taking it all very well, and moreover he was being exceedingly accommodating.

"I don't expect you to support me," she said quickly.

"The health care is more than generous. I have some savings. It's enough until I get my business up and running."

She paced back and forth as she assimilated her thoughts. The very last thing she wanted was for him to think she expected a gravy train since she was having his child. There'd be too many damn strings attached anyway.

"Surely we can work out a suitable arrangement between us." She looked up then to find him staring at her. "Will you want to be…involved? With the pregnancy, I mean. Some men aren't interested. Well, Devon is with Ashley, but I know some have no desire to go to things like doctor's appointments and stuff like that, and it's okay, really."

She was babbling endlessly and the strange thing was, the more she talked, the angrier he seemed to get. His brows drew together until his face resembled a thundercloud.

"Just wait a damn minute. I *will* be involved. I have the *right* to be involved in this pregnancy."

She blinked. "Well, okay. I wasn't saying you couldn't be. Just that I thought maybe you wouldn't want to be."

His expression grew fiercer. "You thought wrong."

"Cam, look. I'm not too sure what I'm doing here. I'm trying to be civilized and cooperative, but you've got to help me. You're sitting there glaring at me and I have to tell you I'm this close to completely losing my mind."

The words rushed out in shaky succession and her hands trembled as she clasped them in front of her.

Cam cursed softly and rose to stand in front of her. "Sit down. Please."

She hesitated only a moment before allowing him to guide her back to the couch. He curled his hand around hers and gave it a gentle squeeze.

"Now, here's what I think we should do. First we'll get you to a doctor so that we can make sure you're in good health and everything is okay with your pregnancy."

She nodded. That much she could deal with. Going to the doctor was a logical first step. At least one of them was capable of rational thought.

"Then I think we should get married."

So much for rational thought.

Before she could ask him if he'd lost his mind he put a finger to her lips. Then he heaved in a deep breath almost as if he was having to convince himself every bit as much as her.

"Just hear me out. We can get married, have separate living arrangements—or rather, quarters. My house is large enough for us to share without tripping over each other. You'd have your space. You'd be provided for. But most important, I could be assured that you and the baby were safe."

She gaped incredulously at him. "Are you insane?"

His eyes narrowed.

She yanked her hand away from his and pushed upward to her feet. The room was too small. She felt caged and like her world was spiraling out of control.

"Don't be unreasonable, Pippa."

She swung around. "Unreasonable? Cam, three weeks ago you told me in no uncertain terms that you wouldn't call me, that this was just sex and you didn't do commitment. Well, guess what. Marriage is a big freaking commitment!"

"I wasn't suggesting we have a relationship," he said tightly.

Oh, this was just going from bad to worse.

"What are you suggesting, then?"

"A mutually beneficial partnership. You and our child will be well provided for and I'll have peace of mind."

Her brow furrowed. "Peace of mind for what, Cam? I feel like there's something huge I'm missing here. You keep harping on wanting to be sure me and the baby are safe. That we're provided for. Look, I appreciate that. More than you could possibly know. It touches me that you aren't turning the other way. I just don't understand your adamancy here. What are you so afraid of?"

Silence fell. So pronounced that she could hear them both breathing. Pain flashed in his eyes and his lips tightened. Then as if someone had flipped a switch, his face became impassive. His expression gave nothing away.

"Isn't that enough?" he finally asked. "That I'm willing to step up here? That I want you and our child to have the protection of my name and everything else that goes with it?"

Slowly she shook her head. "No. It's not enough."

"It was damn well good enough for you three weeks ago," he growled. "You didn't want anything but a night of sex, either, so don't make me out to be the bastard here."

"This isn't about you!"

It came out as a near shriek and she put both hands to the sides of her head in frustration. For a moment she stood there, eyes closed, her nostrils flaring as her breaths blew out in angry puffs.

When she reopened her eyes, Cam was staring at her, concern etched into his brow. "Pippa..." he began.

"No, just listen to me for a minute. Please," she begged. "You made yourself clear before we went to bed together. You were honest. I was honest. But things have changed in a huge, huge way. What I wanted then isn't what I want *now*. And no, I'm not asking you for anything. I need you to understand that. *I've* changed. My *priorities* have changed.

"You were right. That night I wanted sex. With you. I was attracted to you. I wasn't looking for more. A relationship isn't what I want or need at this stage of my life. But I'm pregnant now. And there is no way I'm going to shortchange myself or my child by entering into a cold, loveless relationship for the purpose of convenience. When I get married, it's going to be to a man who loves me and is willing to be a full-time father to my child. I need those things. *Especially* now."

"I can't give you that," Cam said flatly.

"And I'll never settle for anything less," she said quietly.

He shot off the couch and turned away, his hands clenched into tight fists at his side. "I'll be damned if I watch you marry another man when you're pregnant with my child." He turned back around, raw anger lighting his eyes. "I have a right to fatherhood, Pippa. You can't take that from me. I won't allow it. I'll fight you with every breath I have."

Some of her frustration fled. She took a step forward and put her hand gently on his arm. He flinched underneath her touch but she curled her fingers tightly into his skin. There was something terrible and painful in his eyes. Something that knotted her stomach and made her want to soothe some of the torment she sensed within him.

"I'd never take that from you, Cam," she said softly. "I'm merely giving you reasons why I won't settle for a relationship like the one you're offering."

"I want my child safe," he gritted out.

"So do I. I love this baby already. I've lain awake at night imagining its future. I'd never do anything that wasn't in his or her best interests."

"Then let me take care of you both. I don't want anything to happen to you. Move in with me. If you won't marry me so my child has my name, then at least move in with me so you're both provided for."

She wondered if he even knew that he was nearly pleading with her. As vehement as he was that he could never give her what she wanted or needed from a relationship, he seemed just as determined to tie her to him.

She let her hand slide down his arm until she caught his fingers and laced them with hers. "If I agreed to this, I could never respect myself. If I have a daughter, I want her to know she never has to settle for second best or nothing at all. If I'm going to teach her to be strong and resilient and self-reliant, I can hardly have settled in my own life."

He tensed again as if to argue, but she squeezed his hand. "No, listen to me, Cam. Neither of us wanted this. We sure didn't plan it. Think about what you're doing here. Our emotions are heated. Neither of us are thinking straight. Don't do something we'll both regret. That speech you gave me three weeks ago speaks to the heart of you. That's what you want. Not marriage. Not the inconvenience of a wife underfoot when the last thing you want is commitment. Because you know what?

Sooner or later I'll resent you for not being able to give me what I want. And it'll eat away at me until I hate you for it. What kind of environment is that for our child?"

His lips thinned. He looked as though he wanted to argue further. But he remained silent, his hand in hers as they stared intently at each other.

"I'm willing to let it go for now," he said grudgingly. "But there are things that I will want to do to ensure your safety and you're just going to have to deal with it."

She lifted an eyebrow in question. "What on earth is your obsession with safety? I can't live in a bubble. You can't hover over me for the next eight months."

"The hell I can't."

"What are you so afraid of?"

It was the second time she asked the question and for a moment she thought he might actually respond.

But he went silent again, his eyes darkening.

"Will you at least let me move you into a more secure apartment?" he asked.

She shot him an incredulous look. "What's wrong with the apartment I have?"

"It opens to the street. There's no security. The steps are dangerous, particularly in winter."

She blew out a frustrated breath and shook her head. "There's nothing wrong with this apartment. And by the time I'm bigger, winter will be long gone. I like my apartment. I like the location. This is the area where I want to try to start my café. Besides, I can't afford more than what I have right now."

"I don't give a damn what you can afford."

"Well, I do. I can't just halt my life and allow you to sweep in and take care of me until the baby's born. What would I do afterward?"

"I wouldn't just quit because the child was here," he said in outrage.

"Please just stop," she begged. "We're getting nowhere. I'm tired. I'm stressed. I honest to God want to go to bed and cry."

He looked horrified by the possibility. Instant regret flashed across his face, and she knew, she knew deep down, that they weren't really the two people who stood here so volatile and on edge. They had been pushed beyond their endurance. The past weeks had put enormous strain on them both. They just needed time. And distance. A better perspective. Anything but standing here in her apartment arguing endlessly.

"I think you should just go now," she said gently. "We both have a lot to process and we're both too raw to have a sane, intelligent conversation. We're going to have a long eight months together. Let's not start it off by arguing endlessly over details."

"I'm sorry," he said gruffly.

To her surprise he pulled her into his arms. She rested her forehead against the hollow of his throat and closed her eyes.

"I didn't intend this to happen," he said in a quiet voice. "I would have given anything at all for it not to. But it's a reality and it's something we must both come to terms with. Like you, I want this child very much. I have to know you're both safe. Grant me that at least."

She nodded against him before pulling away.

He grimaced and checked his watch. "I didn't bring dinner as I said I would. I was in too big a hurry to get here. I know you're tired and upset, but perhaps we could order in and have a quiet dinner together."

"Would it offend you if I only wanted to crawl into bed and go to sleep? Fatigue is killing me so far."

He looked as though he might argue and then he simply nodded, touching her cheek before he walked past her to the door.

Chapter 8

"So when exactly were you going to tell me the news?" Devon asked in an irritable voice.

Cam turned to find his friend leaning against the door frame of his office.

Even though they shared a suite of offices, Cam hadn't seen his friend in quite some time. With his other partners, it was understandable—ever since they'd gotten married, Rafe and Ryan spent most of their time overseeing projects on their respective islands where they'd settled with their wives. But Cam had to admit that he'd avoided Devon ever since the night he and Pippa had left Ashley's housewarming. Pippa was very good friends with Ashley, and Ashley was nothing if not intensely loyal. She'd probably already filled Devon's head with all the ways in which Cam was a first-rate jerk.

Cam sighed and motioned Devon in with a wave of

his hand. Devon ambled forward and dropped into one of the chairs in front of Cam's desk.

"Well?"

Cam swore under his breath and took a seat in his leather executive's chair. "Well, what? I'm sure you know the whole bloody story by now. With the way Pippa's avoiding me, you probably know more than I do at this point."

Devon raised an eyebrow. "Avoiding you? Don't tell me that fatalistic charm of yours is an epic fail?"

"Charm has nothing to do with it," Cam bit out.

"Evidently."

Cam sighed. "Did you just come to put the screws to me or do you actually need something?"

"More like I was wondering why my best friend doesn't bother to tell me he knocked up my wife's best friend."

Cam winced and closed his eyes. "Christ, Dev, you think I set out to do it on purpose? You of all people should know this is the very last thing I'd ever want."

Devon slowly nodded. "Yes, I do know. Which is why I found this all a bit strange."

"It was supposed to be a one-night thing. I was attracted to her. She was attracted to me. Things kind of came to a head the night of your housewarming and we went to my place."

"You brought a woman back to your cave? I knew you had the hots for her but didn't think you were serious about taking her back to your place."

The utter disbelief in Devon's voice annoyed Cam. It wasn't as though the decision was earth-shattering.

"It made no sense to drive back into the city and get a hotel or go back to her place when my house was a quarter mile away."

"Of course," Devon said mockingly.

"Whatever," Cam muttered. "The point is, this was not planned. In fact, the effort was made to prevent it. Unfortunately, the damn condom broke and here we are, both about to be parents. She isn't any more thrilled about it than I am. I mean, with the way it happened. Hell, I'm making it sound like neither of us wants this baby. We do. We just don't agree… Well, we don't agree on anything so far."

"I'm sorry to hear that," Devon said sincerely.

Cam waved the sympathy away. It did him no good at this point. "Have you seen her? Has Ashley said anything about her at all? She's avoiding me and it's starting to piss me the hell off."

Devon cleared his throat. "Pippa was out at the house the other night. She's pretty upset at the moment."

Cam sat forward. "Upset about the pregnancy? Has she changed her mind about having the baby?"

Devon held up his hand. "Slow down. Nothing like that. As far as I know, she's taking the pregnancy very well. Things aren't going so well for her business plans, though. Apparently the lease she'd signed for her shop fell through and she's not having any luck finding anything else suitable. She's on a pretty tight budget, and now with a baby on the way, she's starting to panic."

Cam swore long and hard. "Damn fool, stubborn, mule-headed female. All she had to do was agree to marry me. Or move in with me. She had options. A hell of a lot of options."

Devon stared at him like he'd lost his mind. "Marry you? Move in with you?"

"I know what you're thinking, and yes, I'm obviously out of my mind. But damn it, Dev, all I can think about is what if something happens? Something I could prevent? I just need..."

"I know, man," Devon said softly. "So what are you going to do?"

"Hell if I know," Cam muttered. "What is there to do? She doesn't seem to want anything to do with me. At least, not yet. And I've tried—really tried—to give her the space she seems to want and need, but I'm getting impatient here. I've tried to call her. Arrange dinner. She always has something else to do. She was supposed to tell me when her next doctor's appointment is but so far I've heard nothing. I need to know she's safe and is taking care of herself and the baby. How can I do any of that when she won't agree to see me?"

"Try letting go of the past and stop allowing it to overshadow every single thought and decision. You can't change the past, but you can sure screw up your future."

Red-hot rage clouded Cam's vision. His fingers curled into tight fists and he sat there, refusing to even look at his friend because he knew Devon meant well but he also knew he'd do or say something he'd regret if he wasn't careful.

How the hell could Devon possibly understand? He wanted to tell Devon that he wouldn't be so quick to give advice if something happened to Ashley and their child, but he couldn't be so cruel as to even make Devon contemplate such a future. He wouldn't do it to his worst enemy.

"I'm sorry," Devon said, regret heavy in his voice. "No one expects you to ever forget. I just think at some point you have to be willing to move forward and take a chance again."

Cam nodded curtly, still refusing to look Devon's way.

"Look, if it's any consolation, Pippa is mostly devoting her time to trying to get her business started. Ashley's been helping her come up with ideas. I doubt her avoidance is personal. She's stressing because now that she's pregnant, she feels even more pressure to get her business off the ground so she can provide for her child."

"She wouldn't have to stress if she'd just accept help from me," Cam growled.

"Have you offered? And I mean in a no-strings kind of way?"

"Maybe my mistake is in asking her. It occurs to me that when given the opportunity to say no, women will, if for no other reason than to be contrary."

His mood brightened considerably as he warmed to the idea that had just taken root.

"The trick is not to ask but just do. Wouldn't you agree, Dev?"

Devon gave him an uneasy look. "You're on your own, man. Don't ask me to get involved. I'm not going to help pave the way for you to have your nuts painfully removed."

"Chicken," Cam drawled.

"Hell, yeah. I'm chicken. I know what side my bread is buttered on. I've discovered in a very short time that Ashley's happiness or sadness has a direct bearing on my own."

For a moment pain sliced through Cam's chest, robbing him of breath. He envied Devon with a ferocity that left him bereft. Devon was happy. He'd discovered the joys of marriage and the love of a woman. He was looking forward to fatherhood with the innocence of a man who didn't realize that happiness was fleeting. That everything could change in a moment's time. And that you could go from being on top of the world to hell in the blink of an eye.

Cam knew. And if he had any say in the matter, he'd *never* know that kind of pain again.

"But I'll wish you luck," Devon said cheerfully. "If nothing else, you'll provide me with entertainment."

Cam sat back in his chair. "You underestimate me."

Devon studied him for a long moment and then pushed forward in his chair. "What exactly do you want here, Cam? You say you don't want a relationship. Don't want commitment. Don't want anything resembling a permanent situation. And yet you're pursuing Pippa relentlessly and are frustrated by the fact that she's giving you precisely what you want, which is a pass on all of the above-mentioned things."

Cam's eyes narrowed. It was a damn good question and one he didn't have a ready answer to. Nor did he really want to examine all the reasons why he was pulling marriage proposals out of his ass. "I want to do everything in my power to make sure she and my child are safe and taken care of."

Devon sighed. "You can't protect them from everything. Bad things happen. You can't live your whole life expecting disaster."

For Cam, the conversation was over. He ignored Devon's remarks and steered the conversation to business. But Pippa was very much on his mind, and even as he discussed the latest progress on the resort in St. Angelo, he was already formulating his idea on how to rein Pippa in.

The sooner he was certain of her safety and well-being, the faster his own life would get back to normal. And he'd keep telling himself that until he damn well believed it.

Chapter 9

Pippa dug her hands deeper into the pockets of her coat and hunched her shoulders forward as she hurried down the sidewalk toward her apartment. Snow flurries blew furiously around her and the wind cut ribbons across her body, chilling her to the bone.

She clamped her elbow down on her purse when the wind blew it up and then readjusted the strap over her shoulder so it was crossways over her body.

It had been a dismal day in a long line of dismal days, and to make matters worse she was battling morning sickness and overwhelming fatigue. It disgusted her how much she needed to sleep in order to feel human.

She rounded the corner and breathed a sigh of relief. Just two more blocks and she'd be home. As soon as she got inside her apartment, she was going to put on her jammies, curl up with a cup of hot chocolate and then sleep for about twelve hours.

What a party animal she was. She was one happening chick. From having endless energy and being able to function on just a few hours of sleep a night to not being able to hold up her head unless she got about fourteen hours in. Pregnancy had turned her into a pathetic, boring lump.

She was so deep into her thoughts that she wasn't immediately aware of the car pulling to a stop on the street beside her. When she did notice, her heart lurched and she stepped hastily back. Just as a hand curled around her elbow.

She let out a startled cry and then quieted when she saw who it was who held her.

"Cam, you scared the life out of me!"

"Get in," he said tersely. "It's freezing out here."

"It's just a block and a half to my apartment!"

Ignoring her, he steered her toward the open car door and she sighed as a wave of warm air hit her square in the face. Okay, so maybe riding the rest of the way wouldn't hurt. She slid across the seat, Cam getting in after her. He shut the door and gestured for the driver to pull away.

"You haven't returned my calls," he said in a clipped voice. "You have an uncanny knack of never being at home when I come by. Your friends, amazingly enough, have no idea where you are at any given time."

The sarcasm made her flinch, but guilt made her wince even more.

When the car didn't slow as they passed her apartment, she leaned forward. "Right here! My apartment is right here."

"We aren't going to your apartment."

She sank back against the seat and sighed wearily. "Look, I know I've been avoiding you. I'm not offering any excuses. But, Cam, please, I cannot deal with you tonight. I'm tired. I'm in a terrible mood. I'll only make you crazy."

To her surprise, he cracked a smile. "At least you're honest."

The sudden change in his demeanor unbalanced her. He was so damn...appealing...when he smiled.

"Where are we going?" she asked irritably.

"Somewhere I think your mood will be much improved."

"Cryptic bastard," she muttered.

To her annoyance, his grin widened. But just as quickly, his brows drew together and he turned to face her fully. There was no anger in his eyes, but there was most definitely determination. Oh, yes, he was clearly telling her that he'd finally cornered her cowardly butt and he wasn't going to let her go this time.

"What gives, Pippa? Why won't you return my calls? I thought we had an agreement. I don't even know when your doctor's appointment is. Or have you already been?"

She frowned. "Of course I haven't. I told you that I'd let you know so you could come with me."

"You said a lot of things that haven't exactly come to fruition," he said darkly.

"I've been busy," she burst out in frustration. "I've got a lot on my mind, including how the hell I'm going to support a baby. Much less myself. I'm stressed beyond your imagination, Cam. Cut me some slack here. Your life may not change so much but mine sure as hell will."

His eyes grew stormy and his lips tightened into a fine line. She knew she'd gone too far. She knew she'd been careless with her words. She wanted to bite at someone and he was the unfortunate victim because he just happened to be in the wrong place at the wrong time. Not that it was entirely her fault. She could be at home where she wouldn't annoy anyone but herself. But he'd played Mr. Kidnapper and Mr. One Thousand Questions, so in her mind he deserved what he got.

Only he didn't deserve it and she knew it. He'd made the effort. He was doing and saying all the right things. Sort of. But it had been hard for her to come to terms with her pregnancy and what it meant for her. How did anyone do a complete one-eighty in their life and just keep on trucking? Maybe some people managed it, but Pippa wasn't one of them.

"You think you're the only one struggling with this, Pippa? Let me tell you, it sucks not knowing what the hell is going on with you. It sucks not to know if you're okay, if the baby's okay, if there still *is* a baby. Would you like living with that kind of uncertainty?"

Guilt gnawed at Pippa like a hungry beast. He hadn't deserved her avoidance, and maybe, just maybe, if she had been more willing to include him, they could have tackled this whole thing together instead of her worrying incessantly about how she was going to manage alone.

"I'm sorry, Cam."

She leaned forward and then threw her arms around his broad shoulders, hugging him tightly. He stiffened at first as if he had no idea how to take the impulsive gesture. Then he gradually relaxed and put his arms around her, as well.

She hugged him fiercely, burying her face in his neck. It felt good to just hold on to someone stronger than herself because she needed that support.

"I'm sorry," she said again. "I'm no good at this.

You don't deserve the way I've treated you, Cam. I'm so sorry."

He gently pulled away and put a finger to her lips. His eyes were soft and so focused on her that she shivered. "How about we just make a pact going forward," he said gruffly. "Don't leave me out of the loop and stop avoiding me."

She nodded, and settled back into his arms.

He stroked her shoulders in a soothing pattern and then said close to her ear, "I've got a surprise for you that I think will alleviate some of this stress you've placed yourself under."

She pulled away, hating to leave that comforting haven, but she wanted to know what the heck he was talking about. He must have seen the obvious question in her eyes because he shook his head.

"We'll be there soon. It isn't far from your apartment."

With that cryptic remark, he closed his mouth and settled back against the seat. He pulled her into his side and directed his gaze out his window as they navigated through traffic.

Just a few more blocks up, the driver slowed and pulled to the curb in front of an upscale cluster of retail businesses. Cam opened his door, stepped into the cold and then reached back for Pippa's hand to help her out.

As soon as she stepped onto the pavement, her gaze went to the shop on the corner of the busy intersection. Her mouth fell open as she saw the sassy storefront sign.

Pippa's Place. Catering Done Your Way.

It was sort of perfect. Hot pink. Flashy. Contemporary. And girlie! It fit her to a T.

She dropped his hand and surged forward to stare into the window. The inside was immaculate. Already set up with a seating area to the left and a large counter with a display for all the yummy things she'd fill it with. There were two registers at each end of the counter.

"Holy crap, Cam, what have you *done?*"

She whirled around to see him standing there, a smug smile of satisfaction on his face.

"Would you like to go in and see if the rest meets with your approval?"

He held up the keys, dangling them in front of her like the proverbial carrot before the donkey.

"Oh, my God, yes!"

She snatched the keys from him and hurried to unlock the door. She nearly squeaked her delight when a bell above the door jingled, signaling her entrance.

The inside was beautiful. The walls had even been decorated with pictures of cupcakes. Cupcakes everywhere. How could he have possibly known what suited her so well?

"Ashley helped," Cam said, as if reading her mind.

"I can't believe you did this," she whispered.

He gestured toward the doorway to the back. "Better go check out your kitchen and see if it passes inspection."

She let her hand slide along the countertop as she rounded the end. She could *so* see herself inside this place. Could practically smell the mouthwatering delicacies she'd prepare.

She burst into the kitchen and came to an abrupt halt as she took in the perfection before her.

Lining the surfaces of the countertops were rows and rows of top-of-the-line appliances. There were multiple stainless-steel ovens, two huge refrigerators and a huge freezer in the back.

Everything she could possibly want or need was right here. In her kitchen. In her shop.

Her knees wobbled. The practical part of her knew she should refuse all of it. She couldn't afford any of it. She shuddered to even think of what the lease cost. She hadn't even inquired about this property because she knew it was out of her reach.

The other part of her chafed at refusing such a generous gift. Cam had put a lot of time and effort into giving her the perfect place to work. She would be the biggest bitch in the world if she threw it back in his face.

"Do you like it?"

Her chest caved in at the thread of insecurity in his voice. There was no way she was refusing his gesture. No way she'd put them solidly back to square one again. If he was so willing to try, then she'd damn well do the same.

"Like it?" she choked out. "Oh, my God, Cam, I love it!"

For the second time, she threw herself into his arms and hugged him with all her strength. He took a step back to steady himself and laughed as she wrapped herself around him.

She closed her eyes as relief poured through her. This was the answer to all her problems. She could start work immediately, or at least as soon as she got all the red tape taken care of. But permits and the like were the easy part.

"I'll make this a success," she said fiercely. "I won't let your investment go to waste."

Carefully, he extricated himself from her hold and then palmed her shoulders as he stared into her eyes.

"This isn't a damn investment. It's a gift. I've prepaid the rent for two years. Plenty of time for you to get on your feet and start realizing a profit."

"I can't believe you did this for me," she said quietly. "After the way I've been acting. I don't know how to thank you. You can't possibly know how much stress this takes off me."

He sent her an admonishing look. "This gift does come with strings. You'll give me two promises. One, you'll stop avoiding me so we can work together on the issue of your pregnancy. Two, you'll hire enough employees that you won't be spreading yourself too thin."

A helpless smile worked over her mouth. He was too cute when he was all stern and forbidding. "I promise." With the money she wouldn't be spending on a lease, she'd be able to afford to hire actual employees!

He hesitated a moment, his hands sliding down her arms in the gentlest of caresses. "I may not be able to give you what you want or deserve, Pippa, but what I *can* give you is yours without reservation. You carry my child and I'll do anything at all to keep the both of you safe and happy."

How easy it would be to love this man who swore he had no love to give. He seemed so determined to keep her at arm's length and yet he exhibited caring at every turn.

Unable to resist, she moved into the circle of his arms, leaned up and pressed a kiss to those firm lips. His breath caught and held, his body going tense against hers. No matter what he said, he wanted her. But she refused to use that attraction against him.

"Thank you," she said again, before slipping away.

He made a grab for her hand, catching only her fingertips as she stepped back. "Let's go eat dinner. We have a lot to catch up on and I'd love to hear your plans for the shop."

It was an offer of friendship, one that warmed her even as it left her bereft on the inside. They could have so much more. She ached for more. But it was something at least.

Maybe all she'd ever have from him at all.

She smiled up at him and squeezed his hand, lacing her fingers more tightly with his. "I'd like that."

Chapter 10

The next morning when Pippa left her apartment, she noticed a car parked directly in front of her walkway and a driver leaning against the passenger door. As soon as he saw her, he straightened and reached to open the door to the backseat.

"Miss Laingley?" the driver queried. "Mr. Hollingsworth wishes me to drive you to your shop and anywhere else you need to go during the day."

Pippa blew out her breath in a sigh. Okay, this was taking things a bit too far. She'd allowed him to give her the shop. She hadn't wanted to be ungrateful. But providing her a car and driver when she had only a few blocks to go?

As if sensing her hesitation, the driver dug his cell phone out of his pocket and hastily punched a button. Then he thrust it in her direction. She stared back in puzzlement as he closed the distance between them, holding the phone out to her.

"He said to call him if it looked as though you'd refuse," the driver explained.

As she took the phone, she heard Cam's deep voice over the line. She put it to her ear.

"Take the car, Pippa. It's cold, the sidewalks are slippery and it's supposed to snow later today."

She smiled in spite of herself. There was something about his gruff concern that was endearing. "Cam, you can't keep doing things like this."

"Can't I? I thought we came to an agreement last night. Are you already calling off our truce?"

Oh, the man was slick. How neatly he turned this back on her. By refusing, she was the bad guy and he was only trying to provide for the mother of his child.

"Oh, all right," she muttered. "But, Cam, quit it. No more. You've already done way too much."

His amusement was readily evident as he replied, "I believe that's for me to decide."

He rang off and she was left standing there holding the phone while the driver waited expectantly for her to get in.

Grumbling about hardheaded males, she ducked inside the car and waited for the driver to walk back around to his side. When he got in, he thrust a business card over the seat.

"This is my cell number," he said. "Any time you need to go anywhere at all, no matter the distance, you're to call me. Mr. Hollingsworth's orders were quite explicit. He doesn't want you out in the cold on the sidewalks. Weather's supposed to get nasty."

She glanced at the card and saw that the driver's

name was John. She shook her head but leaned back as they pulled away. "Okay, John. I'll be a good girl. Somehow I also think you have orders to rat me out if I don't use your services."

He had the grace to blush as he glanced in the rearview mirror. "Yes, ma'am, I do. Sorry, but Mr. Hollingsworth pays my wages so I answer to him."

She chuckled. "Far be it for me to be responsible for you losing your job. I promise to call when I need a ride."

He nodded his approval, then refocused his attention on the traffic.

It had begun to sleet, and she was suddenly really glad she wasn't out in it.

A few minutes later, he stopped in front of her shop and hurried out to open her door for her.

"Remember to call when you're ready to leave," he urged as he handed her onto the sidewalk.

She waved and made a dash to the door. To her surprise, it was unlocked. Had she been a complete idiot the day before and not locked back up when she and Cam had left? She groaned, wondering if she even had any of those lovely appliances left.

She pushed open the door, hit the light switch and then jumped two feet into the air when all her girlfriends popped up from behind the counter and shouted, "Surprise!"

She let out a shriek, dropped her keys and then staggered sideways, her hand flying to her chest to calm the rapid uptick in her pulse.

"Oh, my God, you guys scared me!"

Ashley, Tabitha, Carly and Sylvia hurried around

the counter and immediately surrounded her, hugging and fussing over her.

Carly squeezed her in a huge hug. "We're sorry. We just wanted to help you celebrate the new place!"

Pippa stepped back and stared into her friends' excited faces. "How did you even know? And how on earth did you get in?"

Ashley smiled. "Cam called me. He thought you might like a surprise. He dropped a key by the house early this morning."

"The place is awesome, Pip!" Tabitha exclaimed. "I can so totally see your customers out here sitting and enjoying your yummy treats."

An insistent honk interrupted the women's celebration. At first Pippa wrote it off as normal street traffic, but the horn kept blaring and the women turned, frowns on their faces.

A young man, who couldn't be more than twenty, stood outside the door waving frantically to them.

"What the heck?" Pippa murmured.

"Be careful, Pip!" Sylvia cautioned when Pippa went toward the door.

The women crowded around as she opened the door to stare out.

The guy grinned, then gestured toward the street.

"Oh, my God," Carly breathed.

Pippa stared in shock at the brightly decorated delivery van parked in front of her shop.

It was perfect. Absolutely perfect. How on earth could Cam have pulled this off?

Just as with her store sign, Pippa's Place was splashed in hot pink across the side of the white van. There were lavender, yellow and orange flowers surrounding the lime-green tagline: Catering Done Your Way.

"Here are the keys," the guy said with a grin as he held them out to her.

She held out her palm, tears filling her eyes as she stared in astonishment at her delivery van. It was too much.

Her friends crowded in behind her, hugging and squeezing her as they squealed in excitement.

"Let's go for a ride!" Tabitha suggested.

Sylvia's eyes lit up. "Ohhh, let's do it!"

"Don't you have to have a commercial license or something?" Pippa asked. "Or any license at all?" she added with a laugh.

Ashley chuckled. "How would I know? I think you're supposed to hire someone to drive it for you, but hey, we should totally try it out."

Pippa grinned, excitement overtaking her. "Okay, let's do it. Last one in is a rotten egg."

Laughing like hyenas, the women ran to the van, oohing and aahing as they jumped in.

Pippa climbed into the driver's seat and inserted the key into the ignition. Before she cranked the engine, she turned and shot them all pointed glances. "If any of you rats me out to Cam, I'll murder you. That means you, Ash. He'd have a cow if he knew I was driving around the city without a license. I'd have to endure endless lectures on safety and God only knows what else."

Ash blinked innocently. "Who's Cam?"

"Let's go, Pip!" Sylvia said from the seat next to Pippa.

Pippa started the van and then carefully pulled into traffic.

"Turn on the radio," Carly called from the back. "Put something good on."

"I'll do the radio. You drive," Sylvia said as she leaned forward.

Soon the van streaked along the streets of the city, the radio blaring as the women laughed and sang along. Okay, so this was the most fun Pippa'd had in longer than she could remember. This pregnancy thing wasn't so bad. Nothing had changed. Except for the fact she was going to be a mother.

But she still had good friends. Her career was finally going places. And some of the worry was gone.

She had Cam to thank.

Cam, who swore he couldn't give her a damn thing. Cam, who swore he didn't do commitment, wouldn't call and only wanted sex. She nearly snorted. He sure didn't act like a man who wanted to distance himself.

"Let's drive to Oscar's for lunch," Tabitha said. "My treat today. Then we can head back to your shop after and make cupcakes."

Pippa grinned. It sounded like a perfectly wonderful plan to her.

She LOVED it. You did good, Cam.

Cam read the text from Ashley and smiled despite himself before sliding his phone back into his pocket. He felt a pang as he imagined Pippa's eyes lighting up when she saw the van. He could well picture how beautiful her smile was and how radiant she looked now that she was pregnant.

He curled his hand into a tight fist, then rubbed it

over his chest in an attempt to dispel the uncomfortable sensation.

But it wasn't something he could wipe away any more than he could wipe Pippa from his thoughts. He was consumed with her every waking moment and there wasn't a damn thing he could do about it.

Chapter 11

Pippa stood on her stoop until she saw Cam's car coming down the street. Then she hurried to the curb to wait as it came to a stop.

She slid into the passenger seat, cupping the sundress she wore firmly to her rounded abdomen so the ends wouldn't billow up. The city was on the cusp of spring. Still raw and windy, prone to chilly rains and the occasional snow flurry, but today the temps had soared into the sixties and the sun shone brightly, a promise of what was to come.

The past few months had been…nice. It seemed too tepid a word, but it fit. Accepting friendship from Cam had been hard—it was still hard. There were times when she could so see them together long-term. Then it was almost as if Cam realized how close they were getting, and he would back off and erect the wall between them once more.

Today, though? Today was special, and in her heart of hearts, she hoped their relationship would move forward just a bit. How could it not? Today they'd "meet" their child and for the first time see the tiny little life inside her.

"Are you nervous?" Cam asked as he drove toward the clinic where Pippa had her regular checkups.

Pippa took a deep breath. "Maybe?"

Cam smiled indulgently and reached over to squeeze her hand. "Still want to find out what we're having?"

She nodded. "I do. I have to know. I want to be able to establish that bond early. Figure out a name. I can start buying clothes and decide how I want to decorate."

She didn't even realize she had drifted off into a dreamy smile until she became aware of Cam watching her.

"Have you given thought to what you'd like? Are you hoping for a boy or a girl?"

She grinned ruefully. "Depends on what day you catch me on. Yesterday I was sure I wanted a boy. Today I'm leaning toward a girl. What about you?"

His eyes went bleak for a moment. She watched his Adam's apple bob up and down as he swallowed. Then he attempted a smile, but it was lame at best.

"I think I'd like a daughter."

"Really? I thought guys always wanted sons."

His eyes grew dimmer. "No. I think a daughter would be great. A little miniature Pippa. All that dark hair and green eyes."

Her cheeks grew warm and she smiled at how pleased he seemed over the idea of having a daughter who looked like her.

A moment later, they pulled into the clinic's parking garage and Pippa's stomach burst into nervous flurries.

"Oh, my God," she breathed. "We're going to find out in just a little while."

Cam smiled faintly, then reached over to squeeze her hand again. "Let's go do it."

Maybe it was her nerves, but Cam looked like he'd rather be anywhere but sitting in the tiny room where the sonogram tech was about to perform the scan. He looked…tormented. There was raw emotion in his eyes and he kept glancing toward the door like he was seriously contemplating bolting for it.

She bit her lip and controlled the urge to reach for his hand. He wasn't even paying her any attention. He kept eyeing the tech and growing more uneasy by the minute. Instead, she took several calming breaths as the tech rolled her gown up and tucked it just over the slight swell of her belly.

She flinched when the cool gel smoothed over her skin and then the young man smiled at her as he placed the wand over her belly.

She strained closer as the blob took shape on the screen. Tears burned her eyelids when the tech explained that she was seeing the beating heart. She glanced over at Cam to see him equally awestruck. But there was such deep sadness in his eyes that she wondered what he could possibly be thinking.

Several long minutes later, the tech moved the wand again. "Ready to see what flavor of baby you're having?"

"Oh, yes," she whispered.

"Let's take a look here. Hopefully we won't have a shy one. Oh, hello! No shyness here. Look at the little guy."

Pippa sat forward as she stared in amazement at the tiny appendage that clearly signaled the baby's sex. "Oh, my God, it's a boy! Cam, we're having a son!"

Her excitement dimmed when she caught sight of Cam's expression. And then to her shock, he simply got up and walked out of the room, leaving her on the table with the image of their son still vivid on the monitor.

Cam walked straight out of the building. He shoved at the door, needing freedom, needing air. Tears burned his eyes and he was desperate to get as far away from anyone as possible.

The sunlight assaulted his senses. A cool breeze blew over his face, freezing the unshed tears in place. The knot in his throat was so big he didn't have a prayer of taking a breath. So he stood there, chest burning, throat so raw that it felt like he'd swallowed a razor.

A son. Another son.

Why couldn't it have been a daughter? No threat to the memory of Colton. And it wouldn't seem so damn much like he was replacing his first son with another. How could he even bear to look at this child, knowing he'd lost one before?

He fumbled for his cell, punched in his driver's number and then gave a terse order for him to collect Pippa from the clinic. He was being the worst sort of ass. He was walking away from her when she needed him the most. But he couldn't pretend. He couldn't smile and be excited when he felt like he was dying all over again. He wouldn't stand there and suck the joy from her.

After making sure John would take Pippa home, he turned and walked back to where his car was parked. In the past couple of months, he'd been staying more in the city so he could be closer to Pippa, but right now he wanted more than anything to retreat behind the iron gates of his Connecticut estate.

* * *

"He just left?" Pippa asked in bewilderment.

John looked discomfited as he led Pippa to where he'd parked the car. "I believe something urgent came up, Miss Laingley."

"Like what?" she demanded. "What could possibly be more important than this? And he couldn't simply tell me he had to leave?"

The more she pondered the matter, the more pissed she got. She was working herself into a righteous fury as John ushered her into the waiting car. All the way home, she fumed. This should have been special. They should even now be celebrating. Instead, she was on her way home alone not knowing what the hell kind of bug was up Cam's ass.

The past couple of months had been terrific. Cam had lightened up. He had seemed to relax his guard around her and didn't act so freaking stiff and uptight all the time anymore. They'd had fun together. If nothing else, they had become friends and for the first time Pippa hadn't looked to the future with gnawing uncertainty that somehow Cam wouldn't be in it for the long haul.

So much for that assumption.

What the hell was wrong with him?

John pulled up to her apartment but Pippa sat in the backseat for a long moment. Frowning, she leaned forward. "John, where did Cam say he was going? Do you know where he is now?"

"I believe he's returned to Greenwich."

Home? *Home?* What the ever-loving hell? This big emergency brought him home? Oh, hell, no. She'd had about enough of his volatile moods.

She sat back with a bounce. "Take me to Greenwich, John."

John did a double take in the rearview mirror. "Pardon?"

"You heard me. Take me to his damn cave."

"Perhaps it would be better if you called first. Mr. Hollingsworth doesn't like to be disturbed when he's in residence."

"I don't give a damn what Mr. Hollingsworth likes," she said sweetly. "Either you drive me or I'm taking a cab the entire way."

With a resigned sigh, John pulled back into traffic.

She stewed for another hour, and by the time they rolled up the long winding driveway of Cam's home, she was in a foul mood. He'd messed up everything and she was going to hear what his excuse was or else.

When John stopped in front of the house, Pippa was out before he could open his own door. She marched up the steps, considered knocking, but then decided if she came all this way she wasn't going to chance that he wouldn't answer.

She shoved the door open and went inside.

"Cam?" she yelled belligerently. "Where the hell are you?"

She stood a moment, waiting for him to appear, but she was met by resounding silence.

"Cam!" she yelled louder. "Get your ass down here!"

A moment later she heard footsteps and then he appeared at the top of the stairs, his brows furrowed.

"What the hell are you doing here, Pippa? Is something wrong?"

If it wouldn't take so much effort, she'd march up

the stairs and punch him. He had the nerve to act like he'd done nothing?

She shook her head, her fingers curling into a tight fist. She was already fantasizing about decking him.

"You ruined the most exciting thing that's ever happened to me and you have the nerve to ask if anything's wrong?"

He descended the stairs in a slow, methodical manner, his footsteps sounding ominous in the quiet. When he reached the bottom, he took a few more steps until he was a short distance away and then he stared coldly at her.

She shivered under his scrutiny. There was no warmth in his eyes. None of the friendship and caring he'd demonstrated over the past weeks.

"What on earth is your problem?"

"You came all this way to ask that?"

She refused to be put off by the censure in his tone. She closed the distance between them, poking her finger into his chest.

"I thought we were friends. I thought you cared a little about me or at least about our child. Friends don't pull what you pulled today. What were you thinking? You left me alone in that exam room and then had your driver come for me? I want to know what the hell your problem is."

"Not everything is about you, Pippa."

The ice in his voice just served to piss her off more because she knew he was holding back. Knew that something was wrong and he didn't trust her enough to tell her what it was. But what right did she have to pursue it? They were "friends." Nothing more. He didn't owe her anything. It hurt to remind herself of that little fact.

"I thought we were *at least* friends," she whispered, her voice cracking with emotion.

She turned away, realizing just how stupid she'd been to come here at all. It was the one place she wasn't welcome. Had never been welcome since that night when they'd first slept together. He hadn't been able to get rid of her fast enough the next morning and he'd never, ever brought her back here. They met in the city. Never here.

She *needed* this reminder because she'd come dangerously close to building larger expectations. Creating a fantasyland where she actually had a chance at a future with this man.

"Don't bother coming to the next appointment," she said stiffly, her back still to him. She began walking to the door and had almost reached it when he caught her hand. She hadn't even heard him come up behind her.

"Pippa."

The single word conveyed a wealth of emotion. Regret. Sorrow.

She paused, her hand trembling in his.

"I'm sorry," he said quietly. "Please don't leave like this."

She yanked around, fighting to keep angry, frustrated tears at bay. "Why, Cam? Give me one good reason. You don't want me here. I don't even know why we're pretending to have any sort of a relationship at all. Let's just cut our losses and get it over with now."

"I don't like anyone to come here," he said harshly. "It's not personal to you. But… Just stay. I'm sorry for the way the appointment went. I was an ass. I ruined your moment."

"Our moment," she corrected. "It was *our* moment, Cam. It was our child's moment when he was revealed to his parents. It was a moment that neither of us should have ever been able to forget, but in all honesty, I now don't want to remember. Because how will I ever explain to my child that his father walked out the moment it was told to us we were having a son?"

Cam flinched and went pale and those vivid blue eyes stared back at her, flashing with so much dark emotion.

The tears she'd tried so hard to hold back slid down her cheeks as she stood shaking before him. And then she was in his arms. He hugged her tightly. So tightly she couldn't breathe. His body shook against her. She could feel his rapid pulse jumping against his skin.

"Don't cry," he whispered. "I'm so sorry, Pippa. Please just stay. I'm sorry. You didn't deserve this. Forgive me, please."

And then he was kissing her. Hot, breathless, almost desperate. He touched her, frantically, as if his need for her was the most important single thing in the world. Like she was the single most important thing in his world.

She felt his sorrow, his uncertainty. It rolled off him in waves. His despair and grief. His regret. There was so much emotion churning inside him that it was tangible and thick in the air.

And then his touch became gentler, became more beseeching, almost as if he was begging her not to deny him. To touch him back. To offer him the comfort he seemed to crave.

She was unable to remain cold and distant when he was crumbling before her. She kissed him back, her breath hiccuping softly over his lips. And then she slid her palm across the slight bristle of his jaw, cupping his cheek in a simple gesture of acceptance and understanding. Of forgiveness.

He swept her into his arms as if she weighed nothing and carried her into one of the downstairs bedrooms. Leaving the door open, he moved to the bed and eased her down onto the mattress.

He hung over her, his eyes fierce and hungry. Her breath caught when he came down over her, hard and unrelenting. His mouth claimed hers once more and it was several long seconds before she could breathe again.

Impatiently he pulled at her sundress, tugging it free of her body before tossing it aside. He quickly divested her of her underwear until finally she was naked beneath him.

Then his expression changed. Some of the darkness faded and he stared down in wonder. Carefully his palms slid over her slim form to the gentle swell of her belly. He cupped it, and then to her shock, he lowered his head and kissed the firm bump.

"I'm sorry," he whispered again.

Emotion knotted his throat, making the words almost indistinguishable, but the harsh apology hit her right in the heart. Nobody who heard it could possibly think he didn't regret his actions with all his heart. He was essentially stripped and bare, standing before her starkly vulnerable.

She gently wrapped her arms around him to pull him close. "It's all right, Cam."

She pulled him higher to fuse his mouth with hers. Their tongues flirted and played and then he plunged deeper, overwhelming her with his essence. His body moved possessively over hers, though he was careful not to put his weight on her abdomen.

He kissed her neck, in turns gentle and then rougher until she was sure she'd wear marks the next day. He licked and nibbled at her skin, sucking lightly as he made his way lower.

When he got to her breasts, he hovered just over one of the tips and then tilted his head up so he could meet her gaze.

"Are they more sensitive now?" he asked huskily.

He ran his thumb over one crest as he awaited her response. A shudder worked over her body.

"Yes, definitely."

"Then I'll be extra careful."

With infinite tenderness, he slowly ran his tongue over one rigid peak before sucking it into his mouth. She came off the bed, arching helplessly into him as wave upon wave rolled over her.

It had been a long time since that careless night between them. She wanted him desperately. The past weeks had been a form of torture. He'd been so attentive and caring, yet there was an almost tangible barrier between them.

She was pretty sure this solved nothing, but she longed for physical contact. She needed it.

With a blissful sigh, she surrendered to those skilled lips of his.

But then he moved down, cupping her belly between his large hands and he proceeded to kiss every inch of the taut flesh until tears burned her eyelids.

He moved lower still, spreading her thighs as he settled down on the bed. His mouth found her heat and she nearly came apart on the spot.

He cupped her buttocks, holding her in place for his

seeking tongue. He took long, sensuous swipes, the roughness of his tongue a contrast to his gentle sucking.

Her fingers dug into his hair, and she became more restless, nearly wild as she moved in rhythm with his intimate caresses.

"Cam, please," she begged. "I need you."

His feet were off the bed, and he stood, his hands curled around her legs. He pulled her forward so that her behind rested on the edge of the mattress.

"Wrap your legs around me," he said roughly.

As soon as she did, he slid into her.

The shock of his hardness made her gasp. Skin on skin. No barriers this time.

His groan was a harsh exhalation in the silence.

His fingers dug into her hips, pulling her closer to him. Then he released her and smoothed his hands over her belly, his fingers suddenly a lot gentler than they'd been just moments before.

"Don't let me hurt you."

She reached for him, pulling him down so their bodies met and his heat enveloped her. "I know you won't hurt me, Cam," she whispered. "Love me."

It was the closest she'd come to spilling what was in her heart. She'd held back because she knew he wouldn't welcome her feelings.

He claimed her mouth. His movements were urgent, a layer of desperation buried deep. His hands were everywhere, caressing, stroking, touching, as if he couldn't get enough of what he wanted. As if he wanted her closer still.

She wrapped her body around him, holding him as he drove deeper inside her. Release wasn't as important as the intimacy of the moment. The connection between them that was being established.

This wasn't…sex. It was so much more.

She kissed the side of his neck and then bit her lip to keep the words she so wanted to say from escaping. Instead, she inhaled his scent and molded her body more fiercely to his.

Pleasure was warm and sweet as it slid through her veins. Her release was a slow rise, no sharp edges or tumultuous explosions. Higher and higher she crept until every muscle in her body tensed in expectation.

"Cam!"

It was a cry of need. It was a plea for help.

She felt him in every part of her body. Hard, so very powerful. His muscles bunched and he tensed above her. He whispered her name and she felt him let go.

For a long moment he held himself just above her before finally lowering his body to hers.

He was like a warm blanket, the very best kind. He pressed his forehead to hers, kissing her with light smooching sounds as their lips met again and again.

"Pippa," he whispered.

It conveyed a wealth of things, that single word.

Chapter 12

For a moment after Pippa awoke she was disoriented. It took her a few seconds to realize where she was and that she'd fallen asleep. She rolled, searching for a clock, and then breathed a sigh of relief. She'd napped for only an hour.

She sat up, glancing around the dark room. Cam was nowhere to be found, but she was starting to suspect he didn't stick around after sex.

With a sigh, she got up to look for her clothing, but then she saw that a robe had been laid out on the bed. Apparently he wasn't completely thoughtless.

She pulled on the robe and headed for the bathroom to shower and change. Okay, so maybe she shouldn't have had sex with him. It certainly didn't solve anything, but then again, it hadn't made things any more complicated than they already were. She wasn't going to spend any time beating herself up over it because the simple truth was she wanted it.

Her problem was quite a bit more complicated because she'd been stupid enough to fall in love with a man who had no desire to return that love. Worse, she was pregnant with his child so she'd be tied to him forever. Even when he eventually married someone else.

Her stomach churned and she closed her eyes as she completed her quick shower. She didn't think she could handle another woman participating in the care of her child. A stepmother for her son.

Okay, she had to stop this because she'd just make herself crazy. For now, there were answers she wanted from Cam.

Her lips firmed and she sucked in a deep breath. No one could ever accuse her of taking the path of least resistance. What did she have to lose, anyway? It wasn't as if she had to worry about him telling her to take a hike.

Laughter bubbled in her throat as she walked out of the bedroom a few minutes later, her stride determined. Maybe that crap worked with other women, but it wasn't going to work with her.

She found him in the downstairs office. His back was to the door and he was staring sightlessly into the night. For a moment she studied his profile, reluctant to intrude even if she was determined to force a confrontation.

His hands were shoved into the pockets of his slacks and there was a bleakness to his expression that made her breath catch in her throat. Then he turned fully and saw her standing in the doorway.

"Are you hungry?" he asked.

She was, but that wasn't what she wanted to discuss.

"I'd like to talk first," she said in an even voice.

He blew out his breath as if he knew there was no getting around the inevitable.

She started forward, determined she wouldn't let him shrug this off. "Cam, I need to know why the idea of our son haunts you so. You were perfectly happy at the idea of a daughter, and the moment it was revealed that this baby is a boy, you couldn't get away fast enough."

He went completely pale, and his eyes became dull, dead orbs.

Then he closed his eyes and his lips tightened. For a long moment he seemed to do battle with himself. At one point she was sure he'd throw her out. He looked furious and devastated by turns.

What had happened to make him this way?

And then finally he opened his eyes and stared lifelessly back at her. She knew she'd won, but why didn't she feel like this was a victory?

"All right. We'll talk. After dinner."

She very nearly forced the confrontation here and now, but something held her back. Maybe he needed the time to prepare himself. She could give him that.

He herded her toward the kitchen, seated her at the island that doubled as a bar and then went to the refrigerator. He grimaced as he glanced back at her.

"I'm afraid our choices are somewhat limited. My housekeeper freezes meals for me and stocks the pantry, but I don't do much cooking. I eat out a lot."

She slipped off the bar stool and rounded the corner of the island. She waved him off with her hand. "Let me. I can whip us up something with what you have on hand."

"And have you think my hospitality sucks?"

She leveled a stare at him. "Your hospitality *does* suck. Sit and I'll make us something to eat. Then you're going to talk."

He winced at her bluntness but took the stool she'd vacated while she surveyed the contents of the pantry. She wanted something quick because she wasn't going to wait all damn night for this come-to-Jesus moment with Cam. Nor was she going to give him enough time to think better of his promise and toss her out without explaining himself.

She found fresh croissants and decided on melted ham and cheese. There was an array of fruit so she made a quick fruit salad while waiting for the croissants to toast up in the oven.

She set the table with honey mustard, mayo and the fruit salad and then went back for glasses.

"What would you like to drink?" she asked after checking on the croissants again.

Cam got up and hurried around to the wine cabinet. Then he paused and turned back around. "I guess wine is out. What do you usually drink?"

She smiled. "Water. Decaf tea. Fruit juice sometimes, but it gives me awful indigestion. Mostly water."

"I'll have water, too, then."

She set glasses out and filled them with water from the fridge. Then she went to take the cookie sheet from the oven. After depositing the toasted croissants onto their plates, she took a seat next to Cam.

"This is good," he said after finishing the first croissant. "Seemed easy, too. I wouldn't have thought of doing something like this."

Pippa smiled. "I'm the queen of improvising in the kitchen. Growing up, we didn't have very many family meals together, so I learned early to make do with what we had."

He cocked his head to the side. "You don't talk about your family much."

She nearly snorted. It was on the tip of her tongue to tell him he didn't, either, but she didn't want to shut that particular door before it was ever opened.

"Not much to talk about," she said lightly.

His eyes narrowed. "Why do I think otherwise?"

She shrugged. "No idea."

"Oh, come on. Give me a bone here. Do you see your family?"

She sighed. "Yeah, I see my mother when she doesn't give me enough advance warning so I'm sure not to be around."

He winced. "Ouch. That doesn't sound very healthy."

"Oh, it's a lot healthier when we don't see each other."

"What about your dad?"

Pippa sagged, putting down her half-eaten croissant. "He split when I was younger. Not that I can entirely blame him. My mother was difficult to say the least. He died a few years ago and left me the money I'm currently surviving on until I get my business up and running."

Cam frowned. "You're obviously not close to your family."

"Give the man a cigar," she drawled. "Did anyone ever tell you how observant you are?"

"Cut the sarcasm, Pippa. Talk to me here."

"You know, your gall astonishes me. We're supposed to be talking about you. That was the deal."

His jaw tightened and bulged. "It solves nothing."

"Oh, yeah? Maybe not for you. But see, here's the thing. I'm having your baby, and I kind of need to know

if I can expect more outbursts like today. Like maybe
you run out on his birthday party because you suddenly
can't deal. We're going to talk about it, Cam, because if
we don't, I'm out of here and I won't be back."

"Is that a threat, Pippa?"

She met his gaze without blinking. "I'm not threatening you. I'm making you a promise."

He shoved his plate aside and got up, nearly knocking the stool over. He stalked out of the kitchen and into
the living room, his hands shoved tightly into his pants
pockets.

Undaunted, she followed, coming to a stop a few feet
behind him. For a long moment, Cam faced away from
her, anger radiating in waves. Then he jerked around,
his eyes ablaze.

"I had another son. Colton. And a wife. Elise."

Pippa's eyes widened in surprise. She hadn't expected
this. She opened her mouth, then snapped it shut again.

"Nothing to say?" he snapped.

She ignored the anger that emanated from him, knew
it was how he was maintaining control when he was
barely hanging on. Suddenly she understood a lot of
things. She wouldn't prod the wounded lion and she
wouldn't get angry and defensive over his terseness.

"What happened?" she asked softly.

"I lost them. I lost them both. He was just a baby. The
most beautiful, sweet baby in the world. Elise was…
She was wonderful. Young. Vibrant. So full of life. She
was a wonderful mother."

Pain vibrated in his voice and her heart clenched at
the grief still evident in his eyes.

"I could bear the thought of a daughter," he choked

out. "I even looked forward to it. But not a son. It feels too much like I'm replacing Colton."

Her mouth fell open in shock. She wanted to immediately deny that by having another son he was somehow replacing his first child, but she remained silent. It may make no sense to her, but it was evident by the torment in Cam's eyes that he absolutely believed it.

How could she argue with something so deeply ingrained?

She stood there a long moment, trying to make sense of it. She looked down at the tiny swell of her belly and was overwhelmed by a fierce need to protect her baby. She glanced back up at Cam, her jaw as tight as his had been.

Anger and sorrow warred inside her. Sorrow for him. For such a horrific loss. But anger that her child would pay the price.

"So you'd deny this child your love because he had the misfortune to be born the wrong sex?"

Cam's nostrils flared and his eyes flashed with anger. He advanced toward her, bristling with outrage. "I never said that."

"But nothing you've said or done so far tells me any different."

He dragged a hand through his hair, rumpling it even more than it already was. "I'm trying here, Pippa. I'm trying really damn hard. You know I didn't want this."

"I get that! Okay? I understand. Believe me, you've made yourself more than clear on the matter. You didn't want me. You didn't want our child. But you know what? He didn't have a choice in the matter. It's not his fault his parents are brainless twits who didn't do enough to prevent his conception. But you know what else? I'm not sorry."

She broke off, her chest heaving.

"I'm not sorry," she said again, more fiercely this time. "I'll never be sorry that the condom broke. I want this child. I want our son. If you want to wallow in the past and deny yourself the miracle that this child is, that's your problem. But I don't have to put up with your stupid crap."

She turned around and stomped toward the front door, yanking up the purse she'd dropped when she'd stormed in earlier. She really had no idea if John was around. At this point, she didn't care. She'd walk to Ashley's if she had to.

"Pippa!"

She yanked open the front door, walked out into the night and then slammed it behind her.

Oh, boy, was she an idiot. She'd fallen into bed with him. Even after he'd ditched her at the doctor's office. He'd been clear from the start, and yet she kept agreeing to see him. Like she had some desperate hope that she was going to be the one to heal him.

She stalked down the driveway, determined to put as much distance between herself and the source of her stupidity as possible.

"Pippa! Damn it! What the hell do you think you're doing?"

She flinched as Cam roared at her from the doorway. She pulled out her cell, hoping like hell that Ashley was home tonight. If not, it was going to be a long-ass walk to public transportation.

When she reached the end of the driveway and turned toward Ashley's house, the beam of headlights flashed over her and the growl of an engine sounded. Cam pulled up beside her and rolled his window down.

"Get into the damn truck, Pippa. This is insane."

She turned to look at him, never breaking stride. "What's insane is me staying at your house another minute. I'm going to Ashley's. I'll be fine."

He swore a streak that scorched her ears. Then he pulled the SUV in front of her and stopped on the shoulder. He got out and strode back to meet her.

"Look, at least let me give you a ride to Ashley's. You don't need to be out walking around in the dark alone."

"As long as you promise to drive straight to Ashley's."

"Get in," he growled.

She walked around to the passenger's side, got in and slammed the door shut. She didn't even look his way when he got back in and put the SUV in Drive.

When he started to speak, she jerked around and put her hand out to silence him. "Just save it, Cam. I don't want to hear it."

He fell silent again and turned into Devon and Ashley's driveway. He pulled to the front and she slipped out almost before he came to a full stop. She slammed the door shut and walked toward the front door, never once looking back.

Ashley opened the door before she got there and only then did Cam pull away.

"Pippa? What on earth is going on?"

Tears filled Pippa's eyes as she stopped in front of her friend. "I need a place to stay tonight, Ash. Is it okay if I crash here?"

Chapter 13

"Look, Dev, I know he's your friend, but he makes me crazy," Pippa said.

Devon handed her a glass of juice with a look of sympathy.

"He's a hard-ass, honey. Always has been."

Ashley wrapped her arms around Pippa, or at least as much as she could with a bulging, ginormous belly. The two of them looked like poster children for fertility. Only, Ashley had a loving husband—at least Devon was over the moon about the impending birth of his child.

Pippa sniffled and swallowed some of the juice even knowing she'd suffer for it later.

"I can't believe he's so freaked because we're having a boy."

Devon glanced uneasily at both women, and who could blame him? One pregnant hormonal woman was enough, but two? He was probably ready to either start drinking or run screaming into the night. Maybe both.

"I get that it's hard to lose people you love. I suppose some part of me should be all, 'Awww, you poor thing,' and fawn all over him, pat him on the back and be understanding, but damn it, I can't do that!"

Pippa wiped angrily at her face and leaned forward on the couch to put her glass on the coffee table.

Devon slowly shook his head. "No, Pippa, I think you did right. Sympathy is the last thing he needs. Cam is my oldest friend, but it's time for him to move on with his life and stop rehashing and living in the past."

She nodded miserably. "It makes me seem heartless and I'm not. Really. It breaks my heart to see him so tortured but how does he think it'll make *our* child feel to know he was rejected because his father didn't want to make it look like he was replacing his first son with his second?"

"You're protecting your baby," Ashley said in a fierce voice. "You should never apologize for that. Cam's an idiot."

Pippa cringed. "It doesn't make you an idiot to mourn people you love. I get that. I do. What makes him an idiot is not being able to look past something horrific and see that he's being given a second chance. This baby won't replace Colton. No one could ever do that. I don't know how to make Cam see that. At this point, I don't even know if I want to try. I'm tired. Tired of this stupid game we're playing where we both pretend that we don't want more and that we're happy having this superficial relationship. I'm not happy. I'll never be happy with a man who gives me only a part of himself. I'm a selfish bitch. I want it all."

Devon cracked a grin and Ashley hugged her all over again. Pippa remained in her friend's arms for a long moment, soaking up every bit of comfort she could.

"You may not see this now, Pippa, but I think you're the best thing that ever happened to Cam," Devon said.

Pippa sighed. "Oh, I agree. I'm not some martyr who refuses to see her own value."

"Atta girl," Devon said.

Ashley squeezed her.

Pippa crumpled into Ashley's arms again, her misery overwhelming her. "God, Ash, I slept with him again. Tonight. After he ditched me at the clinic. After that spectacular demonstration of support, I still slept with him. Someone needs to lock me in my apartment for my own good."

Devon cleared his throat. "I, um, think I'll leave you two alone now. If you need anything, holler."

Pippa watched in amusement as Devon all but ran from the room. Then she sighed and leaned her head on Ashley's shoulder.

"I'm stupid, Ash. He's stupid. We're both stupid and I still love him."

Ashley laughed softly. "Not stupid. Sometimes you can't help who you love. God knows there were times I wished not to love Devon with everything I had."

"He was a bonehead there for a while," Pippa acknowledged. "I guess that was what gave me hope with Cam. I thought maybe he'd come around. I'm an idiot. You can say it."

"You're not an idiot! You're smart and brave and I love you."

Pippa smiled. "I love you, too, Ash. Sorry for getting you all wet and disturbing your evening with Dev."

"Oh, like I didn't crash at your place for days and sob and weep all over you like a dishrag."

"Yeah, you did, but it all worked out in the end." Her lips turned down into an unhappy frown. "I don't see that being the case here. Cam seems too comfortable in his misery."

"He's really not so bad, Pip," Ashley said softly.

"You're not in love with him," Pippa pointed out. "You're not facing an impossible future tied to him but relegated to being a nobody in his life. Not that I would have ever acted this way, but I'm beginning to see why some women don't tell the father of their baby that they're pregnant."

"You're hurting now, but you did the right thing. You'll see. It'll work out, Pip. You have to believe it. Cam will come around. He'll take one look at his child and be a complete goner."

Pippa raised her head from Ashley's shoulder. "I hope you're right."

The next day, Pippa rode into the city with Devon and had him drop her off at her café. She was getting so close to the grand-opening date, and as a result, her nerves were near to exploding.

All the paperwork was in order. Her first supplies had been delivered and her kitchen was set up with everything she could possibly need to start baking. All she had to do was…start.

She had a list of items she intended to have out on opening day. She'd already placed ads for the employees she wanted to hire. She needed at least one person to help man the front and an assistant in the kitchen as well as a delivery driver for when she began taking catering jobs.

She was finally, *finally* realizing her dream of opening her own business and she'd never been so scared in her life.

After making a few calls to set up interviews, she unpacked the delivery and put everything away. The more she thought about her grand-opening date, the more she wanted to hyperventilate into a paper bag.

But this is what she'd been working for. Cam had certainly made it a lot easier for her, but she would have accomplished it on her own. It might have taken her a few more months, but she would have done it. He'd only facilitated the matter.

Her cell phone rang and she went completely still. Then she pulled it out of her pocket and stared at the screen for confirmation of what she already knew. Her mother had her own ring tone. It was as unmistakable as Miranda herself.

"Boy, do you have rotten timing," Pippa muttered.

She briefly contemplated letting it go to voice mail, but that would be cowardly of her and then she'd have to listen to Miranda complain that her daughter was avoiding her. Okay, it was absolutely true, but if Pippa didn't answer, Miranda would simply persist. Better to have done with it now.

Besides, Miranda was harmless. Clueless, but utterly harmless.

With a resigned sigh, she punched the answer button and then put the phone to her ear.

"Hello, Mom."

"Pippa, darling! Hello! Long time no talk. How are you?"

Pippa smiled despite herself. She always felt guilty about avoiding her mom. She knew in her heart of hearts that Miranda did love her. It wasn't her fault she was... Well, Pippa wasn't entirely certain how to describe her mother. *Harmless* worked well enough because Pippa truly didn't believe her mother ever *tried* to be malicious.

"I'm good, Mom. How are you? How is Paris?"

"Oh, Paris was wonderful, but we're on to Greece now. It's so warm and sunshiny. I'm sure it's much better than spring in the city. Don't you think?"

"How is Doug?"

Pippa held her breath, hoping that she hadn't just stuck her foot in her mouth. Was her mother still with Doug? She'd left the country with him, but one never knew with Miranda. She was just as likely to fall in love in Paris and go off with someone else. Miranda fell in love like most people changed underwear.

"He's having a wonderful time. We both are. He sends you his love."

That amused Pippa given that she'd never actually met the man. She was sure he was perfectly nice. But she doubted she'd ever know firsthand because it would be a miracle if her mother actually made it back home with the same guy.

In a lot of ways, Miranda reminded Pippa of a child who'd been given more Christmas presents than she knew what to do with. She'd pick one up, ooh and aah, and then promptly drop it and move on to the next one.

That was Miranda's love life in a nutshell.

"When do you think you'll be back?" Pippa asked casually.

She hadn't talked to her mom in months. Miranda

didn't know that Pippa was pregnant and she was racked with indecision over whether to break the news to her. It would likely devastate her mother, who considered herself far too young and beautiful to be called a grandmother.

While some part of Pippa did long to share the news, she couldn't bring herself to ruin Miranda's trip. And it would ruin it. She'd spend the rest of her time wailing that she was too young and asking Doug or whatever guy was her current lover for reassurance that she didn't *look* like a grandmother.

"Oh, I don't know. We're having such fun. There's no hurry, you know? Life's too short. Unless you need me? Is there something wrong, Pippa, darling?"

The hope in Miranda's voice decided the matter for Pippa.

"No, Mom. Have a good time, okay? We'll talk more later."

"Love you, dear Pippa."

"Love you, too," Pippa murmured as she rang off.

After shoving the phone back into her pocket, Pippa stood in her kitchen for a long moment, feeling the weight of emotion settle over her shoulders. It was always like this after she spoke to her mother. Regret that she couldn't have a normal relationship with her own mom. She wanted a mom like Ashley's.

Gloria Copeland fiercely loved her children. She was a rock, always there, offering unconditional love and support. If Ashley needed her mom, she was there. No questions asked.

While Miranda might have the best of intentions, and she really did love her daughter, she just didn't have it in her to be…maternal. The concept was as alien to

Miranda as settling down with one man for more than a few months.

Pippa had always considered her mother to be very much like a butterfly. Flitting from one thing to the next, never staying in one place for very long.

Pippa herself preferred being a homebody. The idea of deviating from her routine gave her hives. She liked the city. Loved her circle of friends. Loved doing the same things every day. Maybe that made her a coward. Maybe she'd never go out into the world and take it on bare-handed. But she knew what she liked. Knew what she wanted. And she simply wouldn't settle for less.

After putting the last of her things away, she went out the front and locked up. When she turned toward the street, she saw Cam's driver standing there waiting beside the car. She shook her head. She should have known.

John looked pointedly at her and then opened the door and gestured her over. With a sigh, she climbed into the backseat.

Her pride wasn't such that she'd turn down even the short ride to her apartment. She didn't mind walking, but now that her belly was protruding more every day, her feet were paying the price.

John dropped her off in front of her apartment and admonished her to apprise him of her schedule for the next day. After arranging a pickup time, she mounted the steps to her front door only to find a basket with a large blue bow on the stoop.

She unlocked her door, pushed it open and then reached down for the basket to take it inside. After dropping her keys and sweater on the table in the foyer, she went into the living room and deposited the basket on the coffee table.

There was a card attached just below the bow and she opened it.

Forgive me.

Cam.

She hastily reached into the basket and pulled out a tiny Yankees uniform in a newborn size. She broke out in a smile as her vision blurred with unshed tears. It was adorable. The very first outfit for her baby boy.

There was a teddy bear. A baseball and tiny catcher's mitt. And two tickets to the next home game at Yankee Stadium.

If Cam had been there she would have thrown her arms around him and all would have been forgiven. Which was why she was glad he was nowhere near her.

It was a fault of hers. She was too forgiving. She couldn't let herself be a doormat while Cam waffled back and forth like some sick version of Jekyll and Hyde.

But the idea of him hurting, even as much as he'd hurt her, made her heart squeeze. He had five more months to get over this notion that their son was somehow replacing the child he'd lost. Surely that was enough time. Wasn't it?

"Oh, Cam," she whispered. "What am I going to do about you? About us?"

All she could do was take it one day at a time and hope and pray that Cam came around. Because if he didn't? She and their son would lose, and she'd do anything at all to spare her son the pain of a father who didn't want him.

Chapter 14

It was the big day and it felt like Pippa had swallowed a giant rock. She'd been up the entire night before—baking, cleaning, arranging and stressing. Being the wonderful friend she was, Carly had hung out with Pippa until dawn. Pippa had shooed Ashley home much earlier. The poor woman was due to pop any day now and she was miserable.

But everyone had promised to return for the 9:00 a.m. grand opening of Pippa's Place.

"Your displays are gorgeous, Pip," Carly said. "What time are your employees coming in?"

Pippa wiped her forehead with the back of her hand. "Any moment now. I could have had them in overnight to help, but to be honest, I'm too much of a control freak. I want everything just so for the first day. After this I can leave the shop in capable hands when needed."

Carly laughed. Then she impulsively hugged Pippa. "You need some rest, hon. You look exhausted."

"No rest for the weary today," she said with a crooked grin. "I don't close until this afternoon and I'm hoping to draw a large crowd. Cam might have gone a little overboard advertising the big event. Let's just hope he didn't oversell me and nobody likes my cooking."

"Not going to happen," Carly said firmly.

The front bell jangled and Pippa stuck her head through the kitchen door dividing the kitchen from the rest of the space. She waved her employee back and gave her instructions for stocking the displays with the remaining cupcakes and cookies.

She busied herself with cleaning the kitchen while Carly greeted the second employee and put her to work. Pippa thought about the delivery van, which was parked in front of the shop today. It provided great advertising with its cheerful color and the shop name displayed predominately on the side.

After her illegal drive through the city, she'd spent the next few weeks getting her driver's license even though she hoped she never had to actually drive the thing herself.

Satisfied that her kitchen was in order, she went into the bathroom to repair her appearance. What she really needed was a shower, but she didn't have time to go home.

"Pippa, you in there?"

She cracked open the bathroom door to see Carly and Tabitha both standing there. They started to crowd in, both carrying cosmetic bags.

"We're here to do your hair and makeup," Tabitha announced.

Pippa smiled, put the seat of the toilet down and sat so her friends could fuss over her. Peace replaced the overwhelming sense of panic. This was it. Her dream was coming true today. It hadn't gone exactly as she planned, but she wouldn't change a single thing.

Already she loved her son with a fierceness that surprised her. She hadn't imagined being so connected to another life in quite this way. She talked to him every day. Sang to him at night. Read him stories while she lounged on the sofa after a long day of dealing with business stuff.

Her child had given her a purpose. She was even more determined to succeed. To be a mom her son would be proud of. She never wanted her kid to feel about her the way she felt about her own mother.

Where Miranda was more concerned for her own happiness than that of her child, Pippa was never going to go that route. Her son would be the single most important person in her life.

For the next half hour, Tabitha and Carly kept up a lively stream of chatter as they applied makeup and touched up her hair. Pippa's heart was full of love for her friends. They were working hard to keep her mind off the impending grand opening and to allay her nervousness.

Just as they finished the last brush of the mascara wand, the door burst open and Ashley and Sylvia tried to shove inside.

"Pippa, you have to come see!" Ashley exclaimed.

She grabbed Pippa's hand and hauled her toward the front. As they stumbled into the eating area, Pippa's eyes rounded in shock.

People. Lots and lots of people!

All crowded outside the entrance to her shop. Waiting for her to open. And her employees, bless their hearts, were outside circulating with cups of hot coffee and samples of her baked goods.

Tears gathered and Carly whispered fiercely in her ear. "Don't you dare mess up that mascara!"

Pippa laughed and then excitedly hugged all her friends.

Half an hour later, the doors opened and the customers surged in. There was much laughter as all of Pippa's friends helped serve the crush of people.

For two hours there was no end to the line of people. As fast as they could ring customers up, others came in droves.

It was past noon when Pippa looked up and saw Cam stride through the front door, shoving his way past a line of customers. He sought her out and then fixed his stare on her as he moved toward the counter.

"Go on," Ashley whispered. "I'll take the register for a while."

"You sure?" Pippa looked doubtfully at her friend. "You've been on your feet for a long time, Ash. Maybe you should take a break. Devon's going to kill me for wearing you out."

Ashley smiled. "I'm having fun and I get to eat all the cupcakes I want. Total win!"

Pippa grinned back and then stepped away from the counter to meet Cam around the side.

"Looks like you've drawn a huge crowd," Cam said when she got close enough for her to hear him.

"It's fantastic! I can't believe it. We've been hopping all morning."

Cam smiled. "Can I get a cup of coffee and a few minutes of your time?"

She glanced over at her friends, who were waving her on and giving her the okay signal that they were fine handling the customers. She waved back and said to Cam, "Okay, you've got me for a few minutes."

She poured him a cup of coffee, grabbed a pastry, a croissant and a cupcake and then motioned him into the kitchen.

They walked through to the office at the very rear of the shop. She closed the door behind them and then took a seat at the small desk. Or rather she sagged into it.

"Oh, my God, I may never get back up." She groaned.

His eyes narrowed in concern. "When was the last time you slept? Have you been here all night?"

"It's been a while," she said ruefully. "And yeah, I was here all night getting ready."

"You should rest. That can't be good for you or the baby."

"I won't argue that point. I plan to go straight home and sleep about twelve hours before I get up tomorrow and do it all over again."

He was silent a long moment. He looked for the world like he wanted to argue. His lips were set in a line and his jaw ticked. He ran a hand through his hair. To her surprise, he seemed unsure of himself.

"I wanted to come by to see how it was going. But mostly I wanted to say once more that I'm sorry for what happened at the clinic. I'm trying, Pippa. I know you probably don't believe that, but I am trying to deal with this."

She pushed the coffee and the plate of yummies at

him, her heart melting just a little at the vulnerability she saw in those troubled eyes of his.

"Tell me how awesome I am," she teased as she held up the cupcake.

He looked suspiciously at the cupcake piled high with fluffy pink icing. Unable to resist the opening, she swiped a finger full and then smeared it over his lips.

He reared back in surprise but his tongue automatically came out to lick away the sticky frosting. Then he took the cupcake from her and carefully peeled away the wrapper. He took a cautious bite and then stared down at it as if trying to figure out the mysteries of the universe.

"Okay, you're awesome."

"I know," she said smugly. "Damn good, isn't it?"

He took another bite and then smiled. "Yeah. Does this mean I'm forgiven?"

She cocked her head to the side and decided to let down her guard. "That depends on where you take me to dinner tonight. I'm starving and I want a steak. I'm sugared out from eating my own goodies. Me and baby want red meat."

She waited for the flinch. The inevitable reaction when he was reminded of the son she carried. But he didn't react. He actually seemed hugely relieved that she'd taken the matter in hand and barged forward. Well, that was typical Pippa. Bull in a china closet and all that.

"I'd like that," he said in a somber voice. "I'll make early reservations for us so you can get home and rest. I have a meeting in a little while but I'll swing back by at closing time, run you by your apartment if you want to change and then we'll go eat."

"That sounds awesome," she said with a sigh.

He rose from his seat and then held a hand out to help

her up. "You've done a great job making this place your own, Pippa. By the looks of that crowd, I'd say they agree with me. You have a solid success on your hands."

She squeezed his hand as she came around the desk. "I owe a lot of it to you. If you hadn't gotten me this great place, I'd probably still be looking for space to lease."

"I was glad to do it. You've worked hard for this."

Part of her was saddened by the slight awkwardness between them and the almost formal way they danced around each other. She longed for the easy friendship that she'd come to rely on over the past few months. If she couldn't have a more intimate relationship with him, she'd at least take friendship. Anything but this unease between them.

She gave him a quick hug to convey that she was seemingly unaffected by all that had transpired and then herded him back through the kitchen and out the front, where there was still a steady stream of customers spilling into the shop.

He hesitated a moment as they stood at the counter and then he leaned in to brush his lips across her cheek. "I'll see you in a few hours. Try to take it easy, okay?"

As he walked away, she raised trembling fingers to the place he'd kissed her.

Hot and cold. She could never figure out where she stood with him and it pissed her off. One thing she knew for certain—she wasn't going to wait around forever while he got his act together.

Chapter 15

Cam drove past Pippa's café to see the open sign go out and lights start to flicker off inside. He gave the voice command to dial Pippa's cell and then turned to circle the block.

After a few rings, she answered, her breathless voice doing odd things to his insides.

"I'll just be a minute," she said by way of greeting.

"No hurry. I'm circling the block. I'll pull up so you can just come out."

He maneuvered the SUV through traffic and waited for the light to turn so he could turn back onto her street. He tapped his thumbs impatiently on the steering wheel and he realized that he was anxious to see her again.

It didn't compute. He had this sick love-hate relationship going on. He wanted to be as far from her as possible. She made him nervous. She looked at him like she could see right past the front he put on.

At the same time, when he was away even a short period of time, he got anxious. He needed to know she was okay, that she had everything she needed. That she was safe. And hell, if he was honest, he just wanted to see her again.

He had to let go of his pain. He had to move on. But how did one ever just decide that sort of thing? At what point did the hurting stop? At what point did one stop being gripped by paralyzing fear over the thought of losing someone you cared about?

He didn't have the answers, and until he did, this thing between him and Pippa would never work. He didn't want it to work.

Which didn't explain why he was circling the block, anxious to see her again. It made no sense. He should be at home. He should have never apologized, though he certainly owed her the apology and more. But he should have let it go, allowed her to remain angry with him. In the end it was kinder to both of them. A clean break. No remorse. No recriminations. No dragging it out only to rehash it all again later.

But he wanted to see her. He wanted… He wanted her. On his own terms. He recognized the selfishness of it and yet he couldn't stop himself from craving her. In or out of bed. It mattered little to him. He just wanted to be near her because, God help him, he felt more alive whenever she walked into a room.

He slowed as he approached her shop and leaned forward to see if she was waiting. She was at her door, locking up, the wind blowing through her dark hair. Then she turned and he was struck by the picture she presented. Young, vibrant, beautiful.

She saw him and waved, her face lighting up with a gorgeous smile. She hurried forward, one hand cupped to her belly and the other hanging on to her purse. He stopped and leaned over to push open the door for her. She climbed in, melted into the seat with a sweet sigh and then turned that dazzling smile on him.

It was like being kicked in the stomach.

"It is sooo nice to be off my feet," she said.

Blinking, he realized he was sitting still while angry horns beeped behind him. He eased off the brake and drove away, listening as she talked in animated fashion about her day and how amazing the turnout had been.

His blood hummed with desire. With need. He wanted her. He didn't want to want her.

He couldn't process a single rational thought.

Suddenly the thought of spending so much time in a restaurant didn't appeal. She looked tired. He was impatient. He needed to have her to himself.

"Change in plans," he said gruffly as he turned left so he could circle back to her apartment.

She roused from her semistupor and shot him an inquisitive glance. "What's up? You standing me up?"

He smiled at the growl in her voice. "Oh, no, far from it. What I'm doing is taking you back to your place so you can put your feet up on the couch while I order us the best damn steak money can buy. Then I'm going to take you to bed, give you an all-over body massage and make love to you until you pass out."

Her eyes widened and then she blinked, momentarily speechless. "Well, okay," she finally said.

He smiled in satisfaction at her acceptance. It was more than okay.

When Pippa let them into her apartment, the air was electric and heavy with anticipation. She wouldn't even meet his gaze because she was sure she was an open book, and hey, a woman had to have some mystery, right?

Only it wasn't a mystery that she wanted him. Or that from the moment he'd laid out his plans for the evening she'd become a quivering ball of anticipation.

She walked ahead of him into the living room, her step lighter than it had been all day. Her fatigue had fled and she felt energized. Ready.

Her skin prickled with tiny goose bumps every time he so much as looked her way. It felt like her very first date. Her very first kiss. The first time she'd ever gotten naked in front of a man. She wasn't sure whether she liked it or not.

"Why don't you sit and relax," he said. "I can find my way around your apartment. I'll phone in our order and get things started. Would you like something to drink?"

This suddenly very solicitous side of Cam was confusing the hell out of her. She liked this new Cam very, very much and she could get used to it.

It wasn't as if he was never generous with her. Quite the opposite. He went to great lengths to take care of her needs but he did so as impersonally as possible.

But now his caring seemed very personal. She didn't know if this was a further attempt to make up for walking out of the sonogram or if he was genuinely softening toward her. Who the hell knew with him?

"I'll take a bottled water. There's one in the fridge," she said as she settled on the couch.

She propped her feet on the ottoman and groaned in sheer pleasure. She leaned her head against the back of the couch and closed her eyes while she listened to him putter around the kitchen. Then she heard the rumble of his voice as he placed their dinner order. A moment later, he returned to the living room and handed her the drink.

"Thank you."

"Your grand opening was quite the success," he said.

He took a seat in her armchair and propped his feet just inches from hers.

"I owe a lot of my opening day success to you. Maybe all of it."

He shook his head. "I gave you a place but it was your talent and hard work that made it happen."

"Thank you for saying that. It means a lot. I've been working toward this for a very long time."

He put his hands behind his head and cupped his nape. "Have you thought about what you'll do after the baby is born?"

She cocked her head to the side and glanced questioningly at him. "What do you mean?"

"Will you keep your current schedule or will you employ others to run the shop so that you have more time with our son?"

For a moment she couldn't respond. She was too struck by the reference to their son. And she was reminded that she and Cam weren't a couple. Of course he would wonder what arrangements she'd made because he wasn't going to be there on a 24/7 basis.

It shocked her how much that hurt. How much she wanted it to be different.

"I haven't decided yet," she said slowly. "A lot will depend on how the café is doing and if I can afford to hire more help. I have to train my assistant so that she can duplicate my recipes while I'm out on maternity leave. But I can't close down. That's not even an option."

"Of course not. If you'll allow me to help, I can certainly put some feelers out. We have a number of pastry chefs that work in our various hotels. I'm sure we could loan one to you for a few weeks."

She stared back at him, mouth open. "Cam, you guys own five-star resorts. There is no way I could afford to pay even three weeks' wages to a world-class pastry chef like the ones you guys employ."

"He or she would of course remain on our payroll."

She sighed. "I can't keep relying on you, Cam. I'm only setting myself up to fail miserably. What you've done is so wonderful and so helpful but it also skews the results. When all your support goes away, I'll be left in a lurch."

He frowned. "No one says it's going away."

"I say it's going away," she said gently. "I have to make a go of this myself, Cam."

He didn't argue, although she had the distinct feeling that he hadn't dropped the subject for good. Then a completely unrelated thought struck her.

"I didn't frame my first dollar."

He blinked in surprise and then seemed puzzled by her dismay.

Her lips turned down into a frown. "You're supposed to frame the first dollar you make. You know, when you start a business. You didn't do that with yours?"

"Hell, Pippa, your first sale was probably a debit card purchase. Nobody carries cash anymore. You could always frame the credit card receipt."

She pulled a face. "You're such a party pooper. You don't have your first dollar?"

He shrugged. "I still have my first million."

She rolled her eyes at him. "Somehow that doesn't

surprise me. Does money mean anything at all to you or has it lost its value?"

"Of course it means something." He scowled, making her almost want to giggle. "It means I can support our child and you. It means I can live comfortably and not worry about where my next meal is coming from. It means you don't have to worry about your lack of health insurance."

She held up her hands in surrender. "Okay, okay, I was being a snot. It was an unfair jab. I'm sorry."

"I'm not out blowing my cash if that's what you were wondering."

Her cheeks warmed and she glanced away. "No, I was just stereotyping you and being flip. I really didn't mean anything by it. People who don't have a lot of money tend to not really understand people who do have money. Or their attitude toward money."

He lifted one eyebrow. "I hope you're not implying I'm a snob."

"No," she said truthfully. "I truly don't think you're a snob. You can be a first-class jerk, but not a snob."

He shot her a glare and she snickered.

The doorbell interrupted and Cam quickly rose to go answer. A moment later, he came back, followed by a delivery person who set up the food on the coffee table. The young man smiled at Pippa and then he and Cam disappeared from the living room once more.

She waited, sniffing appreciatively at the mouthwatering aroma floating from the covered plates. She'd leaned over to take a quick peek when Cam admonished her from the doorway.

"Not so fast."

She yanked back guiltily.

"Want to eat in here or the kitchen? Are you okay on just the coffee table?"

"Oh, yeah. I'm comfortable. I'll just lean forward and shovel it all in."

He chuckled. "Not a pretty image."

She sniffed disdainfully. "Watching a pregnant woman inhale her food isn't for sissies."

He went forward and uncovered the dishes. He poured her a glass of cold water and then shoved the plate across the table so that it was directly in front of her. Then he handed her a steak knife and a fork. "Dig in."

He didn't have to tell her twice. He'd ordered a filet and it was fork tender. As soon as she took the first bite, she closed her eyes and sighed in sheer pleasure.

"Good?" Cam asked.

"I don't have words. Best steak I've ever put in my mouth."

He nodded his satisfaction and then sat down to eat his own steak.

They ate in silence, only the clink of forks and knives disturbing the peace. Pippa had been only half kidding about inhaling her food. These days it didn't seem she could put away enough to eat. Which was just as well because she'd read that in the last trimester, eating was a lot more difficult with a baby's head lodged in your lungs.

Cam finished his steak before she'd gotten halfway through hers. He went to put away his dishes. When he came back, he sat forward in the armchair and grabbed her plate.

She frowned her protest but he gestured for her to sit back. Then he put the pillows from the end of the couch on her lap and plunked the plate down on it so she could continue eating. Just when she had no idea what he was up to, he lifted her feet and propped them back on the ottoman.

He closed his hands around her left foot and pressed his palm into her instep. She sagged precariously and let out a glorious sigh as pleasure seeped into her muscles.

"How can I eat with you doing that?" she complained.

He smiled. "Easy. Just pick up your fork. You were on your feet all day. They have to be sore."

She shoved a bite of steak into her mouth and nodded vigorously.

"Well, then, relax and let me take care of the matter for you."

Oh, hell, yes. She wouldn't say another word. She'd just sit here and eat her scrumptious steak while the most gorgeous man on earth gave her a foot massage.

"Remember what I promised you?" he murmured.

She stopped chewing and damn near choked as she struggled to swallow the bite. Then she nodded because she couldn't seem to find her tongue.

As he gripped her heel with one hand, the other stroked over the top of her foot and up her leg, heat from his touch warming her skin.

"As soon as you're done, I'm taking you to bed, Pippa. How much sleep you get is entirely up to you."

Oh, hell…

She put aside the plate, unconcerned with whether it tipped over on the couch. He stared at her for a moment as if gauging whether she was ready. If she was any more ready she'd be stripped down and holding a sign saying Take Me.

Chapter 16

As soon as Cam pulled Pippa to her feet, adrenaline surged like an electric charge through her veins. For a moment he pulled her close, their bodies touching. His warmth leaped to her and surrounded her. Then he dragged a gentle hand through her hair and leaned down to kiss her.

It was brief, just a brush, but she felt it to her toes. He drew away, his breath harsh in the quiet.

"Your bed," he said.

Swallowing hard, she started to drop his hand to go past him toward her bedroom, but he tightened his hold and rubbed his thumb over her wrist.

She went ahead of him, pulling him behind her as she crossed the short distance to the steps leading up to the small loft where her bed was. Her legs trembled as she climbed and then came to a halt, the bed in front of her, unsure of what he wanted next.

He moved past her, this time taking her with him. He eased her into a sitting position on the edge of the bed and then unbuttoned her top.

He went down on his knees as he pushed her shirt over her shoulders, baring her lacy bra. His gaze dropped to the swell of her belly and he went still. She held her breath, wondering if the moment was lost, but to her utter shock, he laid his cheek over the bump and turned his mouth just enough to press a kiss to her taut skin.

She inhaled sharply, the bite of emotion harsh in her throat. She slid her fingers through his unruly hair, her touch gentle and loving.

Slowly he pulled away and then he lifted her just enough that he could ease her pants off.

"I promised you a massage," he said in a husky voice. "I think I'm going to enjoy it more than you will."

She cast him a doubtful look, but okay, if that's what he wanted to think. Right now his hands on her body was about as good as it got.

He curled his arms underneath her and lifted so he could position her on her side. Then he unhooked her bra and carefully pulled her panties down her legs so she was naked, facing away from him.

During a long pause, she glanced over her shoulder to see him disrobing a short distance away. He had a gorgeous, lean body. He wasn't pretty or polished. There was just enough edge to his appearance to send her girlie senses into overdrive.

He strode back to the bed and got on his knees behind her. When his hand slid over her hip, then wandered to her back and shoulder, she closed her eyes and sighed in contentment.

His mouth followed, pressing hot against her neck and then gliding over the curve to her shoulder. When he pulled away, he put both hands to her back and gently began to stroke and caress until her eyes rolled back in her head.

He worked methodically, leaving no part of her flesh untouched. He stroked down to her buttocks, molding the plump globes with his palms before working lower to her thighs.

Nudging her over onto her back, he lifted one leg and began working the muscles with those to-die-for hands. He worked all the way down to her ankle and then began massaging her foot.

She floated somewhere else, hovering on a cloud of sensory overload. Then he lifted her foot and kissed her instep. She nearly lost it right there. It was the most erotic sensation she'd ever experienced and it was just her foot! But the man made every single touch so damn sexy.

He moved to her other leg but she was only dimly aware. She let out a blissful sigh and surrendered to the euphoric sensation of having a sinfully handsome man cater to her every pleasure.

Each caress sent warmth all the way to her soul. She opened her eyes and watched in fascination as he rose over her, gently parting her thighs before settling his upper body between them.

For a brief moment he glanced up and those sizzling blue eyes connected with hers. His mouth crooked up into a half smile and then he lowered his head to her most intimate flesh.

She couldn't call back the moan. She twisted restlessly but he kept her firmly in place with those hands at her hips. He kissed, licked and made love to her with that delectable mouth. He had such a talented tongue and he was driving her crazy.

She reached for his hair, twisting her fingers with almost desperate strength as she arched into him. He delved deeper with his tongue, loving her with long, lazy strokes. Then he moved one hand from her hip and slid his fingers deep into her warmth.

It was more than she could withstand. She bowed beneath him, tightening to the point of near pain and then she reached her peak in a quick, tumultuous burst.

He tenderly kissed the quivering bundle of nerves, eliciting another shudder from her before he moved his mouth up to her belly to lavish gentle attention on it. His hands molded to the swell and there was such reverence in his touch that she had to swallow back the knot forming in her throat.

She wanted to believe so very much that he was coming around. That maybe he was beginning to let go of his past, but she was afraid to broach the subject. Afraid of his rejection. And she couldn't be patient and understanding. She wasn't going to wait around forever for him to decide he wanted to fight for their future.

"Tell me if I hurt you."

He shifted upward, positioning himself between her thighs. He held his weight off her with one palm pressed to the mattress while he used his other hand to guide his erection to her opening.

Tentatively he pressed forward, his gaze never leaving her face as he probed deeper. She pulsed around him, still hypersensitive after her orgasm. As he pushed even deeper, she closed her eyes and dug her fingers into his muscled shoulders.

"Too much?" he asked.

She opened her eyes to see him eyeing her with concern.

"Oh, no," she whispered. "Not enough."

His pupils dilated. His jaw tightened and bulged and he drew in a deep breath as if he were trying valiantly to maintain control.

She lifted her hands to frame his face, caressing his jaw as she stared up at him.

"Make love to me, Cam. Don't hold back. You won't hurt me."

He closed his eyes and emitted a harsh groan. Then he turned his face into her hand and kissed her palm. Carefully he lowered himself until her belly pressed into his. He rested his forearms on either side of her shoulders and then pushed deeper.

His mouth found hers. Hungry. Hot. Demanding even as he was exceedingly gentle.

He found a slow, sensual rhythm, rocking against her as he filled her again and again. He was patient, working her up that slow rise all over again.

It was less urgent this time. Mellow. A lazy climb upward as pleasure filled her. She felt weightless, surrounded by him. She felt...*loved*.

Even as she knew it was foolish to allow herself the fantasy that he wanted and needed her, she couldn't help but immerse herself in this one moment where everything in her world was utter perfection.

His mouth skimmed down her jaw to her neck where his teeth grazed the sensitive skin underneath her ear.

Then he raised his body just enough to send himself even deeper inside her.

She gasped, then clutched at his shoulders, digging her nails into his flesh. She arched upward, wanting, needing more.

"That's it, baby," he murmured. "I love how you respond. Always with me one hundred percent."

Oh, if he only knew just how with him she was and wanted to be. She bit her lip to prevent the words, those damnable words, from slipping out in the heat of the moment. He wouldn't welcome them.

I love you.

She closed her eyes and wrapped her arms around his neck, pulling him down so they were close. So close that his warmth bled into her body and she had no sense of where he began and she ended.

He shuddered against her. Let out a hoarse cry. She moaned softly and then whispered his name as the world crashed around her. Arching. Sighing. Undulating. Their bodies moved in quiet unison until they were wrapped tighter than braided rope.

She melted back onto the mattress, so sated that she couldn't even contemplate moving. For a moment he rested above her, his weight only barely pressed to hers, and then he rolled to the side, taking her with him.

He pulled her in close, anchoring her head in the hollow of his neck. His heart tripped frantically against her cheek and she inhaled deeply, wanting to capture his essence and imprint it in her memory.

He didn't speak but neither did she. Anything she'd say would only ruin the moment and anything he'd likely say she wouldn't want to hear. So she was content to let things lie.

She closed her eyes, knowing that when she woke again, he'd be gone. Just like the other times. She'd wake to an empty bed and an even emptier heart.

She threw her arm and a leg over him, knowing it was pointless but unable to resist the urge to keep him close for as long as she could. Then she snuggled deeper into his embrace and allowed the veil of sleep to overcome her.

Cam woke in a cold sweat, the horror of his dream still alive and vivid in his mind. For a moment he stared into the darkness, still reliving every moment.

The accident that had taken Elise and Colton from him had been replayed in slow motion. He'd experienced the horrific, numbing helplessness of knowing he couldn't save them. But still, he'd run toward the wreckage, his heart in his throat, praying with everything he had that this time would be different. That this time he'd find them alive.

Only when he'd gotten there, it had been Pippa's bloodied face he'd seen, the last, pained cry of their newborn son he'd heard.

Desperate to get away and to make the awful vision disappear, he shoved hastily out of the bed, Pippa's sleepy murmur of protest dim in his ears.

He yanked on his clothing, nearly tripping in his haste to be gone. He stumbled through her apartment to the front door and lunged into the night, gulping huge, steadying breaths into burning lungs.

He palmed his forehead as he made his way to his car and fumbled with the lock. He got in and slumped against the seat and sat there several long minutes, staring through the windshield, trying to bring to mind Elise's features.

But it wasn't his beloved wife he saw every time he closed his eyes. It was Pippa.

Chapter 17

Pippa struggled out of bed the next morning. She should be euphoric. She'd had a terrific turnout for her grand opening. She'd spent a wonderful evening with Cam and an even better night in bed. But as she'd known, even though she'd awakened before dawn to get to her café, Cam had been gone.

She trudged into her shop, feeling thoroughly down. The two people she'd hired to help her bake in the mornings arrived shortly after she did and they worked in silence, Pippa shunning any attempt at conversation.

She needed time to think. Or rather time to berate herself for being such a weak ninny. Cam was...well, he was manic and it was driving her insane. She couldn't continue like this.

Oh, who was she kidding. All the man had to do was smile at her, offer an apology and take her to bed.

She'd never envisioned herself as one of those gullible women she and her friends liked to rag on. But apparently Pippa was smart in every aspect except men and relationships.

It was just a few minutes to opening when Pippa's cell phone rang. It was Ashley's ring tone and Pippa felt some of her tension ease. Ashley always made her feel better.

"You're up early this morning. Baby keeping you awake?" Pippa asked as she put the phone to her ear.

"Pippa, it's Devon."

He sounded harried and there was a terse quality to his voice that immediately put her on edge.

"Where's Ashley?" Pippa demanded.

"We're at the hospital. She's in labor and wanted me to call you. I can't reach her mother and she's in a panic. I think she just wants some female company. I'm driving her crazy."

Pippa smiled. "It's all right, Dev. I'm on my way. Hang in there."

Devon's relief was palpable. "Thanks, Pippa."

She rang off and then gave her employees instructions for running the shop in her absence. Leaving her business on its second day wasn't at all what she wanted but she wasn't about to leave Ashley when she needed her most.

After making sure they'd call her if any issues arose, Pippa hurried out the door to hail a cab. She could call John, but she didn't want to wait even that long to get to the hospital. She was nervous and excited to be with Ashley on the big day, but if she were honest, she'd admit that the whole delivery thing scared the bejebus out of her.

She wasn't yet prepared for that aspect of her pregnancy; she'd been existing in ignorant bliss. Childbirth itself was the part of all the pregnancy books she skipped over. She knew all about the nine months leading up to it. She knew all about what happened after the delivery. But she'd blocked out any information about the actual delivery of the baby.

Not smart, but hey, a girl did what she had to just to get through.

Once at the hospital she stopped by the information desk to find out Ashley's room number and then headed up to the maternity ward. She tapped on Ashley's door, half-afraid of what she'd see on the other side.

Devon opened the door and looked relieved to see her there. Pippa hesitantly peeked around Devon, happy when she saw Ashley propped in the bed looking none the worse for wear. Ashley's face brightened when she saw Pippa.

"Pippa! I'm so glad you're here."

Pippa smiled and went over to the bed to enfold Ashley in a hug. "Hey, you. How's it going? When's that baby going to get here?"

Ashley pulled a face. "Not soon enough. It could be hours yet. I'm only dilated to four."

Pippa blinked. "Four what?"

Ashley's brow furrowed. "Centimeters."

"Oh."

Pippa really didn't want to know what exactly that meant. It sounded painful. These were things she avoided. She'd much rather read about the baby's first movements and all the development stages after birth.

"Can I get you anything, Ash?"

Ashley shook her head. "No, just stay with me. I'm

driving poor Dev nuts. He wants to make it all better and I'm grumpy."

Pippa laughed. "You grumpy?"

"Here, have a seat, Pippa," Devon offered as he pushed a chair behind her. "You don't need to be on your feet, and like Ash said, it's going to be a while."

Pippa settled in the chair beside Ashley's bed while Devon continued to pace in a small area behind them. She reached for Ashley's hand and offered a comforting squeeze.

"Are you excited?"

Ashley took a deep breath. "Excited. Scared out of my mind. I just want to know how soon I can get my epidural."

Pippa shuddered.

"I kind of wish now that I'd found out what we're having," Ashley said mournfully. "I thought it would be exciting to be all surprised when the doctor said 'it's a boy' or 'it's a girl,' but now I'm thinking no surprises is a good thing."

Pippa nodded her agreement. Of course if she'd opted not to find out, maybe Cam wouldn't have wigged out, but then it probably wouldn't have been good for him to find out on delivery day. The more time he had to come to terms with the fact he was having another son, the better. Or at least that was her way of thinking.

Devon moved to the other side of Ashley's bed and leaned down to kiss her temple. "It'll be all right, Ash. You're going to do great."

Ashley looked up with such love in her eyes, love that was openly reflected in Devon's tender gaze. Pippa had to look away and swallow against the knot forming in her throat. She wanted this. What they had. She and Cam hadn't even discussed if he'd be here when the baby came. She assumed he would, but she was learning it was dangerous to assume anything when it came to him.

She stood abruptly, tears burning the lids of her eyes. "I'll be right back. I need to make a phone call. Check on the store."

She all but fled from Ashley's hospital room, shutting the door behind her and leaning heavily on it as she tried to clear her blurry vision. She pushed off the door and hurried down the hall to the waiting room where hopefully she could regain her composure. Ashley needed her to be strong today.

Throughout the day, visitors came and went. Ashley's mother barged into the room a few hours after Pippa arrived, mortified that she couldn't be reached the minute Ashley went into labor. Pippa was glad to see Mrs. Copeland. She just had a way of making everything better. She'd already hugged Pippa no less than a dozen times and Pippa gloried in each one.

Tabitha, Carly and Sylvia came by but didn't stay long since the room was growing more crowded with Ashley's family. Pippa herself had already decided she'd retire down the hall to the waiting area so she wouldn't be in the way.

She crept out, snagged a cup of water from the cooler and sat in a comfortable chair to wait the arrival of the baby. As the day wore on, more people filtered into the waiting room and it was alive with conversation and excitement.

Ashley had a large family and it seemed that every

single one of them was going to be present for the birth of Ashley's child.

Pippa's heart squeezed because she couldn't imagine such a wonderful fuss when it came time for her baby to be born. How marvelous it must be to have a huge, loving family who gathered for special occasions and celebrated with such vibrancy.

Here in a room full of warm, friendly people, she'd never felt so alone in her life.

"Have you eaten anything today?"

She jumped, pulled suddenly from her thoughts by the sound of Cam's voice coming from behind her. She turned around and shook her head, watching as he frowned his disapproval.

"Let's go down to the cafeteria," Cam said.

He started to take her elbow but she pulled away. "I'm not leaving now. Ashley is going to deliver at any minute. No way am I missing this."

Cam seemed to take in the expectant air that permeated the room. He drew his lips into a thin line and then said, "I'll go get you something. You need to eat."

She shrugged—which seemed to irritate him—but she wasn't exactly concerned with him at the moment.

With another inquisitive look in her direction, Cam turned and walked out of the waiting room. Pippa blew out her breath and settled back in her seat. Yeah, he probably was confused as to why she was snippy. In his mind, he'd probably already blown off the fact that he'd high-tailed it after sex again. And he had no way of knowing just how muddled Pippa's own feelings were and how close to her breaking point she was.

Fifteen minutes later, Cam returned with a foam

carry-out container and handed it to her with plastic utensils.

"I wasn't sure what to get you to drink, so I got you a bottle of water."

"That's fine," she said, retrieving it from his grasp. "You aren't eating?"

"I ate before I came."

He parked himself in the chair next to her, extending his long legs as she opened the container. The spaghetti and garlic bread looked good, but she had absolutely no desire to eat. Her stomach was too churned up.

She managed a few bites and pushed the food around so it would look like she was eating. The only problem was, she could feel Cam's stare on her and knew he wasn't fooled.

She was saved when Ashley's father, William Copeland, burst into the waiting room, grinning from ear to ear. "It's a girl! I have a granddaughter!"

The room erupted with excitement. Pippa put her plate down and rose with the others to converge on Mr. Copeland. The smiles were huge. Lots of hugging. It was everything Pippa wanted for her own delivery.

A few minutes later, Devon appeared holding a tiny bundle in his arms. He was smiling so big that his face had to hurt. But then Pippa watched as Cam converged on his friend, his own smile a match to Devon's.

Her mouth drooped as Cam peered over the blanket at the baby, his eyes glowing as he and Devon exchanged comments. Worse, Devon readily handed the baby over to Cam and they stood together cooing and talking baby nonsense.

Pippa hadn't thought it possible to hurt more than she had the day of her sonogram. She stood locked in stone as she watched the same man who'd walked away from her and her baby make a total moron of himself over that tiny little girl.

Cam handed the baby back, slapped Devon on the back and heartily congratulated him. The room was a buzz of excited chatter, congratulations and oohs and aahs. But Pippa was focused on Cam. Cam, who was smiling. Cam, who was happy. Cam, who clearly had it in him to love.

So why couldn't he love her and their child?

Chapter 18

Pippa was no longer able to stand there and pretend that everything was fine when she was dying on the inside.

In the excitement, she was able to slip away unnoticed. As she headed toward the elevator, she bumped into one of Ashley's cousins and asked her if she'd make Pippa's excuses to the new mother. She walked into the elevator, turning to stare at the jubilation at the opposite end of the corridor. Tears pricked her eyelids as she punched the button for the first floor.

Just as the doors started to slide closed, Cam looked up and their gazes connected. His brow furrowed and he started forward, but the gap closed and the elevator began its descent.

Realizing that Cam would likely come down after her, she headed out and crossed the street, deciding to walk a few blocks before hailing a cab.

The night air was chilly despite the earlier sunshine and warmth. And what a perfect day it had been for Ashley's baby girl to be born. Spring. The beginning of new life. A fresh start. Life after a long winter.

So symbolic, and yet for her, spring meant death.

Okay, so she was being a little dramatic, but sadness had a firm grip on her throat and it wasn't letting go.

She loved Cam. Despite his many flaws.

But she wanted him to smile at her and their child the way he'd looked down and smiled at Devon and Ashley's daughter. She wanted to see him light up and look…happy. Had he ever seemed so carefree when he was with her?

It had been like looking at an entirely different person. Was this the way he was around people he cared about? Ashley had said he was always gentle and even tender with her.

So it wasn't that he didn't care about people or that he was incapable of love. It was just as he'd said. He didn't want to love her. Or their son.

A sob escaped as she raised her hand to hail an oncoming cab. It never slowed and she dropped her hand, staring down the street in search of the next one.

Tears streaked down her cheeks, but she made no effort to wipe them away. What was the point?

She leaned out when she saw another cab approach and slow down. She climbed in, barely managing to tell the driver her cross street. He gave her an odd look in his rearview mirror as he pulled into traffic.

Her cell phone rang but she didn't bother to dig it out of her purse. It was Cam. She'd known he'd call. After a moment, the phone went silent and then a ping sounded, signaling a text message

She was nearing her apartment, when her phone rang again. It was Ashley's ring tone. Pippa dug into her purse, fumbling for the phone.

"Ash?" she said as she put the phone to her ear.

"No, it's Devon."

Pippa went silent for a moment. "Is everything okay with Ashley and the baby?"

"I'm more concerned with whether you're all right," Devon said in a low voice.

"I'm f-fine," she said in a shaky voice. "Really. I hope I didn't hurt Ashley's feelings by not hanging around. I just figured she'd be exhausted and with all her family there I'd just be in the way."

"You're never in the way, Pippa," Devon said gently. It was as if he knew precisely how upset Pippa was. As if he was standing in front of her, watching her cry. "I just wanted to make sure everything was okay with you. I know...I know it had to be hard for you to see that. Cam, I mean."

It was then Pippa realized that Devon had indeed picked up on the very thing she had. She closed her eyes, a fresh resurgence of tears sliding hotly down her cheeks.

"I appreciate your concern, Dev. Truly. But I'm okay. You should be focusing on Ashley and that beautiful baby girl. Tell Ash that I'll come see her tomorrow when things are a little less crazy, I promise. But you're right. I couldn't stay there tonight. I...I just had to go."

"I understand," Devon said. "Chin up, Pippa. If killing him would help, I'd give serious consideration to it. Only the knowledge that I was once the same sort of bastard and that I eventually saw the light is saving me from tossing him off a bridge."

Pippa smiled as her cab pulled to a stop. "Thanks, Dev. I'm home now so I'll let you get back to your family. Give Ash my love and I'll see her tomorrow."

"Take care, Pippa," Devon said. "If you need us, you know we're here."

"I do know," she said softly.

She thrust money at the driver and then ducked out and hurried down the sidewalk toward her apartment. She glanced down at her phone to see she had several text messages. All from Cam.

The last?

Damn it, Pippa. Pick up the phone. What happened? Are you all right?

She slid the phone back into her purse and grabbed her keys as she mounted the steps to her door.

No, she wasn't all right. She'd never been so *not* all right in her life.

The next day was a test of her endurance. She woke early after having not slept well at all and went into the café to get a start on the baking.

She enjoyed a steady stream of customers, many effusive in their praise of her goodies. She should be on top of the freaking world but it was all she could do to keep her head up for the duration of the day.

The only thing that made it bearable was the fact that Cam didn't show up. She was half-afraid he would after she refused to answer his calls or texts the night before.

After locking up, she went home and took a long nap. Or at least she tried. She lay down and went through the motions of napping, but her mind wouldn't shut down and all she could do was replay Cam's smile and his joy from the night before.

She was wrung out, disillusioned, and she knew it was time for her to make a decision. She could no longer afford to hang around hoping that one day Cam woke up, pulled his head out of his ass and realized his life wasn't over.

She pushed herself from the bed, made a halfhearted attempt to straighten her appearance and then trudged to her kitchen to get a drink and try to shake the cobwebs from her brain.

First she'd go visit Ashley and make up for the fact that she'd bailed on her the day before. Her friends came first.

Not bothering with a coat—it was her hope that the chilly evening air would give her a much-needed wake up—she left her apartment and walked to the end of the block to hail a cab. She just didn't have it in her to walk the extra few blocks to the subway.

When she got to the hospital, visitor hours were almost over but she headed up to the maternity ward, anyway. The worst they could do was kick her out.

She knocked quietly on Ashley's door, hoping her friend wasn't asleep. A moment later, the door opened and Devon appeared.

"Come on in," Devon said with apparent relief. His gaze sharpened as he took in Pippa's appearance, and without a further word, he simply pulled her into his arms and gave her a huge hug.

She hadn't known just how badly she needed that until his arms surrounded her. She bit into her lip to keep from bursting into tears on the spot. She was here to see Ashley and the baby, not blubber all over her and her husband.

"Thank you," Pippa whispered against Devon's chest. "How is Ash?"

"Go see for yourself," he said as he pulled away. "She's holding Katelynn now."

Pippa hurried past the private bathroom and approached the bed. She stopped and stared at the beautiful sight of Ashley with her daughter cradled in her arms.

Ashley smiled broadly. "Hey, Pip. Come on over and see her. She's so beautiful."

"You're breast-feeding her?" Pippa whispered as she went to Ashley's bedside and stared down at the tiny infant. "Is it hard?"

Ashley smiled. "A little at first but the nurses here are so great. They helped a lot and then Katelynn did the rest. She's a real champ at it now."

Devon pushed a chair to the side of the bed and motioned for Pippa to sit.

"So Dev said Cam was a real butthead last night," Ashley said in a low voice.

Pippa sighed. "Let's not talk about him, Ash. This is your time to be happy and enjoy your beautiful baby without listening to your friend complain."

Ashley gently broke suction and pulled her gown back to cover her breast. Then she looked toward Devon. "Want to see if she'll burp for you?"

Devon reached over Pippa to take the bundle and went to sit in the recliner by the window.

"Now," Ashley said, crossing her arms over her chest. "Spill. You look terrible, Pip. You're clearly unhappy."

The knot grew larger in Pippa's throat and her eyes clouded with tears once again.

"I'm miserable, but it's my own fault. I totally sct

myself up for this. I walked into this knowing the score. I'm just frustrated and heartsick. I'm going to confront him, Ash. It's stupid but it's something I have to do."

Ashley reached over to take her hand and squeeze. "What are you going to say to him?"

Pippa emitted a harsh laugh that grated on her own ears. "I'm going to tell him I love him."

Ashley blew out her breath. "You're so much braver than I am. You always were."

"Yeah, but you're smarter, so we're even," Pippa muttered.

"Not true. Okay, so after you tell him you love him, what then?"

Pippa sighed. "Then nothing. He'll do what he always does and I'll walk away but this time it'll be for good. I just feel like I have to give him this last chance. Or maybe it's just me and I want one last chance. Either way, I need it to be final. I can't continue this hot-and-cold thing we have going. My eyes were opened last night. I realized that he's happy around other people. Just not *me*. And that hurt."

"Oh, Pip," Ashley said, her whole face a mask of sympathy. "I wish…"

"I do, too," Pippa said. "But wishes aren't real. Wishing is for fairy tales. Cam is no Prince Charming and I'm no princess living happily ever after."

Ashley seemed to be on the verge of tears and the very last thing Pippa wanted was to further upset her friend. Not when she should be on top of the world. So she forced cheer into her voice and a smile onto her lips as she rose to hug Ashley.

"I'm going to steal that baby from Devon for a minute and then I'm going to get out of here and let you rest."

She turned toward Devon, who slowly lifted his daughter away from his shoulder and placed her in Pippa's arms.

She held the baby close, studying every inch of her softness. She touched the tuft of hair on top of Katelynn's head, feeling the silky, delicate strands. Someone had affixed a tiny little bow just in front of her soft spot. Pink and girlie. So much like Ashley.

She ran her finger over the tiny fingertips and watched in fascination as they curled around Pippa's own finger and made a tight fist.

She was instantly and completely won over, heart and soul. She was absolutely in love with this little girl. Who wouldn't be? But then it had been the same when she'd seen her son on the sonogram monitor for the first time. Instant love. Unconditional. A bond that couldn't be broken.

It hadn't been the same for Cam. He hadn't been able to leave fast enough.

She briefly closed her eyes and then lowered her head so she could brush her lips across Katelynn's forehead. She inhaled the sweet baby scent and then brought the baby back over to where Ashley lay.

"She's absolutely perfect, Ash. You did good."

Ashley beamed and held out her arms to collect her daughter. Then she looked back up at Pippa.

"It's going to be okay, Pippa."

Pippa nodded because there was nothing else to do. She turned to offer Devon a wave. "I'll see you guys later."

"Call me if you need anything," Devon said.

Pippa nodded and then walked out of the room, closing the door softly behind her. She checked her watch and stood there a long moment, simply leaning against the wall in the hallway.

There was no way she would sleep tonight. Not until she settled things with Cam. She had to get this over with before it ate her alive.

It would be a long trip on an already late night, and it meant dragging Cam out of his bed, but at the moment she didn't care. One way or another, it would be settled tonight.

Chapter 19

Convincing a cabdriver to take her all the way to Greenwich had been next to impossible, and it was going to cost her a fortune to boot. The ride seemed interminable and traffic was heavy even at the late hour. By the time she reached Cam's gate, it was past midnight. He might not even be there for all she knew, but she suspected he was. He'd retreated to Greenwich with increasing frequency lately.

They waited at the gate while the driver spoke through the intercom. It wasn't Cam who answered. She was pretty certain it was John. A moment later, the gate swung open and the cab pulled up the driveway. He parked in front and she paid him and got out after telling him not to wait.

John opened the front door and came out to greet her, worry on his face.

"Is Cam home?" she asked quietly.

"He is. He retired an hour ago," John replied as he ushered her inside.

"I need to see him. I'll wait in his office."

She didn't give John a chance to argue. She simply turned and walked across the living room to the office. She didn't bother turning on the lights. There was something soothing about the darkness.

She stopped by the window, staring out into the night, at the bright, star-filled sky. Fairy dust. A million wishes. She only needed one. Just one.

The door opened behind her. She closed her eyes for a brief moment and then turned to see Cam standing there in the dark.

"Pippa?"

There was concern and bewilderment in his voice. He took another step forward and then reached down to turn on a lamp that rested on the table by one of the armchairs.

She flinched at the sudden burst of light and turned away, not wanting him to see what she was sure was obvious on her face. But how could she hide it? How could she hide how devastated she was?

"What's wrong, Pippa? What are you doing all the way out here at this time of night?"

She swallowed, squared her shoulders and then took a deep breath. She turned to face him fully, uncaring of what he'd see.

"Are we done, Cam?" she asked bluntly.

He blinked in surprise. He opened his mouth and then snapped it shut again and frowned. "I'm not sure what to say here."

She took a step forward. "Let me make this easy for you, Cam. I love you."

He went pale and flinched. His reaction spoke volumes. It told her everything she needed to know but some demon inside her persisted. She'd gone this far and she'd see it to the bitter end even if it humiliated her in the process.

"I need to know where I stand," she said in an even voice. "One minute you seem to want me and we act like—we *are*—lovers. The next you can't get away from me fast enough and you're cold, like I'm some random stranger."

Cam's lips tightened. "I was honest with you from the onset."

She nodded. "Yes, you were. No doubt about that. But you're sending mixed signals. Your actions contradict your words. I need to know if I have a chance here, Cam."

He started to turn away and it infuriated her.

"Don't turn your back on me," she bit out. "At least give me that. Face me and tell me why you can't give me commitment, why you can't love me. I understand you lost people you loved. I get it. But it's time to move on. You have a child, a son, who needs you. *I* need you," she finished in an aching voice.

Cam whirled back around, his eyes flashing furiously. "Move on? You *get* it? How the hell do you get it, Pippa? You think that by spouting some clichéd armchair psychology crap at me that I'm supposed to say, oh, you're right, and then live happily ever after?"

"What I think is that it's ridiculous to believe you can't love anyone else."

He closed his eyes and his jaw tightened. When he reopened them, he stared directly at her, his tone even. "It's not that I can't love again. I'm not one of these people who believes you only get one shot, that there's only one soul mate out there and if you screw that up you're out of luck for the rest of your life."

Her mouth fell open because, of all things, this was not what she'd expected to hear. "Then *why*?" she whispered. "Why can't you love me and our baby?"

He slapped his hands down on his desk and glared at her with eyes so dark and haunted that she flinched.

"It's not that I can't love you, Pippa. *I don't want to.* Do you understand? I don't *want* to love you."

She recoiled, so stunned that she couldn't even respond. She wrapped her arms around her belly and stood back, hurt spreading to every corner of her soul.

His words when they came were angry and frustrated, as though he hated having to explain himself, as if he hated admitting what he'd just blurted out.

"If I don't love you, then it won't hurt me if something happens to you. If I don't love you, then nothing you do will touch me. I don't ever want to feel the way I did when I watched Elise and Colton die in front of me. You can't possibly understand that. I hope you never have to."

Her arms crept tighter around herself, as if to ward off the unbearable pain of his rejection.

"You would shut out me and your own child because you're too afraid to take that risk?" she asked hoarsely. "What kind of an unfeeling monster are you?"

He jabbed a finger in her direction. "You've got that right. Unfeeling. It's exactly the way I want to be. I don't want to feel a damn thing."

Anger hummed through her veins, replacing the ice that had rapidly formed. "You bastard. You callous, manipulative bastard. What the hell have you been doing for the past months? If you were so determined not to have a relationship, then why did you continue to make love to me?"

His gaze dropped and guilt shadowed his face.

"Am I supposed to feel sorry for you? Am I supposed to be all sympathetic and pet your poor damaged heart just because something horrible happened to you in the past? I've got news for you, Cam. Life sucks. It isn't perfect for anyone and you aren't special. Bad things happen to people all the time but they don't become heartless jerks and piss on everyone around them. They get up, dust themselves off and keep on living. Maybe you never got that memo."

"That's enough," he said tightly.

"Oh, hell, no, it isn't. I'm just getting warmed up and you're going to listen to everything I have to say. You *owe* me that much. One day you'll regret this. You'll regret that you turned your back on me and our baby. You'll find someone you want to marry and you'll think about the fact that you have a son out there who never had a father because you were a coward."

"Somehow I don't think my future wife would care for the fact that my mistress and our love child were in such close proximity," he snapped.

The blood left her face and she took another step back as if he'd physically hit her. His face went gray and he started toward her as if he knew he'd gone too far.

She held up her hand to halt him. She was barely holding on to her composure and only her pride was keeping her upright at this point. This was pointless. They were two snapping dogs trying to hurt each other with quick, angry words. It solved nothing. It never would.

"We're done," she said in a cold voice. "I want nothing from you, Cam. Not your support. Not your money. Definitely not your presence. I don't want you anywhere near me or my child. *My* child. Not yours. You don't want us and quite frankly we don't need you."

"Pippa…"

She shook her head. "I don't want to hear it. But know this, Cam. One day you're going to wake up and realize you've made a horrible, horrible mistake. I won't be there." She cupped her hands over her belly. "*We* won't be there. I deserve more. I deserve a man who'll give me *everything* and not just throw money or convenience at me. More than that, my child deserves more. He deserves a father who'll love him unconditionally. Who'll go to the wall for him every damn day. Not a father incapable of loving anyone but himself."

She turned to walk out but paused at the door. She faced him one last time, ignoring the utter bleakness in his eyes.

"I loved you, Cam. I never asked you for anything. That's true. And yes, you were up front from the beginning, so shame on me for changing the rules. I have equal responsibility for this debacle, but just because I made a mistake doesn't mean that I'm going to punish myself for the rest of my life and I'm damn sure not going to make my child suffer for my stupidity. I'd tell you to have a nice life, but somehow I don't think that's going to be possible because you're far too content to wallow in your misery."

She yanked open the door and walked out, slamming it behind her. It wasn't until she got outside the front entrance that she remembered she hadn't asked the cabbie to wait and now she was stranded at this damn monstrosity of a house.

"Miss Laingley, will you allow me to drive you home?"

She turned to see John standing there, his eyes soft with sympathy. It was the last straw. She burst into tears and then allowed him to guide her toward the waiting car.

Chapter 20

Cam sank into the chair behind his desk and buried his face in his hands.

He'd followed Pippa out the door and seen that John was giving her a ride home. He'd watched as the car drove down the lane, the lights disappearing in the distance.

For how long he stood there, numb, he didn't know. He realized the door was still open and the wind had picked up. A chill had stolen over him but he knew it wasn't the temperature. He was cold on the inside. Dead. Still breathing and yet dead. He had been for a long time.

Now, sitting at his desk, his gut clenched. His chest ached. It shouldn't. He should be relieved. It was done. There was no possible way for Pippa to misunderstand.

Clean break. He'd done exactly what he should have done from the very beginning.

So why didn't he feel vindicated? Relieved, even? He

should be glad. He could go back to his unemotional existence where he didn't have to feel pain.

Only none of that was true. He hurt *now*. He hurt so damn much that he couldn't breathe around the knot in his throat.

He'd lost Pippa.

The very thing he'd tried to protect himself from was the pain of loss. The despair and frustration of not being able to keep a loved one safe was his reality. Right here, right now.

He'd lost Pippa. He'd lost his son.

His *son*.

An innocent, precious life.

A child who deserved to have the world at his feet. Two parents who loved him. A father who'd protect him from all the hurts and disappointments life had to offer.

Oh, God, he was a bastard. He was such an unfeeling monster, just what Pippa had accused him of being. Only he wasn't unfeeling. Right now he'd give anything not to be able to feel this agony.

Seeing Pippa tonight and the evidence of just how low he'd brought her down made him want to die. She'd stood before him, pain in her eyes, and yet she'd still put herself out there. She'd taken a chance. Laid it all out.

And he'd slapped her down because he was afraid.

It was humbling to realize just what a coward he was. What a coward he had been for so long.

He'd been given something many people never got. Something others wished for, would kill for, would live every single day of their life in gratitude for.

A second chance.

Another chance at something so special and wonderful.

Pippa was a breath of fresh air into a life he'd quit living. He went through the motions. He performed. But he'd stopped truly living a long time ago.

Pippa had changed all that. From the moment he'd first seen her walk into a room, she'd been like a bolt of lightning to his senses.

Her smile, her laughter, her take-no-prisoners attitude. Her confidence. Her inner beauty. And her courage.

When he really stopped to consider just how much she'd had to shoulder alone these past few months it made him physically ill. She was young, had plans. She could have anyone and yet she'd chosen him. He'd made her pregnant and yet she soldiered on, making the best of a difficult situation.

She'd fought fiercely, was still fighting fiercely for his son. He was so damn proud of her and so damn ashamed of himself that he couldn't bear to think about it.

He didn't deserve her. She was right about that.

But he wanted her. Oh, God, he wanted her.

It was laughable that he'd actually thought that he could spare himself the pain of loss by shutting himself off and away, by closing the door on a relationship with Pippa.

He'd been so worried about losing her that the very thing he feared the most had happened. At his instigation!

Stupid didn't even begin to cover it.

He pushed upward from his chair, suddenly agitated and more determined than he'd ever been in his life.

He loved her, damn it.

He'd lied to himself and to her. He'd spouted all kinds

of crap about not wanting to love her. Yeah, he hadn't wanted to but he did and that wasn't going to change.

And now he had to crawl on hands and knees and beg her to give him yet another chance.

He hurried out of his office and through the kitchen to the garage. He yanked the keys from the hook, and not giving any consideration to how he looked or how he was dressed, he climbed into the Escalade.

He was driving back to the damn city and he was going to her apartment and he didn't care if it was four in the morning. This couldn't wait. He couldn't wait.

Some things needed to be done immediately, and this was one of them. He'd made her wait all this time. He wasn't waiting another damn moment.

It had taken immeasurable courage for her to come to his house and face him down, tell him she loved him and wait with her heart on her sleeve.

How could he not do the same for her?

It would be the hardest thing and yet the easiest thing he'd ever do. Because when faced with the alternative of living his life without her and their son? Crawling didn't seem so bad.

Pippa trudged into her apartment, weariness overtaking her. Her head ached from trying to hold off the tears. Her eyes were swollen and scratchy. She was heartsick and numb from head to toe.

She felt…lost. Like she wasn't sure what came next. There was such finality to her confrontation with Cam. What was she supposed to do?

She sank onto the couch, tossed her purse onto the coffee table and closed her eyes. Her head throbbed.

She needed sleep. At least there, she could escape for a while and not feel so horrible.

She arranged one of the cushions against the arm of the couch and pulled her feet up, curling up on her side. Exhaustion beat at her, making her remember that between her grand opening, Ashley giving birth and all the angst over Cam, she hadn't had a good night's sleep in longer than she could remember.

She pulled out her phone, looked at the time and winced. She'd need to be up in just a couple of hours. She set the alarm on her phone so she'd be sure to wake and then she reached over to set it on top of the coffee table next to her purse.

Then she closed her eyes and let the comforting blanket of sleep slide over her.

The smell of smoke woke Pippa from a dead sleep. She opened her eyes, confused by the darkness and the acrid smell of something burning. She blinked away the cloud of disorientation and then shoved herself up from the couch in horror.

Flames surrounded her and the scorching heat singed her skin. Everywhere there was a wall of orange fire and smoke billowing heavily. It was so dense she had no idea where she was or which way was out or if there even was a way out.

She breathed in and then coughed as her lungs burned. Panic slammed into her as she realized the horrific danger she was in.

Clutching her belly, she lunged from the couch, trying to see through the flames and smoke to know if she could make it to the door.

Then she remembered that in a fire, the safest place

to be was as close to the floor as possible. She dropped down, as low as she could with her burgeoning belly, and pulled her shirt up to cover her nose and mouth.

Her phone. Where was her phone?

She turned back but lost sight of the couch in the haze of smoke. She was fast becoming so disoriented that if she didn't do something now she was going to die.

She closed her eyes and pictured the layout of the room and forced her panic down so she could focus. She knew every inch of her apartment and she wasn't going to let her hysteria make her do something stupid.

She had to save her baby. She had to save herself.

Still holding her shirt over her face, she began to crawl in the direction of the front door. Above her, flames licked over the ceiling and smoke billowed from every corner. It was becoming harder and harder to breathe and she was sick with worry of what this was doing to her baby.

Thoughts of her child renewed her determination to get out no matter what. She scrambled over hot, smoldering rubble and made it to the foyer. Just a little farther. There didn't appear to be as much smoke close to the door and she put on a burst of speed, ignoring the cuts and burns to her palms and knees.

She was a few feet away when the door splintered and cracked and caved in. Smoke began drawing through the opening, pulling around her and enveloping her. She heard a shout and then strong hands gripped her, pulling her upward.

The fireman cradled her in his arms and barged out the front door into the cool night air. Around her, the world was a sea of flashing lights, smoke and flames shooting toward the star-filled sky.

"Is there anyone else in your apartment?" the fireman yelled to her.

She shook her head. "No," she replied, dismayed by the fact the denial came out in a barely audible croak.

He carried her to a waiting ambulance where she was handed over to another man who promptly put her on a stretcher.

"The baby," she rasped out. "I'm pregnant."

An oxygen mask covered her face, blocking out anything further she'd say. The next thing she knew, she was laid flat, pushed into the back of the ambulance and two paramedics hovered anxiously over.

There was a prick in her arm. They shouted down questions to her. She tried to tell them she was okay, but she couldn't say anything through the mask and her throat hurt too badly, anyway.

Numbly she lay there, trying to process what had just happened. Darkness grew around the edges of her sight and then one of the medics leaned down close, shouting at her to stay awake and with them.

"There's nothing wrong with me," she tried to say, but she couldn't get her mouth to work.

She blinked twice and then the world went black around her.

Chapter 21

As soon as Cam turned onto Pippa's street, his stomach dropped and his mouth went dry. He gripped the steering wheel with white knuckles as he accelerated.

The entire world was ablaze with flashing lights. Police cars, ambulances, fire trucks. The smell of smoke was heavy, and the sky was colored orange with the glow of flames.

He screeched to a halt in front of a police barricade and he was out of his SUV like a shot, running toward Pippa's apartment. The entire row of buildings was ablaze and firemen directed a steady stream of water from multiple directions.

"Hey! You can't go in there!"

He ignored the shout, his only thought to get to Pippa. Oh, God. Not again. Anything but this. He couldn't lose her! A sob tore from his throat.

He'd just reached the front line of fire trucks and ambulances when he was hit by a flying tackle. He hit the ground hard and came up swinging. A police officer hovered over him, shouting something Cam couldn't hear or understand.

Another officer joined in, helping wrestle Cam to the ground.

"Get off me!" he yelled hoarsely. "I have to get to her. Pippa! She's pregnant! I have to save her."

"You aren't going anywhere," the officer growled as he exerted more pressure over Cam's neck. "Get it together, son. The entire block is on fire. You'll just get yourself killed."

"Don't make us arrest you," the other officer threatened. "I get that you're worried, but they're doing everything they can to make sure everyone gets out. Let them do their job. The last thing they need is to have to go in to save your stupid ass."

"Let me up," Cam demanded. "I have to know if she's okay. Did they get her out?"

Slowly the first officer eased up on the arm across Cam's throat. He glanced warily at Cam as he and the other officer hauled Cam to his feet.

"Don't make any sudden moves," the officer warned.

Cam put his hands up, his heart pounding with dread as he eyed the carnage around him. This was his worst nightmare playing out in real time.

Fate was dealing him yet another blow, one he may never recover from. But no, this wasn't fate. He could have prevented this. If only he'd reached out as she had done. If he'd only been willing to take the chance that she had taken by coming to him.

He alone was at fault. If something happened to Pippa and their child, his life was over.

"Pippa," he said hoarsely. "Pippa Laingley. She lived there." He pointed at her apartment, his hand shaking, his voice cracking under the weight of his terror. "She would have just gotten home not so long ago. She was tired and upset. Please, can you just tell me if they found her?"

The officer pointed at Cam, his expression stern. "You stay here. I'll go see what I can find out." He gestured for the other officer to stay with Cam.

He watched the officer wade through the firefighters and other EMS workers. It was all he could do to stand there while his heart was dying with each breath. The officer standing beside him eyed him with sympathy.

"They got several out already," he said in a low voice. "Many have already been taken to the hospital. I'm sure if she was in there that they got her."

A few moments later, the first officer returned, a grim expression on his face. Cam lunged forward, getting so close he was almost pressing up against the policeman's chest.

"They took her away in an ambulance maybe a half hour ago. She was one of the first they got out. I don't have any further details. It's crazy right now, but they said she was conscious and appeared to be unharmed."

Cam's knees buckled and he nearly went down. All his breath rushed out in a violent explosion of relief.

"Whoa, steady there. Maybe you should take a seat."

Cam shook his head. "No. I have to go. Where did they take her?"

He was already turning to run to his SUV when the officer called after him with the name of the hospital.

Cam sprinted from the scene, got into his truck and pulled away from the chaos.

He had to force himself not to drive recklessly when all he could think was to get to Pippa as fast as he could. He had to see her. Had to know she was all right. Had to hold her again and tell her everything that was in his heart. Everything he'd been too stubborn and too stupid to tell her before.

He only hoped to hell she would listen.

Pippa lay on the uncomfortable bed in the small cubicle in the emergency room as nurses came and went. Her horrific panic had settled somewhat with the news from the doctor that the baby was okay. She hadn't been subjected to the smoke long enough to do any lasting damage to her or the baby.

But she kept imagining what could have happened.

What if she hadn't awakened when she had? What if she hadn't gotten out as soon as she did?

The images wouldn't go away.

She rubbed her belly in a soothing circle, reassured by the baby's movements. The past hour had been a blur as she'd been poked, prodded, stuck, checked over. A sonogram had been ordered and she'd gotten to see for herself that her baby was still there, still alive and didn't seem in any distress.

She reeked of smoke. She looked like hell. But she didn't care. All that mattered was that her baby was okay.

Her door opened and to her surprise Devon poked his head in. To her further surprise, Ashley came in behind him and all but ran to Pippa's bedside.

"Pippa! Oh, my God," Ashley choked out.

Ashley threw her arms around Pippa, who lay there, stunned and unable to find her voice.

"What on earth?" she finally managed to sputter. "Ashley, what are you doing here? You just had a baby! You should be in bed."

Devon came around to the other side of Pippa's bed and leaned down to kiss her forehead. "We were worried, Pippa. When we heard, Ashley had to come right down. I couldn't very well tell her no."

Pippa frowned. "You should have. Where's Katelynn? Ash, are you okay?"

Ashley hugged Pippa fiercely and then pulled away, her eyes flashing. "I'm fine! The question is how are you? I had a baby, Pip. Normal delivery. I've been up walking around all day. And Katelynn is in the nursery for now. Tell me what on earth happened!"

Ashley slid onto the edge of the bed beside Pippa and grasped her hand, squeezing tightly. It was the last straw. Tears streaked down Pippa's cheeks and she hiccuped back a sob.

Devon gently stroked Pippa's hair. Ashley gathered Pippa's hands in hers and leaned forward, concern etched on her brow.

"Oh, Ashley," Pippa whispered. "It's been such an awful night."

"Wait, did you go see Cam?" Her eyes widened as she seemed to realize something. "Oh, no. What happened?"

"It's over," Pippa said, her voice cracking under the emotional strain and the rawness from the smoke. "I went to his house, told him I loved him and now it's over."

Ashley held on to her tightly, rubbing her hand up and down Pippa's back.

"I'm going to step outside," Devon murmured. "Give

you girls some time alone. If you need anything, I'll be right outside the door."

He gave her one last affectionate touch on the arm and then left.

Ashley pulled away and gently pushed Pippa's bedraggled hair from her face. "Tell me everything, starting with what the doctor said. You scared me to death. I want to know you're okay first and then I want to know everything that happened at Cam's."

"The doctor says I'm fine. The baby is fine. I went to sleep on the couch and when I woke up, the whole apartment was on fire. But I got out before I inhaled too much smoke. I was lucky. I'm a bit scraped up from crawling, but I'll be fine. The doctor even says that I can go home by tomorrow afternoon...."

She trailed off, realizing that she no longer had a home.

Fresh tears surged, spilling down her cheeks.

"It'll be okay, Pip," Ashley soothed. "I promise you. I don't want you to worry. Mama will be here later in the morning. You know she loves you just like a daughter. She's already making plans to bring you home with her and take care of you."

Pippa smiled shakily. "You have no idea how much I need her right now." She broke off and sighed. "I should be happy. I made a decision. I told Cam off. Rightfully so. But I'm so miserable. I love that jerk and I'm mad that I can't make it stop."

"Tell me," Ashley said quietly.

Pippa looked down at her hands, humiliation and devastation pummeling her all over again. "He told me he didn't *want* to love me or our baby. Not that he couldn't or that he didn't believe he'd ever find another soul mate. Just that he didn't want to love us. He was so…cold."

Ashley scowled. "I hate him. I don't care if he's Dev's best friend. I swear the man fell out of the stupid tree and hit every damn branch on the way down."

Pippa tried to laugh but she dissolved into a coughing fit instead.

"Easy," Ashley murmured. "Catch your breath. You've been through a lot tonight."

"Oh, God. It all feels so unreal."

Ashley squeezed her hands again. "I don't want you to stress about this. I know that sounds absurd. You've had the rug pulled out from underneath you and right now you likely think your entire world is falling apart. But it's going to be okay. You have me. You have Mama. You have Sylvia, Carly and Tabitha to help. Devon will do whatever he can, you know that. Please don't make yourself sick worrying. Right now you just need to focus on you and the baby and making sure you're both healthy."

Pippa gave her a watery smile. "Thank you. I love you, Ash. I don't know what I'd ever do without you."

"I want you to get some rest now, okay? It's almost time for Katelynn's next feeding so I'm going to go back up, but I'll have Dev check in on you. Mama will bring you something to wear home. I want to know the minute you're released. I'm supposed to go home today, too, so maybe we can blow this joint together."

Pippa squeezed Ashley's hand. "Thanks, Ash. You're the best. Kiss that baby for me."

Ashley fussed with the pillow and tucked the sheet more firmly around Pippa before she finally backed away from the bed and started for the door.

As soon as Ashley disappeared from view, Pippa

closed her eyes and melted into the bed. Exhaustion beat at her. She'd reached her absolute limit. She was physically and emotionally spent. There was nothing left except vast emptiness and an unnerving ache in her heart.

Chapter 22

Cam strode through the doors of the E.R. and went to the desk to inquire about Pippa. He blatantly lied, saying he was her husband and then demanding to see her. One of the nurses motioned him through a series of doors and then pointed down the hall and told him she was in room seven.

As he rushed forward, he realized that Devon was standing out in the hall. He was about to call out when the door to Pippa's room opened and Ashley came out.

Devon put his arm around his wife and started to lead her down the hall when he and Ashley both looked up and saw Cam.

He hadn't expected there to be much love for him from Ashley at the moment, but the anger in Devon's tight expression surprised him.

"How is she?" he demanded.

He would have just shoved by and gone into her room, but Devon blocked him. Then Ashley put her hand on Cam's arm, which halted him immediately. He had no desire to risk hurting her. She shouldn't even be running around the hospital after just having had a baby.

"Cam, please," Ashley said softly. "Leave her be."

He backed away and shoved his hand through his hair.

"Leave her be? I need to see her. I need to see for myself that she's okay. You can't possibly understand what it was like to drive up to her apartment and imagine that she was trapped inside that inferno."

It made him sick all over again just thinking about it. It was an image that would live with him for a long time to come.

"She's exhausted. She needs rest. Cam, she's so... fragile right now."

Her hesitant description only made him more determined to get into that room.

Ashley gripped his arm once more and it was only then he realized he'd moved forward.

"Let her rest. You've done enough tonight. You can't barge in there and upset her. She's been through hell. She doesn't know you were the one who called us. She didn't even ask us how we knew she was here."

He closed his eyes as bleakness settled over him. "She hates me."

"No, she loves you," Ashley said softly. "And that's the problem. It's why you can't go in there and take advantage of how distraught and run-down she is. I'll never forgive you if you don't give her some space and let her at least sleep a few hours. She looks terrible, Cam. Part of that is your fault."

"Don't upset her," Devon said, speaking up for the first time. "Ashley's right. She's extremely fragile right now. Barging in there to assuage your guilt won't make that any better. For once think of someone other than yourself."

The angry censure in Devon's voice made Cam flinch.

"This has nothing to do with guilt," he said in frustration. "Damn it, I love her. I have to tell her. I can't let things go the way they ended between us."

Devon put his hand on Cam's shoulder. "If you love her, then it'll wait. You can wait. Don't push right now, Cam. I promise you, the result won't be good. She's past her breaking point."

"I'm not leaving," Cam said fiercely.

"Nobody says you have to."

Cam closed his eyes, his shoulders sagging. "All right. I won't go in now."

The idea that she was exhausted, weak and emotionally spent tore at him. He wanted nothing more than to hold her. To cradle her in his arms, whisper that he loved her and that everything would be all right.

He hadn't been there for her before but he'd be damned if he'd desert her now.

Ashley's gaze found his and her big blue eyes stared imploringly at him. But they also held a warning.

"Make this right with her, Cam. And don't you ever hurt her again."

"I'll spend the rest of my life loving and protecting her if she'll have me."

Devon blew out his breath. "Yeah, that's the big question, man. You're not going to have an easy time of this."

Cam knew it but his heart still sank at the conviction in Devon's voice.

"I'll be down later to check in on her," Devon said.

It was a warning to Cam that Devon would be back and that he better not find her upset. Cam acknowledged him with a nod and then watched as Devon and Ashley slowly walked down the hall.

Cam glanced at the closed door, wishing for the world that he could just see her. Just touch her. He walked to the end of the corridor and grabbed a chair. He set it across from Pippa's door and sat down to begin his vigil.

He wasn't leaving.

And so he sat, staring broodingly at her door. At one point a nurse went in, giving him an apprehensive glance. A moment later, she came back out and Cam surged to his feet.

"How is she?" he asked, his voice almost a croak.

The nurse stared at him a moment, her brow furrowed. "I'm sorry but I'm not allowed to give out that information."

"I'm her husband," he said, and then realized how stupid it seemed for him to be sitting in the hall if he were married to her. "I…I just wanted her to rest and I've been so worried. I didn't want to put additional stress on her."

Her expression softened. "She's sleeping. Quite soundly. She never even moved when I checked her vitals."

Cam nodded and murmured his thanks. He wiped nervous palms down his pant legs as the nurse hurried away and then he tentatively opened the door, careful to not make a sound.

If she was asleep, then she'd never know he was here. He could watch her for a while and know that she was safe. He eased the door open farther and stepped inside, his gaze immediately seeking her out in the semi-darkened room.

She was lying on a narrow bed with her back elevated. She was sleeping as the nurse had said, but she didn't look at all comfortable. She was sagging to one side and seemed precariously close to sliding off the bed.

He took another step closer and for a moment he couldn't breathe. Fragile had been a good word to describe her. She looked so small against the bed. Her hair was in disarray. He could smell the faint scent of smoke.

She was pale and her face seemed thinner. There were dark smudges underneath her eyes. His gaze dropped to her hands and he frowned to see scrapes on her palms.

She looked worn through. As Devon had said, past her limits. Cam had pushed her there.

Unable to resist, he lowered his fingers, simply wanting to touch her. He traced the lines of her face, gently pushing back a tendril of hair that rested close to her mouth.

Then he bent and gently kissed her forehead, closing his eyes and allowing his mouth to rest there for the briefest of moments.

"I love you," he whispered.

Pippa awoke with the nagging sense that she'd missed something. Her dreams had been odd, occupied by Cam and infinite tenderness instead of flames, smoke and fear. They had been nice but bizarre.

There was no clock in the room and if it weren't for the bright sunlight streaming through the small window, she'd have no idea it was daytime.

She automatically smoothed her hands over the bulge of her belly and smiled when the baby kicked. Relief was sweet. She and the baby were going to be all right.

Just then, her door opened and Gloria Copeland bustled through, looking determined and agitated. But the moment their eyes met, her gaze softened and she rushed over to the bed to enfold Pippa in her arms.

"My poor baby," she crooned. "Are you all right? Devon told me what the doctor said but I've been so worried about you."

To Pippa's never-ending shame, she started crying again. It was becoming ridiculous how easily she became a watering pot.

"Oh honey," Gloria said. "Don't cry. You know you're coming to stay with me. I have a bedroom all ready for you. I'm putting you next to Ashley's old room. I'm hoping she and Katelynn will stay a few days and it'll be just like old times. Having my girls around will be such a delight. I can fuss over all of you."

"I love you, Mrs. C." Pippa sniffled.

Gloria smoothed Pippa's bedraggled hair from her face and then kissed her forehead. "I love you too, baby. It's going to be all right. I promise. It may look bad right now but we're going to get you back on your feet in no time."

Pippa squeezed Gloria's hand. "I'm so lucky to have you and Ashley. You're the only family I have."

And Pippa knew it was true. Blood didn't count for much at all. Miranda may have given her life, but family wasn't necessarily about blood. It was about uncompromising love and support. About always being there no matter how hard things were.

This was what she wanted for her son. And she'd give it to him no matter what she had to do.

Gloria hugged her again, and really, Pippa was perfectly happy to be hugged all day. Each time, a little more of her melancholy drifted away.

"Tell you what we're going to do. I'm going to take you home and put you to bed. As soon as you're up to it, we're going to have a spa day. If that doesn't put the pep back into your step, I don't know what will. We'll bring Ashley, too."

Pippa smiled. A girlie day with Ashley and her mom sounded...wonderful.

"There now, see? You're smiling already," Gloria said. "Seriously, honey, I don't want you worrying about a thing. I'll have William sort out your hospital bill. You'll stay with us until the baby's born. There's no sense you shouldering the stress of trying to find a new apartment when you should be focusing on your baby. We'll have great fun. You'll see."

Pippa wouldn't refuse Gloria Copeland's hospitality even if she wanted to. Nobody ever stood a chance against her. She was a force of nature and Pippa loved her for it.

Then she frowned as reality crashed in. "What about my bakery? I can't just leave it."

"Of course not," Gloria soothed. "We'll manage. You have employees who can handle things for a few days while you rest and recover. After that, we'll work out a way for you to get to work each morning. William will be more than happy to provide a driver for you."

Pippa smiled again. "Thank you. Seriously. I don't know what I'd do without you and Mr. C. and Ashley."

Gloria beamed. "William will be glad to hear that. You know he loves you just as much as I do even if he can be an old goat sometimes."

Pippa snickered.

"Now, let me find out when they're going to let you out of this place," Gloria said. "The sooner we get you home, the better. We'll have our physician check in on you daily just to make sure all is well."

Pippa leaned back against the pillows and sighed. Things were already looking up. She'd get beyond this with the help of the people she loved.

A few moments later, Gloria returned. Once again she had that odd look on her face as she came through the door.

"What did the doctor say?" Pippa asked.

Gloria blinked. "Oh, I didn't talk to him. I spoke to the nurse. She says you'll be ready to go home in just a couple of hours."

An uneasy feeling crept over Pippa. Something was up with Mrs. C. "Is anything wrong?"

Gloria looked up at the sharpness in Pippa's tone. She glanced back toward the door and then she sighed. "You'll know soon enough, anyway. Cam's outside the door. Looks like he's been there all night. He refuses to budge. Just sits there in that chair and broods. He wanted to come in, but I told him not to. I didn't want to upset you."

Pippa's heart thudded painfully. Her fingers automatically curled into fists and she went quiet. Her breathing was loud in the silent room and she stared at the wall as if she could see through it to Cam sitting on the other side.

"I don't want to see him," she whispered.

Gloria put her arm around Pippa's shoulders and squeezed. "You don't have to, baby. I just didn't want you to get a shock when you left and he was there in front of you."

"No, it's okay. Thank you for the heads-up. It's just that we have nothing left to say to each other."

Gloria kissed her temple and squeezed her a little harder. "Ashley's being discharged today and is bringing Katelynn home. We'll all just go to my apartment together once you're released."

Pippa nodded numbly, her mind still on Cam. She wasn't a coward, but the very last thing she wanted right now was another confrontation. His words had cut her to the core and it was a wound she wouldn't recover from in a day or even a week.

One day at a time. Things would get better. She had to believe that.

Chapter 23

Cam paced the hallway outside of Pippa's door, wondering at one point why he didn't just walk in and force a confrontation. Then he shook his head. It wasn't the time or the place. Devon and Ashley were right. Pippa was holding on by a thread. This wasn't about him.

He glanced up when he saw Devon coming down the hallway.

"Have you been in to see her?" Devon asked as he stopped in front of Pippa's door.

Cam shook his head. "Ashley's mom is in with her. She didn't want me anywhere near Pippa. I don't blame her. Where's Ashley and Katelynn?"

"They're in the car. I pulled it around to the exit. Ashley's father is out with her. He's going to drive Pippa and Gloria home."

Cam grimaced and rubbed a hand through his hair.

Pippa had no home to return to. But she should. It was with him. Always with him. She should have never been anywhere else all these months.

He blew out his breath, not knowing what to do. It was a feeling he wasn't accustomed to. He was always decisive even when he was dead wrong. He never had a problem knowing what to say even when he was putting his foot in his mouth. Right now he lacked for words.

And then Pippa's door opened and there she stood, Gloria hovering just behind her. His gaze zeroed in on Pippa. She was pale and wan, deep shadows under her eyes. Her hair was pulled back into a rough ponytail and her cheekbones were more pronounced than ever. Her arms even seemed more slender. The only part of her that seemed normal was the bulge in front where their son rested.

"Pippa," he said in a low, unsteady voice. "Thank God you're okay."

He reached out, wanting to touch her, to somehow confirm that she was really standing before him, but she flinched away. He withdrew his hand, curling his fingers into a tight fist at his side.

She started to move past him and he closed his eyes knowing he couldn't let her walk away. Not again. Not like this.

"Pippa, wait, please."

She halted in midstep and stood there a long moment, her back still to him. Then she slowly turned, her eyes dull and lifeless as she stared back at him. Then her chin came up and she squared her shoulders.

"Wait outside for me," she said to Devon and Gloria. "I'll just be a minute."

Gloria Copeland looked very much like she wanted to argue but she kept her mouth tightly shut.

"I'll wait down the hall so I can walk you out," Devon said.

Pippa nodded and then turned back to Cam as Devon and Gloria walked away.

No longer able to keep from touching her, Cam reached out to capture Pippa's hand. He pulled her close so he could feel the steady reassurance of her heartbeat against his chest. She sagged against him, her sigh hitting him right in the gut. It was a forlorn, tired sigh that told him she was at the end of her rope physically and emotionally.

She closed her eyes and turned her face into his neck for just a moment before she pulled away, her expression locked in stone once more.

"I need to go. They're waiting for me."

Cam's protest was automatic. "You can come home with me, Pippa. I'll take care of you. We have a lot to talk about. There's a lot I need to say to you. But my first priority is you."

"No."

He expected more. An argument. Something he could counter. But all she uttered was a clipped *no* and stared woodenly back at him.

His heart lurched. This was so much worse than he'd imagined. All the emotion he'd held back since the night before came rushing forward, bulging in his throat.

He put his hand to her face. "My God, Pippa, I thought I'd lost you when I saw the fire and the smoke and all those fire trucks and ambulances."

The cold, lifeless eyes that stared back at him sent chills down his spine. This wasn't the Pippa he knew.

This was someone else entirely. Someone he'd made with his indifference and his determination not to get emotionally involved with her.

"I knew this would happen. I knew something would happen and I'd lose you both, and that fear controlled me. It made me do and say horrible things. Things I didn't mean, Pippa."

"You're a moron," she bit out. "You already lost me. The only difference was I didn't die in the fire. But for all practical purposes I'm dead to you. You lost both of us long before this happened. You spend so much time trying to shield yourself from hurt and you don't give a damn who you hurt in the process. How's that working out for you, Cam? Because from where I stand it sucks. Now if you'll excuse me, I want to go home and go to bed."

You already lost me.

It was a crippling blow even as he knew it was the truth.

As she pushed by him, he caught her hand, allowing his fingers to trail over it. Then the connection was lost and she turned away.

Cam watched her go, numbness creeping through his body with insidious speed. Her words had penetrated the wall around his heart, the one he'd erected after losing Elise and Colton.

Tears burned his eyes until he blinked to ease the discomfort. She'd stormed right past that supposed barrier the first time he'd ever seen her across a crowded room. There had been no defense no matter how hard he'd tried. No keeping her out. No lying to himself.

He loved her. Had loved her from the start. He'd never really believed in love at first sight until Pippa.

His dumb ass had known even then that she was a threat. And so he'd pushed her away. Tried everything in his power to tell himself he didn't love her, that he didn't want to love her.

But he did. He wanted to love her more than he wanted to live.

And now it was too damn late.

A hand came down on his shoulder. Startled, he looked to the side to see that Devon had come back to get him.

"I think it's time you and I had the same talk that I had with Rafe right after I screwed things up so badly with Ashley that I feared I'd never get her back."

Cam shoved his hands into his pockets, despair and hopelessness weighing down on him from all sides.

Devon pulled him along, herding him toward the doors. When they got to the parking lot, he shoved Cam inside the car and then walked around to get into the driver's seat. When they were on their way, Devon glanced over at Cam.

"Go big or go home."

Cam rubbed a hand over his eyes. "Stop talking in riddles. Just say it, man."

"I'm saying it. You gotta go big or go home. This is it, Cam. You're playing for all the marbles. For your future. For your son's future. This is your last chance. You won't ever get another. It's time to pull your head out of your ass and start living again. You're going to have to crawl to Pippa on your hands and knees and lick her shoes if that's what it takes."

"I said some unforgivable things."

Devon shrugged. "Define unforgivable. It's only unforgivable if *she* refuses to forgive you. And you don't know if she will because you haven't begged for it."

"I wouldn't blame her if she never spoke to me again."

"Neither would I, but are you going to throw in the towel just because you're a huge ass and don't deserve another chance with her? Hell, man, we've all screwed up. Rafe, Ryan, me and now you. We seem to have a common thread of being the biggest bastards on the face of the earth when it comes to the women we love. But you know what? Bryony forgave Rafe. Kelly forgave Ryan. Ashley forgave me and Pippa will forgive you. You just have to give her the opportunity and the right motivation."

"I love her."

"I know you do. I think you're the only idiot who didn't know it until now."

"I can't believe what I almost did," Cam said painfully. "I tried to deny her. I tried to deny my own son. How do you ever get over something like that?"

"The key word is *almost*," Devon said. "Tell her you're a dumb ass and then swear you'll wise up and never be a dumb ass again."

Cam sighed. "I just hope she'll listen."

"You make her listen. If she means enough to you, then you won't give up so easily."

Mean enough? She was his damn world. Her and their son. It was time to take a chance. The biggest chance of his life. It could end badly. They could be taken from him just like Elise and Colton had been.

But it could also end wonderfully. A long life filled with love and laughter. More children. Pippa's love and her smile. Wasn't that worth the risk?

Chapter 24

"Pippa, darling, Cam is here to see you, and I should warn you that he's vowed to sleep outside our door until you agree to talk with him."

Pippa stared back at Gloria Copeland, her mouth dropping open in astonishment.

"Are you serious?"

Gloria nodded. "I'm afraid so. He does seem quite determined. I would have thought it an empty threat but he's carrying an overnight bag with him."

"He doesn't give up," Pippa muttered.

In the past two days, Cam had haunted Pippa's existence. He'd called. He'd come by the Copelands' apartment. He'd gone by her bakery. He'd made it a point to show up in every conceivable place she could possibly be.

When none of that appeared to work, he'd resorted to text messages. I love you. Flowers. Tons of flowers.

Every card signed *I love you*. The few times she'd actually come face-to-face with him, he's just stood there, looking so haunted and determined, his eyes never leaving her face.

She felt hunted but not threatened. She was baffled by his persistence, confused by the messages.

After hanging on to desperate hope for so long, she'd made the painful, difficult decision to sever her ties to Cam. And now he was storming back, demanding her attention. Wanting things he'd vowed he'd never want from her.

It made no sense and she was at her wits' end.

She nibbled at her bottom lip and stared nervously over the back of the couch toward the door. She had no doubt he'd be stubborn. The past two days had proven that much.

"What should I do?" she asked anxiously. The very last thing she wanted was to cause trouble for the Copelands when they'd been nothing but kind and generous to her.

Gloria smiled indulgently and then came to sit beside her on the couch. She pulled her into a tight hug and patted her comfortingly on the back.

"My dear, you do whatever you wish. If you want to talk to him, I'll be happy to show him in and give you some privacy. Or if you don't want to be alone I'll stand guard like a mama lion. If you prefer not to see him, I'll simply have security remove him from the premises."

"I do love you, Mrs. C. If only…"

She broke off with a sigh and looked down.

"If only what, dear?"

Pippa raised her gaze and smiled. "If only my mother was like you."

Gloria smiled back and then leaned forward to enfold her in another of her glorious hugs. "You know you're like a daughter to me, and Miranda loves you as much as Miranda is capable of loving anyone."

Pippa sucked in a breath. "You know what? I'm not ready to see him. Not yet. He'd just run over me. When or if I decide to talk to him, it'll be on my terms. Not his."

"That's my girl. Okay, let me go make a call to the building security. Now don't go looking like that. It'll be quiet and discreet."

Pippa frowned unhappily all the same and hunched her knees toward her chest as Gloria got off the couch to go make the call.

She wasn't being vindictive. She wasn't being anything at all. She'd said what she'd wanted to say to Cam. There was nothing else.

But even as she reassured herself, doubt nagged at her, because somehow she knew this time Cam wouldn't walk away as he'd done in the past.

Go big or go home.

The past few days had been the most frustrating days of his life. Hell, he'd tried everything he knew to get Pippa to talk to him. Or just acknowledge him in some way. Getting thrown out of the apartment building where the Copelands lived had certainly capped off an already crappy day and earned him a warning from Devon.

Yet Pippa's continued resistance just strengthened his resolve. He wasn't going to give up no matter how long it took.

Which is how he found himself standing in the reception area of an exclusive salon. A very *girlie* salon filled with women of all shapes, sizes and ages waiting to be pampered.

Somewhere in one of those back rooms was *his* woman, and come hell or high water, today was the day she was going to listen to reason. If he had to lay bare his soul in front of countless strangers, then so be it. But Pippa *was* going to listen this time.

But first he had to get past the dour-faced dragon lady who stood guard over the doorway leading from the reception area.

He'd simply be honest. Weren't all women softies when it came to groveling men and the grand gestures they made for the women they love? If that didn't work, he'd get on his knees and he damn well knew no woman would turn down that kind of an opportunity.

He started toward Dragon Lady only to see her cross her arms and scowl directly at him. He sighed. This was so going to suck.

Pippa was covered in some sort of muddy goo—or at least her face and belly were—but she couldn't find it in herself to complain. Besides, it felt good. She was relaxed.

Somewhere down there someone was massaging her feet. She closed her eyes in bliss just as someone else put nice, cool cucumber circles over her eyes.

She almost laughed at how ridiculous she must look, but then it occurred to her that she was in heaven, and really, did it matter if she looked like a cream puff in a bikini with cucumber eyes?

The hands left her insteps and she grumbled her protest but then a new set of hands—firmer, larger, not nearly as smooth as the others—closed around her heel and began massaging.

Warmth spread up her legs and her lips parted as a sigh escaped where moments before she'd protested.

She liked these hands better. They weren't as practiced or smooth. But they hit all the right spots.

The hands moved up her leg, tenderly applying just enough pressure. Rubbing, kneading, leaving no spot untouched as they ventured higher.

It occurred to her to be alarmed at the familiarity of this person's touch, but it felt too wonderful to end just yet.

The hands left for the briefest of moments and then a warm cloth wiped gently at her belly, cleaning away the fluffy mixture of God only knew what.

Then those wonderful hands palmed the bulge of her belly and she sighed again. But when lips pressed to her firm abdomen, she reared up, cucumber slices flying from her eyes.

To her complete surprise it was Cam who stood there, his hands molded to her belly. And it was his lips that had pressed to her skin.

She tried to scramble up, but it was difficult and Cam put a hand to her shoulder, gently pressing her back down to a lying position.

"Why are you here?" she squeaked. "And what are you doing? Where's my attendant? How long have you been here?"

Cam spread his hands out, palms up. "I'm it. I'm yours. Completely and utterly at your service to fulfill your every whim and desire."

Her eyes rounded and her mouth flapped open and shut like she was a senseless twit.

He looked…broken. Hopeful and yet hopeless all at the same time. He looked tired. Worn. Worried. But more than anything he looked determined. There was a glint in his eyes that told her he wasn't backing down this time.

"I'm not having a conversation with you with all this crap on my face and wearing nothing more than a bikini," she muttered.

He bent down, captured her face in his hands and proceeded to kiss her breathless. When he finally released her, there was as much fluffy goo on his face as there was on hers. He looked…ridiculous.

She couldn't help but smile. Then she laughed.

"I don't care what you look like," he said hoarsely. "You're still the most beautiful woman I've ever known in my life."

She sighed, ignoring the flutter in her chest. "What are you doing here, Cam? I mean, really. What is it you want? We've said all that needs to be said. There's nothing left to do but get upset all over again."

His eyes became fierce blue orbs that burned a trail over her face. "No. Not even close. I have plenty to say and I want you to listen, Pippa. Really listen to me."

She blinked at his vehemence. Well, she wasn't having this conversation lying down. The very last thing she wanted was to feel at a disadvantage.

She struggled for a moment and finally reached her hand out to Cam. "Help me, please. If we're going to talk, I don't want to do it with us both looking like cream puffs."

He clasped her hand and helped her forward until she swung her legs over the side of the reclining chair. She slid off and went to the sink to wash the remainder of the cream from her face. Then she dampened a cloth and returned to dab at Cam's face.

He stood, completely still, while she wiped at his cheek. His eyes never left her, though. When the last bit of goo was gone, she took a step back, suddenly feeling the need to cover herself so she didn't feel quite so vulnerable.

She grabbed a robe off one of the hooks and wrapped it around herself, tying the ends tightly over her swollen belly.

And still Cam was staring at her, unshakable. She was sure there was a message in his unshakable gaze, but it wasn't one she could discern.

Then it was as if he couldn't stand it a moment longer. He crossed the distance, dragged her into his arms and kissed her like there was no tomorrow.

He wrapped his arms tightly around her body, holding her so close to him that she couldn't breathe. He shuddered against her. His lips moved over hers, devouring, hungry, *desperate*.

When he finally pulled away, she was shocked by the emotion so prevalent in his gaze. He had the look of a tortured man, someone who'd lost everything.

"I can't live without you, Pippa," he said in a low voice. "Don't make me live without you and our son. I love you both so damn much. It's eating me alive. I wake up thinking about you. I worry for you all day. I go to bed at night aching to hold you. Being without you is gnawing away at my soul. You are everything to me. *Everything*."

She swallowed, her nostrils flaring as she tried to control her own emotions. She wanted to lash out but knew it solved nothing. But his words—words he couldn't take back—still hurt. They cut deeply, a wound that was still open and raw.

"It's awfully cliché to realize you can't live without me and that you've seen the light after something life-threatening happens," she said in a low voice.

"You're wrong," he said fiercely. "I already knew it. I fought it. But I knew. I already loved you. I never said I didn't love you, Pippa. Never. What I said was that I didn't *want* to love you. I didn't just figure this out because of some damn fire. Did that scare me? Hell, yes. I haven't been able to sleep at night for imagining you in that apartment and the unbelievable fear you must have experienced. I was coming for you that night. Ask me how I knew you were in the hospital, Pippa. *Ask* me, damn it!"

Her fingers trembled as she stared back at him. "H-how?"

"Because I drove like a bat out of hell to get to you after you left. I knew I'd just made the biggest mistake of my life letting you walk away. I was gutted. But I knew if I could just get to you that I could make everything all right. And then when I got to your street, all I saw were those lights and the flames and smoke and I wanted to die because I thought it had happened all over again but this time I could have prevented it. Just by telling you what was in my heart. Just by not being so damn afraid."

Her eyes widened and her mouth popped open in shock at the vehemence in his voice.

"Hell yes I was terrified that I'd lost you. But that's not why I'm here. It's not why I'm putting myself at your feet and hoping to hell you'll give me another chance. I love you, Pippa. I've loved you for so damn long and

I didn't want to. I fought it. But some things just are and one of those things is my love for you and our son."

She opened her mouth to respond, but he came in close again and put a gentle finger to her lips.

"Don't talk. Just listen to me. Please. I have so much to say. So much to make up for."

Mutely she nodded.

He framed her face in his hands and stared down at her with such torment in his eyes that it made her chest ache.

"I'm tired of fighting myself. I want a life with you and our son. I'm tired of always expecting the worst, of trying to forget the pain of losing someone and protecting myself from the worst sort of agony. If I only have a year with you, I'd take it and treasure it for the rest of my life and I'd die a happy man having that time with you even if it meant living the rest of my life alone."

The words, so heartfelt, so bleak and raw and powerful, shook her to the core. There was no mistaking the sincerity. The truth was there in his eyes to see.

His thumbs caressed a line over her cheeks. His hands were gentle on her face, and he stared down at her with so much love that her throat knotted and tears burned her eyelids.

"I've been such a bastard to you, Pippa," he said hoarsely. "I've done everything possible to alienate you. I don't deserve another chance with you or my son, but I'm begging. I'll get down on my knees. I'll do whatever it takes to convince you that I'm not that man. I'm better than that. I want to be better than that. I'll spend the rest of whatever time I have with you proving to you that you can count on me."

Her heart surged with love. So much her chest ached.

"Oh, Cam, what you can do for me is stop expecting the absolute worst. I'll never leave you if I can possibly help it. Me and our child will love you and stay with you."

She reached up to stroke her hand over his jaw. "I'm so sorry for what happened before. But you've been given another chance. What you do with that gift is up to you."

He caught her hand, turned his face into it and kissed her palm. "You *are* a gift, Pippa. I never imagined having someone like you. And now our son." He choked off, caught his breath and for several long moments just breathed into her hand. "I love you. Please forgive me."

Her heart nearly bursting, she pressed into his arms and wrapped herself tightly around him, squeezing hard until he had no choice but to feel her love from every angle.

"I do forgive you," she whispered. "I love you, Cam. I love you so much."

He stroked her hair and kissed the top of her head as they simply held each other.

Then from behind came the sound of applause. They both whirled around, Pippa tucked protectively into Cam's side, to see Gloria, Ashley and several other women standing in the doorway of the room.

There were smiles and tears on the other women's faces.

"Well done, my boy," Gloria said, giving him a thumbs-up.

Cam smiled back and squeezed Pippa a little closer to him. He was shaking against her. She glanced up, shocked to see just how close he seemed to breaking down.

She reached for his hand, twining her fingers with his and then pulled him toward the door that led out to the little tranquility garden. She waved to the others to let them know she was all right and then tugged Cam the rest of the way from the room.

The only sound in the lush open garden was water cascading over a fountain. The air was heavily scented with blooming flowers, their splash of color dominating the small area.

It was as if a hole had been cut out of the center of the building, leaving an isolated slice of peace for whoever ventured out.

"Sit," she ordered Cam.

He sagged onto the bench by the fountain but he wouldn't relinquish her hand. He tugged her toward him as if afraid she'd leave.

"I love you," he said raggedly. "Say it again, Pippa. Tell me you love me and that you forgive me for being such a bastard to you. I need to hear you say it."

She smiled, then leaned forward between his legs. He wrapped his arms around her and rested his cheek on the bulge of her abdomen. She ran her fingers through his mussed hair.

"I love you, Cam. And I forgive you. I do."

He let out a groan and his hold tightened on her. Then he raised his head so their gazes met.

"Come home with me, Pippa. Stay with me. I don't want to spend another hour without you. Marry me. Love me. Spend your life with me. I swear I'll make you happy."

Her chest caved in a little more and she smiled until her cheeks ached. "Oh, yes. I don't want to spend another hour away from you, either."

"And you'll marry me? I know it wasn't the best proposal. I'll get it right, I promise. I'll get the ring and get on my knees. Whatever it is that makes you happy."

She touched the lines of his forehead, easing them with her fingertips. "What makes me happy is you loving me."

"Then you're going to be one happy lady," he vowed. "Because I'm going to love you with every breath I breathe, every minute of every day for the rest of our lives."

Epilogue

The living room was alive with conversation and laughter. Cam's house no longer resembled a somber cave; instead, it was light and airy. It was a house filled with love and happiness.

She settled onto the couch and hoisted her feet onto the ottoman, watching fondly as Cam and his friends oohed and aahed over a whole passel of babies.

Rafael de Luca and his wife, Bryony, had arrived two days ago with their daughter, Amy. Ryan Beardsley and his wife, Kelly, had been the last to get here and they'd flown in today from St. Angelo where they lived permanently. Their daughter, Emma, was nearly the same age as Amy. The two were born mere weeks apart.

Though it had been touted as a time for everyone to get together and visit, Pippa knew that Cam had arranged it to give her the kind of delivery surrounded by friends and family that she'd so wistfully dreamed of.

In addition to the love and attention he lavished on her at every opportunity, he'd set it up for her café to be staffed for the last month of her pregnancy and for a period of three months after the baby was born until she decided to return to it full time or not.

Finally, she was living the ultimate fairy tale. One she'd thought she'd be forever denied. It was the most wonderful feeling in the world.

Pippa liked Cam's friends. They hadn't been exactly as she'd expected. She'd thought they would be more like Cam had been in the beginning. Reserved. Stand-offish. But they were warm, outgoing and exuberant people. She'd first met them when they all came in for Cam and Pippa's wedding. It hadn't been a huge affair. They'd both opted for a quiet gathering of close friends and family only.

Kelly was probably the quietest woman in the group, but Pippa liked her a lot. She had a sweet smile and she clearly adored her daughter. Her husband, Ryan, never strayed far from their sides.

Pippa smiled and then promptly grimaced when she was seized by another contraction. She recovered quickly, pasted back on her serene smile and glanced at Cam.

He was standing next to Ryan, holding Emma in his arms while the men talked and laughed. The interesting thing was that they weren't discussing business. No, they were all trading baby stories and boasting about how their daughter was smarter, prettier and more clever than any other baby in the world.

Bryony rolled her eyes and flopped onto the couch beside Pippa. Ashley settled on the other side while Kelly sat in an armchair right beside the couch.

"I'm amazed by the change in Cam," Bryony said

quietly. "He seems so…happy. He's not as dark and brooding as I remember. I don't ever remember hearing him laugh. He rarely even smiled. You've performed a miracle, Pippa."

"He's great. He's still way overprotective and he can get worked up when he thinks about something happening to me or the baby, but he's really learned to let go and not dwell so much on the negative."

Ashley reached for her hand and squeezed. "He loves you, Pip. You've been so good for him. You saved him."

Another contraction tightened her belly, and she nearly groaned aloud. Kelly frowned and leaned forward in her seat.

"Pippa, what's wrong?"

"Shhh!" Pippa hissed. "Don't let Cam hear. He'll freak."

"Then tell us what's wrong," Ashley said in a quiet voice. "I saw that look, too. Are you having contractions?"

Pippa blew out her breath. "Yeah, for a while now."

"What?" Bryony demanded. "Why didn't you say anything?"

"Because I didn't want Cam to freak out and be stressed for longer than necessary. I'm not supposed to go into the hospital until they're two minutes apart, anyway."

"Uh, Pip, I'm pretty sure you're supposed to be there before they're that close together," Ashley said.

"My doctor told me that I should come in when my contractions were five minutes apart, regular and lasting at least a minute," Kelly offered.

Bryony's brow wrinkled in concentration. "I think mine told me five to seven minutes apart and regular."

Pippa swallowed uncomfortably and then put a hand on her belly.

"Another one?" Ashley demanded. "Pippa, how far apart are they coming?"

"Closer than five to seven minutes," she grumbled. "I know I read somewhere that I should wait to go in until they were two minutes apart."

Ashley gave her a look of exasperation. "Where would you have read that? You refused to even look at the chapter in the childbirth book that dealt with the ninth month or any part of labor and delivery."

Bryony was on her feet, pulling at Pippa's arm. "Cam," she called. "Pippa needs to go to the hospital."

All four men whirled around and Cam's brow immediately furrowed. Then when he seemed to realize the significance, he went pale and concern burned bright in his eyes.

He handed Emma back to Ryan and hurried over to Pippa.

"Honey, is it time?"

"Hell, it's *been* time," Ashley said in exasperation. "She should have gone hours ago."

Cam's gaze flicked from Ashley to Pippa. "What is she talking about?"

"I may have misunderstood when I was supposed to go to the hospital," Pippa muttered.

She grimaced and closed her eyes as another contraction started low in her back. By the time she opened her eyes again, she was panting lightly and the entire room was looking worried.

Cam reached down, plucked her into his arms. "Let's go," he said as he strode across the room.

She laughed but settled against his chest as he made his way to the garage. Behind them there was chaos as everyone juggled babies and diaper bags and hurried to get to their vehicles.

Cam placed her in the passenger seat, then carefully put the seat belt around her and buckled her in. As he was about to pull away, she put her hand on his cheek and cupped it lovingly.

"Hey," she said softly. "It's going to be okay. We're going to be okay."

He kissed her fiercely, then let his fingers linger on her face as she'd done to him. "I know. Now let's get you to the hospital so we can meet our son."

"Push, Pippa! That's it. Now breathe. Okay, one more time, breathe in deep. Hold it! Now push and count to ten."

Dear God but this baby delivery stuff was for the birds. Pippa puffed and strained and she really did try to hold her breath but it all came rushing out by the time she got to five.

If it wasn't for epidurals, she would have given this up already and begged for someone to knock her out.

"You're doing great, sweetheart."

Cam's voice, low and reassuring, gave her a much-needed jolt of energy. He had his arm behind her back, holding her tightly as he breathed through each contraction with her. His hand was tightly curled around hers and he murmured words of encouragement in her ear in between kisses.

"When is he going to be here?" Pippa wailed.

The nurse on her right smiled and then the doctor looked up from between her legs. "One more push and we'll have the head. Concentrate hard and bear down with this next contraction."

That sounded better. She was almost finished with this.

As the contraction began, she felt the mounting urgency to push, almost as if her body took control and she no longer had any say in the matter.

She sucked in her breath, closed her eyes and put her chin to her chest.

"Push, baby. Push," Cam whispered over and over. "You can do this. We're almost there."

"The head's out. Okay, Pippa, relax for a moment while I suction. We'll get him all the way out on the next push but the hard part's over."

"So says you," she grumbled.

The nurse laughed and the doctor just smiled.

A moment later, the doctor told her to push again and suddenly it was as if her belly caved in. The enormous pressure was gone as the baby slid from her body.

She gasped, overwhelmed by the sensation, and a baby's cry echoed across the room.

"Oh, my God," she whispered.

"Ready to meet your son, Pippa?" the doctor asked.

It took just a moment to finish suctioning and to wrap the baby in a blanket before the nurse laid him in Pippa's arms. Tears burned her eyelids as she stared down at the red-faced squalling baby.

Then she looked up at Cam and slowly held the bundle out to him.

Cam took the baby gingerly, his expression one of complete and utter awe. He stared down in fascination and then he smiled.

It was the most beautiful, honest smile Pippa had ever seen. There was so much joy in his expression that it choked her up and she had to swallow away her tears.

"He's beautiful," Cam whispered.

And then to Pippa's complete surprise, a tear slid down Cam's cheek, followed by another and then another. His hands shook as he cradled the baby closer to his chest.

Then he leaned forward, touching his forehead to hers as he held the baby between them.

"I love you," he choked out. "Thank you for this, Pippa. Thank you for my son. Dear God, he looks so much like you. He's so perfect. Every part of him."

Pippa closed her eyes as tears of her own trickled down her cheeks. There was never a more perfect moment than this. Never would she forget this time in their lives.

"What are we going to name him?" she whispered.

Cam carefully put his son back into Pippa's arms but leaned forward on the bed so he could watch every movement.

"What about Maverick?" Cam suggested. "Maverick Hollingsworth."

"Our little Mav," Pippa said with a smile. "I like it."

Cam found her lips again as the baby settled to sleep against his mother. As he drew away, he caressed her face with trembling hands.

"I'm going to love you and Maverick every single day, with every single breath I have, for the rest of my life. I'll glory in every single memory we make."

Despite her fatigue, Pippa's smile was so big that her cheeks ached.

"I know you will, Cam. But you know what? I'm going to love you every single minute of every single day of my life and I plan to live a damn long time. When you're eighty I'm going to be the biggest pain in your ass you ever had and I swear you're going to love every single minute of it."

Cam threw back his head and laughed. His eyes

twinkled merrily. "I absolutely believe every bit of it. I have no doubt that when I'm old and gray you'll still be telling me to straighten up and fly right."

The nurse interrupted to give Pippa instructions and get her ready to move to a regular room.

"Why don't you take Mav out to see his family?" Pippa suggested. By now the Copelands would be here and all of Cam's friends had followed them to the hospital and had kept vigil the entire time Pippa was in labor.

Cam rose and once again took Maverick from Pippa's arms. He stared down at his wife—he'd never grow tired of that word—and thought she'd never looked as beautiful as she did right now.

Tired, beautiful, so very courageous. He leaned down, kissed her brow and then stood to his full height again.

"We'll be back before you know it."

She smiled tiredly and gave him a look so full of love that it was like a fist to his stomach. She still did that to him. Every damn time.

He turned and walked to the door, his arms cradling his new son protectively. The knot grew in his throat as he walked down the corridor to where the others waited.

His son. His miracle. His second chance at life and happiness. At being a father.

His eyes burned and he blinked to keep his vision clear.

The others looked up and then surged to their feet when Cam entered the waiting room. Cam stopped and then smiled. Smiled so big that it was like stepping into the sun after living in the dark his entire life.

"I want you all to meet my son."

* * * * *

We hope you enjoyed reading this
special collection from Harlequin® books.

If you liked reading these stories, then you
will love **Harlequin® Desire** books.

You want to leave behind the everyday.
Harlequin Desire stories feature sexy,
romantic heroes who have it all: wealth, status,
incredible good looks…everything but the
right woman. Add some secrets, maybe a
scandal, and start turning pages!

Enjoy six *new* stories from
Harlequin Desire every month.

Available wherever books and
ebooks are sold.

COMING NEXT MONTH FROM

Available June 2, 2015

#2377 WHAT THE PRINCE WANTS

Billionaires and Babies • by Jules Bennett

Needing time to heal, a widowed prince goes incognito. He hires a live-in nanny for his infant daughter but soon finds he wants the woman for *himself*. Is he willing to cross the line from professional to personal?

#2378 CARRYING A KING'S CHILD

Dynasties: The Montoros • by Katherine Garbera

Torn between running his family's billion-dollar shipping business and assuming his ancestral throne, Rafe Montoro needs to let off some steam. But his night with a bartending beauty could change everything—because now there's a baby on the way...

#2379 PURSUED BY THE RICH RANCHER

Diamonds in the Rough • by Catherine Mann

Driven by his grandmother's dying wish, a Texas rancher must choose between his legacy and the sexy single mother who unknowingly holds the fate of his heart—and his inheritance—in her hands.

#2380 THE SHEIKH'S SECRET HEIR

by Kristi Gold

Billionaire Tarek Azzmar knows a secret that will destroy the royal family who shunned him. But the tables turn when he learns his lover is near and dear to the royal family *and* she's pregnant with his child.

#2381 THE WIFE HE COULDN'T FORGET

by Yvonne Lindsay

Olivia Jackson steals a second chance with her estranged husband when he loses his memories of the past two years. But when he finally remembers *everything*, will their reconciliation stand the ultimate test?

#2382 SEDUCED BY THE CEO

Chicago Sons • by Barbara Dunlop

When businessman Riley Ellis learns that his rival's wife has a secret twin sister, he seduces the beauty as leverage and then hires her to keep her close. But now he's trapped by his own lies...and his desires...

HDCNM0515

SPECIAL EXCERPT FROM

 HARLEQUIN®

Desire

*Will Rafe Montoro have to choose between the throne
and newfound fatherhood?*

*Read on for a sneak preview of
CARRYING A KING'S CHILD,
a DYNASTIES: THE MONTOROS novel
by USA TODAY bestselling author
Katherine Garbera.*

Pregnant!

He knew Emily wouldn't be standing in his penthouse apartment telling him this if he wasn't the father. His first reaction was joy.

A child.

It wasn't something he'd ever thought he wanted, but the idea that Emily was carrying his baby seemed right to him.

Maybe that was just because it gave him something other than his royal duties to think about. He'd been dreading his trip to Alma. He was flattered that the country that had once driven his family out had come back to them, asked them—him, as it turned out—to be the next king. But he had grown up here in Miami. He didn't want to be a stuffy royal.

He didn't want European paparazzi following him around and trying to catch him doing anything that would bring shame to his family. Including having a child out of wedlock.

"Rafe, did you hear what I said?"

"Yeah, I did. Are you sure?" he asked at last.

She gave him a fiery look from those aqua-blue eyes of hers. He'd seen the passionate side of her nature, and he guessed he was about to witness her temper. Hurricane Em was about to unleash all of her fury on him, and he didn't blame her one bit.

He held his hand up. "Slow down, Red. I didn't mean are you sure it's mine. I meant…are you sure you're pregnant?"

"Damned straight. And I wouldn't be here if I wasn't sure it was yours. Listen, I don't want anything from you. I know you can't turn your back on your family and marry me, and frankly, we only had one weekend together, so I'd have to say no to a proposal anyway. But…I don't want this kid to grow up without knowing you."

"Me neither."

She glanced up, surprised.

He'd sort of surprised himself. But it didn't seem right for a kid of his to grow up without him. He wanted that. He wanted a chance to impart the Montoro legacy…not the one newly sprung on him involving a throne, but the one he'd carved for himself in business. "Don't look shocked."

"You've kind of got a lot going on right now. And having a kid with me isn't going to go over well."

"Tough," he said. "I still make my own decisions."

Available June 2015 wherever Harlequin® Desire books and ebooks are sold.

www.Harlequin.com

Love the Harlequin book you just read?

Your opinion matters.

Review this book on your favorite book site, review site, blog or your own social media properties and share your opinion with other readers!

Be sure to connect with us at:
Harlequin.com/Newsletters
Facebook.com/HarlequinBooks
Twitter.com/HarlequinBooks

HARLEQUIN®

A *Romance* FOR EVERY MOOD™

Stay up-to-date on all your
romance-reading news with the
Harlequin Shopping Guide,
featuring bestselling authors, exciting new
miniseries, books to watch and more!

The newest issue will be delivered right to you
with our compliments! There are 4 each year.

Signing up is easy.

EMAIL

ShoppingGuide@Harlequin.ca

WRITE TO US

HARLEQUIN BOOKS
Attention: Customer Service Department
P.O. Box 9057, Buffalo, NY 14269-9057

OR PHONE

1-800-873-8635 in the United States
1-888-343-9777 in Canada

Please allow 4-6 weeks for delivery of the first issue by mail.